Skinjob

BRUCE McCABE

BANTAM PRESS

LONDON · TORONTO · SYDNEY · AUCKLAND · JOHANNESBURG

TRANSWORLD PUBLISHERS
61–63 Uxbridge Road, London W5 5SA
A Random House Group Company
www.transworldbooks.co.uk

First published in Great Britain
in 2014 by Bantam Press
an imprint of Transworld Publishers

A CIP catalogue record for this book
is available from the British Library.

ISBNs 9780593074084 (hb)
9780593074091 (tpb)

Addresses for Random House Group Ltd companies outside the UK
can be found at: www.randomhouse.co.uk
The Random House Group Ltd Reg. No. 954009

The Random House Group Limited supports the Forest Stewardship Council® (FSC®),
the leading international forest-certification organisation. Our books carrying the FSC
label are printed on FSC®-certified paper. FSC is the only forest-certification scheme
supported by the leading environmental organisations, including Greenpeace. Our paper
procurement policy can be found at www.randomhouse.co.uk/environment

Typeset in 11½/14½pt Caslon 540 by
Kestrel Data, Exeter, Devon.
Printed and bound in Great Britain by
Clays Ltd, Bungay, Suffolk.

2 4 6 8 10 9 7 5 3 1

MIX
Paper from
responsible sources
FSC
www.fsc.org   FSC® C016897

To Jane, Elise and Sean

The Pentagon will issue handheld lie detectors this month to US Army soldiers in Afghanistan . . . The Defense Department says the portable device isn't perfect, but is accurate enough to save American lives by screening local police officers, interpreters and allied forces for access to US military bases, and by helping narrow the list of suspects after a roadside bombing.

– msnbc.com, April 2008

With the growing availability of images that can describe the state of someone's brain, attorneys are increasingly asking judges to admit these scans in evidence, to demonstrate, say, that a defendant is not guilty by reason of insanity or that a witness is telling the truth.

– *Scientific American*, April 2011

SANTA CLARA, California – Applied Biometric Instruments Inc. is pleased to announce that the Police Nationale, France's principal national law enforcement agency, has adopted the Handheld Multimodal Detection Array (HAMDA) as its standard field polygraph device. The first 750 units will be delivered in March. US trials are underway.

– Press release, February 2019

Wednesday

Chapter 1

The high-rise office workers in San Francisco's finance district sensed it as an eerie sway. It passed quickly beneath their feet, but a good many started towards the fire escapes anyway, in case it was the seismic prequel to something worse. A moment later the tourists walking the Embarcadero and children eating ice-creams on Pier 39 looked up as a muffled *ka-rump* broke the summer stillness. In the opposite direction the residents on Russian Hill watched walls shake and cutlery skitter across tables.

Retailers and shoppers within three hundred yards of the intersection of Jackson Street and Grant Avenue experienced sound and shock as one. The thud shattered their afternoon like a hammer, and they watched, wide-eyed, as windows dissolved into cascading waterfalls of glass. After the thunderclap, fragments of masonry peppered from the sky like hail.

At Maggie's on Grant, a cafe fifty yards from the intersection, the waitress placed a tray of coffee and danishes on a front table and a second later found herself thrown to the ground. Her first reaction was to get up, embarrassed, and brush herself off. Then she saw other astonished faces rising from behind upturned chairs and tables. She shook her head, trying to throw off the high-pitched monotone shrilling in her ears, and stared at where the front window had been. She stepped shakily into the street, feeling shards crack and splinter under her shoes. People lay scattered, hunkered, coughing. Dust billowed, depositing a fine, sooty film over every surface. Above, an angry black cloud boiled over a pristine blue sky.

Without lowering her eyes, the waitress fished in the pockets of her uniform and withdrew a cell phone. She did nothing for a few seconds, then looked down and dialled 911.

Sergeant Shahida Sanayei was halfway through her shift as surveillance duty officer at SFPD Central Station when she felt a vibration through her seat and heard yelling in the corridor. Then her communications panel lit up. As she donned her headset she noticed one of the patchwork of camera views on the Wall – the cinema-sized display dominating the room – was black. She selected the line from the dispatch centre. 'Viddy ops.'

'We're getting reports of an explosion. Downtown. Near the corner of Jackson and Grant. What can you see?'

'Wait one.' Shari's hands moved rapidly over the electronic map on her console. In seconds she selected sixteen cameras in and around the intersection. She stared at the Wall as they came online. Five, ten, fourteen. Plus two black squares. Two dead. The live ones were filled with dust and smoke that varied from a light brown haze to an ugly, impenetrable black.

'Okay, location is correct. It looks big. I've got two cameras out in a hundred and fifty yard section. Looks like you're going to need fire units.'

'On their way.'

'I'm going to need a minute to adjust the angles and get you a good assessment. Can you hold?' Shari snapped her fingers at her team but specialists Angie Mertz and Lynn Symonds were seasoned operators and already making pan and zoom adjustments, working to construct a sensible picture as rapidly as possible.

'Roger that. I have to direct mobile units. Call me back as soon as you have something.'

'Sure thing.'

Shari watched as the collage came together, piece by piece. Her team started with the more distant cameras to frame the smoke plume and get a sense of the size of the affected area, then worked inwards, experimenting to get the best angles. They hit paydirt with camera 643, less than thirty yards from the scene and tilted crazily at the sky, but still functioning. When they rotated it, an image came into view straight from the London Blitz.

The other buildings along Grant Avenue suggested that the shattered structure had, until a few moments ago, stood four storeys tall. Now it was more like three and a half. The second floor had been punched out. Ragged holes belched flames and soot from where the windows had been. The upper storeys sagged in the middle. The street was a sea of bricks and glittering glass.

Shari called dispatch and described the scene in a few terse sentences. It hardly mattered: she could already see the first emergency vehicles arriving. In a few moments they would report from on site.

With the help of her two specialists, Shari switched to the task of securing evidence. They placed a priority data hold on all cameras in the area. That ensured the footage they were watching live, as well as all stored footage going back forty-eight hours, would be retained permanently for later analysis. Then the team methodically captured images of every living thing within five city blocks. They did not discriminate: men and women, young children and elderly pedestrians were all tagged.

Angie yelled.

Shari looked up. The building was no longer centred in view. She reached out to adjust 643 before realizing that it was not the camera moving – it was the *building*. The entire structure twisted and buckled in a sickening, slow-motion waltz. Walls and joints popped and puffs of brick dust fired outwards like a last broadside from a sinking galleon. Firemen ran.

The second floor crumpled, sending shock waves reverberating upwards. Then, in a horrible concertina, the first and third levels gave way and the entire stack, in a gathering rush of colliding masonry, pancaked downwards. Thick grey clouds boiled out and up, enveloping the camera.

They stared, speechless.

Shari's console flashed.

'Viddy ops.'

'Shari, it's me.'

The informality took Shari by surprise. Of course she knew the voice – she had been friends with Yolanda Payne for years – but now was not the time to be personal. 'Go ahead, dispatch,' she said.

'It's Adam. It may be nothing, but I thought you should know. He . . . his GPS is down. He was with Terry Strong on foot patrol. Their last known position was on Jackson, heading towards Gra—'

'Call him.'

'We did. He's not responding. Look, we don't know anything yet, he may have just switched off, but I thought . . . Shari?'

Shari ran for the door.

She dashed down the corridor, past the front desk and into Vallejo Street. Officers were running everywhere. A squad car tore past. Another peeled away from the kerb and she leapt in front, arms outstretched. The bumper lurched and dipped, stopping an inch from her knees.

'Shari! Jesus, I almost ran you down.' The driver, Tony Villiers, one of the station veterans, was white with shock.

'I'm coming with you,' she yelled. She ran around to the passenger side, one arm stretched out across the windscreen in case he changed his mind and left without her. She yanked open the door and dived in. 'Go!'

They tore down Vallejo, siren wailing, and took a right into Stockton. All four tyres screamed in protest. They skimmed the side of a FedEx truck as they blasted past – Shari just had time to see the startled look on the driver's face and they were gone.

Waves of nausea flooded through her. Her last words to him had been angry, unkind. He had listened patiently, mumbling reassurances that he would always do the right thing by her, that he loved her. Then he had to go, and that was how they left it. And now, Shari thought, he could be under that mountain of concrete. *I never said sorry, Adam. Don't you dare die before I say sorry.*

They hit the bumps crossing Broadway, and again at Pacific, and the suspension crunched, lifting her from the seat. The radio squawked a stream of updates. Multiple casualties. Spot fires. Request for K-9 units.

They skidded onto Jackson and accelerated down the hill before Villiers slammed the brakes.

The car squalled to a stop.

A haze of tyre smoke drifted in front of them. Jackson Street was one-way, and the traffic had funnelled down to a blocked intersection with nowhere to turn. Beyond the wall of backed-up vehicles, a black pall spread across the afternoon sky like ink. Shari knew every inch of these streets, every camera, angle and distance. They weren't far. She got out and ran.

She arrived at the Grant Avenue intersection, legs and lungs burning. As she stood, hands on hips, gasping for breath, she saw a street from hell.

In the centre of what had once been a neat row of buildings was a yawning gap. The building was gone, replaced by a rubble pile belching thick black smoke. Fire trucks directed long jets of water into sputtering orange hot spots.

A group of people, brown with water and grime, huddled near the corner receiving first aid. Shari scanned for a police uniform. Nothing. Then she noticed bodies, two of them, right in the middle of the street. One was a woman, her arms and legs oddly twisted. No one had even bothered to cover her. The other was shielded by a pair of kneeling paramedics.

Shari moved closer, arms slack by her sides.

One of the paramedics shook his head. 'No use. Too many damn holes.'

'Don't stop,' said the other. 'Sometimes they surprise you. Give me another bandage. No, unwrap it. My hands are slippery.'

'Pressure here. Here!'

Shari could see now that the victim was – had been – a man. His right arm was missing to the elbow. If that had been his only injury he might have had a chance, but the entire right side of his body was black, the hair gone, and his face had ballooned into pillows of weeping flesh. Pink froth fluttered from a ragged hole in his chest, and through her daze Shari could see the bandages were useless against the flow.

The paramedic working the man's chest was completely covered in blood. The other, his uniform caked with dirt, looked at his colleague with a resigned expression that said, *Yes, sometimes they can surprise you, but not this one.*

Shari bent and forced herself to stare, but there was nothing to recognize in the swollen, blistered mess that had once been a face. She took in the blood-soaked rags wrapped around the neck and shoulders. Grey pin stripes on white. Not a uniform. *Not Adam.*

The first paramedic stopped pumping. He leaned back and wiped his face with the back of his arm, smearing blood and sweat across his cheek. His colleague stood, took a breath, and mumbled a few words of prayer. A tiny stylized crucifix dangled from his ear.

Shari's emotions began to crystallize, condense and take direction. There was no logic, just a rising, overwhelming resolve. *Adam is inside. Underneath.*

She moved towards the rubble. The siren of an arriving ambulance sounded muted. The officers making a barrier against the gathering crowd seemed disconnected and distant. She walked underneath the water jetting from the fire engines and was vaguely aware of curtains of mist soaking through her uniform.

Moving to the side of the rubble pile furthest from the flames, she began to climb. It was hard going. She slipped several times, banging her knees. Finally she resorted to a crab-like approach, spreading her weight across her hands and feet.

She peered into a hole and yelled, 'Hello! Is anyone in there?' She crawled towards a beam caught across two slabs of concrete so the pieces formed a crazy, jagged arch, and shouted into the cavity, 'Can anyone hear me?'

She began wriggling her head and shoulders into the gap.

'Get the hell out of it!'

Shari turned. A fireman waved frantically from the street, his face twitching between fury and wide-eyed horror. 'What do you think you're doing? Get out of there! You wanna get killed?' He wasn't shouting, he was *screaming*. She stared back at the arch of broken concrete, the logical side of her brain fighting to break through. Suddenly, with stunning clarity, she realized how precariously balanced everything was. She reversed her course and began descending. As she neared the fireman, he reached for her.

It was then she saw the hand.

It was a woman's hand, poking out from under a sheet of plaster. It lay still, relaxed. The skin was smooth and unblemished, with a vaguely pinkish hue. Each finger was tipped with a perfectly manicured nail.

The fireman, frustrated that Shari had stopped, followed her gaze. He paused, weighing the safety of the position, then climbed up to help. They lifted the plaster together. It was just a hand. No body. Shari was surprised to realize she felt nothing.

But there was something wrong. It took a moment before she knew what it was. In her rookie year she had served in a clean-up crew after an Amtrak train thundered over a sleeping drunk. The driver of the *Southwest Chief* didn't slow, and Shari had found herself picking up pieces a half-mile from the impact. Each was a torn-up mess. Flaps of skin had clung to her gloves.

What she was looking at now had no ragged tissue, nor even a single spot of blood. She knelt for a closer look. The stump was pale green. In the middle, where there should have been bone, a knob of metal caught the sunlight.

'Skinjob,' said the fireman.

'What?'

'It's a skinjob. Thank Christ. I thought we had another corpse.' She looked at him blankly.

'It's the dollhouse. Someone blew up the dollhouse,' he said, shaking his head. He was trying to grin, but it came out as a grimace. 'We found a couple more parts down the bottom.

Separating the real from the fake ones is going to make for a real dandy afternoon.'

Shari stared down at the hand. Revulsion pressed upwards from her stomach as words and images propelled her towards sickening comprehension. She began to vomit.

Chapter 2

FBI Special Agent Daniel Madsen cranked back the driver's seat a couple of notches and studied the side mirror of his battered blue Dodge. *Anytime now,* he thought, *then another two after this guy, then I'm on vacation.*

A group of pedestrians approached from the direction of the campus. Unlikely his target was coming from there, but hard to tell because overhanging trees partly obscured the view. He pressed the 'off' button on his cell phone for the third time in as many minutes and checked that the comms unit was tucked behind the dash. His Beretta made no bump under the flap of his jacket. The sales brochure he was supposed to be reading was right side up. His gaze dropped to the passenger footwell and he wrinkled his nose at the week's accumulation of paper cups, burger wrappers and spilled fries. He'd have to get around to cleaning that up sometime. Arguably, the litter suited the Dodge. It was by far the oldest vehicle in the fleet, with dented doors and large slabs of paint missing from both bumpers. Not that this bothered him. Mechanically it was fine. And it blended in.

In the mirror the pedestrians resolved themselves into young women in jeans and blue-and-gold Cal sweatshirts. Snippets of conversation floated through the open window.

'. . . Saturday . . .'

'. . . told me she was going.'

'When you see . . . tell them.'

They passed, deep in conversation and oblivious to his presence. Madsen watched appreciatively as a brunette, tall with nice curves, sashayed past, trailing a little behind the others. She caught his stare and smiled, and he glanced away. The girls continued down to the corner, disappearing towards the nearby BART station.

Madsen shook his head. An hour ago he'd been interrogating a banker in a back room of some sleaze-pit in the Tenderloin district, now he was being distracted by pretty girls in a leafy avenue in Berkeley.

He reached into his jacket to touch the cigar-shaped stainless steel cylinder hidden there, nestled warm against his ribs. His thumb traced the Applied Biometrics logo and the five letters he knew were stamped into the polished surface.

H.A.M.D.A.

'The mark one handheld multimodal detection array,' his instructor had said, walking down the line of recruits, 'is going to take you into all kinds of interesting places. The simultaneous analysis of voice stress, eye movement, pulse, pheromones, skin flush and breathing takes polygraphy to unprecedented levels of accuracy. The sensor array can also be used to test narcotics and sniff for explosives. The technology is solid. You can rely on it. The *program*, however . . . is experimental, with a capital E, which means you guys need to get ready for a steep learning curve.'

No kidding. After thirteen months of trial and error, strategic rethinking and tactical tinkering, two-thirds of the guys standing in that line had been washed out, never to be seen again. 'Steep' didn't begin to cover it. Still, they *had* learned, and the first time they'd combined the little field polygraphs with saturation video surveillance and rapid response, the results blew everyone away. That was when Washington fell in love with its tiny band of HAMDA agents, labels like 'experimental' quietly disappeared, and every other federal agency was suddenly clamouring for a piece of the action.

Which was why he was so tired.

Today's DEA-led operation would be his fourteenth in five weeks. He couldn't remember when he last had a weekend. He was a day shy of a well-earned break. Just a few days off. He'd probably sleep through most of them, and that would be fine.

A distant figure appeared in the mirror.

Electricity crackled up Madsen's spine as he tilted his head for a better look: tall, male, grey suit. He glanced at his watch, then back to the figure.

Marc Aaron Silverberg. Bang on time.

Silverberg moved along the sidewalk with the measured steps of a man trying to look natural. The suit was expensive, the shirt tailored and the hair groomed. The gold cufflinks would most probably be blue-edged, to match the stripe in the tie. It was a shame, really. The guy was thirty, almost the same age as himself, with a cute wife, two kids and a ridiculous salary – his bonus alone would be six figures. A man of standing. And now his heart would be thumping as he told himself not to jump at shadows, not to panic.

Silverberg looked left and right before stepping from the kerb. He crossed the road with exaggerated care. Madsen tracked him in the mirrors, then, as his quarry drew level with the Dodge, out of the corner of his eye. Silverberg approached a pair of black glass doors with 'TORRIDO'S BAR AND GRILL' stencilled across them in gold capitals. He stopped with his hand resting on the left-hand door, glanced quickly over his shoulder, and pushed his way in.

Madsen sighed. You do the crime, you better know the rhyme.

He counted to ten, climbed from the Dodge and strode briskly across the road.

Torrido's was dimly lit and it took a few moments for Madsen's eyes to adjust. A couple of early drinkers propped up the end of the bar. The voices of excited basketball commentators boomed from a screen mounted up near the ceiling. Laughter floated from one of the tables. Office workers, celebrating something. Silverberg sat alone in a booth, staring out the window.

Madsen took a stool and ordered a beer. No one gave him so much as a second glance. The mirror running behind the bar allowed him to monitor Silverberg while pretending to watch the plays of the week.

His beer arrived and he settled in to wait.

Balls looped and swished. Commentators yelled. Impossibly tall people in baggy shorts danced and high-fived.

A minute ticked by. Then another.

The door to the street opened.

The man who entered was serious looking, in his mid twenties with slicked hair and a jacket over one arm. His eyes lingered briefly on Madsen's back.

Madsen sipped his beer. His other hand tripped a switch in his jacket pocket to activate an array of pinhole cameras sewn into his collar. He didn't bother aiming; the software would sort it out later.

The new arrival spotted Silverberg, nodded a greeting and slid into the booth so they faced one another. The waitress came over and placed a coke in front of Silverberg. She asked the other man a question and he shook his head. She left them to it.

A moment later the man stood, shook hands, and walked out.

It must have happened under the table. Even had he been standing alongside the booth Madsen wasn't sure he could have picked the moment.

A burst of laughter came from the party in the corner.

Madsen took another sip. Patience. The dealer would already be crossing the street, gaining distance each second, fingering a fresh bundle of notes and headed someplace he could count it. It didn't matter. Silverberg came first, quietly and where no one could see. Shake him down, share the data, geo-locate the targets up the next level of the supply chain, repeat. Cyclical triangulation was what they called it in the new manual. Knowing how to wrangle a handheld polygraph in the field was only part of it. It also demanded speed, timing, and an instinct for staying just inside the boundaries of the law. And patience.

The old hands couldn't get their heads around it. Madsen had it down to an art.

Silverberg headed for the men's room, leaving his drink untouched. His front right trouser pocket looked heavy. Madsen downed a mouthful of beer and followed. He pushed open the swing door.

Silverberg stood at a urinal. Madsen glanced under the stalls to confirm they were empty, then strode up behind him, drawing his gun at the same time. He reached out with his left hand, grabbed a handful of hair and pushed Silverberg's forehead into the wall, pinning him against the tiles. His other hand pressed the Beretta into the small of his back. 'Marc Aaron Silverberg, FBI. If you move I will put a fucking bullet in you. Do you understand?'

Silverberg stood petrified, propped awkwardly against the wall. A squeak came from his throat.

'Nod your head if you understand,' said Madsen. Silverberg nodded, the movement almost imperceptible. 'In a moment I will show you my ID. You will not move a muscle. Got that?'

Another nod.

Madsen released his grip and fished out his badge, slapping it flat to the wall next to Silverberg's face. 'Are you armed? Anything in your pockets I need to know about?' Silverberg shook his head.

A fast pat-down revealed a billfold, a set of keys and a paper bag – a fat, pink paper bag bearing the logo of one of the donut chains. Madsen unrolled the neck and peered inside: it was stuffed with blue pills. Tossing it to the floor, Madsen fished the metal cylinder from his pocket and held it near Silverberg's nose. A bright light winked at the tip. 'Do you know what this is?'

Silverberg nodded.

'You need to say it.'

'Yes. I know. It's a lie detector.' The voice was a whimper, barely audible. A tiny microphone in the cylinder picked up the soundwaves. Pin-sized lenses captured the pulse, the rise of the chest, each tiny eye movement. A thermal eye scanned the veins in the irises and mapped the flush patterns across the face. Software compensated for Silverberg's involuntary shake.

Madsen studied him carefully. 'Okay, calm down. If you answer my questions then in a minute you get to go. No strings. You need to tell the truth. I will not use what you say against you, I will use it to roll up your dealer and the dealer above him. Do you understand?'

'Yes.'

The winking light flashed green.

'But if at any stage you lie to me, I will arrest you for possession and dealing and I will do my level best to make sure you do time. Do you understand?'

'Yes.' Another green flash.

'Right. Are you standing in a men's room?'

'Yes.'

'Is your name Marc Silverberg?'

'Yes.'

The baseline questions were inane, but essential for calibration, especially when a suspect was stressed, which, in Madsen's experience, was always.

'What's your dealer's name?'

'Enrico.'

'What's his surname?'

'I don't know him by any other name.'

'How do you contact him?'

'I post a message in the public comments on a web page. The page is different each time. When I see him he tells me which one to use next. He posts a reply and we meet.'

'Always here?'

'No. We have three places. His post includes a number. The first digit is the place, the second is the day of the week, the third and fourth are the hour.'

Madsen nodded. Enrico, or whatever his real name was, was careful. It wouldn't matter. 'Where did you meet last time?'

'Golden Gate Park. At the east entrance, where all the bums hang out.'

Too hard. 'And the time before that?'

'A donut place. The one near my house.'

Much better. The fast-food chains archived all security footage and gave unfettered access to law enforcement. 'When?'

'Three weeks ago. A Friday.'

The flashes were still green. 'Anything else to tell me? Anything at all that will help us find him? Think about it.'

'No. Wait – yes. I was introduced to him by Mike Colley, a friend at work.'

Madsen nodded. Colley was the banker he had interviewed earlier.

'Nothing else?'

'I – I can't think of anything.'

'Okay.' Madsen pulled Silverberg's head from the wall and spun him around. The guy was shaking violently. There was a stain down the front of his trousers.

Madsen re-holstered the Beretta. 'Zip up. Pull yourself together. You are going to walk out of here like this never happened. But, remember, you are not going to contact Enrico. You are not going to tip him off. We will be watching. Do you understand?'

Silverberg nodded. Tears spilled down his cheeks. He stole a glance downwards. Madsen followed the look and bent to retrieve the paper bag. For a moment he contemplated offering it back. *Here, take a handful, just to get you through the week.* Silverberg would no doubt accept, his expression that of a grateful puppy and then . . . and then the tables would be turned, and when the Office of Professional Integrity boys next swung by Madsen's office, he'd be the one sweating red lights.

Madsen pocketed the bag, ignoring the pain cutting across Silverberg's face. 'Count slowly to twenty, okay? Then go home.'

Silverberg wiped his eyes and nodded.

Madsen suddenly had an odd feeling.

It was quiet outside. Too quiet.

Leaving Silverberg to straighten himself out, Madsen cautiously eased open the men's room door. He could hear neither laughter nor the blare of the basketball. The chairs where the office workers had been sitting were empty. He heard low, agitated voices coming from the bar. Everyone was there, crowded around the screen. Madsen moved up behind them for a closer look. On the screen, under a 'Breaking News' banner, was a shaky aerial shot of central San Francisco. Right in the middle of the shot was a great big smoking hole.

Swearing, Madsen pulled out his cell phone and switched it on.

Instantly, a message flashed up: DROP EVERYTHING. COME IN NOW.

Five minutes later, Daniel Madsen sped west over the Bay Bridge, weaving in and out of the traffic. Ahead, a thick column of smoke punctuated the downtown skyline. Tiny specks – news drones – circled like vultures around carrion. He did his best to piece together what had happened from the radio calls. A building was down, somewhere in Chinatown. The cops were calling it a bombing. Unknown number of fatalities. Urban search and rescue had been activated.

Madsen recalled a slideshow at the academy in Quantico, gory images of the World Trade Center and Oklahoma City presented by a grizzled expert with a facial tic that might have come from attending one scene too many. As the expert traced the gutted outline of the Murrah federal building with the red dot of his laser pointer, Madsen had been distracted by the frozen snowstorm of fluttering paper, thinking it a sadly appropriate metaphor for the departed souls of a hundred and sixty-eight government employees. He had tuned back in just in time to catch the instructor's matter-of-fact summation: the real casualties come after the bang, when the building collapses.

Someone came on the radio asking for confirmation that the building was a dollhouse. A dispatcher said yes, that was an affirmative.

Dollhouse.

Skinjobs.

Madsen shook his head. The dollhouses had caused a stink from the beginning, when the first one opened in a refurbished office block south of Market Street. The company, Dreamcom Interactive, had been dismissive, claiming they were just the next logical innovation in an adult entertainment industry that had been an accepted and even celebrated part of American culture since the 1970s. What the Dreamcom execs hadn't figured on were churches and women's rights groups deciding that it didn't matter a damn that the whores were plastic, the whole exercise constituted a new form of prostitution. The politicians and talk show hosts, having carefully plumbed the sentiments of their constituents, flooded the airwaves with bitter debate. With each new dollhouse that opened the protests had grown louder and angrier. Punch-ups were common. Only last week, patrons in Chicago were splashed with red paint, and a pit bull was let loose on a group of picketers in LA. The animal mauled a protester's seven-year-old son before an officer clobbered it with his nightstick.

And now this.

Madsen turned onto Golden Gate Avenue.

Ahead was the monolith of grey granite and glass that housed the San Francisco offices for the FBI, DEA and a host of other federal agencies. He shot a wary glance up at the thirteenth floor, where his desk was. If ever a nutcase felt the need to send The Man a message wrapped in fertilizer, diesel and a Ryder truck, then the Phillip Burton building boasted more feds per square foot than anywhere else in the city.

A few minutes later he arrived at the briefing room to find it packed. Everyone was on their feet. A wall-mounted screen displayed smoke, debris and confusion; there was an occasional flash of colour as rescue workers darted back and forth in their high-visibility coveralls. Live chatter from the emergency services radio network squawked from the speakers.

A wiry, dark-eyed woman in a blue suit pushed her way over.

Mary DiMatteo was special agent in charge at the San Francisco FBI field office. She was a tough, sometimes terrifying boss, with a way of lighting fires under people when she didn't feel they were being sufficiently proactive. On the plus side, she embraced enthusiasm, had the courage to stand up for her people, and insisted that every success, big or small, was properly celebrated. Boisterous nights at Pacelli's, a restaurant a few streets away, had become legendary during her tenure. In a week, DiMatteo would be handing in her gold badge to be mounted on a plaque. Whatever consulting job she picked up, Madsen thought, it wouldn't give her a tenth of the satisfaction, and the rest of them would see a lot less of Pacelli's.

DiMatteo glowered at him. 'Nice of you to make it,' she said. Her voice was gravel-harsh, like a godfather don's. 'Someone hit the dollhouse in Grant Avenue. We don't know how many people were inside, but the chances of anyone coming out are slim to nil. Provisionally this one's going down as domestic terrorism. That means we're in.' She paused to allow the message to sink in.

Madsen nodded, waiting for more.

'The SFPD brass asked for assistance from evidence response and said no to everything else, but I've suggested in the strongest terms that they also take our best and brightest HAMDA agent. I'm still waiting to hear.'

There was no need for Madsen to ask who she meant. San Francisco, like all the other big field offices, only had one HAMDA agent. He cocked an eyebrow. 'And the DEA?'

'They'll cope. I already took you off their operation. I want you ready to roll the second we get word.'

The hairs on Madsen's neck pricked up. If she was prepared to deal with the headaches that came with swapping him out of an operation in progress, then she expected things to move very quickly indeed.

'We need speed,' DiMatteo said, reading his thoughts. 'Because whoever did this may be planning more firecrackers. Get down there and get out on the street as soon as possible. Just keep in mind, this one is going to be high-profile.'

'What's that supposed to mean?'

'It means that with all the heat in this dollhouse bullshit, everyone in our towering pyramid of authority will be watching.' She prodded an index finger at his chest. 'So be fast but be *good*.'

Madsen squinted at her. Be good. Which means stay under the

radar, don't upset anybody and, whatever you do, do not, under any circumstances, embarrass the Bureau.

DiMatteo slapped him on the shoulder. 'You'll do great. With luck SFPD viddy have already pulled footage of the guy and you'll nail him tonight. This one's made for you. Am I right?'

Madsen's eyes drifted back to the screen. *We need speed*. Despite his tiredness, he felt a familiar itch. The camera jockeys would already be scanning faces. One or several of those faces would belong to the killers, and those killers might already be preparing to strike again. His skills could make a difference. He wanted to get down there and get to work. The sooner the better.

Grant Avenue wasn't far. He could jog it in ten.

'Absolutely,' he said.

A bespectacled clerk hurried over and handed a sheet of note-paper to DiMatteo.

She glanced at it before passing it to Madsen. 'You're up.'

Chapter 3

Central Station at 766 Vallejo Street was just one of five stations in the San Francisco Police Department's Metro Division and by no means the biggest, but on this day, Madsen thought, it could probably claim to be the busiest.

Inside surveillance operations, a cramped, darkened room with the faint whiff of body odour, squares glowed within squares on the Wall. The three operators – two specialists and a sergeant – looked like black-uniformed virtuosos as they caressed controllers and dials and mixed a visual symphony from a thousand camera feeds. Behind, crowded in the small viewing area, a half-dozen broad-shouldered detectives looked on.

Madsen sat to the side, in a steel-framed chair with the padding long beaten out of it. He had been there precisely nineteen and a half minutes and his patience was wearing thin; he couldn't help it – every minute that passed meant fewer witnesses, lost points of triangulation – but he kept his frustrations to himself. Everyone was doing their damnedest. You only had to look at the diminutive sergeant at the master console to see that.

She was soaked. Her long dark hair, streaked grey and brown with muck, clung to the side of her face, and her uniform looked like it had been dragged through a sewer pipe. She must have been at Grant Avenue pulling bodies out of the rubble, and now here she was setting up the video analysis. The plate on her desk said Sgt Shahida Sanayei. An Iranian name. Or Afghan. Madsen had heard the others call her Shari.

Perhaps sensing his stare, she turned in his direction. Madsen met her gaze and started in surprise, quickly looking away. He had anticipated dark eyes to match the dark complexion, but her irises were a bright electric green.

Recovering his composure, Madsen switched his attention to the man peering over Shari's shoulder: a great big grizzly bear with jowls and a silver-sided crew cut that said don't-fuck-with-me almost as loudly as his brick-sized fists. For thirty minutes Madsen had followed Inspector Mike Holbrook as he pulled his team together, bellowing into a cell phone and snapping off instructions like rifle shots. Holbrook seemed to know what he wanted and how to get it.

Unfortunately he also had a pretty good idea of what he didn't want, and one of the things he didn't want was Madsen on his team. Right now the temperature between them hovered at about thirty below.

Ordinary street police had a nickname for the brand-new category of law enforcement officer created by the HAMDA: *plotter*. Madsen had already heard it whispered several times since his arrival at Central Station. The dislike was driven partly by professional jealousy, partly because Madsen and his small band of colleagues were perceived to be undisciplined, unrigorous and egotistical (a view that had been well reinforced by a few bull-headed agents in the early days of the programme), and partly – mostly – by fear. The fear came when HAMDAs were issued to the FBI's Office of Professional Responsibility, the Bureau's equivalent of internal affairs. The martinet in charge had applied them with a vengeance, firing and demoting hundreds of otherwise distinguished agents who had made one-off mistakes or bent rules that should never have been made in the first place. He had even gone so far as to rename his department the Office of Professional Integrity. Every law enforcement officer in America was appalled, and knew it was only a matter of time before random 'integrity tests' were carried out in their own workplace.

Of course Madsen was a field agent with nothing to do with OPI, but few outside the Bureau made a distinction.

I understand, Madsen thought as he watched Holbrook. *You don't want a plotter on your turf. You took me under sufferance. But don't worry, big guy. You're still the boss. You can still do it your way. I'll just do my thing and work the express route.*

He'd have to find a way to break the ice, but to do that they had to have an actual conversation; the dozen words they'd exchanged so far didn't qualify.

Shari looked enquiringly at Holbrook, who nodded. She pressed a button on her console.

Life-sized images of Grant Avenue flashed onto the Wall.

The scene was pre-explosion. The street was intact, its late-afternoon inhabitants alive and well and frozen mid-stride. Each square offered a different perspective of the building that would soon be transformed into a layer-cake of concrete and masonry. The views from municipal cameras were supplemented by views from security cameras inside the stores across the street.

Holbrook turned and cleared his throat. 'Now, before we start, listen up. Some of you may already know that two of the people in there were officers from this station.'

Shari had her back to the detectives, but from where Madsen sat he had a better angle. The corner of her mouth was twitching.

'I guess they thought it was quiet,' Holbrook continued, 'and they could sneak a break before their shift ended. Obviously they broke some rules. Maybe that's a regular thing here. Maybe a friend in dispatch covered for them. I, for one, don't give a shit. Adam Carmichael and Terrence Strong were decorated veterans, well liked. They served with distinction. Officer Carmichael left behind a wife of fifteen years. So when you mention their names just remember the guys at this station lost two of their buddies . . .'

Madsen was no longer listening. He was watching Shari. A solitary tear, shiny from the reflected light of her console, washed a grimy track down her cheek. *One of those guys was a friend*, he thought.

She wiped the tear away with the back of her hand.

Holbrook had stopped talking. The other detectives shuffled and stared. Madsen suddenly realized he had been asked a question. Something about whether he had any objections.

He flashed a warm smile and shook his head.

'Fine. Let's get started,' Holbrook growled.

'I've synched all the streams,' Shari said in a voice that betrayed none of the emotion Madsen had just seen. 'We've consolidated all data from Grant Avenue cameras for the last forty-eight hours, but what you are seeing now is T minus ten minutes. The footage is good enough to identify some of the people without composite matching.' She rotated a dial. 'Here is the mechanic leaving.'

On the Wall, the still images came alive.

Madsen leaned forward for a better look.

A man wearing grey coveralls strolled across the road. He lit a cigarette when he reached the opposite sidewalk, then turned left, exited one camera frame, appeared in the next, then walked out of view altogether.

'He was in the coffee joint down the road,' Holbrook said. 'A piece of brick hit him. He's at St Francis Memorial now with a suspected skull fracture. Got off lucky, considering.'

The playback continued rolling. A woman and two small children walked in from the left, passed in front of the dollhouse, and exited at the right. They were followed by an elderly couple. Two men strolled into view, their black uniforms in stark contrast to the other pedestrians.

Holbrook pointed. 'There go our boys.'

The two officers smiled and laughed silently as they walked up to the dollhouse entrance and pushed their way inside. The door swung shut.

No one spoke.

Only hours ago, Madsen realized, those two men had started their shift in the patrol room just down the corridor. Their gear would still be hanging in their lockers.

The footage shuffled forward. More pedestrians. A young man left the dollhouse, ran a comb through his hair, stepped off the kerb and crossed the street. Another arrived and stepped inside quickly with his head down, perhaps embarrassed about being seen entering an adult establishment.

Shari twisted the dial further and the vision kicked into fast-forward. She let it fall to normal speed just as the door opened. 'T minus three and a half minutes. This was the last person to leave.'

The man stepping out was large, balding, and wore baggy trousers with a white business shirt, no tie or jacket. He checked his watch. Dangling from his right hand was a soft brown leather briefcase with straps and buckles, the kind favoured by academics. One of the straps hung loose. Madsen wondered how much explosive could be crammed into it.

'Numbers?' demanded Holbrook.

Shari checked her console. 'The computer count says six hundred and fourteen arrivals for the last forty-eight hours, and six hundred and two departures. That's customers, staff, cleaners, deliveries . . . everyone.'

There was a low whistle from one of the detectives. 'That's how Dreamcom makes the big bucks.'

Holbrook shot him a look. 'I make that twelve dead, plus or minus.'

'We've got a sub-count of thirty-seven carrying bags of one type or another,' continued Shari, 'and twenty-five flagged as possibles for a bomb concealed under clothes. We've yet to double-check any of these manually.'

'When do we get IDs?' asked Madsen.

'The first ones should be coming through in a few minutes.'

Holbrook waved his hand. 'Okay, let's see the in-house footage.'

'Sorry, sir, no inside vision just yet,' Shari said. 'Dreamcom premises are exempt. They're going to review it to make sure it doesn't compromise customer privacy—'

Holbrook snorted. 'Bullshit. Twelve of their customers just got vaporized and they're worried about privacy?'

'They'll have it to us first thing tomorrow.'

The exemption Shari referred to was from Stream Share. The Stream Share Act, a federal law passed during the second Al Qaeda surge, extended the powers of the original Communications Assistance for Law Enforcement Act of 1994. The new law compelled businesses to make all their CCTV networks – in commercial retail and trading areas, showrooms, waiting rooms, servicing rooms, thoroughfares and lobbies – accessible to law enforcement agencies in real time. Most businesses complied by installing a standard, police-approved electronic gateway, which was how Shari's team had already tapped recorded CCTV footage from all the stores along Grant Avenue, but a few industries, such as healthcare and adult entertainment, had secured exemptions because of heightened privacy obligations to customers. Getting their footage always took longer.

Holbrook began barking instructions. 'I want a new file opened as each ID comes in. Start with those carrying bags or making deliveries. Collect all the background info you can get. Share names and places as you get 'em. Gerry, you're on victim profiles. Anyone important or different – big money, connections, you name it, we need to know . . .'

When he had finished he clapped his large hands together and shot Madsen a lopsided grin. 'Agent Madsen, would you like to start with the victims' wives?'

Madsen winced. He could picture it now. She, pale, distraught, tissue dabbing at her eyes as he asked, ever so gently, Mrs Smith, did you resent your husband banging a skinjob because you couldn't give him the extra kick he was looking for? Did it make you want to blow him to smithereens? A green light is good. It rules you out, you understand, so we can go after the real killer . . .

Aloud he said, 'How about we deal with wives later. I'm sure we'll have higher priority candidates.'

Holbrook ignored him. Addressing his men again he said, 'Home base for the duration is this station. There's a room being cleared for us. Upstairs, first on the left. Be there for a swap and tell at nine a.m. sharp. Let's go!'

As the detectives dispersed, Madsen fell into step beside

Holbrook. 'Mike,' he said, as amiably as he could, 'I'm here to help. If you just have your team feed me names, I can—'

'You'll get your names,' Holbrook said. 'Just be sure to share the results. Everything comes back through me. Don't get any ideas about flying solo.'

As the voices of the detectives receded down the corridor, Shari Sanayei struggled to rationalize her actions. *That was the time,* she thought. *I should have taken Holbrook aside and excused myself from the case. When it involves family you declare it. Don't kid yourself that lovers don't qualify. You declare it and you step away. Then others decide what role you have, if any. I've no business being here.*

But I am *here.*

And he might be back . . . the rescue teams are still digging, sending micro-bots down crevasses, bringing in heavy cutters, lifters . . .

No. They have to go through the motions. And I saw for myself: there won't be any miracle survivors stretchered from the depths, gasping clean air and blinking in the sunshine.

He's gone.

Fresh emotions welled up, and with them questions. *Why a dollhouse? Explain that to me, Adam. Wasn't I enthusiastic enough, attentive enough? And why now? Was it the pressure? Did the stress drive you to it?*

He had complained sometimes, about things he saw on the streets that distressed him, usually followed by a lame joke about how she, safe behind her cameras, wouldn't understand.

Pressure. The word echoed harshly back at her.

And if you are honest, Shari, you know it didn't come from the work.

It came from you.

She had been pushing him, gently but firmly, to do what was right. It had gone on too long, she said. The carefully planned trysts, once exciting, now felt furtive and dishonest. Time to get it into the open. If people didn't understand, then so be it. Soon, he had replied. A few more days. Next week. Be patient. He was scared of the confrontation with his wife, and when that was over, her retribution.

Shari had seen her just the once, when she stopped by the station. Taller, older, but still attractive. She was speaking to Adam in the entrance lobby. Not rude, not friendly. Businesslike. Hints of the bitter personality beneath? The one sketched by her husband in brief moments of post-coital reflection? Or maybe she was just having a bad day.

Whatever, she would be devastated now. She was probably crying somewhere, probably alone.

What will it do to her now? Shari wondered. Finding out that her husband was embroiled in a passionate, longstanding, full-blown affair, and was preparing to leave her. Being in a dollhouse was nothing compared with that bombshell.

And his parents' memories, the respect of his colleagues, his decorations. They too would be sullied and tarnished.

And herself. She would be ostracized. The humiliation . . .

She savagely pushed the thought from her mind.

No, she thought. It was over. No one knew and no one needed to know. And it wasn't just to spare herself. It was for the others. There was too much pain already. And she wasn't going anywhere. She was going to stay right there and do her job and get the bastard that killed him and be there to stare into his eyes when they brought him in.

No one needed to know.

A tiny alarm triggered.

Yolanda. She knew.

And while she was a friend who kept her confidences, something this big could change that. Best to talk to her, make sure she understood.

Addressing her two subordinates through her microphone, Shari said, 'Guys, I'm taking a break. Back in two.' They nodded, too busy at their tasks to turn. Shari slipped off her headset and hurried down the corridor to the dispatch room.

Chapter 4 _____

Three thousand miles to the east, Tom Fillinger, the seventy-two-year-old silver-haired CEO of Dreamcom Interactive, sat in the darkness of his apartment and stared out at the canyons of Manhattan. The specially manufactured flawless glass panel before him gave no internal reflections, creating the illusion that nothing lay between him and the twinkling lights of the city. The rest of the apartment, which occupied the entire floor, was equally unique. Every wall and partition had been removed to create a single space, with only a few pillars and an elevator shaft to interrupt the three hundred and sixty degree panorama. Fillinger came here to be alone, to think and to reflect on his achievements. He came here to relax.

But he was not relaxed tonight. A war had started.

A cell phone buzzed on the small table beside him, its face flashing green in the darkness. He put down his glass and answered with a wave.

'Speak to me.'

The caller was unfazed by the bluntness. 'They've confirmed it's a bomb.'

'So what are they doing about it?'

'Swarming all over. There were two cops in there, so it's maximum effort. They're shaking down everyone they can lay their hands on.'

'Fallout?'

'It's going to hurt, but we can contain it – the entire marketing team is working full throttle. We might take more dips depending on how NeChristo works the media.'

NeChristo. The New Christian Organization of America was the fastest growing church in the country, having taken little more than a decade to leap to the forefront of mainstream religious culture. It had a huge membership, and its charismatic leaders were fiercely opposed to the dollhouses.

'We'll just have to outwork them,' Fillinger said. 'What's the security situation?'

'Should have extra manpower outside office buildings, the plant and fifty per cent of the dollhouses first thing in the morning. We're contacting police departments in each city to request extra drive-bys and any other assistance they can give. We'll have to handle most of it ourselves.'

Fillinger contemplated this for a long time, clenching and unclenching his fist as he tallied the costs. 'The people investigating this,' he said finally. 'Are they any good?'

'The SFPD inspector leading it is Mike Holbrook, a twenty-two-year veteran. Half that time uniform, half in homicide. He's been given plenty of resources. An FBI plotter has been assigned as well. One of those hotshots with—'

'I know what a plotter is. What I want to know is, can they wind it up in six days?'

'I think so.'

'They'd better.'

Eleven months earlier Fillinger had cut a deal with a Texan billionaire named Jim Bonitas to gut, refurbish and relaunch his casino – the biggest on the Vegas strip – as an adult entertainment mega-complex. With massive themed playrooms and a long list of exotic indulgences unavailable in any other casino, or regular dollhouses for that matter, Ten Worlds promised to deliver huge revenues. It had to, because the renovations had taken twice as long and cost twice as much as projected. Each day that passed added to an already crippling financial burden. The opening was Tuesday. Nothing could be allowed to get in the way.

Fillinger said, 'This plotter guy, what do you have on him?'

'Name's Daniel Madsen. Some kind of rising star. Reputation for making fast arrests. That's about it.'

'He deals with me personally. No one else. Anything comes up, any decision, anything important at all, send it direct to me. Understand?'

'Got it.'

Fillinger asked a few more questions, demanded updates every hour, then hung up. His face twitched with the intensity of his emotions. He would out-think and out-dare them, he told himself. Like he always did.

Tom Fillinger was a survivor. He had grown up without a father; his mother drank her wages and secured shelter by floating between seedy boyfriends while Tom eked out what cash they had with his knack for repairing radios and record players. When he was thirteen one of his mother's beaus, a hustler named Zack, had transformed his life. Zack heard about the money in skin flicks and decided to build his own booth or, more precisely, source the components so Fillinger could build one for him.

A clapped-out projector was bought for a few dollars and a coin mechanism scrounged from an old vending machine. Plywood sheets were lifted from a construction site. The film canister arrived covered in Zack's dried blood after he used his fist to punch it out of someone else's booth. And Fillinger did as he was told, fixing, aligning, assembling and adjusting the pieces into a working unit.

They installed it on a Thursday, just in time for the weekend action, at a strip joint owned by an ex-con and one-time cellmate of Zack's. Late Saturday night the friend called to say the machine was already broken. In the early hours of Sunday morning Fillinger, sporting a black eye and purple bruises down both arms, was dispatched to make repairs.

That morning would stay with him for ever: running down

deserted streets in the cool dawn, graffiti-plastered walls, the dirty spaghetti of unlit neon, fumbling in his pocket for the key, then the eerie silence inside as he tiptoed past a stage scuffed and scratched white by the countless girls who had gyrated and strutted upon it, shedding everything but their high heels.

The booth – a crude box with a matt black paintjob and matching curtain – was in the back room. Fillinger unlatched the metal cover at the rear. He rocked the reels to ensure they had not slipped off their hubs, then checked the film was correctly threaded between the rollers. He flicked a lever. The projector rattled into life. After a few seconds he switched it off. Puzzled, he closed the cover, pulled the curtain and stepped inside. Slimy wads of tissue covered the floor, mixing with spilt beer to create an almighty stink. Kneeling in the mess, he unlocked the kick panel and reached into the cavity, groping for the steel coin bucket. It wouldn't budge. Cursing his own design he bent lower and tried again. Eventually he lay flat, with a cheek pressed into the stickiness so he could use both hands. He levered the bucket out, inch by inch.

The shock came first. Then elation, more powerful than any he had experienced. The quarters were piled so high they dribbled over the edges of the bucket. Jammed behind and down both sides of the cavity were twice as many coins again.

A slow smile spread across young Fillinger's lips, growing and widening until it became a full, contented grin. The grin of a slave just handed his ticket to freedom.

In the darkness, staring out through the flawless glass, Fillinger picked up his phone again. He punched a button.

'Get a hold of our guy in Washington . . . Yeah, him.'

A few minutes later he stepped out of his private elevator onto the rooftop. A breeze whispered across his skin. Distant sounds of traffic echoed from the streets. Squatting in the darkness was a helicopter, sleek and menacing in red and black Dreamcom livery.

Alerted by the light from the elevator, the pilot began performing checks and flicking switches.

Fillinger listened to the spooling turbines and waited until the rotor blades chopped at the air before stepping aboard. As he strapped into the rear compartment he wondered if this was how all men felt when they departed for battle, and losing meant dying.

Twelve minutes later he crossed the general aviation ramp at JFK International to where *Dream Flyer*, his personal Gulfstream G3000, waited with lights flashing and big Pratt & Whitney jet engines turning and burning.

Shortly after that he was flying west, towards San Francisco, at six hundred miles an hour.

Chapter 5

The store resembled a mini mart. It had its own parking lot, occupied by only a few cars this evening, and was surrounded by a high privacy wall. The sign in red and yellow neon out front said it all.

EDDIE'S ADULT EMPORIUM
'Eddie gets it!'
Open 24 Hours

Madsen pushed through the plastic curtain and stood in the doorway, letting the air conditioning wash over him. He had conducted nine field polygraphs in two hours, beginning with the last men seen leaving the dollhouse and ending with a convicted arsonist picked up loitering near the crime scene. Somewhere in the middle he stopped by St Francis Memorial for a bedside interview with the mechanic. He had a good feeling about that one, bolstered by the dark looks that greeted his arrival, but the mechanic pulled clean greens on the polygraph like all the others.

Eddie, a middle-aged rogue with a perpetual twinkle in his eye, stood behind the counter in one of his trademark shirts – this one a collage of sunsets, palm trees and hibiscus flowers in bright tropical hues. He was serving a customer. Tonight's sales assistant, a thin, clean-cut young man like all the others, was holding up what looked like a black rubber space suit.

The customer shook his head.

Madsen looked at his watch and resigned himself to waiting. According to Eddie, there was nothing so important to *optimize* as one's next sexual experience, especially for men, but with all manner of subtle variations on offer this meant some customers took an interminably long time to make up their minds and buy something. Eddie called it the timeless challenge of adult retail.

Madsen moved away from a showcase of super-sized electronic appendages to a display of restraints, each of them more elaborate than anything he had seen in law enforcement.

His first encounter with Eddie had been more than a year ago, when a strange creature in sky blue slacks and a fox fur coat appeared in front of his desk one morning and feigned horror at Madsen's rumpled jacket, gave a dissertation on fashion and the modern agent and meandered through a series of random observations on sexuality and morality in San Francisco. At first Madsen thought it a joke played by his colleagues, and was angry at the interruption because he was working on an urgent case. Two little boys had disappeared and a stranger, subsequently identified as a sex offender who had skipped bail in Michigan, had been seen near their elementary school. Madsen was in a frenzied race to find them, and the last thing he needed was a goofball wasting his time. Very quickly, however, he realized that Eddie was establishing his rules of engagement.

There were three.

First, Eddie did not – not now, not ever – judge people for their peccadilloes, no matter how extreme. If someone had been dealt an unusual hand, then Eddie's only role was selling them paraphernalia to help them along the way. Second, so far as morality went, Eddie couldn't care less about the statutes. His boundaries were defined by the words *consenting* and *adults* and even they could be nuanced. You had to give latitude on the former, for example, when trying to establish that extra *frisson* that some relationships demanded. Third, there was an obvious commercial downside to being seen helping anyone in Madsen's profession, so he would attend no courtroom, accept no question about his information and make no further visits to a federal building. If Madsen wished to stop by for a social call he was welcome – law enforcement boys were among his best customers – but if Madsen dared pull out his polygraph, ever, then their relationship was over.

After this hurricane of words, Eddie placed a single sheet of paper on Madsen's desk, made a bow and left.

Across the top, in neat copperplate handwriting, was an address.

Within hours a baby-faced man, naked except for a leather apron, screamed for his life as six burly SWAT operators slammed him to the ground, and Madsen was choking up as he tried to convince two terrified boys he really was there to take them home.

Eddie, true to his word, refused to discuss the case again. He was always happy, however, to debate the vicissitudes and moral ambiguities of sexuality, and more than once these discussions gave Madsen useful insights about the dark places inhabited by his fugitives.

Which was why, with no deep knowledge of dollhouses and no joy from his first round of targets, Madsen had stopped by tonight.

A set of large blacked-out goggles caught Madsen's eye. They would have looked at home in a welder's shop. He lifted them, felt their weight, and discovered they were tethered to a complicated-looking device designed to be strapped over the lap. A yellow sunburst label proclaimed it the last word in portable, 4-D haptic erogenous wear that guaranteed a *Silky-Smooth, Sensory-Saturated EXperience!!!* Another, more prosaic label dangling from the power cord spelled out a long list of health warnings.

'Personal or professional use?' purred a voice.

Madsen replaced the goggles and turned to face Eddie's wicked smile and suggestively arched eyebrow.

'Purely professional tonight, Eddie. Sorry.'

'Mmmhmm. Shame. I got some leather chaps in that you should look at. Real high-grade cowhide. You'd stand a much better chance of catching bad boys in those.' His gaze tracked downwards. 'All I need is an inside leg measurement.'

Madsen smiled. 'I'm here to get some advice, if that's okay.'

'Depends what it is, darling.'

'The dollhouse bombing. Today. You heard about it?'

'Heard about it? I felt it! I hid under the counter with Scotty and told him it was an earthquake and we were all going to die. Made him stay under there with me for a half-hour, just to be sure.' The cheeky smile appeared again. 'It's all everybody's been talking about.'

Madsen wasn't sure whether Eddie was referring to the doll-house or the interlude with Scotty. 'I'm on the investigation.'

'Congratulations. I should think that's a pretty big coup for an FBI plotter man like you.' Eddie affected a gushing, Scarlett O'Hara accent, pronouncing 'I' as an extended *aaah*. 'But I didn't do it, sir, I promise!' He laughed.

Madsen was serious, though. 'The way I look at it, some people got killed today for nothing more than exercising a little sexual freedom.'

Eddie's smile became strained. He nodded. *Point taken.*

'I'm after general insights,' continued Madsen, 'about the whole doll scene for starters. Who's up who, that sort of thing. Can you give me a primer?'

'Perhaps you would care,' Eddie said salaciously, 'to spend a few minutes alone with me in the storeroom.'

Madsen grinned. 'That would make my evening.'

As they passed the counter, Eddie shot his clean-cut assistant a cat-that-got-the-cream smile. The younger man stared daggers back.

Only half of the storeroom was taken up by stock. The rest was an Aladdin's cave of erotic memorabilia. Autographed first edition magazines, posters, films and video cassettes, and a disorganized selection of vintage sex toys, lay alongside wind-up vibrators propped up on antique bondage furniture. A collection of plaster-cast phalluses jutted provocatively from a shelf labelled 'Organ Donors'.

Eddie locked the door and dragged out a pair of plastic chairs. He retrieved a Tequila bottle and glasses and poured two generous shots.

Madsen gestured at the door. 'Will he be all right?'

Eddie chuckled. 'Scotty? He'll be fine. Do him good to think he's got a little competition.' He handed Madsen a glass. 'So, darling, where would you like to start?'

'Who hates Dreamcom enough to do this?'

Eddie knocked back his shot in one go, then poured himself another. 'The churches. Polygraph those white-cassocked hypocrites and you'll get enough to put every one of them in jail.'

Oh no, we're not going there, Madsen thought. He had suffered through at least a dozen of Eddie's lectures on how religious revivalism was the end of adult entertainment, freedom and everything worth living for generally. 'Who else?' he asked.

'Dreamcom are hurting everyone, Danny boy. The entire industry. Me included.'

'How? Don't you sell their products?'

'Last year I moved a thousand sim-sets a month. A month! They loved me. I was their best friend. When they came out with the dollies, who do you think they called first?' He held up an index finger and made an elaborate show of tapping his chest. 'That's right, they wanted little Eddie to help, just like you do. Questions and then more questions. How should we promote our dollies? What price? Where's the sweet spot in the market?' Eddie downed his second shot and wiped his mouth. 'So I helped. I told them which ideas were good and which ones would never work. I even let them use my store to get customer feedback on the prototypes. But when they were all done, when they had all their answers . . .' He put on a sad face. 'Do you think they let little old Eddie get even a teeny-weeny slice of the action? No. Just like some other people I know, lots of take, but never any give.' After a pause he said, 'Actually, that's not fair. You may be a plotter man, darling, but at least you aren't a pretender.'

He pointed over Madsen's shoulder. 'All we got out of them in the end was that promo dolly. They asked me to send her back too, but I told them to get lost.'

Madsen turned. In the corner, partly obscured behind a stack of boxes, was a curvaceous figure in a sequinned blue bikini. She was standing in the classic hand-on-hip pose of a fashion model.

Eddie walked over and shoved the boxes out of the way, revealing the doll's face: she had long eyelashes, full, moist lips, and thick, glossy curls that cascaded over her shoulders and made Madsen think of shampoo commercials. Most striking was the skin: smooth, soft-looking, and complete with tiny imperfections – a freckle here, a dimple there – that drew the eye and tricked the brain into thinking that perhaps she was a real woman after all.

'Of course she's only a showroom model, and first generation, but even then you could tell they had something special.' He gently pulled the bikini top aside and cupped a breast. 'This is where the magic is, you know. In the skin. Go ahead, feel.'

'I'm fine,' Madsen said.

'No, you should, Danny boy,' Eddie whispered. 'I insist. I'm not being silly old Eddie. If you really want to understand. If you want to know what Dreamcom had that was so special . . .'

Madsen had heard all about the patented skin from the advertising, but he had never felt it, and he had to admit he *was* curious. He stood and moved towards the doll, reaching out to touch a shoulder.

'No, Danny, like this.' Eddie grabbed Madsen's hand and, before he could react, pressed it into the breast.

The surface was silky smooth. The flesh beneath – for it did feel like flesh – yielded under his fingers exactly as a real woman's would have, but what surprised him, what was wholly unexpected and *electrified* his senses, was the heat. It radiated out of her like she had just jogged a mile, or come in from the gym, or was flushed with sexual energy. And it ran deeper than the skin. If he closed his eyes he could almost imagine he could feel . . .

'What the *fuck!*' Madsen jerked his hand free and leapt back, eyes wide.

Eddie doubled over, convulsing with laughter. 'Oh, Danny, your face! If you could only see yourself . . . Oh, oh dear. She's just a dolly, I promise. But the heartbeat is so perfect, don't you think?'

Regaining his composure, Madsen cautiously reached out and placed his hand against the doll's slender neck. There was a pulse there too. Slightly fast, in tune with the elevated body temperature. Hypnotic.

'The whole point of the display version,' Eddie said, 'was to wow shoppers with look and feel. One touch and you had to have one. It worked for me: I keep her plugged in all day . . .'

'So what happened? Why didn't they let you sell them?'

'Oh. Well, first there was the pricing. The dollies were expensive, especially when you added in the servicing, and only our wealthiest clients could afford one. But that wasn't insurmountable. I came up with – well, myself and some other retailers came up with – a new rental-based business model which solved those issues.'

'The dollhouses.'

'Yes, darling. You're jumping ahead but yes, renting dolls by the hour, on the premises. That was our concept. We worked with our customers to get it right. In return we expected first option on a franchise, but Dreamcom decided they didn't want franchises, they wanted control. They did it themselves. Cut us out.'

He gazed sadly at the doll, then, with the gentleness of someone handling a newborn kitten, he began to plait her hair. 'It would have been lovely . . .' Suddenly, he let out a loud sob. 'I would have looked after you, sweetie. You and all your friends.'

There was a scuffling on the other side of the door. 'Eddie, is everything okay?'

Eddie responded with another sob, louder and even more theatrical than the first.

'Eddie, I'm coming in there.'

Madsen said loudly, 'Scotty, it's my fault. I'm afraid I've asked a bit much of him and he's worn out. Would you mind getting him a nice cup of tea? There's a good boy.'

A derisive snort came back through the door. It seemed to restore Eddie's spirits a little. Madsen ushered him back to his chair and took up where they had left off. 'You said they were hurting everyone, but surely someone stands out?'

'Yes, Danny. Me. Arrest me and take me away . . .' He pressed his wrists together in readiness for the handcuffs, then dropped them in his lap. 'Look, I don't know why you have to ask me,' he said, suddenly serious again. 'It's obvious, isn't it? The boys in Tokyo.'

'Tokyo?'

'Nomura? Hello?' Eddie threw his hands up in exasperation. 'Where have you *been*, darling, don't you have time to watch the news while you're out chasing bad boys?'

Nomura. It took Madsen a moment to remember. Not a person, a Japanese conglomerate. It had been in the headlines six or seven months back, for importing products barely tolerated even in its home market.

'They do kiddie dolls, right?'

'They make all sorts. Kiddies, doggies, cartoon characters. If you want to fuck it, they make it. They even make women.' Eddie gestured at the corner. 'Not nearly as good as that, but it won't be long – you know the Japs. They've rolled out their own dollhouses across Asia and half of Europe, and they're hopping mad they can't get in on the action here.'

'What's stopping them?'

'They got slapped with an import ban on their dollies, not just the kiddie versions, all of them. Three years.' Eddie studied his fingernails. 'Dreamcom knew perfectly well the sort of backlash the kiddie dolls would inspire. They screamed loudest of all, and behind the scenes they worked politicians, bureaucrats, everyone. The sinners remade themselves into saints. I don't think the Nomura boys saw it coming, frankly.' He shook his head. 'Think about it. Three years was a big punishment for something that might be bad taste but technically wasn't a crime, and it effectively gave their biggest competitor an unbeatable head start in the market. Nomura have been desperately lobbying for a reversal, but they haven't got a hope against that kind of influence.'

'Whose influence?'

'Dreamcom's, darling. You really should pay attention.'

Outside in the parking lot, blue-white light from a dashboard screen flickered over Madsen's face as he sat in the Dodge skimming a downloaded file on Nomura Entertainment Enterprises. It was much as Eddie had told him. They had put up a fight, hired the best PR agency money could buy, but in the end they never stood a chance against the images flooding the media. The pathetic, cherubic faces of kiddie dolls had sickened the nation. Nomura continued the fight out of an office in Beverly Hills. It had hired a barrage of lawyers to challenge the ban on anti-competitive grounds, but they weren't making much progress.

The file contained another piece of information that caught his eye: a note, appended by a senior agent in the Bureau's Tokyo office, on Nomura's connections to the Japanese mob. From what Madsen knew about the Yakuza, they generally favoured a businesslike approach to crime, operating like a vast, highly efficient parasite beneath the surface of mainstream society. Generally, but not always. When necessary, they were perfectly comfortable employing vicious and extreme violence to get what they wanted.

Madsen began dictating a request for an administrative subpoena *ad testificandum*, more commonly known as an ASAT. Introduced to expedite urgent investigations during the war on terror, the ASAT was an instrument that compelled individuals to testify in a matter or face charges of their own. They had proved their value time and again, prompting a series of extensions on how and when they could be used. Nowadays a federal agent could request an ASAT on any operation where lives were endangered and time was a factor. Requests were routed to a special FBI tribunal which sat twenty-four hours a day, and approvals were usually turned around in forty-five minutes.

Madsen expected no delay on this one.

He finished setting out his case logic, pasted in the background on the Yakuza connections and uploaded the request. He copied it to the LA field office with a cover note explaining his intentions. Then he started the Dodge, backed out of the lot and turned south, towards San Francisco International Airport.

Chapter 6

It was nearly midnight when the US Airways flight touched down at Bob Hope Airport in Burbank, nine miles north of Beverly Hills. Madsen was met at the gate by a small, sharply dressed man with a flat-top haircut and a black Camaro. He introduced himself as Kenji Kobayashi, a special agent from the LA office.

Considering the lateness of the hour, Kobayashi was surprisingly upbeat. He happily filled Madsen in on the situation while he drove.

'LAPD viddy ops pinned both targets at the address you gave. It's actually a residence. A nice one – these guys aren't short of bucks.'

'Both targets?' Madsen asked. He had only named Butch Traviano, the CEO of Nomura's US operation, in his ASAT request.

'Yeah, Traviano is just the American face, the one you see on the news. Does all the press interviews, fronts the hearings. God knows why they picked him: he's a hell of an ugly frontman, especially for a company whose main mission right now is making friends and influencing people.' Kobayashi chuckled. 'Then again, Nomura Entertainment isn't famous for its good taste and subtlety. The other guy is Hideki Yoshida. Strictly low-profile.

The trusted man from Tokyo who keeps an eye on things. The real boss. I figured you'd want both, so I extended the subpoena. Hope you don't mind.'

Madsen didn't.

'Yoshida speaks English,' Kobayashi added, 'but will almost certainly insist on Japanese in the interview.'

'Do you happen to—'

'Fluent. That's why you got me. I was on a date, by the way. Nice restaurant, candles, the whole shebang.'

'Sorry about that.'

'Forget it.' Kobayashi flashed a smile. 'Probably did me a favour.'

The Nomura residence was in a compound surrounded on all sides by a solid, ten-foot-high wall. Above that the upper storeys of a garish mansion poked up through a thick canopy of trees. Spotlights lit up dusky pink ramparts, reminding Madsen of the Disney castle. A single entrance guarded by a pair of enormous wrought-iron gates breached the perimeter. Through the bars, a white pebble drive could be seen receding into a small forest.

A streetlight reflected off a windshield fifty yards further down the street. A parked LAPD cruiser. *Nice to have a little backup for a change*, Madsen thought.

Kobayashi drove directly up to the gates and announced himself into a grille.

A metallic voice replied and a camera zoomed in on his badge.

The back of Madsen's neck tingled. *They've got motive, criminal connections and capability*, he thought. *And I'm landing on their doorstep within a few hours, express delivery, to catch them off balance. No time to prepare, no chance to sleep. Close to ideal conditions.*

The gates swung open. Pebbles crunched softly under the tyres as the Camaro idled past cherry blossom trees, manicured gardens and an endless series of ponds, each connected to others via miniature canals and sluices. Stone lanterns glowed at regular intervals along the banks. Orange carp slid silently through the light pools, their tails tracing lazy patterns along the surface.

They drew up to the mansion and two stocky men in navy suits materialized from the shadows. One stepped into the headlights with his hand up. The other peered into the driver's side window, inspecting the occupants.

Madsen and Kobayashi were escorted through a front door almost as grand as the gate. After a brief wait, they were ushered through a second set of doors.

The room was lavishly furnished, brightly lit and enormous, with a ceiling higher than Madsen had ever seen inside a private residence. The interior decorator must have had a flair for the dramatic because suspended just inside was a bronze eagle with a ten-foot wingspan. It was poised mid swoop, talons extended, as if ready to pluck unwanted intruders from the ground and spirit them to its nest. A heavy mahogany dining table occupied the space directly in front of the visitors.

Three men sat at the far end of the table, radiating hostility.

Madsen immediately recognized the sagging bloodhound jowls in the middle. Butch Traviano. To his left was a Japanese man in his fifties, his hair styled into short, yellow-dyed spikes, like a punk's. That had to be Yoshida. The third man was younger, a blue-eyed Californian type wearing delicate steel-rimmed glasses and sitting slightly apart, as if in deference to the others. He looked like a lawyer.

All three wore suits; not a dressing-gown in sight.

The man with the glasses slid a business card across the table. 'Agents Madsen and Kobayashi, I believe? Gerard Collett, of Collett & Saunders, attorneys at law. We've been retained by Mr Traviano and Mr Yoshida for legal counsel. I'll be sitting in on your interviews this evening.' Yoshida gave a small nod at the mention of his name. No one offered to shake hands.

So much for surprise. Madsen stole a sideways glance at his colleague. Kobayashi gave a tiny shrug.

Traviano smiled. 'What took you so long?' he drawled.

'Can I please see your subpoena?' continued Collett smoothly, motioning for them to sit.

Madsen slid a copy of the ASAT across the table. In theory, interviewees didn't need lawyers because they couldn't be compelled to testify against themselves, and answers to any question outside the scope of the subpoena were inadmissible in court. In theory. In practice, career crims always wanted one because they had learned, the hard way, that plotters remembered every red light, admissible or otherwise, and filed it away for future reference. A well-prepared lawyer could at least ensure the questions stayed within tight boundaries.

Traviano went first. He spoke slowly and deliberately, employing the fewest words he could get away with while still answering the questions. As expected, Collett interjected frequently, challenging any question that could be construed as testing the scope of the subpoena. Each time this happened Madsen was forced to pause and negotiate an adjustment. Traviano was clearly an old gangster with plenty to hide, and Collett was skilled at ensuring it remained hidden.

Traviano drew a steady sequence of greens.

Coming to the last of his questions, Madsen decided to toss in a hand grenade. What the hell. He had nothing to lose, and sometimes shaking things up revealed an unexpected weakness, a chink in the armour which could be probed and exploited. Without changing tone or pace he said, 'So level with me, Butch, ever had anyone killed?'

Traviano's eyes widened.

Kobayashi stiffened and looked like he wanted to be somewhere else.

Collett's hand shot out. 'Don't answer that,' he spluttered.

Yoshida remained impassive, his eyes half-closed. If he understood the question he gave no sign.

Madsen switched off the HAMDA and casually tossed it on the table. 'It's just between us now, what do you say? C'mon, you're a tough guy. Impress me! How many times have you had someone rubbed out?'

'I object. This is harassment!' Collett exclaimed.

Traviano's eyes flashed and his jowls reddened, but he said nothing. He clasped his hands together over his belly and sat back from the table.

'Your polygraph interview is now complete, Mr Traviano,'

Madsen said, as if nothing had happened. 'Thank you for your cooperation.' He retrieved the HAMDA and hit the reset button. Turning to Yoshida, he said, 'Agent Kobayashi, if you would be so kind . . . Mr Yoshida, do you know what this device is?'

Madsen ran through the same series of questions, adapting them as Collett had requested to avoid further interruptions. Collett, who was also apparently bilingual, listened carefully to the translations but did not intervene. He had done his job, and he could hardly protest what had already been agreed. Madsen briefly considered picking up the pace a little to put his interviewee on the back foot, but Yoshida had his own delaying tactics. Each time Kobayashi translated, the older man sought a clarification, which he then pondered at length before answering.

Yoshida gave his answers in Japanese, enunciating the syllables precisely and softly, and with his eyes locked to Madsen's.

When it was over, Madsen fished out a card and dropped it on the table. 'The people who hit Dreamcom could target your interests too. If you know anything, or you hear anything, this is how you contact me.'

He stood to leave, trying not to show his disappointment. Butch stank of the mob and Yoshida, although more refined, gave off the same foul odour, but neither had triggered so much as a glimmer of a red light. If Nomura Entertainment was behind the bombing, then it must have been planned and executed out of Tokyo with neither of these two knowing about it. That was unlikely.

He was halfway to the door with Kobayashi close behind when a rush of Japanese words, harsh and admonishing, stopped him in his tracks. He turned. Yoshida was on his feet, ramrod straight with his arms close by his sides, as if on a parade ground. Madsen shot a raised eyebrow at Kobayashi.

Kobayashi shifted uncomfortably. 'Mr Yoshida says he is most disappointed that you finished your interview and never asked him your additional, special question. The one you asked Mr Traviano.'

Madsen fought back a smile. The HAMDA, safely nestled inside his jacket, remained on. It would only pick up the audio, and the results would be useless in any case, but he was curious. He said, 'Please, Yoshida-san, will you do me the honour of telling me how many people you have had rubbed out?'

Kobayashi began to translate the question, but this time Yoshida did not wait. Instead of speaking, he raised both hands: five fingers outstretched on one, two on the other. Then he bowed and burst into a long, loud laugh.

The navy-suited goons appeared and escorted Madsen and Kobayashi back outside. Kobayashi said nothing as he started the Camaro, and a few moments later they were rolling back through the trees and past the fishponds. As Madsen listened to the pebbles crunching beneath the tyres, he felt deflated. The day was finished, he had worked through all his best candidates and he had nothing to show for it. So much for speed. It was late, he was tired, and somewhere nearby a motel bed awaited. The other candidates would have to wait until morning.

Thursday

Chapter 7

In the half light of the Washington dawn, two men walked together between hundred-year-old elms at the western end of the National Mall. A light rain spotted the long expanse of the Reflecting Pool and layers of mist swirled around the monuments and memorials, muting the white marble to a dirty grey.

The men walked slowly, their umbrellas touching, pausing occasionally to take in the view. From a distance they looked like two bureaucrats taking an early stroll to ruminate before the day's manoeuvrings in the Capitol. But they looked without seeing, and their conversation did not touch on bills, debates or votes. As always, it was about money.

The tall man with striking blond hair did most of the talking. His companion, short and stout, was making heavy work of the listening. Inwardly, Erol Arbett, the imposing senior senator for Ohio, fumed.

As an influential man in Congress, Arbett had endured countless meetings of this kind in his colourful career. Many, it had to be said, he had initiated. But even people representing major donors were supposed to exhibit a certain polite decorum. Right now it was absent. It hadn't helped that this ungrateful shit had called in the middle of the night, nor that his request for a meeting sounded like a summons. Arbett should have hung up. Except he shouldn't, and hadn't, because his term was almost up, and the campaign fund was looking anaemic, and the guy was not only in the front rank of Washington's 17,500 lobbyists but represented someone with whom Arbett had enjoyed a very satisfactory relationship over the years.

Had. The arrangement was looking pretty shaky right now.

The senator laboured along in the rain, listening and gritting his teeth as the lobbyist explained, in detail, just how much money his client had poured into those ridiculous dollhouses. Arbett had heard the numbers before and they only reminded him that Dreamcom could have been more generous.

'. . . and those are just the outlays over the last year,' the lobbyist was saying. 'You can see what's at risk. And after yesterday, well, it's imperative that we maintain the confidence of customers.'

Was that a statement or a question? Arbett wondered.

He said nothing.

'What they would like from you, Senator, is a little top-down assistance.'

Arbett frowned. 'What kind of assistance? I appreciate they had a bad day, but I can hardly call out the National Guard.'

'We were thinking of something less dramatic. A speech perhaps, or even a statement condemning the violence, reaffirming Dreamcom's right to do business.'

'Maybe we should save that for another time.'

'We need you now. Not tomorrow or next week. If we can't even get a lousy speech, then what exactly are we paying for?'

'That's enough,' snapped Arbett. 'You've had plenty of help.'

That was true. Arbett chaired the Senate Subcommittee on Competitiveness, Innovation, and Export Promotion, an appointment that sounded bland but had proved highly lucrative, and out of the dozen or so Silicon Valley corporations seeking his special assistance, Dreamcom was undeniably the one that had asked for, and received, the biggest favours. Just this year he fast-tracked a bill, drafted by the man walking alongside him, that had effectively excluded a big Japanese competitor from the US market for three years.

Arbett said, 'This is not a good time. There were protests in Washington, Chicago and Seattle yesterday. There will be another in New York this morning. The revivalists are scoring points, and the media haven't been shy about pointing out how close I am to your client.'

'Close? Right now you are so far away we hardly know you exist.'

They trudged in silence up a grassy slope and stopped at the Korean Veterans Memorial, contemplating the columns of life-sized GIs frozen in steel. The soldiers were dressed for the weather. Rain ran down their helmets and dripped from wind-ruffled ponchos and greatcoats.

Arbett tried again. 'What I'm trying to tell you is that it will be far more effective to lie low, until the revivalists lose steam. After that I can emerge as the voice of wisdom. I make a few carefully considered pronouncements. No new laws required. No changes. Back to business.'

Friends and enemies alike called Arbett a born hustler who could make money tap-dance from other people's pockets into his own. It explained his success as a real-estate executive – the last real job listed in his official résumé – as well as his meteoric rise to the Ohio State Legislature and thence to the Capitol. Those closest to him knew that behind this reputation lay a far simpler talent: he could convince anyone, no matter what their creed, agenda, problem or position, that he truly believed in their cause.

The lobbyist, however, was not just anyone, and his cynical smile spoke volumes.

Arbett sighed. 'There must be other ways of helping.'

The blond man rubbed his chin. 'Are you still on the Homeland Security Committee?'

The question was rhetorical; you didn't get to be any kind of lobbyist without knowing the members of every committee, Senate and House, by heart. 'Sure,' Arbett said. 'Although I don't know why.' He wielded little influence among the ribboned and medalled ex-military senators and had been trying to get off the damn thing.

'Perhaps you could do something to help expedite the investigation. This is domestic terrorism, after all. Nasty. The kind of thing that could have national implications. Until we get closure, a safety concern hangs over Dreamcom facilities across the country.'

Arbett nodded. This was more palatable, and more practical, and therefore very likely what the lobbyist had in mind all along. At least he wasn't talking about speeches any more. 'Go on.'

'To begin with, there is the question of resources. Are the police and FBI giving this case what it needs? What about assistance from other agencies? And is this guy Daniel Madsen—'

'Who the fuck is Daniel Madsen?'

'Exactly. He's the FBI plotter assigned to it. We need to make sure he's A-grade. Someone who knows how to crack heads to get things done.'

'My influence doesn't extend to rank and file appointments.'

'No, but you can ask questions, shake the tree a little. Interest from the top gets people jumping and sends a message that second best isn't good enough. I don't really care how, Senator, but we need arrests, fast. Give me a straight answer. Can you help or not?'

Arbett thought it over. The Bureau would find it irritating, but he was perfectly justified in asking questions about how a case of domestic terrorism was being handled. Two of San Francisco's finest had been killed, after all, and there was the possibility of more bombings to come. No one could blame him for taking an interest.

No, shaking the tree wasn't a big deal.

The big deal was how it would look to his new acquaintances.

The initial contact had been a fortnight ago. An offhand remark dropped at a fundraising dinner by a quiet fellow with a New England accent. Arbett couldn't even remember what was said, and it was only afterwards he realized that the remark had been a tentative probe. Later that evening, when Arbett was standing on the marble steps of the Excelsior waiting for his car to be brought around, the man reappeared alongside him, casually mentioning that he represented people who would very much like to meet the good senator, if he had time. The conversation was short. He handed Arbett a business card before stepping into a cab and disappearing.

The card identified the man as a partner in a small but prestigious DC law firm. It took one of Arbett's staffers less than five minutes to dig up a profile and client list, and to establish that the principal preoccupation of the firm was progressing the interests of a certain religious organization – the New Christian Organization of America.

The hotel rendezvous that followed had impressed Arbett a great deal. Considerable lengths were taken to preserve its secrecy. The NeChristo people present were unfailingly polite and charming, and alive to the subtleties of Arbett's position. Instead of tiptoeing around the elephant in the room they came right out and acknowledged his longstanding relationship with Dreamcom and said there would be no hard feelings if he wished to preserve it. Of course if, by chance, he was interested in a new relationship, then he would have to cut those ties, but for now this was mere conversation. Theoretical. Most impressive of all were the dollars. They were bigger, much bigger, than anything Arbett had ever seen.

Arbett had played for time, asking for a week or two to consider their offer. Not that much more consideration was needed. NeChristo's ascendancy as the largest of the new churches had been spectacular beyond belief. And public sentiment had been sliding away from Dreamcom for months, thanks to the protests. But there was still lingering uncertainty about whether the latter shift would be permanent. Arbett liked certainty, if he could get it.

Now Dreamcom wanted a favour. The question was, did he have time to squeeze a little more out of the old arrangement, or would it send the wrong signals and potentially block a more profitable arrangement with his new friends, should he decide to go that way?

They left the ghostly faces of the Korean Veterans Memorial behind and strolled downhill, back in the direction of Arbett's limousine and waiting driver. The rain was coming more steadily, at a slant. Arbett tilted his umbrella forward to shield himself, but only succeeded in exposing his back and shoulders.

The NeChristo representatives seemed to understand his current allegiances. Of course what they said and what they thought could be two different things, but they appeared to be genuine. And anything he did on behalf of Dreamcom now would be behind the scenes. Nothing public. Put the thumbscrews on a few FBI people. Tell 'em to pick things up a little. Straightforward. The other side were unlikely to even know about it.

'Sure,' he said. 'I'll see what I can do.'

Chapter 8

Madsen awoke with a start. He groped in the dark for his watch but there was no watch, and no bedside table either. A strange rattling hum came from the far corner of the room. A truck thundered by, only yards from his head. He sat up and rubbed his face until his brain put it together. He was in LA. In a cheap motel. The rattle was the air conditioning, such as it was. He rolled over and felt along the other side of the bed. Finding a table, he pushed buttons at random until he found a light.

He had slept for four hours.

He dialled up a news channel and settled back into the pillows to watch. The lead stories cycled, regular as clockwork. An oil rig fire in the Gulf of Mexico, pretty orange flames shooting hundreds of feet into the air. A breaking scandal involving the governor of Illinois and a Hollywood starlet. The dollhouse bombing. There wasn't much new. Re-runs of yesterday's interviews with the mayor, emergency workers and a wide-eyed waitress from Maggie's on Grant. Footage from a citizen's cell phone was introduced under the banner 'Close Shave in Chinese Market' and Madsen watched a brick fly between a gaggle of elderly shoppers and pulverize a ten-foot-tall display of fresh fruit. This was followed immediately by several re-runs of the same clip in super slow motion.

The next item was billed as live and breaking news, and the broadcast cut to shots of an angry crowd. A young female reporter spoke breathlessly into her microphone. 'As you can see, a major protest is getting underway outside the Dreamcom building in New York. The numbers are bigger than expected and downtown traffic is severely disrupted.'

The marchers, mostly women, chanted and waved placards. A deeply unflattering effigy of Tom Fillinger, the Dreamcom CEO, complete with horns and a long, forked tongue, was thrust into the camera.

The reporter shouted to be heard above the din. 'The event was organized jointly by the Coalition of Feminists Against Dollhouses and the New Christian Organization of America. The call is the same: for state and federal legislators to outlaw the dollhouses. So far the crowd has been disciplined and there have been no arrests. In the wake of the San Francisco bombing CoFAD has this morning issued a press release emphasizing their commitment to non-violence, at the same time reiterating that Dreamcom had incited outrage in the community and needed to take responsibility for—'

Madsen grunted and switched off the screen. CoFAD happened to be next on his list. He dressed and called a cab.

He managed a ten-minute nap at the airport and another half-hour on the flight, arriving at Central Station not especially refreshed, but in time to sneak into the nine o'clock swap 'n' tell before it got underway. The second-floor room that had been set aside for the Grant Avenue Task Force, as it was now called, was packed with detectives, crime scene specialists and uniforms, far too many for the available chairs. The latecomers loafed against walls or perched on the edges of the government-issue steel-top desks. Madsen found a space between two officers at the back of the room.

Mike Holbrook began by recapping the roles and responsibilities of everyone in his task force, after which each of the inspectors stood in turn to briefly summarize their activities and findings. Madsen duly gave an update on his interviews of the previous day. No one had turned up anything interesting. Much hope was pinned on the dollhouse CCTV when it came in.

Next up was Carl Steinmann. Short, never out of his lab coat, and with the ruddy complexion of a heavy drinker, Steinmann was the stalwart of San Francisco's evidence recovery and processing unit. For eleven years he had been responsible for providing ballistics, photography, fingerprinting, DNA, computer forensics and chemical analysis services to the Bureau and anyone else in law enforcement who asked for it, and for eleven years he had delivered. It was a hell of an accomplishment because, while crime rates had been falling steadily, his resource pool had been shrinking at an even faster rate. From four teams of eight specialists each, he was now down to two teams of seven. Budget cuts mostly. And attrition. Either way, Steinmann's rubber band was constantly stretched to the limit and he still managed to keep coming up with the goods.

Steinmann tapped his watch. The room fell silent.

'You will all be aware,' he said, 'that the sniffers have confirmed the presence of explosives. They've picked up large quantities of D-5 residue. We've now got definite confirmation on the chemical composition. It's a high-grade military variety, made here in the United States. We should have the specific manufacturer and batch isolated in the next twenty-four hours. No bomb fragments yet. We've begun sifting, but the search and rescue teams still have priority so you will appreciate it may take a while.' Steinmann paused and looked around fiercely, as if daring someone to challenge him. Gesturing at a screen on the wall behind him he said, 'Seven bodies have been recovered so far. All located in the upper levels, where the customer rooms were. The manager's office was at street level. We expect to get to him last.'

The screen displayed a jumble of pale blue lines and boxes. From Madsen's distant vantage point they might have been wiring diagrams or a schematic of a metro system, but he assumed they were blueprints of the Grant Avenue dollhouse.

'As far as the placement of the bomb goes,' Steinmann continued, 'we know for sure it was on the second level. And we are confident,' he tapped his index finger on one of the blue boxes, 'it was here.'

Madsen craned forward, but it was impossible to distinguish one room from another.

'It's a customer room,' Steinmann added helpfully. 'Second to the right of the stairwell.'

Holbrook closed the briefing. As everyone headed for the door, he came over to Madsen and said, 'Dreamcom's security department called. Their CCTV footage has been cleared. We pick it up at eleven.'

Madsen nodded. 'You want me to come?'

'No, they do. They specifically asked for you by name.'

'Why?'

Holbrook shrugged. 'Maybe they're excited by the prospect of meeting one of Uncle Sam's famous plotter men.'

'I seriously doubt it.'

'So do I,' Holbrook said, flashing a cold smile at his own joke. 'If you want to catch a ride, I'm leaving here at ten-forty.'

Madsen checked his watch. He still had well over an hour. 'No thanks. I'm going to squeeze in one more interview. I'll meet you there.'

Chapter 9

The CoFAD address turned out to be two blocks from the Haight-Ashbury intersection. Hippieville. Madsen half-expected it to be above an anarchist bookshop, or tucked behind a grungy T-shirt merchant trading on reinvented memories of LSD, Woodstock and Jimi Hendrix. He fully expected the principal occupant to be young and butch and wearing denim overalls and Doc Marten boots. Instead, he found himself standing outside an immaculate row house receiving a courteous greeting from a polite, conservatively dressed woman in her fifties. Eva Hartley, the founder and director of the Coalition of Feminists Against Dollhouses, would have looked right at home selling cookies and kitchenware to Middle American housewives – except for her eyes, which displayed the sort of intelligence, purpose and strength that can only come from seeing and surviving a great deal.

Hartley examined Madsen's badge closely before unlocking the security door and letting him in.

The house obviously served double duty as residence and workplace. Half the living room was given over to desks, computer equipment and filing cabinets. Shelves groaned with books and papers. The walls were covered with photo-portraits of feminists and civil rights leaders.

Propped on a sofa was a chart with dates and tasks marked off. Some kind of project plan. Above the chart was a map of the United States, glued to a corkboard and liberally sprinkled with blue and red pushpins. The blue pins, Madsen noticed, corresponded to the locations of dollhouse protests over the preceding six months. The red pins were probably for planned protests. The reds outnumbered the blues three to one.

When Madsen explained that he was on the dollhouse bombing investigation and had come to interview Hartley, she offered no complaint. Nor did she show anger or emotion of any kind. She simply listened. And when he was finished she stood and went to the kitchen and did something that was about as far from Madsen's notion of a militant feminist as he could imagine: she made tea.

She made it the old-fashioned way, scooping leaves into a pot. She waited for the jug to boil, then filled the pot and allowed it to brew. She poured two mugs. Handing one to Madsen, she waved him to a seat and cleared a pile of folders off the lounge for herself. Directly above where she sat was a framed photograph in which a younger version of Hartley stood shoulder to shoulder with a second, formidable-looking woman. They were in front of what appeared to be a London terrace. The photo was autographed, 'Looking forward to making every home a women's refuge! Love, Erin.'

Hartley sipped from her mug and waited.

Madsen said, 'I'd like to begin with the feminist perspective on the dollhouses. The question for me is, why the big reaction? I mean, I understand why you find them offensive, but it's not as if they involve real women. Your members have been marching in cities across America for six months to protest what is essentially a jumped-up sex toy.'

Hartley frowned in a way that made it hard to tell if she was annoyed or amused. 'You don't know much about feminism, do you?'

'No, not really.'

'Do you know why women hate prostitution and pornography?'

'I think so, yes.'

'Well, I'm not sure you do, because the answer to your question lies there.'

Madsen said nothing.

'It's not just because they exploit and degrade the women directly involved. It's because of larger evils they perpetuate indirectly. They change expectations and redefine social norms on a much, much bigger scale. They redefine what's natural.' She examined him closely. 'The basic sexual orientations – gay, bi, hetero – we are born with. It's in our genes. You get what you get, so don't fret. But when it comes to the finer details of sexual behaviour – what you like sticking your penis in, if you like your skin caressed by lace or smacked by leather, whether you think it's okay to choke someone while you have an orgasm, or piss on them afterwards – these things are shaped to a very large degree by society.'

She said *choke* and *piss* without emphasis and in the same matter-of-fact tone as everything else.

'Sex industries,' Hartley continued, 'condition men to reduce women to objects. Objects without feelings or needs of their own. Objects that exist for the sole purpose of male gratification. They teach men to believe in a right, an *entitlement*, to be aggressive, to take, to rape. They poison ordinary relationships in ordinary American households. They create violence.'

Madsen interrupted. 'But why dollhouses? They're just one part of a huge industry. There are so many other elements that are . . . nastier.'

Hartley regarded him thoughtfully. 'Have you ever heard of the escalation effect?'

'The what?'

'That's what we call it, anyway. Not everyone uses the same term. Let's see . . . Think of consumerism. It has become part of the modern human condition to always want more, right? Whatever we have, we can't feel completely satisfied if we know others have more, when our neighbours have something we don't have. People go to malls and buy crap they don't need just because everyone else has it. They don't even know why. They just don't want to get left behind. It's a curse.'

Madsen nodded.

'A similar principle operates in sexuality. Not the same, similar. Basically, people should be satisfied with a sexual relationship with a compatible partner. But if they are continuously exposed to strong suggestions that others have more frequent, more intense sexual experiences, then it isn't long before they seek that for themselves. The big accelerant has been hyper-realistic, immersive, fully interactive 3-D porn. Unfortunately, there is no end point. When they get variety, they crave the exotic, and when the exotic becomes commonplace, they want extreme. This has brutal consequences for women. Over the course of a relationship men demand more and more in the bedroom from their partners. When they are no longer satisfied they become resentful and abusive. It breeds infidelity, violence, divorce – if the woman is lucky. Are you with me?'

'Yes, but not all men, right?'

'More and more, and the cycles are getting shorter. Men are being exposed to so much sex that their whole idea of what constitutes normal has been rewired. They start escalating when they hit puberty and they don't stop.'

'And Dreamcom products contribute to this.'

'Everything Dreamcom does contributes. The company has a deliberate strategy of escalation. It didn't get to be the world's biggest adult entertainment company without knowing everything there is to know about yanking dollars from the male wallet. It's always the next upgrade, the next experience that keeps them coming back for more. The dollhouses took everything to a whole new level. A fully physical act, all senses engaged, that takes place in the real world. There is nothing "virtual" about it, no cues left to even vaguely suggest what is happening is fantasy. Which makes the change faster. Much faster.'

'So you hold Dreamcom responsible for changing men . . .'

Hartley leaned forward. 'When a man can no longer get it up without the prospect of inflicting pain or violence, women suffer.

There are various theories on what goes on in the brain, but there can be no doubt about the outcome. The dollhouses create monsters. That's why we're shutting them down.'

The statement hung there. Unequivocal. Was it an unshakeable belief that when enough people march, good must ultimately prevail? Or did her conviction come from knowledge of surer and deadlier strategies? If the latter, then Hartley gave no sign of feeling threatened by the FBI agent in her living room.

He changed tack. 'Are the protests working?'

'Not yet.'

'Why?'

'Money, influence, blindness. In roughly that order.'

'Do you think they will work?'

'Yes. Eventually. What Dreamcom is doing isn't illegal. It should be, but it isn't. We have to keep going until the law changes, or we shame enough customers away to put them out of business. We lost the war on pornography a long time ago. We have to win this one.'

'What about the churches?'

'What about them?'

'NeChristo and the others. You work with them. What's their philosophy on this?'

'You'd have to ask them. We coordinate our protests because we have the same goal, that's all. Oh, and they have deep pockets and a big audience.' She laughed. 'Who would have thought revivalism could be a good thing?'

'You don't see eye to eye on everything, then?'

Hartley sipped her tea. 'We've teamed up on dollhouses – I'm a practical person, an enemy of my enemy is my friend and all – but we don't agree on much else . . . Some of their attitudes are, how can I put this? Medieval.' She paused, as if considering whether to go on. Madsen waited.

'Personally,' she said, 'I stopped believing in God when I was nineteen. My husband started pimping me out for stag films and beating the living hell out of me. Asking for help was a big step. He threatened to cut my throat if I went anywhere, but I was desperate, and I was *this close* to suicide.' She held up her thumb and forefinger so they almost touched. 'So I turned to the only person I could think of that was safe, who wouldn't talk, wouldn't give me up. Father Kavanagh was his name. I could reach out to him secretly, in the sanctity of a confession . . . And can you guess what he did when I finally summoned up the guts to tell him what I was doing? What Al was making me do?'

Madsen shook his head.

'He asked me for a blow job.'

'Jesus.'

'Jesus was nowhere to be found, I'm afraid. Oh, I don't have a problem with people believing in God if it gets them through the hard times. And yes, there are good priests, diamonds there for the finding if you look hard enough. But if anyone asks, I tell them nine-tenths of religion is exploitation.'

They ruminated on that for a moment before Madsen brought the discussion back to the matter at hand. 'You gave an interview once in which you said you would like to see Fillinger burn in hell.'

'It was on CNN, and what I actually said was we would crush his business and send him to hell, and when the flames were lapping at his armpits and he was begging for mercy I wouldn't piss on his grave to give him relief.' She laughed. 'But I see your point. Odd words from an atheist. Or perhaps that wasn't your point. It felt good to say it, anyway.'

'How desperate are you to stop him?'

'Desperate is not the right word.'

'What is?'

'Committed.'

'Committed enough to plan a bombing?'

'I guess you have to ask that, but no, not committed enough to kill. Ever.'

'Would you mind?' Madsen drew the HAMDA from his pocket and held it out for her to see.

She tilted her head and appraised Madsen like a headmistress sizing up a wayward schoolboy. 'That's most impolite. We were having a perfectly friendly conversation. When you whip that thing out a conversation becomes an interrogation. Didn't you know that?'

Madsen had no subpoena to compel Hartley to give her testimony – and she clearly knew it. He fed her his standard line. 'The faster we eliminate possibilities, even far-fetched ones, the easier it is to focus our resources on the real killer.'

'So I am a possibility?'

'Of course.'

Seeing her expression harden, he added, 'It's not completely out of the question, is it? Abortion clinics, after all, were—'

'Abortion clinics were bombed by demented losers who couldn't see the contradiction in calling themselves pro-lifers while killing doctors. As I'm sure you're aware, feminists fought the opposite side, for a woman's right to choose.'

'Look, it's quick and painless and it helps. It's nothing personal.'

'*Nothing personal!* Nothing I can think of is more personal. I'll tell you what. I'll continue to be congenial and open and you keep on asking anything you like. Happy to answer, enjoying the conversation. Who knows? If we talk long enough we might become friends. You could ring me at night to talk about your tough day and I could ring you to tell you about mine. Or you can take out that thing and turn me into a suspect. It carries a big price. You want to pay it?'

Madsen hesitated. He was used to rebukes, whining, angry protestations about civil liberties, complaints about due process and commentary on his parentage, and without a subpoena Hartley could have simply said 'no', but instead she had turned the entire act around, forcing him to make a moral decision. He couldn't remember anyone doing that before. And, as uncomfortable as it was to admit, there was some truth in what she said. You made an invisible, irrevocable change in a relationship when you pulled a polygraph. Hell, didn't he feel the same way sometimes when the OPI boys dropped by and asked him to sit one of their random integrity tests?

But what she didn't see, or didn't want to, was the difference they made, the incredible value that came from converting intuition into certainty. Field polygraphs were driving unprecedented case closure rates. Bad guys were off the streets faster. Families were getting the answers they needed. Police resources were being freed earlier, to tackle more cases. And they *did* save innocent people the distress of being a suspect for more than a few minutes. He wished she could see that side of it.

He stared at the stubby cylinder, feeling its weight and coolness as he tried to make up his mind.

Reaching forward, he placed it in the centre of the coffee table. He thumbed the ON switch. The light winked.

A few minutes later he saw himself out.

Chastened, unsettled, and still without a single lead, he headed downtown, driving quickly to make his eleven a.m. appointment.

Chapter 10

Across the other side of the country, in an oversized office at 935 Pennsylvania Avenue, Washington, DC, FBI Director Gus Tomkinson was also feeling unsettled. He skimmed through a blue plastic folder that had just been handed to him and tried to push Senator Arbett's phone call from his mind. Outwardly his demeanour was calm.

Unfortunately, his chief of staff, sitting opposite, was not similarly predisposed to hiding her feelings, and her pursed lips, in Tomkinson's estimation, were doing a pretty fine impersonation of a cat's ass.

'Yes or no,' he asked again. 'Is he the best available?'

'He's the best on the spot.'

'What does that mean?'

'It means he's a good investigator. He's fast, he knows the city, and he's there.'

'But there are better choices?'

'I can find one in another state with more pre-HAMDA experience, if that's what you want. We'll fly him in tomorrow to join a team he's never worked with, in a city he's never worked in, and we'll see how he gets on, but in my assessment that is not "better".' She raised an eyebrow. 'Do you want me to do that?'

Tomkinson frowned and turned back to the file.

Thirty-two years old, smart and married to the job, Madsen had come in just as handheld polygraphs were approved for operational use. Maybe he sensed the opportunity. Whatever the reason, he had applied for direct entry to the programme. His training in psychology matched the profile they were looking for, and his aptitude scores were off the scale. Right place, right time, right skills. Right attitude too, if the comments were anything to go by. The guy worked at full throttle, often around the clock, and scored an arrest rate impressive enough for his boss to flag him for accelerated promotion. The way things were going in the Bureau, he might wind up a division chief if he wasn't careful.

There was only one blemish. Two different supervisors had cautioned him for not taking sufficient care to sustain his personal needs while working extended periods.

Tomkinson read the comments and tried to remember the last time he was that gung-ho. Probably when the field polygraphs went live. As the closure rates soared they had all become overnight heroes. Happy times. Right up until all the civil libertarians, community leaders, churches and sundry do-gooders had clubbed together and insisted that if instant polygraphs were good enough for citizens then they must be good enough to keep G-men honest too. Their logic was unassailable, but the consequences had been devastating. Nowadays Tomkinson lay awake nights thinking about monthly integrity averages and skyrocketing agent resignations.

He'd have to talk to his wife again about retirement. He could take that trip to Lake Champlain with his sons and fish for rainbow trout, steelhead and bass. He might even let her drag him to that new church she was always on about.

His chief of staff coughed, a reminder he had yet to answer her question.

And that was the other thing the integrity tests had fucked up. They were filtering the place like a giant sieve, taking out all the interesting people and leaving behind all the colourless, by-the-book sticklers. Like the one across his desk.

Tomkinson looked again at the two cautions, then placed the file on his desk. It was hard to fault a guy who worked himself to exhaustion.

'Based on this information here,' he said, looking up, 'I don't see any reason to disagree with your assessment.'

The chief nodded.

'Now, is Agent Madsen fully apprised of the – ah – urgency of the case?'

'Everyone in the Bureau is aware of its seriousness,' said the chief icily. 'A bomber is on the loose.'

'You know where I'm coming from, so don't be a pain in the ass. I need to go back to the senator and let him know we've passed the message on. It's not up to agents to assess for themselves the urgency of their cases.' He leaned forward, spacing each word out for emphasis. 'I need to know Madsen knows.'

'Yes, sir, I'll see to it personally.'

'Good idea.'

She took the file, shut it with a snap, and stalked out.

Tomkinson sighed. All but the Hitler salute.

Chapter 11

Madsen arrived at the Dreamcom tower a shade before eleven. The glittering edifice occupied one side of Justin Herman Plaza, near enough to the Embarcadero for the office workers with easterly views to set their watches by the ferry building clock. Above the entrance a silhouette of entwined lovers was laser-etched in forty-foot-high stainless-steel panels. Holbrook was waiting out front, scowling.

Fountains burbled in the lobby and the space echoed with the clip of heels on marble as well-dressed corporate types came and went with self-possessed urgency. Holbrook and Madsen flashed their credentials at a front desk receptionist with a face that could have graced the covers of a fashion magazine. She responded with a regulation smile and placed a call.

Seconds later a striking brunette arrived. She opened with an apology. 'I'm afraid I'm only authorized to take one of you up, and Mr Fillinger has requested Agent Madsen.' Turning to Holbrook she said, 'Would you mind waiting?'

'Yeah, I mind,' Holbrook said. 'Call Mr Fillinger and tell him I'm in charge of this investigation.' Getting no reaction, he puffed up his chest and repeated himself, but the woman's apologetic smile remained. Eventually the big inspector rolled his eyes and, red-faced, sauntered off to the far side of the lobby.

The brunette escorted Madsen through a screening point where he politely refused an invitation to surrender his firearm. He noticed that some of the security guards wore the Dreamcom logo and others wore the colours of a private firm. Dreamcom was taking extra precautions. After the screening point came an elevator ride. A long one, all the way to the top. The elevator doors opened and they stepped into a spacious waiting room with a single oak-panelled door at one end. In front of the door sat a secretary, blonde and alluring in a sleeveless white cocktail dress. Her desk was completely bare, with not even a keyboard or screen to suggest she did anything other than spend her day waiting for the elevator to dispense visitors.

The secretary appraised Madsen carefully. Without speaking a word, she pressed a button. The oak door swung open.

'Welcome to Dreamcom, Agent Madsen.'

A tall, slender man with angular features and a full head of silver hair stepped forward, hand extended. He was sharply dressed in a black designer suit, high collar with no tie, and looked younger than the seventy-two years Madsen knew him to be. The face was instantly recognizable.

Tom Fillinger, adult entertainment king.

Madsen entered an office as long as a basketball court. The far end was solid glass, affording an unbroken view of San Francisco Bay. The left side was occupied by a showcase of Dreamcom achievements. Countless adult industry trophies, many resembling bizarre parodies of Hollywood Oscars, were displayed alongside patents and scientific and engineering awards from universities as far away as Russia and South Korea. And looking down from gold-framed posters, a selection of Dreamcom's most popular porn stars and avatars.

A younger version of Fillinger stared out from a *Forbes* magazine cover under the caption 'Is this the future of Silicon Valley?'

The side of the room to Madsen's right looked like a cross between a museum and an old library. Rows of heavy leather-bound books competed for space with antique microscopes, chronometers, balance scales, theodolites, sextants and several instruments Madsen didn't recognize. Madsen inspected a large, complicated-looking apparatus with numerous balls suspended from metal arms. Light gleamed off the polished brass.

'It's an orrery,' Fillinger said, following Madsen's gaze. He wound a mechanism and depressed a lever. The balls came to life, swinging into orbit with a series of tiny clicking noises. 'Here is the Earth and the Moon, there is Mercury, there Venus. A master clockmaker in Amsterdam built it in 1770. It cost me a fortune. Here, allow me to show you my favourite . . .' He ushered Madsen to another device resembling a series of clocks set one inside the other. 'This is the Antikythera mechanism. It's only a copy. The original is a lump of corroded bronze in the Athens museum. It calculates years, months, lunar and solar eclipses and the position and phases of the moon. It is much more sophisticated than the Dutch piece – if you look you can see it has more than thirty gears – yet it is fifteen hundred years older! The Greeks built it. The world's earliest mechanical computer. Remarkable, don't you think?'

Madsen nodded. He had expected to meet a security officer, pick up some recorded CCTV on a memory cube, and get out of there. Instead he was getting a lesson in ancient history from a CEO.

'These instruments,' Fillinger continued, 'are precious for their physical beauty, for the knowledge embodied within them, and for their deep and lasting contribution to society. I expect you appreciate them as much as I do. Science is, after all, a form of detective work.' Fillinger gestured to the opposite wall. 'What if I said that everything over there stands for the same thing?'

Madsen surveyed the rows of adult trophies. 'Deep and lasting contribution to society' were not the first words that came to mind.

Fillinger said, 'Dreamcom is a science and engineering organization. Half a billion dollars in R & D in the last three years alone. Dozens of labs, thousands of jobs, and we license our technologies to all kinds of companies for all kinds of applications. And yes, our adult products do make a contribution. Men who are not sexually satisfied get distressed, or depressed, or sacrifice everything in the search for fulfilment. Some are driven to take it by force. Dreamcom offers outlets, answers. We make society healthier by reducing abuse, prostitution, sexually transmitted disease. Do you see?'

Madsen said nothing. According to Eva Hartley, sexual disorders, depression and dysfunctional marital relationships were on the rise, not on the wane, and he couldn't help thinking she was probably right.

Fillinger said, 'Perhaps your experiences in law enforcement make you doubtful? I imagine you are confronted with the very worst examples of vice and violence.'

'With all due respect, it doesn't matter what I think. I'm here to investigate a bombing.'

'But it does matter. Right now our enemies blame us for every evil imaginable! Our business does not hide from what it is, but those hypocrite revivalists put guilt in people's minds and give them ideals they can never live up to. Then they tithe them fifty cents in the dollar for the privilege! I'd like to know where you stand . . .'

You may have a point there, thought Madsen, *but my clock is ticking*. Aloud he said, 'Mr Fillinger, I didn't come here to debate the social consequences of having sex with machines. In my line of work it's important to keep the investigation moving. Perhaps we can talk about Grant Avenue—'

Fillinger raised his hands in submission. 'No one is more anxious than me. It's my business, after all, that is being attacked. Have a seat. Please.' He sighed and flopped down into his own chair, a high-backed executive model generously upholstered in blood-red leather. He propped his elbows on the desk and rubbed his temples with his fingertips. His eyes were clamped shut. 'Forgive me. There *is* a point. I need you to keep an open mind about Dreamcom and what we do.'

'Why?' Madsen asked.

'Because now is a delicate time. The world is taking sides. It's too easy for people to judge. Because police departments leak.

And because all these things can add up to the difference between survival or ruin. Reason enough?' Fillinger opened his
eyes. He reached down and pressed something under the lip of
his desk. 'Will you humour me for just one more minute?'

Before Madsen could answer, the door swung open. The secretary from the waiting room entered, closely followed by his hostess
from the lobby. The two women stood in front of Fillinger's desk,
apparently awaiting instructions.

'Melanie is one of our latest,' said Fillinger, nodding towards
the blonde. 'What do you think?'

Madsen stared. She was classically beautiful, with long hair
worn loose to the shoulders. She moved with a natural grace. He
hadn't suspected for a second. The hostess was real, the secretary
artificial. She had to be light years ahead of the model he had seen
at Eddie's.

She smiled shyly and glanced away.

'Much of it is in her eyes, and in the movements,' Fillinger said.
'Notice that they never stop. All these things are very important,
especially when she is looking at you, responding to you. The tiny
gestures of the hands, the glances . . .'

Melanie's cheeks reddened. She bit her lower lip.

Fillinger nodded to Madsen's hostess.

Without a word the brunette reached out and began to gently
run her fingers through the doll's hair, letting her long nails trace
down her neck to the shoulder.

Melanie swallowed. She began to shake slightly.

Madsen fidgeted. He felt guilty for staring, but at the same
time couldn't look away.

The hostess let her hand glide down the line of Melanie's spine
and over her buttocks.

Melanie's eyes moistened. Her breaths quickened. Flushed,
she caught Madsen's eye, then lowered her eyelids.

It was almost impossible to think of her as a doll. She was
embarrassed and vulnerable. He wanted to reassure her, to say
something to make her comfortable. To his consternation, he
found himself shifting in his seat to hide his arousal.

Fillinger spoke again: 'You talk about sex with machines, but does that do justice to such an elegant creature? My ladies evoke desire, yes, but they also captivate the senses and fire deeper emotions. They inspire and console. Everything about her is perfect . . .'

Fillinger made a dismissive gesture. Abruptly the show stopped. The women left.

Madsen struggled to regain his composure. Turning to Fillinger he blurted the first thing that entered his head. 'Melanie doesn't actually do secretarial work, does she?'

'Good heavens, no,' Fillinger said, laughing. 'What you have seen – opening doors, walking, moving about – is the extent of it. She is simply designed to be beautiful on every level. Her features will find their way into all our models.'

'So she is still a skinj— still designed to, ah . . .'

'She performs all the standard sexual functions, if that is what you are asking. Yes.'

Fillinger waved at a panel on his desk. The lights dimmed and a large screen slid down from a recess in the ceiling. Blinds whispered across the glass panels, blocking out the sunlight. 'I suppose we had better show you what you came for.'

The screen showed a landing with two closed doors and the top half of a flight of stairs. There were no furnishings and few features to distinguish it from the interior of any number of city offices or apartment buildings, but it had to be the stairwell in the Grant Avenue dollhouse.

A man came into view. He laboured up the last few steps and leaned heavily against the wall, side-on to the camera, catching his breath. The sweat stains under his arms suggested he had done more than just climb a few flights of stairs. He was of medium build and wore plain trousers, brown leather loafers and a dark grey hoodie. The hood was raised, covering his head, and he wore sunglasses with large lenses, making it impossible to see his face. Over his shoulder was a red backpack.

Madsen's pulse quickened.

The figure was familiar. Madsen had seen it among the images flashed up in the Central Station viddy room. He was one of those flagged as carrying a large bag onto the premises, but for some reason Madsen couldn't recall, the guy had been left off his interview list.

The man stood, made for the second of the two doors, and stepped inside.

Fillinger said, 'That was the first clip. Here is the main one.'

This time the view was of a bedroom, seen from one corner, high up near the ceiling. The king-sized bed in the centre had a sheet, no covers, and two pillows. In the furthest corner a woman stood side-on to the camera. She was nude. Directly in front of her was an open closet, except it was not a closet, because black rubber tubes extended from it. One tube was plugged into her open mouth, giving her the appearance of a scuba diver. The other looped down and up between her legs.

'Room four of the Grant Avenue Pleasure Palace,' said Fillinger. 'Pre-client procedure. Not very glamorous and not something we advertise, but a necessary part of the service. The lady is just finishing up.'

Any client that saw those hoses, Madsen thought, might not be inclined to come back. He watched, fascinated, as the doll shut off a tap and removed each tube herself, hanging it back in the closet. She reached up to the left side of her face and unplugged another, thinner cord from her ear.

'Now you know where we hide the power socket. Our ladies top up their charge after each client.'

It dawned on Madsen that Fillinger never once referred to the dolls, even when describing their basest functions, as anything other than ladies.

The doll reached into the closet and withdrew a lace-trimmed satin slip. The garment was fitted with Velcro tabs down the side and she dressed in a few quick movements. She moved to the bed and lay still, head propped on elbow, curves accentuated. A seductress waiting for her lover.

The door opened.

The man entered, his hoodie and sunglasses still on. The jaw was set, unsmiling. It was impossible to be sure of his age, but at a guess it was late thirties, early forties.

The man closed the door and gently eased his backpack to the floor. It was clearly heavy. Ignoring the doll, he knelt and began to unfasten the straps. Then he paused, as if changing his mind, and rose and moved over to the bed. He stood there, with his back to the camera, for a long time. He might have been talking but there was no sound and no way to tell.

The doll batted her eyelashes and patted the bed provocatively.

He unbuckled his belt.

She smiled and began crawling across the bed towards him, mouth open.

The man raised his right arm, high.

Madsen jolted. With a sweep the man landed a shattering blow squarely across the doll's face. Her head bounced and fell to the side. Her jaw hung slackly. Her eyes, when they re-opened, were creased with panic.

'Jesus Christ,' Madsen whispered.

The man grabbed the doll by the hair and hauled her around so she faced away from him. He shoved her down on the bed. He continued hitting her with one hand even as he fumbled between her legs with the other. Then he pushed himself onto her with animal violence. Perhaps senseless from the blows, she put up no struggle. As her head jerked to the side, however, the camera caught an expression of pure terror. Madsen felt nauseous.

Fillinger looked across at him. 'The fear is simply a programmed response, and of course there is no physical pain. She doesn't feel anything. We design our ladies to take reasonable levels of abuse from clients without damage. Although . . .' He turned back to the screen. 'This one is a little over the top.'

The frenzied thrusting and hitting dislodged the man's hood slightly. Only an inch, and only for an instant before he pulled it forward again, but enough to yield a glimpse of dark hair and part of an ear.

Suddenly it was over.

The man backed away. He buckled his trousers.

The doll lay motionless.

Madsen wondered if she was also programmed to feign unconsciousness or death. He watched as the man leaned forward and lingered above her. It wasn't clear what he was doing.

A gob of spit splashed across her cheek.

Involuntary images flashed through Madsen's mind. A baby-faced man in a leather apron. Two little boys.

The man moved to his pack. He knelt and opened the flap. The camera had a clear line of sight, revealing tightly packed bricks of what looked like plasticine. Each brick had a wire projecting from it. The wires flowed together to become a single twisted bundle, and the bundle led to a fist-sized gadget that resembled a pistol grip without a barrel. The man picked up the grip and began to fiddle with it.

The screen went black.

'That's it,' said Fillinger.

'What?'

'That's the end of the footage.'

Madsen pointed to the timer at the bottom of the screen: 3:42 p.m. 'The explosion was at three forty-four.'

'The CCTV is compressed into packets and burst back here for archiving every two minutes. I'm afraid that's the last we received.'

There was a long silence. Madsen placed his notebook deliberately in front of him and started jotting notes. It took an effort to stop his hands from shaking. 'Okay,' he said. 'I need copies of both clips.'

Fillinger opened a drawer and withdrew from it a cube. It was small, the size of a die, and transparent. He pushed it across the desk.

Chapter 12

'What do you mean, victim?' Holbrook said. 'This is our guy!'

Shari Sanayei winced. Holbrook and Madsen were leaning over her console, staring at the Wall. The inspector was still breathing heavily after running in with the memory cube, and his voice had risen steadily in both pitch and volume. A few moments ago she had plugged in the cube and pulled up a Dreamcom CCTV image of a hooded man, frozen in the act of stepping into room four of the Grant Avenue dollhouse.

'I'm sorry,' she said again. 'But we tagged this guy as unidentified male victim number three.'

'You're sure?' Madsen asked.

'Absolutely certain. Here, let me pull up our footage.'

She selected a file and another image flashed on the Wall. An exterior shot of the dollhouse with the same man – dark grey hoodie, shades, red backpack – frozen mid stride ten yards from the front door. 'He entered the building at T-minus six minutes. As far as we know, he never came out.'

'Or your cameras missed it,' Holbrook said.

Shari shrugged. Anything was possible, but she would stick to her version until proven wrong.

She pressed play. The image sprang to life. The man strode in from the right with his head tilted forward, hood up, watching the ground. The tip of his nose was visible, but otherwise the face was completely shielded. He covered the last few paces to the door, pushed his way in, and disappeared. She watched him intently. A minute ago he was benign, just another John Doe, now he was a man on his way to commit mass murder.

'How much face data do you have?' Holbrook asked.

'Zip,' Shari said. 'Our analysis picked up some markers from his nose and chin and general body shape. That's it. That's why we never ID'd him.'

Madsen said, 'You'll find plenty more on the Dreamcom cube.'

Shari nodded. 'Okay, I'll feed it all in. I'll call you when I get the results.'

Satisfied they would soon be acting on an influx of new information, the men left to round up more officers.

Shari took a moment to collect herself. The previous evening she had lain awake crying as visions of debris, dust and body parts swirled in her head until two in the morning. When she'd switched on a screen to distract herself, there they were again, this time in full colour and fronted by news reporters trying to mask their excitement behind false frowns and sombre tones. The conversation with Yolanda kept replaying too. Yolanda understood and would never mention the affair, those were her words. But the way she averted her eyes suggested something else. Or perhaps she was just upset at having to repeat a promise already made. When this was over, Shari would have to mend the friendship.

Sometime after midnight Shari had gotten out of bed and stared into her bathroom cabinet, then changed her mind and gone to the kitchen, where she poured herself several generous shots of Bacardi. Alcohol was predictable, sleeping pills were not, and she wasn't about to risk sleeping through her alarm. Nor was she going to take a chance on Captain McAlister, the Central Station commander, ordering her back home to rest, so when the alarm did sound she scrubbed and showered and found a freshly pressed uniform and downed two cups of the strongest coffee she could handle so at least she wouldn't *look* like she was running on empty.

This new footage had given her fuel to draw on. Adam's killer had covered his face, but ultimately the disguise wouldn't protect him.

Angie assisted with the set-up while Lynn took over real-time monitoring of the street cameras.

They started with the image already on the Wall.

Shari replayed the video loop, slowing it until the figure moved along Grant Avenue one frame at a time. When she found a frame she liked she froze it. She left her console and stepped over to the Wall. Reaching up and touching it with her fingers, she placed markers at key positions until, a few moments later, a red outline flowed around the figure. A small box appeared next to the outline. It contained a unique string of letters and numbers. Angie copied them with a few quick keystrokes.

Next Shari opened the Dreamcom viddy file. She watched it until the man entered the bedroom with his face to the camera. Freezing it, she repeated the mark-up procedure on the Wall. This time when the red outline appeared, the label was blank. Angie pasted in the letters and numbers she had copied earlier.

The figures in the two viddy streams were now linked. The software now knew they were two different views of the same person.

Shari set the search parameters – time, location, context and a dozen other variables. She asked Angie to double-check them. It was easy to mistype, or switch two digits, and Shari had once watched a SWAT team smash down a door and tackle a man to the ground in front of his screaming children, only to realize – in the darkness of a surveillance room ten miles too far away and ten seconds too late to do anything about it – that she had pinned the wrong man. It was an experience she did not want to repeat. When Angie was satisfied, she had Lynn check them a third time.

Satisfied there were no errors, Shari bound the parameters and viddy files together to make a single request package.

Then she reached across her console and pressed SUBMIT.

*

The stream of bits shimmered at the speed of light down optical fibres, reflected off junctions and gates and flashed south-east to a remote part of the Almaden hills, fifty-five miles from San Francisco, where it hit a panel of photo-receptors. The receptors were imbedded in a decoding unit in a windowless, spotless room with an atmosphere maintained at precisely sixty-eight degrees Fahrenheit. Thick bundles of cable connected the decoding unit to twelve black boxes, each a yard tall and proportioned like a domino. A small white sticker affixed to one of the boxes said, *TrackBack Master Core / NCCCD Asset No. C46-8551.*

The boxes were in a room under a nondescript building of grey concrete with a modestly sized plaque at the front door identifying it as the National Center for Collaborative Crime Detection. Underneath the plaque were the logos of a multinational computer company, an obscure but generously funded section of the Defense Department, and approximately one hundred participating law enforcement agencies.

The building was surrounded by an expanse of scrubby ground which was in turn bordered by a fence festooned with razor wire and signs promising a 10,000-volt wake-up to the unauthorized visitor. It could have passed for a prison, except there were no guard towers and the grounds were always deserted.

The cluster of dominoes hummed. Blue lights blinked.

In less than a second, TrackBack scanned every section of every frame of the newly submitted video footage, using the slight differences in camera angles between each frame to create working 3-D models of the suspect's face, body shape and clothing.

A second later it had connected with a mainframe at the University of California at Berkeley, verified its authority, and temporarily reserved a third of the machine's capacity for police work. It sent the 3-D models for reference, then activated a program telling the mainframe how to find matches in the footage coming its way.

Then it arranged for stored video from two dozen cameras in and around Grant Avenue to be streamed to the Berkeley campus.

The mainframe ingested the footage – which covered the period from forty-eight hours prior to the blast right up to the present moment, almost seventy hours in total – and analysed every frame for a glimpse of the suspect. It catalogued each hit noting time, place, direction of movement, nearby vehicles, objects, people and anything else the target was interacting with.

It returned its findings.

TrackBack paused for several milliseconds, using the new data to subtly revise and improve its models.

Then it went into overdrive.

It increased the radius around the crime scene to include a hundred street cameras, then five hundred, then a thousand, then cameras in trains and buses, attached to squad cars, dangling below traffic drones and worn on the helmets and uniforms of police officers and city employees.

With each widening of the circle it coopted more mainframes, feeding each as much stored footage as it could handle, until seventeen supercomputers in four states were chewing through the data.

Time passed.

One by one, the machines reported back.

TrackBack cross-analysed the results and performed ID checks against state and federal databases.

It released the supercomputers back to their day jobs, emailing itemized accounts to seventeen system administrators and depositing funds in seventeen university bank accounts. The payments, calculated against a standard government schedule of rates, were not generous.

Then it compiled all the catalogued fragments into a single video sequence suitable for viewing by human eyes.

Twenty-two and a half minutes after Shari pressed SUBMIT, it streamed this video back to surveillance operations, Central Station, Metro Division, San Francisco Police Department.

Chapter 13 _____

Shari wrinkled her nose. Holbrook and Madsen had rounded up a posse of seven uniforms and inspectors and all had crammed themselves into the viddy room. They were pumped up and ready for action. One or two cradled shotguns. Helmets and gear cluttered the floor. Sweat trickled down the necks of those wearing body armour.

No one spoke.

A light crackle of static came from the live conference link with SFPD SWAT command. Holbrook drummed his fingers, stopping every ten beats or so to check his watch.

One of the inspectors chewed gum, and Shari noticed the chewing had synchronized with Holbrook's drumming.

She surreptitiously surveyed their faces, glowing in the light from the Wall. The uniformed officers were typical of the Central Station roster: clear-eyed boys clocking on to a job that was five per cent pure gold and ninety-five per cent shit while maintaining every minute that it was the other way round. They were serious and tense, eager to get the guy who had taken down two of their own. She felt close to them. Less so the inspectors, who never seemed to shake that holier-than-thou attitude that came with a gold star in a black wallet.

Madsen was intriguing. Other agents were clean-cut clones in suits who might as well have had 'FBI' stamped across their foreheads in large capitals. His faded jacket looked slept in and his hair was all over the place. And he didn't take himself too seriously. He seemed unfazed by Holbrook's abrasiveness and yesterday, when snide comments about *plotters* and *thought police* had echoed down the corridor, his only response was to flash a smile and get on with it.

He had zeroed in on her distress, which was disconcerting. Nothing had been said, but his eyes were full of sympathy and unspoken enquiry.

A chime rang.

The drumming and gum chewing stopped. All eyes turned to the Wall.

TRACKBACK COMPLETED

The words were only there a second before images flashed up in their place, each from a different street or shop camera, each centred and synchronized to exactly the same moment. The man in the hoodie, his right foot on the doorstep of the Grant Avenue dollhouse.

Shari's heart skipped a beat.

She could feel the eyes of the other officers swivelling towards the killer. There were soft clicks as body armour was buckled and tightened.

The air conditioning rasped uselessly.

No one spoke.

TrackBack had been created when Al Qaeda sleeper cells were an ever-present threat; rapid response to an unfolding terrorist attack had been foremost in the minds of its makers. It was programmed to present its best and most actionable information first, especially information relating to a suspect's current location. This meant tactical teams could be launched immediately to intercept them.

They were staring at an image of the dollhouse, just a five-minute walk from Central Station.

Which meant he was close.

The footage sprang to life and there was another surprise. It played in reverse. TrackBack apparently considered the information on where the suspect came *from*, before the bombing, more relevant than the information on where he went *to*, afterwards.

The man in the hoodie strode backwards, away from the dollhouse. He passed a boarded-up entrance under a grimy sign advertising the Fung Long Import Export Co. A couple brushed past, going in the opposite direction. Middle-aged. A man and a woman. Tourists, given the camera in the man's hand and the way she was pointing. He passed another store. *Jewellery and Fine Gifts*. Frames opened and closed on the Wall as the suspect moved from one field of view to another. He walked steadily, ignoring everything and everyone, face to the front, never varying his pace. The thin lips beneath the sunglasses were pressed together. Even in reverse his purposefulness was unmistakable.

A man on a mission.

Shari had witnessed more bashings, stabbings and acts of cruelty on her cameras than she cared to count, and she was rarely affected. She had a strong constitution. Or strong coping mechanisms. But this was the first time she had watched a man prepare to murder someone she loved.

He reached the souvenir store on the corner, passing stacked T-shirts and wooden buckets filled with cheap umbrellas and Chinese fans, then backed across Pacific Avenue without breaking stride. He reached the opposite kerb and stopped. The pedestrian signal switched to red. Cars reversed away down Pacific. A young woman pulled a stroller downhill.

The man pivoted on his heel and strode backwards up Pacific.

The straps of the backpack dug into his shoulders. It was heavy. He had to be fit. Everything else about him – build, clothes, shoes – was pure ordinary. Nothing to make anyone give a second glance. Mr Average.

Shari sat up expectantly. Past the dim sum house was a bank. The city cameras were positioned high up, but cameras at bank entrances were set low. Face height. And banks gave unfettered access to law enforcement. In seconds they would get their closest look yet. Perhaps close enough to glimpse the face behind the dark lenses.

A new frame opened on the Wall. Low angle, high definition. The bank camera. The hooded figure backed in from the left, but his head was turned away to look at something across the road, leaving a close-up of the back of his hood. Shari frowned. It was the first time he had done anything other than look where he was going. No matter. The second camera was a few yards further on.

The second low-angle frame opened and Shari's jaw dropped in astonishment. He was facing away again, and a few seconds later a frame from a wide-angle rooftop unit caught his head turning to the front the instant he was clear of the bank.

He knew the camera locations.

She heard a grunt. Holbrook had picked it up as well.

The man passed a sign with a large yellow arrow and the declaration *Public Parking 24 Hours – Early Bird Specials!* Without warning he pivoted and backed into a doorway. The door closed. Shari held her breath. On the Wall, frames disappeared in rapid succession until there was only one, an interior shot of a poorly lit stairwell with a figure plodding backwards up the stairs. He exited a level up and the stairwell frame was replaced by another, darker view inside a cavernous parking bay. He looked grainy in the low light as he backed down a row of cars, deeper into the shadows. The frame disappeared. The clock counter, which had been steadily counting backwards, stopped.

'What happened?' asked Holbrook.

Shari said, 'Pacific Garage normally has full CCTV coverage on all levels. They must have a unit out.'

They waited. Five seconds passed. Ten. Shari felt a constriction rising in her throat. Any moment she expected to see a vehicle reversing out under the Pacific Garage boom gate. The TrackBack scope was huge, almost three days' worth of footage from more than ten thousand cameras. He must have passed dozens more lenses. They had to get a name, a house, a garage, a warehouse, *something.*

Restless murmurings came from the others.

'What about afterwards?' Holbrook asked angrily. 'Didn't we get any sightings after the explosion?'

Shari tapped her console. A stream of data scrolled up the Wall:

```
TRACKBACK ID:        SFPD#6303724


PRIORITY:            AAA
SATURATION:          ALL STREAMS ALL CAMERAS
SPATIAL:             ALL AREAS SAN FRANCISCO PLUS
START:               INCIDENT [T] MINUS 48 HRS
END:                 INCIDENT [T] PLUS 21 HRS 08 MIN


FIRST MATCH SUSPECT:   3:35:03 P.M.
LAST MATCH SUSPECT:    3:38:19 P.M.
TIME ON CAMERA:        0:03:16
ID MATCH:              NO


ACCUMULATED COMPOSITE FACE DATA: [ __ %]
```

Shari's heart sank. Three minutes and sixteen seconds was apparently all the footage they were going to get.

The cursor on the last line stopped blinking:

```
ACCUMULATED COMPOSITE FACE DATA: [ 57 % ]
```

No house, no face, no name. Nothing. All her hopes of pinning him down disintegrated. 'That's all,' she said, deep dejection apparent in her voice.

Profanities and sounds of disbelief echoed around the room.

'I can't believe it,' Holbrook snapped. 'All city cameras, top-priority compute time, and that's *all*? Did it run properly? Did you set it up properly?'

'We checked it twice.'

'Check it *again*.'

The SWAT commander's voice crackled over the speaker.

'I guess you won't be needing us just now. Call when you have something. Sorry, guys, and good luck.'

Disgruntled oaths were accompanied by the scrape of metal and plastic as men collected equipment and began to disperse.

Holbrook snorted in disgust and turned to follow.

A message popped up on the desk console.

'Wait,' Shari said.

'What is it?' Holbrook asked.

'TrackBack has an artifact it thinks we should look at.'

'What kind of artifact?'

'Don't know. It may be nothing. I'll pull it up.'

A moment later she stared in bewilderment. It was the suspect, seen from above and to the rear. His body was contorted and his trousers lowered. His fist was raised high, apparently about to strike the female beneath him.

Madsen cleared his throat. Until then Shari had thought he'd left the room with the others. He said, 'That's from inside the dollhouse. His hood came back a little, just for a moment. You can see some of his ear.'

On cue, TrackBack zoomed in. At full magnification part of a blurry shape became visible under the earlobe. It was small and a dull yellow colour, a shade brighter than the skin surrounding it. TrackBack stepped through an enhancement sequence, frame by frame, using the slightly different angles made by the head relative to the camera to re-interpolate lines and curves. Each iteration added fidelity and sharpness. An edge appeared. A gold band. Then the unmistakable outline of a tiny, stylized crucifix.

Shari saw dozens each day on her cameras. The paramedic in Grant Avenue who prayed as his patient slipped away had worn one, as did millions of members of the New Christian Organization of America. God's earrings, they called them. G-rings. They made a visual statement, but they had a more important practical purpose: a tiny wireless earpiece embedded in the gold kept the wearer connected to the flock and allowed him or her to listen to the daily homilies on demand.

'I'm getting a picture here,' Holbrook said heavily.

'What's that?' Madsen asked.

'Guy's religious, follows a church preaching against dollhouses, goes in there with a bomb big enough to take a building out and puts on an act that, based on what you described on the way over, is deranged. Then, to the best of our knowledge, and assuming we set TrackBack up correctly, he never leaves . . .'

Shari said nothing. Long seconds ticked by.

Madsen said, 'You're thinking maybe he wasn't concerned about the leaving part?'

'Exactly.'

Chapter 14

Madsen chewed slowly as he stared out at the traffic on Columbus Avenue. Across the table, Holbrook picked at his fries.

It was Madsen's suggestion to adjourn and regroup over food. Bad news or not, he needed calories. His total intake since waking in LA amounted to two stale donuts from an airport kiosk and half a cup of Eva Hartley's tea. Holbrook nominated his regular eatery, a cafe a few hundred yards away, wedged into the acute angle where Columbus crossed Vallejo. The red, white and green decor and the opera posters suggested Italian, but the waitress interrogated them in a thick Russian accent, the bearded men at the table alongside argued in Yiddish, and the menu was main-stream Americana. A little slice of the world.

'The son of a bitch robbed us,' Holbrook growled. Some of the redness had left his face, but he was still angry. He had been saying the same thing over and over. On the plus side, the two of them were having an actual conversation. Perhaps the bear's frostiness was finally beginning to thaw.

Madsen took another bite of his sandwich. 'Two minutes is a long time,' he said, thinking of the gap between the end of the Dreamcom footage and the time of the explosion. 'Even a big guy like you could get down those stairs and make a hundred yards if you had a ticking sack of D-5 for motivation.'

'I checked out the parameters and Sergeant Sanayei was right, we had camera coverage. We didn't get a peep. If he got out we'd know. He's still in there, squashed down to skin and jam. End of story.'

Madsen shrugged.

Holbrook stabbed the table with his finger, knocking over a salt shaker. 'You think he waited inside until a couple of street cameras were blown to shit, survived the entire collapse, then crept out of the rubble and vanished in the dust cloud?'

Madsen righted the shaker and took another bite of sandwich. 'No, but a couple of things don't fit a suicide bomber—'

'He wasn't a john who had a bad dolly experience and came back to take it out on the manager.'

'No, but—'

'And he didn't bring a handgun, he brought a big fuckin' bomb. He aimed to kill as many people as possible, customers included. Your type A, garden variety fanatic.'

'But if he was planning to kill himself, why did he give such a damn about being identified? I mean the hoodie and shades, avoiding the cameras . . . He must have taken elaborate precautions to get into Pacific Garage unseen. Why would he care? Don't suicide bombers want to make the biggest statement they can, the more glory the better?'

Holbrook gave up on his fries. He took a napkin and wiped ketchup from his hands.

'Because he wasn't rational,' he said. 'All that crap in the bedroom proves it.'

'Or he planned to get away with it.'

'I don't think so.'

Madsen said nothing.

'Probably his twisted idea of a morality lesson,' Holbrook continued, signalling the waitress. 'More your Old Testament way of thinking, but NeChristo gets its fair share of perverts and nutjobs, and some of their pastors don't mind preaching that heavy eye-for-an-eye stuff.'

Madsen nodded. That was true. What had Eddie called them? White-cassocked hypocrites. It wasn't hard to picture the bomber wearing his G-ring in a congregation of enraptured, hymn-singing worshippers, his eyes closed as he swayed, his face serenely content, then later sitting ramrod-straight and wide awake as he absorbed a militant sermon from a fiery pastor. Madsen imagined him joining a line of men, all identically dressed in grey hoodies and sunglasses, holding out hands, but instead of blessings, each receiving a red backpack . . .

A thought struck, suddenly and with ice-cold clarity.

'If it was suicide, I can think of one reason to hide his identity,' Madsen said.

'What would that be?'

'To slow us down. Because there are collaborators. Either to give them a head start to get out of Dodge, or buy them time to do the next one.'

They split the check, then hurried back up to Central Station, where Madsen watched as Holbrook barked out new assignments. They had their suspect, he said, and dead or alive they still needed to find out where he came from and establish an identity. Fast. Pacific Garage was the immediate focus. If the suspect had exited, then he must have entered, and since TrackBack had failed to spot any candidates on foot, that left vehicles.

The task force collated the tags of every vehicle that had passed under the Pacific Garage boom gate in the forty-eight hours preceding the explosion, then queried the onboard GPS systems. Two vehicles were found to be still inside the garage. Both were impounded for examination. They retrieved the licence and registration records of hundreds of owners, as well as associated criminal records, warrants and other details. Holbrook's detectives then began the task of chasing down each owner, one by one.

Madsen did no chasing. The unchecked names on his initial list of targets had been rendered irrelevant. Holbrook was ignoring him, and until the team found someone or something linked to *backpack man*, as they were now calling him, he had nothing to go on.

He gravitated to the surveillance operations room to watch the operators wading through stored footage.

The operators set about capturing and analysing images of drivers and front seat passengers. Of course their suspect could have lain on a seat while an accomplice drove, but they did it anyway.

They manually reviewed the dollhouse footage. Madsen felt a twinge of regret that they had to see the ugliness of the scene, then chastised himself for being so sensitive – it was only a god-damn skinjob.

It was hard to believe Shari was the same person. Twenty-four hours earlier she'd looked like she had just come off a double shift in a coalmine. Now she was in a fresh uniform and her hair, pinned neatly at the back, was jet black and shiny. There was no outward sign of her earlier emotional stress, just coolness and clipped tones as her fingers danced over the console. A procession of black uniforms dropped by, singly and in pairs, to eyeball the man who had killed their two colleagues. Some spat anger, others made dark, cynical jokes. Shari kept her distance. *You need to talk to them*, Madsen thought. *If you can't find solace in the people in the trenches with you, you sure as hell won't find it someplace else.*

They exhausted the science and fell back on intuition and guesswork. A search for partial matches on backpack man's clothing returned an astronomical number of hits. They tried a search based on body shape and did no better. Gradually, by filtering all the output based on when and where the candidates were caught on camera, they managed to coax the number of potential matches down to four hundred and three.

In desperation they packaged up the entire database – every name, place, description and vehicle caught in the net so far – and sent it down to the National Center for Collaborative Crime Detection at Almaden. A powerful computer program called Crossmatch-2 compared the database against petabytes of data sucked from telephone towers, email servers, electronic tollways, public microphones, credit card records, news tubes and web pages. It searched for any pattern or coinciding information that might conceivably suggest a link with the crime. It sent a list of names back with the qualifier 'Low-probability hits, further enquiries recommended.' The list was so long as to be useless.

Madsen's cell phone buzzed. A Washington number.

He sighed. Word that they had a suspect was spreading. Over the past two hours he had received a barrage of calls and messages soliciting clarification, details and explanations. The calls from his boss, Mary DiMatteo, were expected. They were also mercifully brief and to the point. The rambling messages from further up the chain of command he could do without.

He brought the phone to his ear. 'Yes.'

A woman's voice. 'Agent Madsen? I'm calling from the director's office.'

Madsen's heart sank. Jesus, the closest he had come to those hallowed halls was a graduation handshake and a signature qualifying him as a field agent. Now, apparently, he was on speed dial.

The woman identified herself as the director's chief of staff, then delivered a rambling stream of encouraging words peppered with unsubtle reminders about the need to get on with it. Exactly the kind of horseshit he hated most.

He rang off. It was almost five o'clock. He was doing nothing, contributing nothing, and the inbound calls would keep coming. He felt like a greyhound in a locked cage being prodded in the ass while the rabbit disappeared in the distance.

The only clue he was going to get, he decided, was the one he already had. The G-ring.

But where to begin? The New Christian Organization boasted twenty-three million members in the United States alone and more than a hundred million around the globe. Even if the wearer was a resident of California – and there wasn't a shred of evidence to say he was – then that only cut it down to three million.

There was only one place to start that made sense. At the top.

He didn't bother with a subpoena request because he knew it would never be granted.

For the second time in twenty-four hours, he headed for the airport.

Chapter 15 _____

Shortly after Madsen left surveillance operations, Shari Sanayei tossed her headset aside and stumbled out into Vallejo Street. She walked, not thinking about where she was going, finding comfort in the rhythmic thud of her footsteps. Blood pumped through her fingers and toes. The natural light soothed her eyes, and the warm city air tasted sweet compared to the fug of the surveillance room. She filled her senses with tiny snatches of conversation, the scritch of broom on pavement, the waft of perfume. Precious traces of real, living human beings.

Watching the scene in the dollhouse had been like receiving an electric shock. As much as she tried, Shari could not think of the girl as a doll. The cowering, pleading expression was no different to what she saw on the faces of real women who bled and died and disappeared into ambulances. Questions tumbled through her head. *How far did you go, Adam? Did you hit them too? Did you spit on them?* The thought revolted her, and she was angry with herself for allowing it. There was no evidence Adam did anything like that. But if she was honest with herself, hadn't there been more aggression, more demands in the bedroom over time? How well had she really known him? And there *would* be evidence, wouldn't there, if she dared dig for it: Dreamcom probably kept everything. Somewhere, in some memory cube, there would be video showing what Adam did in that dollhouse . . .

No more! With a shudder Shari wrenched her mind away. Earlier, she had heard Madsen make an offhand remark about the importance of debriefing, getting things off your chest by talking with colleagues. It had obviously been meant for her. But Yolanda was normally the person she confided in and after their last exchange that probably wasn't a good idea. Briefly she considered opening up to Holbrook or Captain McAlister and coming clean about the relationship, but the thought of facing their questions now was too awful. They would want to know everything. It was too late for that.

Now Madsen was flying east, and she found herself wishing she had confided in him.

Shari trudged on. She tuned in to the distant wail of a fire engine, watched shoppers bustle for groceries and peered into gloomy noodle houses. She tried to clear her mind by mentally checking off metro cameras as she passed. She knew them by heart – unit numbers, fields of view, units equipped with microphones, the broken ones and those with dirty lenses. It wasn't therapy, but it was something.

With a start she realized her meanderings had brought her close to Grant Avenue. Another block and she would come face to face with people sifting for body parts. She did an about-face and abruptly collided with someone coming the other way. It was a shoeless man carrying a large plastic bag. The bag split in the collision and metal cans cascaded to the sidewalk.

A string of profanities rang out before the man saw her uniform. He froze, eyes wide, then crouched and started tossing cans back into the bag with quick, panicky movements. Shari bent to help, holding her breath against the reek of mouldering trash. When they had finished, he tied a knot in the plastic and beat a hasty retreat.

Shari felt sad as she watched him go. She knew him. Not his name, but everything else: where he went for food, where he slept and who his friends were. On these streets, she knew them all.

A few moments later she was stepping from a kerb when she was checked by a horn blast and flash of chrome. She leapt back. A limousine sped past, midnight black, with its occupants shielded behind tinted glass. It was followed closely by a second, identical vehicle. Her heart hammered as she watched them zoom down the hill. At the next corner they turned right, tyres protesting, and disappeared. It finally dawned on her just how exhausted she was. She wasn't going to be any use when she got back to the station. It was time to go home. Time to rest.

Inside the rear compartment of the second limousine, Tom Fillinger took no notice as his driver slewed around the corner. The Dreamcom CEO stared at his notes with an intensity that could have burned holes in them.

He rarely spoke in public. Not because he was afraid – he had a cast-iron stomach for risk-taking and tough decisions and had learned to embrace the daily, sometimes hourly, confrontations that came with running a business empire. His satisfaction came from winning, not talking. When it came to trade shows, product launches, press conferences, advertisements and courtrooms, winning results came from paying the best advocates to do the talking for him.

On some occasions, however, the only way to give a message the punch it deserved was to deliver it in person.

Today was one of those days.

The driver gunned the motor, closing on the lead vehicle until they travelled nose to tail. The brakes squealed. Fillinger's seat-belt tightened. The driver's door thumped. The rear door swung open.

Fillinger stepped out into a tight circle of aides and bodyguards. The late-afternoon sun, still fiercely hot, hammered on the shoulders of his suit.

The entourage moved towards a long stream of police tape that blocked the road. A small crowd of journalists waited, cameras rolling. Between the cameras and tape was a small roped-off area, set aside hours before to reserve the best sightlines to the rubble.

As requested, it was unshaded. The rope disappeared. Fillinger's aides melted away.

Fillinger gazed at the shattered scene. His suit, specially chosen for the occasion, was dark and plain. His silver hair was slightly ruffled. Deep lines scored his brow. The sun drew little rivulets of sweat from his temples. He knelt to inspect a small mountain of cards and floral tributes. When he stood, dust clung to the knees of his trousers. He did not brush them clean. No longer a Silicon Valley legend, he was but a humble mourner, come to pay his respects.

He mentally double-checked the camera angles relative to the backdrop, then nodded to the nearest lens. 'I would like to say a few words, if I may.'

The assembled journalists fell silent.

'Yesterday,' he began, 'twelve people lost their lives. Twelve ordinary people, just like you and me. They left behind sons and daughters, mothers and fathers, wives, brothers, sisters, friends. I want, first of all, to offer my condolences to their loved ones and say how sorry I am for their loss.' He paused, looking from camera to camera. 'Two of these people worked for my organization. They died for nothing more than trying to earn a living, for doing the right thing for themselves and their families. The others were our customers. They died for . . . what? For daring to desire a moment's escape from the hardness and loneliness of their lives. For a feeling of companionship. For a few moments of pleasure.'

Another pause. A long look into each lens.

'Who among us doesn't deserve these things? The victims weren't hurting anybody in the world. They did not judge others nor expect to be judged. They respected the fact that we can hold different views and still get along, and that people in a free society are allowed to lead different lifestyles and make their own choices. They held to the essential truth that neither they, nor anyone else, has the right to impose their will upon others.'

Fillinger's frown deepened. 'The same cannot be said for the people who did this. They believe they have a *divine right* to judge, and to impose their will on others. They believe . . .' Fillinger lowered his voice. 'They believe they have the right to kill.'

He let the words hang in the air. The only sound was the distant buzz of a news drone, high overhead.

Fillinger's face clouded over. He lifted his chin. 'Let there be no mistake who is responsible for this atrocity. It is those who led the protests, month after month, and who put hellfire in their speeches and sermons.' He pointed at the ruins. 'It is those who called for violence *in God's name* against the ordinary citizens who dared step into that building!'

In his palatial Washington residence, Senator Erol Arbett heard his children coming downstairs to say goodnight. It was their strict evening routine, not just because four- and six-year-olds like to tear around in a whirlwind of limbs and giggles at bedtime, but because transporting his portly frame upstairs was a task best undertaken only once, when he himself retired.

Tonight the children found him in the hall between the study and the living room. He juggled his cell phone in one hand and a single malt in the other as he returned their hugs, then the nanny hushed the children away. As the squeals receded, Arbett fell into the lounge beside his wife. She was absorbed in the pages of a glossy magazine and did not look up.

Blonde, skinny and twenty years his junior, Rebecca Arbett had brought to their marriage two assets of inestimable value: she knew how to work a room with batted eyelashes and a flash of neatly capped teeth, and she could bear children. His first wife could do neither. Like most things in the senator's life, these assets came at a price. Tonight's stack of catalogues suggested her sights were currently set on a designer kitchen and another Caribbean getaway. St Bart's by the look of it.

As Arbett sipped his whisky, he felt his phone vibrate. An alert from his sentiment monitoring service. For a small fee it mined the chatter of a hundred thousand electronic conversations a minute, notifying him of significant shifts in public mood on any issue he cared to follow. With it he was capable of delivering a subtly altered press release one day, a tweaked speech the next, and by the end of the week a diametrically opposed viewpoint to the one he started with. The service had pushed its maker into the Nasdaq's twenty-five hottest stocks two years running. Capitol Hill marched to its drumbeat.

Arbett frowned. In the last five minutes the public mood on dollhouses had blipped against the recent trend. It was a big blip. He switched on the lounge-room screen and started flicking. The news channels carried the usual mixture of the trashy, the lascivious and the inane. A skydiver hung up in powerlines somewhere in North Carolina seemed to be the big story. A news drone zoomed in as sparks showered down from above. *Without the sparks*, thought Arbett, *you'd be on your own.*

He kept flicking. A banner caught his eye. He flicked back. DREAMCOM CEO VISITS BOMBSITE.

Tom Fillinger appeared to be making some sort of speech. Arbett turned up the volume. '. . . we respect their views and we respect their right to disagree. We always have. We do not reserve the right to invade their churches, to shout in the faces of their parishioners, or to turn people away from their doors. Is it too much to ask for the same respect?'

Rebecca Arbett glanced up, annoyed. She tossed her magazine to the floor and picked up another.

'These hypocrites preach love but then attack. When did sexuality become abhorrent and violence accepted? We have suffered these self-styled moral crusaders, these opportunists, bigots and extremists, and we've stood up for our rights and the rights of our customers, but make no mistake, this is a much greater struggle. It is a struggle to preserve our liberties. It is a struggle to preserve the first amendment rights of every citizen . . .'

Fillinger quivered with emotion, the embodiment of righteous defiance. His face glistened with perspiration.

'This morning I told my people they could stay at home, but instead they came into their offices and sat at their desks and went back to work. I'm proud of them, and I have a message to deliver, on their behalf, to the people who did this. Americans do not bow to violence and terror. We are committed to the preservation of our hard-won freedoms . . .'

Arbett glanced back to the sentiment chart. The worm continued to climb steadily. More networks were picking up the feed. The speech was winning public support for Dreamcom at a prodigious rate and stripping it away from NeChristo just as fast. Fillinger was giving a worthy performance, he thought – more Martin Luther King than Larry Flynt.

He rubbed his chin thoughtfully. The scale of the sentiment shift from a single speech was alarming, but the response would come quickly, funded by NeChristo's bottomless war chest. When those boys got cranked up their messages went out via every channel, every hour, for days. Fillinger's voice would be swamped.

Or would it?

Arbett thought back to his early-morning walk with the lobbyist. Fillinger was smart. He was pulling every lever at his disposal to hit back at his enemies, seen and unseen. With this kind of rhetoric, and the whole bombing thing still wide open, who knew where it would go? It was unpredictable. Shit. Arbett had a deal on the table. NeChristo's people were checking in at regular intervals to see if he had come to a decision. The last thing he needed was unpredictable.

Friday

Chapter 16

'There it is, sir. Pretty impressive, huh?'

Madsen looked to where his driver, probationary agent Steven Galloway, pointed. They had left Salt Lake City and were now travelling south-west along a highway that bisected a vast, flat, industrial landscape. Slightly to the right of where they were heading, just visible above the horizon of smokestacks and concrete, was the top of a dome.

In the side mirror, a dazzling morning sun hovered above the Wasatch Mountains. A couple of hundred years earlier those peaks, coupled with an unshakeable conviction that everyone deserves a place to worship unmolested, had inspired Brigham Young and his Mormon pioneers to settle here. Recently, a different kind of spiritual leader had claimed the same inspiration. This one had never turned a sod or worked with his hands. He travelled in limousines and private jets instead of wagons. And he communed with his followers around the globe via a hundred million earpieces called G-rings. Shortly, when they arrived at the dome, Madsen would meet him.

Overnight he had read everything he could lay his hands on about the New Christian Organization of America. NeChristo, he now knew, had started out as a small independent church in

Dallas, and its founder was an ex-management consultant named Brandt Engels, two facts no longer included in the official guide-books.

Engels had wanted to find out whether making connections between compatible people – for friendship, partnership, romance or marriage – could form the central doctrine of a church. Connec-tions were the key to driving large congregations, he reasoned, and large congregations led to large revenues.

The experiment was not, initially, a success. After a year of haranguing the good people of Dallas from pulpits, billboards and the screens in their living rooms, attendance was low and contributions even lower. He paused to regroup.

After a careful analysis he came to two conclusions. The first was that neither he, nor any other religious leader on the planet, had come close to exploiting the potential of information technology to recruit, connect and bring spiritual value to congregations. The second was that he did not have the personal charisma necessary to successfully front a religion.

Engels knew just the people to tackle the first challenge. Using his old business contacts he recruited a team of experts and put them to work. Within six weeks they had come up with the com-bination of G-rings and social-networking platforms that would come to define the church.

Finding a new frontman frustrated Engels for a further five months, until he heard about a charismatic, larger-than-life preacher in Missouri. His name was Luke McConnell, but he billed himself as Pastor Luke. Engels turned up unannounced and sat in one of Luke's congregations. He listened to the man's warm baritone voice. He watched the worshippers alternately transfixed with burning intensity and bursting in joyous celebration. He felt the energy and magnetism. He knew he had found his man.

A contract was drawn up. Engels' management consulting experience had taught him that to be successful you not only needed the right people but you needed to give them the right incentives, so the document offered a partnership and full profit-sharing rights. Luke signed on the spot.

When the Dallas church relaunched with its new leader, new network and new name – the New Christian Organization of America – it exploded. In the first year it expanded to seventeen cities. A year later it was forty-nine.

Engels and his pastor stuck with the partnership model. The preferred method of recruiting new partners was finding especially charismatic and talented preachers, conducting deep background checks and getting to know them in person over six to eight weeks. If they passed muster, they were invited inside the tent. Membership was conditional on attending a crash programme on the NeChristo formula for communications, marketing and congregation networking. New preachers had to agree to comply strictly with the formula – and to bring their existing congregations into the fold. After a glimpse of the cash flow, none refused.

As word got out, Engels and Luke no longer had to go recruiting. Preachers began coming in from all over the United States to beg their way into the money machine. Soon they were flying in from places like Australia and Brazil.

In the sixth year Engels' doctor diagnosed a mild heart condition and told him to slow down. He had made more money than he could have imagined. The church had eclipsed all his other accomplishments. Ever the pragmatist, he decided to call it quits. He pulled together a team of lawyers and thrashed out an agreement for the other partners to buy him out. A billion dollars reputedly changed hands. Pastor Luke, already the public head of the church, was anointed senior partner in charge of the entire operation. Engels flew to Monaco, dropped three hundred million on a yacht the size of a small ocean liner, and sailed into the Mediterranean sunset.

Pastor Luke proved a capable successor. He maintained an aggressive programme of expansion and reinvestment. As the organization grew he added layers of management and more sophisticated controls. NeChristo soon outgrew its Dallas headquarters, and when a sprawling slab of industrial real estate came up for sale not far from Salt Lake City, Pastor Luke jumped on it.

He had a vision: a new centre of operations befitting the church's brand, a symbol of its power and strength.

The site was big enough. The place was associated with religious independence and it offered a measure of isolation while still being conveniently accessible to NeChristo's largest markets on the west coast. The church courted the Utah governor's office, the state legislature and the Salt Lake City government with site rehabilitation plans, an enormous building programme, job projections and charts that showed millions of clean-living, cashed-up pilgrims coming their way. All the approvals were granted and shortly afterwards work began on the now famous dome.

Madsen noticed that probationary agent Galloway was biting his fingernails again. He'd been gnawing on them on and off all the way from Salt Lake City.

'What's bugging you, Steve?' Madsen asked.

Galloway dropped his hand back to the wheel and glanced across. 'Me? Nothing.'

'Don't like bothering the nice NeChristo people?'

'No. I mean, they don't cause any trouble and I've got nothing against them, but it's no problem.'

'I'm kidding – I know that's not it. How about, you don't much like being the junior guy who has to play cab driver for a visiting agent and, if that wasn't bad enough, it has to be a plotter, a liar-man, a wand waver. One of those guys that you tell a joke to about popping mood pills and, before you've finished, has you in front of a review board admitting you *did* pop one, on your vacation, three Christmases ago?'

Galloway grinned sheepishly.

'And next thing you know,' Madsen continued, 'you're out on your ass, filling in applications for door security work at your local Bank of America. Is that it?'

'Kind of,' Galloway said. 'I guess I was wondering if you were one of those integrity Nazis like everyone said.'

'Who's everyone?' Madsen asked, staring out the window.

'The guys. They were giving me a hard time about it this morning.'

'Why, you got something to hide?'

'No, sir.'

Madsen sighed. 'Relax. I'm sure you're a good agent and I'm equally sure you're human. Maybe you managed to slip something past the polygraph exam at Quantico. Maybe there's one tiny thing you did – way back – that you wish you hadn't, and it scares you to death. But I can tell you, absolutely and for one hundred per cent certain, that I don't give a shit. I'm not OPI and I'm not interested.'

Galloway glanced across at Madsen and seemed to unwind a little. 'Uh, yeah, that's about the size of it.'

'That's all of us, Steve. That's you, me, everyone that ever carried a badge. My advice is to stop worrying. Flip the OPIs the bird. If you're a half-decent agent – and I'm sure you are – just treat every day on the job as a good day and you'll be fine.'

Galloway grinned, more widely this time.

'Hey, don't think guilty thoughts or my radar will go off,' said Madsen.

The factories, warehouses and truck depots ended abruptly and they found themselves driving past parks crisscrossed with cycleways, orchards and vegetable plots. The few visible buildings were low, modern and integrated with the landscape. Some, Madsen saw, had turf grown completely over the top. Everywhere he looked there were small groups of people wearing brightly coloured clothes digging, carrying, pruning or planting.

Galloway said, 'NeChristo volunteers. They come here from all over to work on the urban reclamation and get into the community spirit. They look happy, don't they?'

Madsen had to admit they did. Bright clothes were complemented by brighter smiles and plenty of lively interaction between the workers. The ratio of males to females looked roughly equal. NeChristo had taken kibbutzim to a new level, launching thousands of projects to re-green America and recruiting millions of people to work on them, selecting members for working parties based on a deep analysis of compatibility and common interests. It did this so efficiently that people joked it was the world's largest and most sophisticated dating agency. Looking around, Madsen would be hard pressed to argue.

They were close enough to the dome to get a sense of its stupendous size – higher and wider than the Louisiana Superdome – and to make out the patterns on the surface. Madsen realized it was not a dome at all, at least not in the conventional sense. Rather it was a porous latticework of steel, like an upside-down tea strainer of outlandish proportions. The girders, each covered in solar panels, formed hundreds of interconnected triangles that soared majestically skywards, dominating the surrounding landscape. Lush cascades of green could be seen through the gaps. Hanging gardens. On the inside. It was surreal, a horticultural impossibility in a climate like this.

Suddenly a million tiny rainbows swirled into existence, and Madsen saw how the impossible had been made possible.

'The NeChristo monsoon,' Galloway said. 'Once an hour. They say they installed a hundred miles of piping to feed Wasatch snow to all the sprinklers. In winter they use those solar cells to warm the water to just the right temperature. Can you believe that?'

The colours shimmered and danced. It was magical. Madsen couldn't drag his eyes away. 'You know, once upon a time churches used to be plain white,' he said.

Galloway laughed. 'Not this one.' He slowed to enter an enormous parking lot. 'This is it. They don't let cars any closer. See the tunnel over there?' he said, pointing. 'All visitors walk through that to reception. 'Bout a hundred yards. Look for the smiley people in the big ball bearing and you're there.'

The tunnel turned out to be an opening at the base of the dome, a thirty-foot-high mouse-hole compared to the colossus overhead. Several footpaths and cycleways converged into one and passed through before branching off again on the other side. Above, in the latticework, the sprinklers hissed, but not a drop reached the path. Staircases of ingenious glass panels deflected the falling water while preserving an uninterrupted view of flowering vines, yellow-green ferns and lush, broad-leafed climbing plants.

Madsen passed through the tunnel and stepped into a scene from Jules Verne's *Journey to the Centre of the Earth*. The hanging gardens curved up to the heavens, crisscrossing the sky with greenery. Directly in front of him, in the centre of the vast enclosed space and almost as tall as the dome itself, was a sphere. It was clad in reflective panels and did indeed resemble a ball bearing. The structure had to be more than twenty storeys high. People came and went from openings around the base. They travelled in twos or threes, some walking and some riding bikes. They were fit, wholesome types and among the most attractive people Madsen had ever seen.

Madsen climbed a short set of stairs, entered the sphere and stared upwards. Like the dome itself, the ball was hollow, a shell. The offices were built into the sides, facing into a central well, their lights painting each level with a bright white ring of luminescence. Escalators serviced the bottom half of the sphere and a row of freestanding elevator shafts serviced the top half, each shaft connecting a different level back to the ground. The shafts were transparent and lit from within, giving them the appearance of searchlights probing a night sky. Floating above, in the very centre of the well, without any apparent means of suspension, was a diffuse, gaseous, glowing ball. Islands of blue and green swirled across its surface. The colours made it vaguely reminiscent of Earth, although the shifting shapes bore no resemblance to any of the continents. It might have been forty feet across, but it was hard to be precise.

A ball within a sphere within a dome.

Madsen let his gaze fall back to ground level. He spotted the reception desk, but before he could get to it an impeccably dressed young man approached. He had broad shoulders and a chiselled jaw straight out of a Marine Corps recruiting poster. He held out his hand.

'Agent Madsen, I presume? We've been expecting you. Welcome to NeChristo.'

As they ascended the central and tallest elevator shaft, the man began a running commentary, like a tour guide. Pointing upwards at the glowing ball of gas he said, 'That's the Ball of Connectedness. We're going to pass right through it. But don't worry, it's just a hologram. The size reflects how many members are connected at any point in time. Bringing people together is our mission. That's why we place the ball at the centre, where everyone can see it. The members *are* the church. We designed the ball so that if every NeChristo member connected simultaneously it would fill the interior of the sphere. As you can see . . . approximately ten per cent of our congregation are communing as we speak.'

'Have you ever seen a hundred per cent?'

'No, but we dream about it!' he laughed. 'We come closest when we run our multi-zone Christmas services.'

'And the colours?'

'They symbolize the richness of interaction. Blue is for one-way connections – members listening to our broadcasts and messages of the day – and green symbolizes deeper interpersonal interaction. Members talking to other members, getting together for services, that sort of thing. People need people, so the greener the better. When we get close the individual faces become visible . . . There! Do you see?'

The elevator passed into the ball and the coloured patches resolved themselves into a sea of finely glowing threads. At the end of every thread was a tiny face. Millions of portraits, each the size of a postage stamp, smiling out at the world. It was an astonishing spectacle.

'When you finish your meeting, I'd be happy to show you around some more. Just ask at reception.'

I'll bet, thought Madsen as they exited the top of the ball. *And you'll have a G-ring waiting with my name on it.*

Pastor Luke's office resembled a collision between a stock exchange and the bridge of an aircraft carrier. A conference table with high-backed leather armchairs dominated the middle. Electronic displays dense with numbers and charts covered the walls. The office's position near the top of the sphere made the bank of inward-facing windows steeply angled, providing a stunning view to the bottom of the cavernous interior. Even seated at the conference table Madsen could see the luminous green and blue ball hovering at the centre.

Luke glided in wearing a long robe embroidered with an explosion of flowers. He was almost as wide as he was tall, and his round face radiated friendliness. A big man in every sense.

His voice boomed as he clasped hands with Madsen. 'Welcome! Sorry about the outfit. I just finished a broadcast. We're promoting our reclamation project in Kuala Lumpur and I thought I'd get in the spirit of things. It's a big deal for us, very exciting.'

Madsen nodded. 'Thank you for seeing me.'

In fact he was still surprised to be seeing Luke at all. He had telephoned his request on the way to San Francisco International the previous afternoon, fully expecting to be fobbed off to a senior pastor, but when he arrived at his hotel in Salt Lake City a message had been waiting. Request granted. And now Pastor Luke's face was all lit up like the visit was the highlight of his day.

Luke took the robe off, revealing an expensive tailored suit. He hung the robe near the door and pulled a chair from the end of the conference table. It was large and appeared to have been specially customized to accommodate his width. He lowered himself into it and at the same time his expression switched from cheerfulness to deep concern. 'I know you had to go out of your way to come here, Agent Madsen, and I want you to know I appreciate it. This is a terrible business.' He spoke with an unusual cadence, emphasizing every third or fourth word. 'How is the investigation progressing?'

'It's progressing,' Madsen said. 'But not as fast as I'd like.' He began talking about the scale of the tragedy, watching Luke closely as he lingered over the terror the victims must have felt in their final moments, and the suffering of their loved ones.

Luke nodded and made sympathetic noises. 'The whole thing is so terrible . . . To think that some may have been buried alive . . . Everyone in our congregation has been praying . . .' His words sounded sincere but Madsen noted that the pastor was preoccupied by a nearby electronic display filled with columns of bright red numbers. From time to time the display emitted a soft bleep and Luke seemed unable to resist stealing a glance as updates rippled down the columns.

Madsen waited for one of the bleeps, then leaned forward suddenly and asked, 'Weren't they sinners?'

Luke's eyebrows shot up. His smile faltered. 'Pardon me?'

'Weren't they sinners? Didn't they get what they deserved?'

Luke's expression was strained. Madsen had his full attention now. 'They may have been sinners, but people who have been led astray are there to be saved, not killed. None of them deserved that.'

'And the protest campaign? Is it achieving everything you wanted?'

'It's been a long road, but we are finally getting attention in the right places. Public opinion is starting to swing.'

'So there are no plans to call it off?'

'We thought about putting it on hold. I see you are sceptical, but we did think about it, I assure you. It wasn't an easy decision by any means. In the end we decided that stopping would do more harm than good. This tragedy does nothing to change the fact that dollhouses inspire and perpetuate sin of the worst possible kind. We have a chance to put America back on a more enlightened path and we can't let the work we've done go to waste.'

Sin of the worst possible kind. If the last act of the man in room four was anything to go by, then that was exactly what the dollhouses had inspired. Madsen asked, 'What instructions are going out to your members?'

'About what?'

'About the protests.'

'First of all, we don't instruct our members. What they do is entirely their own choice. We send out alerts letting them know about protests in their city and asking them to consider participating. We also ask them to be peaceful, and to set an example that the world will respect.'

'Don't you tell them to stand in front of dollhouse premises and stop customers going in?'

'Our members try to slow them down so they hear our message.'

'Isn't delaying people in front of news cameras as they arrive and leave a kind of public shaming?'

Luke leaned back in his chair. It popped and creaked under his weight. 'No, I don't think so.'

'Which,' Madsen continued, 'has led to violence.'

'The violence has been directed at our people. They are not the perpetrators. NeChristo members, I am proud to say, have always exercised restraint.'

Madsen knew that wasn't true. Some of the protests had led to all-in brawls with arrests on both sides. Time to turn up the heat. 'Do you think your anti-dollhouse campaign has inspired violence?' he asked.

'Of course not.'

'How confident are you of that?'

There was a bleep, then another. Luke's eyes flicked to the display and back. 'Very confident. Our message, all our messages, are entirely non-violent.'

'Can you think of any reason a member would commit a violent act against a dollhouse?'

'None.'

'Do you think any member has the potential to commit such an act?'

'No.'

Madsen sat forward. 'That's not realistic. A membership as large as yours has to have its fair share of unstable people.'

A knock interrupted. An aide entered and whispered in Luke's ear, glancing towards the display that had been causing the distractions.

Luke excused himself and the two men went to the screen and conferred quietly, using a touch-sensitive panel to retrieve and manipulate several charts. The aide withdrew. Luke remained where he was, staring at the charts. After a few moments he turned to Madsen. 'I take it you think someone in NeChristo was involved in this crime?'

'We have reason to suspect that, yes.'

'Can I ask why?'

'You can ask, but I can't say.'

The corners of Luke's mouth turned down. After a moment he said, 'Of course many of our members are troubled when they join. They come to us for community, love and direction, and we give it to them. So no, I cannot truthfully say that no member has the potential for violence. What I can say is that when they have been with us a while, if we do what we do well, they are no longer prone to violence.'

'Let's get back to you, then. Did you, or any other church leader, do or say anything at all that could have incited the bombing in San Francisco?' Madsen sat absolutely still, outwardly impassive, his senses tuned in like a high-gain antenna.

Luke glared back. 'Absolutely not.'

'Then can you think of any NeChristo leader *capable* of inciting the bombing in San Francisco?'

'That's offensive.'

'So was the previous question. Will you please answer it?'

Luke closed his eyes and squeezed the bridge of his nose with his thumb and forefinger. 'No, of course I know no one capable of such a—'

'Would you repeat that under polygraph?'

Madsen already knew the answer, because no religious leader ever voluntarily submitted to a polygraph. They cited all manner of excuses: confidentiality, sanctity, respect and the preservation of faith. According to the cynics, the real reason was a fear of interviewers straying into the existential and proving they didn't believe in God.

The answer was a given, but Madsen was more interested in the pastor's reaction.

Luke reddened. His nostrils flared. 'That would set a dangerous precedent,' he replied evenly.

'It would go a long way towards clearing the good name of your church,' Madsen said. 'My colleagues and I can get on with more fruitful lines of enquiry. I can assure you the test will be private.'

Luke clasped his meaty hands behind his back and turned to the windows, staring down at the Ball of Connectedness. The back of his neck was the colour of a ripe tomato. Madsen wondered idly what would happen if a NeChristo leader suffered from vertigo.

'There is no such thing as a secret polygraph,' the pastor said, directing his words to the chasm on the other side of the glass. 'Even if you are sincere, your colleagues are not. I won't do one. And before you ask, I will not authorize anyone else to do one either.'

Madsen shrugged. 'Then I have a request. We'd like to perform an identity match for a suspect against images of your members. Would you facilitate that?'

'Access to our database?'

'Yes.'

'A hundred million people have placed their trust in us. They did not become members on the basis that their information will be shared with the police.'

'I appreciate that, but will you consider the request?'

'I can put it to the executive committee, but I know what their answer will be.'

'I see. Then will you help me arrange interviews with flock leaders for the greater San Francisco area? No polygraphs, just interviews.'

'That's two requests. I'm afraid I won't support that one either.'

'Why not?'

'Because I don't like fishing expeditions, which is what this is, and I will not place the reputation of my church in jeopardy. If you want interviews you will need subpoenas.'

Madsen nodded. 'Then I'll get subpoenas.'

'I doubt it. Now, is this interview over? I have other business.'

As they drove from the lot, Madsen looked over his shoulder and eyed a white utility van with dark windows backing out from between two other vehicles. Hadn't he seen it on the drive down? The van exited, then turned and followed them, staying a hundred yards behind. Galloway turned onto the highway on-ramp for Salt Lake City. The van kept straight on. Madsen decided he was imagining things and forgot about the van, concentrating instead on replaying the conversation with Luke in his head. He was onto something. He could smell it.

Chapter 17

Six hundred miles to the west, on the crowded rooftop of the Dreamcom tower, Tom Fillinger spied the top of a white cowboy hat above the sea of talking heads and adjusted course.

The rooftop was an entertainment director's wet dream. In the open-air section, giant stainless-steel wind deflectors gleamed in the midday sunshine, like sails on a space-age clipper ship. Built by a specialist firm in Norway, they ensured the brisk breeze coming off the bay could be heard but not felt. The wind whistled up each sail, tumbling over specially designed gills and shedding energy until only mild waterfalls of cool air were left to ruffle the coiffed hair of the guests. In the covered section, where the crowd was densest, dozens of white-trimmed tables groaned with food. Ten giant banners hung from scaffolds, each carrying an artist's impression of an exotic location with a label such as 'Hadrian's Villa', 'Tahitian Paradise' or 'Louis XIV's playroom'. An eleventh banner, strung horizontally between two scaffolds, read 'Thank you for supporting Ten Worlds!'

Fillinger's strongest emotion was relief. The mood was a little subdued, and he picked up occasional snatches about the bombing in the buzz of background conversation, but the turnout was strong. For the most part his guests had embraced his fighting spirit and made it their own. Drinking unlimited glasses of his Bollinger probably helped.

Someone yelled his name and jumped forward to shake hands. Yet another puffed-up celebrity he couldn't care less about. He stopped and pretended to be flattered. A raucous laugh came from his right, where a retinue of admirers surrounded the new James Bond. The actor was posing provocatively with one of the waitresses. His rugged looks and ice-blue eyes melted women's hearts, but the guy was as thick as he was conceited. Fillinger never completely understood why Hollywood types gravitated to the adult entertainment industry, but it had been that way ever since Johnny Carson, Sammy Davis Junior and other A-listers made a point of attending screenings of *Deep Throat*. Not that he was complaining. Having stars photographed with his ladies was about the most effective publicity you could get. And it was free.

He excused himself and pushed on.

As he squeezed closer to the cowboy hat he sighted the man underneath. Jim Bonitas. Sixty-five, Texan and rich as hell. And, as always, dressed too casually for the occasion in a canary yellow shirt, boots, and jeans, with an enormous belt buckle masquerading as a pair of steer horns. Completing today's ensemble was a skinny girl not a day over nineteen. She clung to his arm like a life-preserver. Her face wore the blank expression of the bored and out-of-depth.

On Tuesday, Fillinger and Bonitas would stand side by side to cut the ribbon at Ten Worlds.

Bonitas was deep in conversation with a tall man with red hair and a beard. Mark Pemberton, Fillinger's head of production. Pemberton saw Fillinger coming and excused himself. Turning, Bonitas startled his bored girlfriend with a slap on the rump and told her to shove off.

'How're you doing, Tom,' he said. His Texan drawl flowed the words together so they came out *howyadoon*.

'Not bad under the circumstances,' said Fillinger. 'I assume Mark has been updating you on the delivery schedule?'

'Yup, forty more dollies tomorrow, last shipment arrives on

opening day. Cutting it mighty fine, boy, if I may say so. But hell, you know what you're doing, right?'

Fillinger nodded. 'They finished the last room. Did you get a chance to see it?'

'All that Roman shit doesn't do it for me. But my boys liked it, and I hire 'em because they know what they're talking about.'

'How about another drink?' Fillinger asked, taking Bonitas' empty glass and holding it high.

A waitress with platinum-blonde hair and ample cleavage approached and proffered a tray with a menu. Bonitas bent forward and examined the menu, letting his gaze linger on the girl's chest. 'Jack Daniel's. Neat,' he said.

'Same, on the rocks,' said Fillinger.

The waitress wriggled away towards the bar, the Texan staring after her appreciatively.

Fillinger was pleased. She was the same model Ten Worlds was getting. His market research people had canvassed five thousand first-time visitors and established that one of their biggest Vegas disappointments was their first sight of casino waitstaff. Hollywood taught them to expect babes, so when their drink orders were taken by grandmas in short skirts it felt like they had arrived in the wrong city. Ten Worlds would be the first casino where reality *exceeded* their expectations.

Bonitas flashed a wicked grin at Fillinger. 'You'd think you could get 'em to at least repeat back your drink order. What if I get a gin and tonic or something? A customer could get mighty pissed at that.'

Fillinger winced. No one appreciated the challenge in realistically synchronizing each syllable with the myriad tiny movements of the lips, face, neck and chest. Getting it even slightly wrong was the difference between ultra-realism and spooky, and no one got turned on by spooky. Until there was a major breakthrough, Dreamcom's designers were sticking to sighs and moans. Customers didn't care. They weren't paying for conversation. He and Jim had been over this before. 'She recorded your order and it plays back in the barman's earpiece. You get the right drink every time. A German lab has a new synchronization algorithm and I'm sending a team to Hanover to take a look . . .' He trailed off. He could tell by the way Bonitas was squinting that he was no longer listening.

'Who did it, Tom?' Bonitas asked.

'If I knew, they'd be dead already.'

'You sounded pretty certain in that speech of yours yesterday.'

'If they didn't do it they sure as hell inspired it.'

'Uh huh.' The Texan squinted again. After a moment he said, 'Listen, Tom, I can't afford to have someone blowin' the fuck out of my casino.'

'That isn't going to happen.'

'And I can't afford for customers to be scared.'

'No one is going to blow up your casino, Jim.'

'I'm thinking we should delay. A week, maybe two. Once the mess is cleaned up, and people know they're going to be safe, then we launch. What do you say?'

'Christ, Jim. The media. All the celebrities flying in. Some are already there doing the preview. It'd be a disaster. We can put on more security—'

Bonitas waved him off. 'We've got enough security. That's not the point. The point is I'm getting word from my survey people that the customers are worried.'

Fillinger felt a prickle of anger. He detested answering to anyone, and the word 'partnership' had been excised from his commercial lexicon decades ago. He'd made an exception for Ten Worlds because it promised to be a titanic cash cow, and it would act as a flagship to lift the profile of all the other dollhouses. Bonitas knew this. They had talked about it. And yet here they were, before it had even opened, and this asshole was *telling him how it was going to be.*

'Listen,' he said. 'I met a guy on the investigation yesterday. He's sharp. They'll make arrests, I'm sure of it.'

Bonitas shrugged. 'If they're behind bars, we don't have a problem.'

'So there's no need to do anything drastic. Give the cops a chance to do their job.'

Bonitas studied Fillinger's face then broke into a laugh and slapped him on the back. 'I'm just yanking your chain, pardner. Now come on, what say we go find that skinjob and ask her what she did with our drinks?'

Fillinger declined the offer on the pretext that he had a media interview scheduled, and headed in the direction of the lounge. There was a service door on the way. Finding it, he ducked inside and closed the door behind him. His temples pounded. Jim Bonitas could take his cowboy hat and two-bit under-age whore and go fuck himself. Without Dreamcom, Ten Worlds would be just another grubby slot machine palace. Where was the gratitude? Where was the *respect*? He thumped his head against the wall, put a fist in his mouth, and bit.

The door opened.

Fillinger stared in astonishment. It was the waitress. Beneath the platinum hair and shiny smile and big cleavage, she held out a tray, his Jack Daniel's placed perfectly in the centre. With a snarl, he struck out. The glass hit the wall and shattered, showering them with amber droplets, glass and fragments of ice. The doll's eyes widened. Her smile faltered. She made a small, nervous bow and backed out the door . . .

Exactly as programmed. In a few moments she would also connect with maintenance and request cleaners to deal with the spillage. He couldn't stand the thought of being there when they came. Brushing off his jacket, he forced a smile and followed her out.

An ugly man with a greasy grey ponytail and unsettling coal-black eyes broke away from a cluster of guests and approached. Radim Ivanovic, Fillinger's numbers man and most trusted lieutenant, had worked in the business for thirty years. He knew everything there was to know.

'Didn't go well with Bonitas?' Ivanovic asked, perusing his boss over an exotically decorated cocktail.

Fillinger shot him a look. 'I had to get some air.'

Ivanovic's expression didn't change.

Fillinger rolled his eyes. As far as explanations went, leaving the roof of a skyscraper to get fresh air in a service corridor left a lot to be desired. 'He asked about delaying the opening.'

Two flashy Chinese men nodded politely as they passed. They were part of a delegation from Macau, in town to propose an arrangement for their own casino. Fillinger nodded in return. He wasn't interested. Not until Ten Worlds took off. Then he would cut a deal on his terms.

Ivanovic sipped his cocktail. 'What did you tell him?'

'I told him to hang in there. It'll be fine.'

Chapter 18

Four and a half hours after leaving Pastor Luke's office, Madsen was back in San Francisco, sitting in an orange plastic chair, waiting for a reply from Captain Pete McAlister, commander of Central Station, Metro Division, SFPD.

McAlister, a tall, intimidating black man who had once played pro football, leaned back against the edge of his desk. His folded forearms rippled with muscle. On the wall behind him, tiny blue dots, some paired, some single, crept along the streets and highways of an electronic map of the city. Above the map was the declaration MINIMUM FORCE, MAXIMUM EFFECT. A speaker crackled with radio calls.

Madsen was tense. He had come direct from the airport, stopping only to choke down a stale sandwich and visit the john. On the way he had received an alarming message from Carl Steinmann in evidence recovery. The lab had matched the explosives signature at Grant Avenue to a specific batch of D-5, a consignment that had recently disappeared from a military train. The army had initially assumed a clerical error, but after wasting weeks trying to track it down, and prodded by the enquiries from the Bureau, had grudgingly conceded theft. At the end of his message Steinmann appended some maths that was both succinct and chilling: *Best estimate is 40 to 60 pounds of D-5 carried in the backpack. Missing consignment was 500 pounds. Enough for eight or nine more Grant Avenues.*

Next to Madsen, in an identical plastic chair, was Holbrook, and next to him sat a thin, plain-clothes man with a three-day beard and a twinkle in his eye that gave him something of the appearance of a leprechaun. He had been introduced as Inspector Brown. Madsen had never met him before and, all going to plan, would never talk to him again.

It was McAlister's turn to speak.

'What you're telling me, Agent Madsen,' the captain said carefully, 'is that you formed the strong impression that these guys merit further investigation?'

'That's correct,' Madsen said. 'The pastor displayed sympathy for the victims but a greater preoccupation with his finances. Frankly, I wouldn't be surprised if they were somehow making money out of this. When I asked for further assistance he was uncooperative. He refused a polygraph, and he reacted strongly when I asked if any NeChristo leaders might be capable of inciting the bombing.'

'Which leads you to what conclusion?'

'Luke McConnell may not be directly involved, but at the very least he believes some of his colleagues could be. He has plenty to hide and fears what might come out if we start polygraphing senior members of the church.'

'Mike?'

Holbrook had one foot crossed over a knee. The fingers of his right hand tapped against his shoe. The tapping stopped. 'There's the inflammatory anti-dollhouse crap the church leadership has been spouting, the protests they've organized . . . these guys have form. And the suspect was wearing a G-ring. It's hard to say how high up it goes, but we can't ignore the possibility that church leaders were involved.' The shoe tapping resumed.

The ritual had been underway for fifteen minutes. With the exception of Brown, who had yet to speak, they had circled back over the same observations several times already, taking turns to seek a minor clarification or repeat a statement in their own words. Very carefully and very gradually a symmetry had been established.

McAlister turned to Madsen. 'How many church leaders might we be talking about?'

'It could be one, it could be a dozen. There's no way to know. In my view, the most efficient line of enquiry is to polygraph a couple of senior ones in San Francisco – it doesn't really matter who. I just need a sniff, then I can follow it, find any conspirators and flush them out.'

McAlister said, 'Tell me again why you can't go after the database?'

Holbrook cleared his throat. 'We put in a warrant request via the Bureau, but religious records apparently give judges indigestion. It's going to take time. And now Luke and his people know we want access, who knows if all the records will still be there . . .'

McAlister leaned forward. 'Okay. So, based on the urgency of the situation, our need to do everything possible to prevent another bombing, we all agree that a few additional polygraph interviews by Agent Madsen here are the fastest way to proceed, is that right?'

Everyone nodded.

'Of course, you can't get a subpoena to polygraph the top religious men in the country just because one homicidal maniac happens to have worn a G-ring.'

'No, you can't,' Madsen said.

Choosing his words with exaggerated care, Holbrook said, 'But *if* someone came forward, someone with inside knowledge of the church, and testified, under polygraph, that he believed certain NeChristo leaders ordered the bombing, and if this person named those leaders . . . That would be enough for you to get an administrative subpoena, right?'

'Yes, it would,' Madsen said. Everyone was on the same wavelength now. Time to wind up the ritual.

McAlister studied his fingernails. 'I only wish my department knew of such a person.' He addressed the remark to no one in particular, but all eyes turned to Inspector Brown.

'As it happens,' Brown said, beaming, 'I understand someone like that came forward just this morning. Guy by the name of Reginald Ryle.'

It was his only line, and his delivery was perfect.

Bootstrapping, it was called. It stemmed from a tactic taught at Quantico for penetrating crime syndicates. The idea was to find a disgruntled foot soldier prepared to mouth off about someone else in the organization. It didn't matter if he was motivated by jealousy or rivalry or a grudge, if he pulled clean greens on a HAMDA while listing a colleague's crimes, then you had enough to apply for an administrative subpoena to lay on the next guy and you were on your way.

In the field, however, Madsen and his colleagues had made an interesting discovery. For *any* given individual with power and profile, there were people who believed, in their heart of hearts, they were guilty of something.

These people often believed other things too – for example, that the president listened in on their phone calls, the moon landings were faked and the 9/11 attacks were masterminded by Freemasons – so it was best to limit your questions to the subject at hand to avoid dealing with awkward transcripts later. And prior to going to trial an agent had to swear his evidence was secured legitimately, which meant procuring such a witness yourself was a bad idea. You wanted distance, the less you knew the better. The ideal way was to drop a hint to a trusted colleague or someone in another department or, as in this case, another law enforcement agency. If you were lucky, a friendly stranger soon stopped by and said, offhand, *By the way, an interesting witness came forward you might want to talk to . . .*

Hence the charade. Madsen would never ask who found Reginald Ryle, because he didn't want to know. With two police officers in the morgue there would have been no shortage of volunteers, but this way it was still possible, at least theoretically, that the man had come forward himself.

Madsen thought of bootstrapping as a workaround, a tactic to be reserved for situations of absolute necessity, but with a single legitimate lead, the distinct possibility of more bombs going off, and the Bureau hierarchy clamouring for results, this was not a time for niceties. He had to penetrate NeChristo.

Downstairs in the surveillance operations room, Shari Sanayei's hands were shaking. She had just realized that a certain conversation, one she wanted to keep secret, was right there in the Grant Avenue evidence files. She was sure of it, because her own team had uploaded stored data from every camera in the area.

With her heart pounding, she entered the unit number for the dome camera outside Central Station and dialled in the time: the start of Wednesday's shift. She checked again that what she was about to view would be isolated to her console. Accidentally displaying it on the Wall, where others could see, would be catastrophic. Actually, it wasn't so much seeing as *hearing* that terrified her. The camera in question had a microphone.

She hit the play button.

Her own face flashed on the desk console. Angry. Animated.

Shari shut her eyes as emotions came flooding back. Swallowing, she mustered the strength to look at the figure standing alongside her in front of the station. The creases in his trousers were knife-edged, the black collar freshly starched. The silver seven-point star on his chest gleamed. In contrast to her own demeanour, Adam's expression was calm, with only a slight frown to betray his feelings about what he was hearing.

Shari's arms were weak and the headset felt heavy as she put it on. She flipped on the audio. Her own voice, irritable and assertive, rang through the earphones: '. . . *waited long enough. If you don't tell her now, then what am I supposed* '

She cut the sound. Cupping her hands to her mouth, she rocked silently back and forth in her chair. She didn't want to hear his reply. It would be too much. She would go to pieces.

The vision rolled on, her silent ultimatums and cutting words alternating with his mouthed platitudes and reassurances. Adam turned. Shari remembered that Terry Strong had called out from across the road, saying it was time to rock'n'roll, and that she had resented the interruption. Adam turned back, cocked his head apologetically and opened his hand in a brief palm-up gesture of helplessness.

Then he was gone. For good.

So long, Adam.

With all the manual scanning underway, it was a wonder someone hadn't come across it already. Forty-eight hours ago she could have explained it. It was personal. It was an affair. They had argued just before he died. Her bosses might have understood. But not now. The questions would be fierce. Why didn't you declare it? What else are you hiding? She would be off the case immediately.

The scene would be on other cameras too, but they didn't matter. They were too far away to hear.

It had to go.

Her index finger hovered over the delete key.

Tampering with an evidence file, of course, was a crime. If she was caught, there would be dire consequences.

But she wouldn't be caught. She knew what she was doing. It would be a brief dead spot, a microphone glitch. And it was small, scarcely more than one minute of audio on one camera nowhere near the scene, nothing to do with the case. If she pressed, it was gone. No one would miss it.

She pressed.

Shari took a deep breath and felt her anxiety ebb away. Toggling her monitor to a live camera on Green Street, she slipped off her headset and rose from her seat.

Yolanda was blocking the doorway.

She was leaning against the doorframe with her arms folded. Her expression was blank, neutral, unreadable. Shari's mind raced. How long had she been there? A few seconds? Longer? She smiled uncertainly, hoping for a positive response.

Yolanda casually uncrossed her arms. Saying nothing, she walked off in the direction of the dispatch room.

Chapter 19 _____

In Washington, DC, Senator Erol Arbett made his way down the steps of the Capitol to where his driver waited with the door held open. He handed his briefcase to the driver and backed into the limousine. As they pulled smoothly into the traffic flow he leaned back, closed his eyes and tried to relax. The briefing from his sentiment guru had lasted an hour. He was exhausted. Jet Barnes spoke too fast and used too many charts, and his Aussie accent and in-your-face manners grated almost as badly as his loud ties and louder sports cars. And the way the kid leered at Arbett's secretary was unseemly. Without the freakish combination of statistical genius and electoral intuition he'd be nothing. Out on his ass.

According to Jet's analysis, Fillinger's speech was nothing to worry about. The impact had been temporary. The dollhouse issue was already trending back to its old pattern. Just as Arbett predicted, the NeChristo publicity machine was smooth and well oiled and working fast. A few more days and you would never know there had been a speech.

The senator wasn't sure Barnes was right this time, though. *Fillinger isn't finished with this yet*, he thought. *The old fox is a survivor, and he won't let his dollhouses go down without throwing everything into the fight.* Just the fact that the man was prepared to launch a head-on attack on NeChristo was unsettling. Could he inflict lasting damage on the church's reputation? It was impossible to know, but until they caught whoever planted the bomb, and the story drifted out of the spotlight for ever, nothing could be ruled out.

That notwithstanding, a decision on NeChristo's offer was due.

He needed advice.

Arbett's driver knew the route by heart. He threaded north, taking shortcuts to bypass the late-afternoon traffic. Government offices gave way to commercial buildings. They wound their way into the suburbs. The streets became leafier and the houses larger.

When it came to the big decisions, Arbett only trusted two people in the world. One was Otto Finkeld, an ex-lawyer with slicked-back hair, spectacles and a rod-up-his-ass bearing that could have earned him a walk-on part as a 1920s banker. Otto loved politics. Every aspect of it turned him on, from wheeling and dealing in the House to winning hearts in the tenements. When he wasn't advising on politics, he was thinking about it, and when he wasn't thinking about it, he was teaching it, as professor of political science at Georgetown University. They met when Otto was engaged as a temporary consultant on one of Arbett's early campaigns. He astonished the team by advising a complete reversal on a contentious city planning issue. Arbett would win more votes from women, he said, than he would lose from senior citizens. He was right. And he kept on being right.

His other trusted advisor was Kenny Bosco, a ginger-haired firebrand who wore gold rings like knuckledusters and looked like he drove trucks for a living, which in fact he had. He'd gone on to start his own rent-a-truck operation, followed by six more businesses in transportation, storage and industrial cleaning. Kenny watched three of his businesses fold and sold the other four for enough cash to buy a string of waterfront mansions stretching from Cape Cod to Fort Lauderdale. Nowadays he referred to himself as semi-retired. Arbett had known Kenny in high school, where they had both been street smart and competitive to the point of viciousness. It was years later, when they no longer warred over the same turf, that they realized how much they had in common and became friends.

Otto the intellectual and Kenny the pugilist – different backgrounds but motivated by the same things. The cut and thrust of the fight. Winning. Spilling the blood of the vanquished.

Meetings were sometimes held in a luxury apartment Kenny kept in downtown Washington. The apartment had the advantage of being completely private. If Kenny had a woman staying he would hand her a credit card and evict her for the evening, and the three men would play poker and smoke cigars while they schemed into the early hours.

Other times they met in a decidedly more civilized setting. Arbett's favourite, in fact.

The driver turned onto a wide, straight drive and Arbett caught a glimpse of immaculate white colonnades and faux Roman edifices. They caught the rays of late-afternoon sun and glowed gold against a deepening blue sky. The interior of the North Washington Country Club was equally grand. More importantly, so was the membership, thanks to two simple mechanisms: a requirement for applicants to obtain written sponsorship from three current members, and an initiation fee of two hundred and fifty thousand dollars, non-refundable and payable in advance. In short, everything about the place reminded Arbett of his perch on life's long ladder of achievement, alongside the very few who can proclaim, hand on heart, that they really do run the show.

Arbett extricated himself from the limousine and laboured his way along corridors lined with French paintings, Italian marble and liveried staff. He ascended red-carpeted stairs to the upper terrace where Kenny and Otto were waiting. They had reserved the same table for years. Much of Arbett's career had been decided right here, sipping bourbon under potted palms and gazing out over the golf course and scarlet oaks.

They talked baseball first, as was their protocol. Then women. Arbett waited until the second round of drinks before getting down to business. 'Dolly-fuckers or God-botherers, gentlemen. We need to make a call.'

'It's a no-brainer as far as I'm concerned,' Kenny said, fiddling with his gold rings and playing his usual role as point man in any debate. 'Luke and his crew are good, and they're in it for the long term. I've never seen such a slick operation. Jeez, they might as well be printing the stuff.' He used his finger to stir the ice in his glass. 'You can't lose.'

'That's the thing, Kenny,' Arbett said, reaching into his briefcase. 'I'm still not sure about that.' He withdrew two binders and tossed them on the table. 'Jet compiled these today. Take a look and tell me what you think.'

Kenny riffled through the pages and turned to the executive summary. After skimming it, he tossed the binder back onto the table. Otto took his time, lingering over each page, studying the tables. After a few minutes of this, Arbett became impatient. 'Otto?'

'Yes? Oh. Well, sentiment is trending back to normal. So that's fine . . .'

'But?'

'But . . . the data also show that yesterday's swing was very big. Bigger than you would normally expect from one lousy speech. In my opinion that hints at underlying volatility.'

'For volatility do I read unpredictability?' asked Arbett.

Otto took his time before answering. 'I'd say so, yes. In this case. Because there are so many unknowns. With Fillinger pointing the finger—'

Kenny interrupted, 'Why don't you release a statement defending the Jesus freaks? Something like, Fillinger has no right to slander our revivalist friends, look at all the good the church does with the projects, et cetera. You become a leader standing up for Christian integrity and good sense, and as a bonus you get a head start with your new buddies.'

Otto threw his head back and laughed

'I'm serious!' Kenny cried, putting his hand over his heart and pretending to be hurt.

'And what if there *is* a link somewhere between the church and the bombings?' Otto asked. 'Who's the upstanding leader then?'

Kenny snorted. 'Bullshit. There's no link. It's some loopy fringe cult responsible, not a mainstream church. Think about it: shutting down dollhouses would be bad for business. All these rallies, the protests, the live debates. They love it. They never had so much cash. The longer they stretch it out the better.'

Otto chuckled. 'Actually, it could go the other way too. When those repressed and cashed-up Bible thumpers need to loosen up they can't go to hookers, so what's the first thing to do? Open their wallets and spend big at Dreamcom!'

'Symbiosis!' said Kenny.

Arbett joined in the laughter.

A waiter arrived and they fell silent. He wheeled a cart alongside the table and set out trays of oysters. Beyond the terrace balcony the sky was deepening to a soft violet where it met the treetops. Gardeners fussed around the edges of the fairways and the distant buzz of their lawnmowers mingled with the clink of ice cubes. The waiter made a small bow and wheeled his cart away.

Otto put on his best professor's frown. 'We should take the worst case seriously. Say you go with NeChristo and some link is established between the church and the bombing. Or the bombings continue and Fillinger keeps pushing blame onto them. Public support for NeChristo will fall. Sure, we'll have funds, but we'll be stuck in unpopular territory and losing votes—'

'Will you listen to yourself?' Kenny said. 'If, if, if! You're too pessimistic.'

'And Fillinger will become a powerful enemy,' Otto continued.

'That's if he's still around,' Kenny said, tipping his head back and sucking down an oyster.

'Pardon me?'

'More attacks might cost him his business.'

Otto rolled his eyes. 'I don't think so. Dreamcom is huge. It has diversified revenue streams and deep pockets. They can cross-subsidize. No matter what happens to the dollhouses they can ride it out.'

Kenny grinned. 'I'm not so sure.'

Arbett stared at Kenny with narrowed eyes. 'What do you know, Kenny-boy?'

Kenny examined his oysters, picking his next victim with elaborate care.

'What,' Arbett repeated, twirling a pudgy finger in Kenny's direction, 'do you know . . . that we don't know?'

Kenny chose an oyster. He took his time chewing. Finally he said, 'I hear he's spent more and borrowed more than he should have. Much more. Research labs, making dollies, fitting out dollhouses. Not cheap, and he's been doing all three in too much of a hurry.'

'Meaning?'

'Let's just say he's put himself out on a limb, and if his cash flow doesn't improve soon he'll fall off.'

Arbett digested this information. No wonder the payments had dried up. And no wonder the lobbyist had been so damn blunt. They must be sweating blood. 'Let me get this straight. Fillinger is in so much debt that if he doesn't fix it he's going to have creditors move on him?'

'That's about the size of it,' Kenny said, pleased with his little bombshell. 'He's pinning everything on Ten Worlds. After Tuesday it comes online and should turn things around financially. It's that big. But he's had to shovel a lot into it. He's in the hole with his business partner. There's no room for delay. If anything goes wrong . . . at best he'll be forced to sell off a big chunk of his business. The word is the business partner will pounce.'

'The word from who?' Arbett asked softly.

'What?'

'You just said the word is his business partner will pounce. What word? Where did this come from?'

Kenny grinned. 'I heard it from an old Texan pal of mine. Happens to have a stake in the outcome.'

Arbett nodded. Jim Bonitas. The casino mogul gambled with everyone's money but his own. He was going to make sure he won out no matter what.

He tilted his head back and slipped an oyster between his lips. He squeezed it with his tongue, feeling the slippery texture, savouring it. The thought of Fillinger being forced to sign over part of his precious empire was delicious.

'So if anything else happens to the dollhouses,' he said, 'Fillinger is a spent force anyway.'

'In that case going with NeChristo is your safest option,' Otto said.

Kenny grinned. 'And they don't have any cash flow problems.'

'And they don't have cash flow problems,' Otto agreed.

Arbett raised his glass. 'Here's to our new friends in Salt Lake City.'

Chapter 20

Madsen located Mr Reginald Aaron Ryle, forty-seven years of age, unmarried, father deceased, estranged from his mother, and recently excommunicated from the San Francisco diocese of the New Christian Organization of America, at his ramshackle rental near the corner of Peralta and 12th, West Oakland.

Ryle didn't answer the knock, but the front door was unlatched and swung inwards. When Madsen entered he came face to face with a slightly built man sitting calmly in a worn recliner, hands by his sides. He was dressed in khaki trousers, a crisp short-sleeved shirt and neatly knotted plain brown tie. The lounge-room screen was off and the house silent.

Ryle registered no surprise at the intrusion, giving Madsen the impression he had been waiting for some time. When asked politely if he would mind coming to answer some questions about his former employer, Ryle nodded and followed like a lamb to the street, where Holbrook held open the passenger-side door of the Dodge.

On the drive downtown, none of them spoke.

In Madsen's book, the best way of camouflaging one bent rule was to demonstrate a meticulous adherence to every other one, which was why he took Mr Ryle to the FBI office and conducted him to an interview room specially fitted out with extra sensors to supplement those on the HAMDA, and why he had a polygraph technician on hand to ensure the entire exercise was properly recorded and documented.

Ryle was seated in a large, comfortable chair. The chair was white, as were the floor tiles and the ceiling and the walls. Except for a reflective rectangle of one-way glass, the entire room was painted to precisely the same grade of stark luminescence, to optimize the sensitivity of the watching instruments.

Ryle was asked if he would like some music to help relax. He chose Bach. Bach was his favourite, he said.

The chair was reclined.

Madsen pulled up a regular chair and perched his carefully prepared clipboard of questions on his knee. He looked like a psychiatrist counselling his patient.

The interview began.

Each time Ryle spoke, the sensors recorded the rise and fall of his chest, the twitch of his eyelids, the heat radiating from his neck. They listened to the intonation of each word and counted the beats of his pulse. They sniffed the pheromones rising from his pores and monitored the electrical activity in each region of his brain from sixteen different angles.

Fifteen minutes in, Madsen knew he was in trouble.

'Let's try that again,' he said. 'I asked you if Pastor Paul was capable of ordering an attack on the Grant Avenue dollhouse.'

'Oh, yes, absolutely. And he steals from his flock. He's a great big fat thief.' Ryle spoke like a grandfather telling tales of a mis-spent youth: warmly and with a glint in his eye. He was happy and relaxed. Madsen, despite the controlled room temperature, was sweating.

Ryle continued, 'He tricks people into giving much more than they can afford. Then he spends it on himself and his fat wife.'

Madsen sighed. *Fat* was turning out to be a favourite word. 'I only asked if he was capable of murder.'

'He is. And he steals. Not small change, either. He must have pocketed more than ten million extra last year alone, oh yes indeedy.'

Madsen shot a withering look at the one-way mirror. Bach played softly in the background.

'Mr Ryle,' he said. 'Do we need to go over this again? A yes or no is quite sufficient. There is no need to give additional information when you answer my questions.'

'I understand.'

Then why do you keep doing it? Madsen thought. He glanced at his watch. 'How about a break? We've been going a while. Help yourself to some water.' He tossed his checklist on the table and made his way out to the observation room and filled a paper cup for himself. He chugged it, aware of Holbrook standing beside him with a puzzled expression on his face. Madsen double-checked the soundproof door was closed, then wheeled on the inspector. 'Okay, here's the news,' he hissed. 'The former flock leader for the good people of Sunnyvale is pouring shit on anybody and everybody.'

'Is that a problem?' Holbrook ventured. The big cop was in alien territory and looked uncharacteristically nervous.

'Yes, it is a problem, because the shit is coming so fast I can't shut it off!'

Holbrook frowned at him. 'Mr Ryle has a lot to say. Based on his inside experience he is well qualified to give impressions of what NeChristo leaders—'

'Fuck his experience. In case you've forgotten, this here is a by-the-book, fully documented polygraph.' Madsen glanced at the technician working at a nearby console and lowered his voice. 'Which means I can't ignore any of it. I'm buying into a truckload of work just writing all this shit up. *Not* to mention the wasted resources doing follow-ups between now and next Christmas. Jesus, Mike, where did you get this freak?'

Holbrook jerked as if struck. His balled-up fists looked ready to pulverize Madsen. The technician suddenly found something intensely interesting in the little squiggles on his screen.

In an instant, Madsen realized his mistake. Losing his temper had affected his judgement. Holbrook had made a concession and stepped way out of his comfort zone to support Madsen's line of enquiry. And what did the extra work matter anyway? Did it really bother him that much? Maybe he was just tired. Either way, it was a serious error. He took a deep breath. 'Sorry, Mike. Really, I'm sorry. That was stupid. Entirely the wrong question. No need to answer it. Actually I recall now that Mr Ryle was put forward as a possible witness by a different inspector.'

Holbrook unclenched his right fist, then his left. He flexed his fingers. Very slowly, he began to breathe.

Madsen turned to the specialist. 'Your professional opinion, please. Is he going to check out?'

'He believes everything he has said. All traces are clean green.'

'Yeah, I know that. But just between us boys, is he going to check out as *compos mentis*, or is some hot-shot defence lawyer going to eyeball those charts and show him to be so pathologically screwed up he'd swear Jesus Christ himself is a kiddie fiddler?'

The specialist stared at his screen a long time. He stuck out his bottom lip and gave a noncommittal shrug. Finally he said in a tone that was far from convincing, 'He should check out.'

Madsen peered in through the one-way glass. Mr Ryle's face was a picture of pure contented bliss. His eyes were closed. He might have been asleep except for his hands. They drew rhythmic, parallel arcs in the air as he conducted the rising crescendo of Bach's symphony opus six, number one, in G major.

There was indeed a lot of work.

Ryle had fingered fourteen men and two women in the NeChristo hierarchy for crimes relating to theft and racketeering. Half of these, according to his testimony, were also candidates for ordering a bombing. Seen through the eyes of the former flock leader, the New Christian Organization was only a step removed from the Cosa Nostra. It didn't matter that Madsen was only interested in one crime. Procedure demanded that every allegation had to be documented, and all sixteen people had to be interviewed. They were spread right across the United States.

Be careful what you ask for, Madsen thought. *You just might get it, tenfold.*

He worked late into the night, long after the last of his colleagues had gone and the air conditioning had switched itself off. The thirteenth floor of the Phillip Burton building was silent except for the sound of his breathing and the soft clack of his keyboard.

People invariably supplied much more interesting information when they were unprepared, and unaccompanied by lawyers, and the best way to prevent one subject from alerting others was to schedule interviews simultaneously. Madsen pondered the earliest this could realistically be achieved in all cities. He set the operation for noon, west coast time.

He couldn't kick off the operation without subpoenas, so as soon as he finished the write-up he started preparing ASAT requests. The panel would want to see as much supporting documentation as possible, given the religious affiliations of the targets. He laboriously trawled through the transcript of Ryle's testimony and pasted in the statements relevant to each application. It took the best part of three hours.

While waiting for the ASAT approvals, he wrote an operational brief for the interviewing agents. He asked them to focus on establishing whether their interviewees knew anything at all related to the bombing or a potential bomber. Ryle's other allegations were to be canvassed and shut down as swiftly as possible. If no relevant knowledge was established, then they were to clear the target as quickly as they could.

He drafted a list of questions, then redrafted it, refining and tightening until he was sure it could not be simplified any further.

Just after midnight, the first approval came back. It was for a pastor in Boston. Madsen filled out a computerized request form for a polygraph-qualified agent in that city to conduct the interview. He included a detailed justification, emphasizing the urgency and importance of the case. In the section marked 'Additional Supporting Documents' he finally found a use for all the messages and reminders he had accumulated from the director's office. He attached the operational brief and list of questions, then sent it to Washington DC for approval. His colleagues in Washington would forward it to the Boston field office.

At three in the morning he completed his sixteenth request form, loaded it onto the FBI intranet, and pressed send. Then he rolled his jacket into a makeshift pillow, curled up under his desk, and fell asleep.

Saturday

Chapter 21

The special agent in charge of the Boston field office read through his Saturday morning bulletins at home, over his first cup of coffee. As always, the bulk of the bulletins were routine case updates. He skimmed them rapidly, deciding which to delegate and which could be safely ignored. Halfway down the list he arrived at a brief labelled 'Most Urgent'. It was from the San Francisco office. After reading it he flicked to the accompanying subpoena and resource request. He grunted with irritation when he saw both had been pre-approved.

A few minutes later he woke Boston's only HAMDA agent. The agent listened carefully, hung up, then read the brief himself. He immediately notified Boston PD surveillance operations and asked the duty officer to pin down the target's location and look in the viddy archives, if available, to establish the man's typical movements on the preceding three Saturdays. Next he broadcast a short message to other agents in case anyone wanted to ride shotgun. He didn't expect any takers. Personnel shortages meant low-risk jobs were almost always handled solo. Then he sat down to commit the questioning sequence to memory.

The pattern was repeated in Miami twenty minutes later. Then Baltimore. Then a succession of cities further west.

*

At eight a.m. in San Francisco, Madsen awoke to a kick and DiMatteo's raspy voice grumbling about vagrants littering her office. Forgetting where he was, he sat up and promptly banged his head against the underside of his desk. He tried again, more cautiously this time, and managed to get to his feet without further injury. If he didn't count a throbbing back and a bad case of pins and needles as injuries.

A harsh morning light cut through the east-facing windows, casting jagged shadows down the avenues of empty cubicles. DiMatteo was already at her office, unlocking the door, doubtless intending to spend the morning devouring case reports. For her the job had always been seven days a week, and even now, with just a few days to go, she couldn't shake the habit. Opening the bottom drawer of his desk, Madsen retrieved an electric shaver and headed for the men's room.

The bleary face in the mirror wasn't going to win any beauty contests, but he saw an edge there just the same. *Today*, he told himself, running the shaver under his chin, *we finally have some momentum*.

The next few hours passed slowly, liaising with SFPD surveillance command mostly. There was the additional complication that Ryle had fingered no less than three of his former NeChristo colleagues living in and around San Francisco; as the sole field-polygraph-qualified agent in the area, Madsen would have to do all three interviews himself. Because he couldn't be in more than one place at a time, and he didn't want one subject warning the next, the best he could do was carry out the interviews in quick succession. Holbrook had offered to drive, which was helpful. Apparently he wasn't holding a grudge over yesterday's brain snap in the polygraph room. Or, more likely, he still saw this as his best chance of a breakthrough and didn't want to be cut out of the action. At any rate, Madsen would be free to concentrate on his interviews.

At eleven-fifteen, he convened a brief conference call with all agents to cover off last-minute queries.

Shortly after, Holbrook called to say he was waiting downstairs. It was time for Madsen to choose his first target.

He asked viddy ops to send the targets' latest locations direct to his desk monitor. One target was following a movement pattern identical to each of the five preceding Saturdays. Assuming he did the same today, Madsen knew exactly where to find him when the first two interviews were done. He would be last. Madsen switched his attention to the others. One was in Forest Hill, the other further south, in Daly City. Both targets were stationary. Their relative positions to the third target, coupled with faster-flowing northbound traffic, meant that the quickest route to cover all three would be south to north. Daly City it would be.

Quickened by the first hint of adrenalin, he pulled on his jacket, checked his HAMDA, and headed for the elevator.

Six hundred miles to the east, in a reclaimed park south-west of Salt Lake City, NeChristo's senior media director searched for wind-rippled trees. His crew had already spent an hour humping gear from one park to another while he checked backdrops and tested the light, but they were well paid and too professional to gripe.

He gave a nod. Equipment cases, coils of electrical cable and reflective umbrellas thumped to the ground and the crew bustled to set up shop. His sound man put on oversized headphones and plugged them into a box of knobs and dials. A gust jostled the branches above. The sound man frowned and twiddled one of the knobs.

A table and chair, suitably unpretentious, were moved from another section of the park into the foreground. Luke would stand, but the white wrought-iron garden furniture added a homely element. Two crew members combed stray leaves from the lawn. Another taped an 'X' over the grass. A pair of joggers stopped to watch.

The sound man gave a thumbs up.

But it wasn't complete. The director had the trees and the setting, and he could frame the dome nicely in the background, but it needed something more. He glanced about, looking for inspiration. With one minute to go he spied a couple and their two young children playing frisbee. They looked happy and, more importantly, attractive. He sent one of the crew to ask if they would be so kind. They would. The family was moved carefully into the background.

Pastor Luke arrived wearing tan trousers, navy jacket and a crisp white shirt with no tie. Trailing in his wake were three assistants and his head of communications.

The director held his breath. The boss was not above asking for a last-minute change. The head of communications offered no objection. Luke gave a nod of approval. A make-up artist hair-sprayed a last few errant strands into place. An assistant knelt and aligned the creases of the pastor's trousers.

Luke turned to the camera. The assistants disappeared. Every-body donned headphones and took up positions. The director waved to the family. They began to play. All smiles and fun. He gave the crew a thumbs up. Turning to watch the monitor at his feet, he began whispering into his microphone. 'Dome shot . . . pan right from the dome across the trees to a wide shot on Luke. Hold that. Get the chair in, and some of the table. A tad closer. We need to see his pleasure as he addresses the multitude.'

A rich baritone voice boomed in his headphones. 'Friends of the New Christian Organization of America, welcome! It is a beauti-ful, peaceful day here this morning, and I hope it is just as warm and wonderful wherever you are in the world.'

'Start zoom in,' the director whispered.

'I have a simple message today. It is about the sinful scourge of the dollhouses. You, my dear friends, have campaigned so vigorously these past months. You have succeeded in building a barrier against immorality. And it has paid dividends. Through your protests, your work, your commitment, you have lifted the scales from the eyes of our politicians. This very morning the senior senator for Ohio, Erol Arbett, who has been so influential in Washington on this matter, issued a statement. He said, and I quote, "It is time to consider whether our latest efforts to defend the rights of the individual have come at the expense of morality and public decency, and whether it is Dreamcom that has taken a step too far." Wonderful words . . .'

Luke paused. He lifted his hand. The director whispered frantically, 'Zoom out. Accommodate the hand. He's inviting us to see the family. Frame them in, get the kids! Hold!'

'You have always known the America you want to live in. An America for families. For children. Where the values of love and warmth and friendship are cherished above all else. For decades the battle between hedonism and Christianity has been cloaked by a growing apathy. But the morals of the American people have not been destroyed. They still exist. They only needed a spark to rekindle the fire and burn away that cloak. That spark has finally been supplied. By you!'

Luke dropped his hand. His expression became serious. The director whispered, 'Okay. Centre on Luke. Slow zoom to his face on my mark . . . Mark!'

The pastor looked straight into the camera. 'Yesterday, the man responsible for inflicting this wretched curse on our nation proved you are winning. And do you know how he did that? He lashed out, trying to use the terrible tragedy in San Francisco to put blame on this church! Your church! And he tried to remake himself as the innocent. But he should have read what it says in the book of Job. "Who can bring a clean thing out of an unclean?" And he needs to take heed of the proverb, "Who causes the righteous to go astray in an evil way, he shall fall himself into his own pit." Because he has tried to lead the righteous astray through his corruption, and now he has looked into his pit. He doesn't like it there! It is a long way down! It is hot! But he has no one else to blame. He dug the hole with his own hands. My friends, today's call to action is this. This afternoon we continue the fight. We march. We stand vigil. Listen for your nearest event after this message. Stand and be counted. If you cannot go in person, send a friend. Spread the word. Tell your congressman! And tomorrow go to your church. Pray, celebrate, enjoy the music, spend time with dear friends. Be peaceful, and let Jesus be your guide. Thank you.'

'Hold . . . hold . . . cut!' The director checked the clock counter: two minutes exactly. Good to go out unedited in both video and audio broadcasts. He shook his head in admiration, not just at the timing but at the way Luke had seamlessly incorporated the family as a visual prop. Always the professional. He glanced at his crew. The cameraman held out a thumbs up. So did the sound man. The director turned to congratulate Luke, but he had gone.

The big man and his entourage were already strolling back towards the dome, its giant steel frame shimmering in the sun.

Chapter 22

'It's just Little League, right?' asked Holbrook.

'Yeah. Why?' replied Madsen, not bothering to raise his head. He was reading over his questions, preparing for the third inter-view of the morning. They were in Holbrook's unmarked Chrysler, with the inspector driving.

'Because it's too nice for Little League.'

Madsen looked up, expecting to see a grassy space with a chain link fence. Maybe a few sagging bleachers with the paint flaking off. Instead he beheld a stadium. Half-sized, but professionally constructed and thoroughly modern. The sun flared off light towers. The top of an electronic scoreboard peeked over the surrounding wall. Over the entrance, six-foot letters proclaimed they had arrived at *Gladeview Ballpark – home of the mighty Dynamos!* He shook his head slowly. 'Viddy ops said he was a supporter – they didn't say how big.'

'You think he paid for this?'

'Why not? Just loose change for a pastor.'

Holbrook cruised down the rows of expensive cars until he found an empty bay. He backed in, so they had a view of the stadium entrance, and switched the engine off.

The motor ticked. A heat haze rose off the hood. Without the air conditioning, the temperature inside the Chrysler began to climb.

'How long do you want to sit here?' Holbrook asked.

'End of ball game. We won't miss him.'

'Maybe we should go in.'

'It'll only be a few minutes.'

Madsen felt wetness spreading from his armpits. He rolled down his window. A distant cheer went up. Jaunty notes from a pipe organ floated from the stadium. Going in there would be a quick way to screw up the man's social calendar, he mused. Judging from the vehicles, the people in this neighbourhood did pretty well for themselves. The type of people likely to view with consternation, if not downright alarm, their local pastor and Little League benefactor being interviewed by the FBI.

But Madsen had already ruined one person's day, and that hadn't been fun. The junior flock leader had dissolved into a quivering wreck as soon as they stepped into her apartment. The sobs were so loud he had to get her to repeat her answers. Even so, it took no time at all to establish she had absolutely no knowledge of anything related to the bombing, or indeed anything even mildly illegal. She was innocence personified. God only knew what she had done to earn the enmity of Mr Ryle. In the end Madsen was promising he wouldn't take her to jail just to get her to stop crying.

The accountant was better. At least he had something to be guilty about. He sweated through the entire interview. By the end, Madsen knew NeChristo money flowed in all kinds of directions that would surprise and horrify the rank and file members. But again, nothing on the bombing.

Of the three, Pastor Joe Sorrell was the most promising. He sat well up the hierarchy and Ryle was especially adamant about the depth of his criminal proclivities. Plus he had an actual record. A string of charges and a conviction for domestic battery. His wife had packed her bags long ago, but maybe the violent streak was still there. Maybe it manifested itself in other ways.

Madsen checked the Chrysler's GPS. The blinking dot on the display placed Sorrell's cell phone just fifty yards away, dead ahead. Right – he smiled even as he thought it – in the ballpark.

Madsen could feel his shirt sticking to his back. He longed to peel it off. 'Did you ever play baseball?' he asked Holbrook, trying to take his mind off the heat.

'Nope. Too busy working.'

'What, even as a kid?'

'Yep.'

Madsen waited for the inspector to elaborate. He vaguely recalled that Holbrook had grown up in a tough part of town.

Holbrook said nothing.

'Shame. You would have slugged 'em out of the park.'

There was a muffled roar, followed by drawn-out applause.

'Ten bucks says our guy's wearing a baseball cap,' Madsen said, kicking open his door.

'Everyone will have a cap.'

'A Dynamos cap then.'

'Very funny.'

Spectators began surging out through the entrance. Madsen and Holbrook stood to the side, scanning faces. Although they were in plain clothes they still drew stares. One or two people quickened their pace as they passed.

After a few minutes, the crowd thinned. No sign of Sorrell.

Madsen began to tense up a little. Maybe the guy had been warned. He nodded to Holbrook and strode through the archway. They stepped onto the field, turning and searching for a glimpse of their target. A couple of kids chased one another, dodging around the bases. Cleaners had begun sweeping. A few stragglers were still in their seats, talking animatedly about the game, making phone calls. Halfway up the right-field grandstand was a tight cluster of men. The one in the middle was holding court, laughing. Madsen recognized the face. Sorrell.

Madsen took the stairs three at a time, Holbrook fighting to keep up. The men looked up as they approached.

'Joe Sorrell?' Madsen said.

'Yeah, that's me.' Sorrell was small, well dressed and clean-shaven. The expression on his face was half surprised, half irritated. Madsen noticed with satisfaction that he wore a baseball cap with *Dynamos* emblazoned across the front.

Madsen held out his badge. 'I'd like to talk to you for a few minutes.' To Sorrell's companions he said, 'Gentlemen, would you mind excusing us?'

The men left quickly, pushing past a puffing Holbrook, not looking back. Sorrell remained seated, his eyes full of suspicion. When the others were out of earshot, he rounded on Madsen. 'This better be good. Those were investors you just scared off.'

'I have a subpoena to question you under polygraph. If you cooperate, we should have you on your way in a few minutes.' Madsen pulled the metal cylinder from his pocket. A light flashed at the tip.

Sorrell glared at him. 'Question me about what?'

'Domestic terrorism.'

Sorrell frowned. He looked confused. Then, gradually, his face cleared. His lips twisted into a grin. 'The dollhouse, the one that was blown up, is that what you mean? You're crazy.' He held out his hand and snapped his fingers. 'Let's see the subpoena.' He took the document and examined it closely, taking his time. Madsen stole a glance at Holbrook. The big cop looked on impassively. Sorrell folded the subpoena in half and handed it back. He waved his hand dismissively. 'Fire away.'

Madsen flipped through the baseline questions and quickly got down to the ones that counted. 'Are you aware that twelve people were killed in an explosion downtown last Wednesday?'

'Yes.'

'Were you in any way involved in any conspiracy to place an explosive device at those premises?'

'No.'

'Were you aware of any plan to place an explosive device at those premises?'

'No.'

The questions and green lights came at a brisk pace. Far from being intimidated, Sorrell seemed to find the whole exercise hilarious, injecting occasional acid comments to underline his disdain for both polygraph and interrogator. Madsen's optimism began to fade. In no time at all he was down to his last question. 'We have a polygraph statement from someone who nominated you as capable of planning the attack. Do you know any reason why someone would believe that?'

Hesitation. A flicker of the eyelids. 'No.'

Red light.

Madsen stared at the light, surprised. He rubbed his chin thoughtfully.

'Would you care to revise your answer, Mr Sorrell?'

'Sure.'

'I'll repeat the question. We have a polygraph statement from someone who nominated you as being capable of planning the attack. Do you know any reason why someone would believe that?'

'Yes.'

Green light.

'Please elaborate.'

'I happen to think that dollhouses and the people who frequent them are utterly pathetic. Frankly, I'm not sorry about what happened. They deserved it.'

Madsen took a few seconds to process this. 'You've shared this with others?'

'I have shared those feelings widely among my colleagues, yes.'

'Do any of your colleagues have the same feelings?'

'I'm sure many do, but thinking isn't doing. Unless you guys are now in the business of charging people with thought crimes, in which case you're going to be pretty busy.' He laughed.

'So let me get this straight—'

'I just happen to think anyone who fucks dolls is a useless piece of shit. Period.'

Holbrook twitched. Something within Madsen stirred. He knew Sorrell didn't have anything to do with the bombing. And Sorrell knew he knew. But the man was arrogant, and now that his interview was finished he wanted to vent, and the true colour of his feelings happened to be a very ugly shade of red. *If that's where the arrogant shit wants to go*, Madsen thought, *then who am I to discourage it?* 'Those are some pretty strong feelings you've got there,' he said.

Sorrell was clearly enjoying himself. 'Not really. No more than anyone who says the world would be a better place if we handed out the death penalty more often. The people in that dollhouse were sad, lonely fucks who couldn't get a real woman to save themselves. They were a waste of space, oxygen-thieves, and I say we're better off without them.'

'Two of them were police officers.' It was the first time Holbrook had spoken since the interview began.

'So much the better,' Sorrell said.

Holbrook's eyes flashed. He looked ready to administer a little summary justice of his own. Sorrell looked like he couldn't have cared less.

'Don't you like police officers?' asked Madsen.

'Based on firsthand experience, I'd say there's not a lot to like. You, for example, run around waving that silver stick in front of your nose. Cheap, lazy policing, that's what this is. I mean, you come here, scare off my business partners and ask me about fucking domestic terrorism! You've got to be kidding!'

'You got something better for us to investigate?' said Holbrook softly.

Sorrell laughed. 'You can't go there. You can't go anywhere outside the scope of your subpoena. I could confess to anything, and as long as it's not on that list, your subpoena isn't worth shit. I robbed a liquor store last week, and a bank, and I assaulted a parishioner – a grandmother, no less. Oh, and tonight I'm meeting up with five senior pastors, we're going on a cruise, and we're going to snort more coke in an hour than you boys could afford in a lifetime.'

'I see,' said Madsen, shaking his head as if in admiration. There was a subtle change in his tone. He was thinking fast. He had to make a decision and he had only seconds to do it.

Sorrell stood. 'I think we're just about done here.'

'Just a minute,' said Madsen.

Sorrell began walking briskly towards the stairs.

'I said, just a minute.'

Sorrell spat and flipped him the bird without breaking stride. He reached the end of the row and started down the stairs, towards the exit.

'Hey!' Madsen stepped over a seat to the next row, jogged several paces, then stepped down another row. From behind, he heard Holbrook mutter something unintelligible. He probably thought Madsen was mad. He'd have to wait for his explanation. Sorrell quickened his pace, taking big strides down the stairs. Madsen alternately ran laterally and jumped rows, zigzagging to cut Sorrell off before he made the exit. The gap closed. A broom clattered as a cleaner stopped and stared slack-jawed at the unfolding spectacle. Madsen sprinted across the last couple of seats and launched himself bodily through the air. Sorrell gave a *yelp* as the breath slammed from his body.

They crashed to the concrete. Madsen twisted Sorrell face down. He seized his right wrist and cuffed it. Then he repeated the procedure with the other hand. He patted the pastor down, flipped him, and hauled him into a seated position. Holbrook arrived a few seconds later, chugging like a train.

Sorrell's mouth opened and closed like a freshly landed trout's. 'You'll . . . pay . . .' he gasped, fighting to regain his breath.

'I don't think so,' said Madsen.

'I haven't . . . done anything.'

'That's correct, Mr Sorrell.'

'You can't handcuff me. I'll have your badge. I'll make sure you never work—'

'Save it,' said Madsen sharply. Inwardly, his mind raced. He needed to slow the pace, to gain time to think. He had seen an opening and reacted. Now he needed to follow procedure, stay inside the law. The next sixty seconds would be decisive. Holbrook shot him a bemused look. The big guy had to be as confused as hell, but if he spoke it might ruin everything. It was vital to keep talking, to control the conversation.

'If I take these cuffs off,' Madsen said carefully, 'can you give me a guarantee you will not try to call or contact any of your colleagues?'

'I'll guarantee nothing. You go to hell.'

Madsen nodded. 'Then they stay on.'

'Take the fucking things off,' yelled Sorrell. 'Now!'

'I'm afraid I can't do that. Not until we have you in a secure location.'

'What the . . . what are you arresting me on then? What charge?'

'Mr Sorrell, I'm not charging you. I'm holding you for a brief period.'

'What the fuck are you talking about?'

The look on Holbrook's face said the same thing.

Madsen squatted down so he was eyeball to eyeball with his captive. 'According to the statement you just gave, illegal narcotics are being supplied on a cruise. A crime is in progress. Given the very large quantities involved, the crime poses a threat to life and wellbeing. On the basis of the information you've given me, I must assume that if I leave you at liberty you will interfere with the investigation.'

Sorrell looked stunned. 'I never made that statement, and anyway you don't have any subpoena for that. It's bullshit. If you had a subpoena you were supposed—'

'Not only did you make that statement, you made it under polygraph, and the polygraph indicated you were telling the truth. The law obliges me to intervene, especially with lives in danger, and it allows me to detain you temporarily to prevent you interfering. Inspector, will you give me a hand?'

Holbrook cocked his head at Madsen in disbelief, then shrugged and took a step forward, reaching down for Sorrell.

Sorrell's eyes widened in panic. 'You're twisting this around! I want to revise what I said. I want a lawyer!'

'Plenty of time for that. Right now we need you downtown.'

They took an arm each and together hauled Sorrell to his feet, then half-walked, half-carried him out of the stadium. As Madsen held the door of the Chrysler open, Holbrook bundled the pastor into the back, placing one of his enormous hands on the man's head to keep it from bumping the roof on the way in. Several by-standers stopped to gawp.

Madsen stuck his head inside the car. 'It's only for a few hours,' he said soothingly. 'And my office is perfectly comfortable. The coffee isn't so great, but you get used to it.' He backed up and shut the door. Sorrell stared out through the glass, dumbstruck. His face was a deathly white.

On the drive back Madsen replayed the sequence, probing for flaws. When Sorrell began his tirade Madsen had instinctively lowered the HAMDA. Not too far, lest its microphones and lenses lose their lock on Sorrell, and not so far that he could not continue monitoring the indicator lamp out of the corner of his eye. Just enough to separate the device from Sorrell's line of sight. The instinct came from experience. When people got angry and emotional they blurted surprising and interesting things. Sometimes you got lucky. Sure enough, Sorrell must have decided he'd get a kick out of mentioning something real, putting something over on the two dumb cops sent out to harass him. He thought he was safe because he had read the subpoena. He thought he knew the law. Except he didn't. Not well enough, anyway. And when, right in the middle of the rapid sequence of red flashes, Madsen caught a brief flash of green, the game changed.

Everything that followed – crime in progress, lives in danger, temporary detention – was legal. Rubbery as hell, barely defensible, enough to make a judge foam at the mouth, but legal.

Madsen smiled. His interviews had at least bought an opportunity to dig further and deeper. Between them, five senior pastors were likely to have a pretty good picture of everything important going on inside NeChristo. With narcotics charges hanging over them, they'd be eager to help out on Grant Avenue any way they could.

Chapter 23 _____

In his San Francisco office on the top floor of the Dreamcom tower, Tom Fillinger was in a foul mood. On his desk were the latest financial projections. They were detailed. They captured all forms of expenditure and all sources of revenue and set out last month's position, the current position, and the estimated future positions for the next three months. The future positions were further supplemented by best- and worst-case scenarios. Fillinger had been scrutinizing the worst-case scenarios for some time while his vice-president of marketing waited on the other side of his desk. The man hadn't delivered the projections, but he shifted from one foot to the other as if he had. He had been standing there for ten minutes.

Fillinger looked up. 'Is it ready?'

The VP licked his lips nervously. 'We're all set.'

'Creative?'

'The messages and visuals were finalized this morning. They scored well with the test audiences. We drew people from all eighteen customer profiles.'

'Coverage?'

'Coast to coast, as you requested. We've briefed the advertising brokers that we want them delivered to all screen types.

Electronic posters, billboards, personal phones, vehicles, truck stops. Everything.'

'Targeting?'

'We're spot buying, as you requested. Maximum number of repeats, every time we get a live one.'

Fillinger nodded. As soon as his campaign kicked off, Dreamcom's advertising brokers would have their systems bidding for vacant advertising slots as they came up, minute by minute. They would bid based on two factors: the number of ideal viewers present – as reported by screen-mounted audience detectors – and the proximity of those viewers to the nearest dollhouse. Which slots they successfully managed to purchase would depend on who else was bidding and how high they were prepared to go. Spot buying guaranteed every advertisement screened hit the target audience. There was a downside, though. The media companies charged more. A lot more.

It didn't matter. This was the right way to do it.

Judging by the marketing man's demeanour, however, he didn't share his boss's view. 'You look bothered,' Fillinger said. 'Something on your mind?'

'Yes . . . I wouldn't be doing my job if I didn't say something.'

'Go on.'

'These settings make it the biggest and most expensive campaign we've done.'

'I know.'

The VP swallowed before ploughing on. 'The analysts are saying the return will barely cover the cost. That's if everything goes well.'

'And?'

'And once we start we're committed. We can't stop halfway, not without losing a bundle. I'm not privy to our overall financial position . . .' He darted an anxious glance at the paper on Fillinger's desk. 'But I understand, that is, I'm led to believe . . . this isn't necessarily the best time.'

Fillinger stared at him. 'And?'

'And I have to recommend we don't do it.'

Fillinger stood, clasped his hands behind his back, and turned to face the window. He gazed out over the bay. Two ferries, one with blue stripes, one with yellow, crossed paths far below. He didn't need a goddamn marketer reminding him he was taking the mother of all risks. There was so much he couldn't control. He could still lose. If there were any incidents, if the police didn't do their job . . . No, he shouldn't be angry. His marketing chief was trying to do the right thing, and it took balls to question a directive from his CEO. He just couldn't see how stunning Ten Worlds was going to be. The settings, the ladies, the grandeur, the services, the sheer scale of every part of it. Nothing like it had been done before. It would set everything right. And Fillinger still had a few shots left in his armoury, shots his subordinate didn't know existed.

Without turning he said, 'Just go and launch the damn campaign.'

Chapter 24

Madsen secured Sorrell in an interview room on the thirteenth floor of the Phillip Burton building. The fight had gone out of the pastor. Still wearing his Dynamos cap, he seemed small and ordinary. Hard to believe he was such a big shot in front of a congregation. Madsen offered coffee and received no reply. He brought one anyway and Sorrell regarded the steaming styrofoam cup as if it was poison. After locking the interview room, Madsen took Holbrook aside and explained his actions a second time.

The inspector listened, then said, 'We got nothing.'

'We got enough. And it opened another door, worth pursuing.'

'There's such a thing as pursuing too far.'

'It'll hold up. And you needn't worry. It's my call.'

'You got that right.'

Holbrook excused himself and headed back to Central Station, his troubled face suggesting that the episode had reinforced every misgiving he ever had about plotters.

Back at his desk, Madsen called SFPD surveillance command and asked them to dig up what they could relating to a bunch of pastors meeting on a boat. Then he settled in and began reading the reports coming in from other cities.

San Diego, Baltimore and Dallas were already in. *All clear, target has no knowledge of the bombing.* Boston and Memphis came soon after. Same results. Chicago reported that they had cleared one target but had yet to find the second. For an hour they trickled in. Detroit, New York, Portland, Los Angeles, Miami, Seattle. Nothing.

Madsen spent a further forty-five minutes retrieving and skimming each of the interview transcripts just to be sure the other agents hadn't missed anything. They hadn't.

His phone buzzed. Surveillance command. The shift operator cut straight to the point. 'We've run traces on every NeChristo senior pastor we can identify residing in the greater San Francisco area. Incidentally, one of them is in your building.'

'I know that,' Madsen said. 'I brought him here.'

'Oh. Well, three have indeed been tracked to a vessel, and two more appear to be en route.'

'Good. Where's the vessel?'

'Right now, about three miles off the Point Reyes lighthouse. Cruising in a southerly direction.'

It took a few seconds for that to sink in. 'That doesn't make sense,' Madsen said. 'The guy I detained was supposed to join them. How could he do that if they're already at sea?'

'I expect the same way as the two that are on their way. By helicopter. It's a big boat.'

Madsen hung up. He racked his brains. To get anything useful out of the exercise he had to catch them red-handed. How in hell was he supposed to do that in the middle of the Pacific Ocean?

After pondering for a few moments he picked up his phone again. He knew someone who could answer that.

Curt Zetter pounded the pavement in the late-afternoon heat, enjoying the slow burn in his thighs and the hot-cool evaporation from his face. Anyone else might have skipped a session, waiting for the predicted change in the weather. For the FBI SWAT commander, however, running had long ago evolved into something transcending exercise. The steady thumping of worn sneakers recharged his mind even as it tired his muscles. It gave him time to think.

Right now he was thinking about how to keep his team intact. The best years of his life had been invested in drilling, honing and leading his men, but thinning ranks across the rest of the Bureau meant they were being siphoned off, one by one, to other duties. The San Francisco unit had once boasted forty-six operators. Now it was twenty-five. To top it off, he'd just lost one of his best to an integrity test. Some crap about not reporting a felony committed by his nephew. OPI had offered a grade demotion and four weeks on the sidelines, but the guy resigned instead. Twenty-one years of crime-fighting experience gone. How could the public be better off? The psychopaths, rapists and killers were still out there. The Chinese and Russian gangs weren't going away. High-integrity policing, they called it. It was a fucking disgrace.

Zetter felt a vibration in the small of his back. He stopped running and pulled the cell phone from his belt pack, half-expecting another request for resources. The caller ID said Daniel Madsen. His frown lifted.

His mood improved further as he heard the details.

Narcotics. Five targets. NeChristos.

Five of the same self-righteous pricks who'd lobbied so enthusiastically for integrity testing of law enforcement officers.

A tricky insertion and a tight deadline.

Sugar *and* spice.

He rang off and hit the number for the office. His second-in-command answered and Zetter rattled off a list of people he wanted waiting in the squad room. He resumed jogging, altering course for a direct route back. His brain worked the problem, mulling over equipment and transport options. Surprise was critical. It took only seconds to dump narcotics overboard. Madsen had mentioned a helipad, but helicopters made a hell of a racket. Plus a boat that size would have radar . . .

It was after seven p.m. west coast time when the missing guy in Chicago was finally found. Chicago PD surveillance operations had accidentally mixed up his reference images. Instead of searching for a NeChristo accountant, they had been chasing their tails looking for a convicted felon already locked up in a federal penitentiary. When they realized their mistake the correct target was located in five minutes. Perhaps to try and make up for the delay, the agent had peppered her report with hints that the subject could be pursued for embezzlement at any time, if there was ever a need, and that the charges would probably stick. As far as Grant Avenue was concerned, however, the guy was clear.

Soon afterwards, DiMatteo stopped by Madsen's desk for an update. She was tense and unhappy. Being told that they had nothing more than a narcotics search and an excuse to interview a bunch of senior pastors meant she left exasperated as well.

Madsen slumped forward in his chair, elbows on knees, staring at the floor. He felt bad for his boss. Her last week was supposed to be about dinners, drinks and war stories. Instead she was being serially harassed from above about a case that needed solving yesterday, didn't look like being solved anytime soon, and was sucking up scarce resources in twelve other field offices. So far the only thing his operation had proved was that, behind the happy facade, NeChristo hid more than its fair share of nasty activities and unsavoury people. Oh, and that one Reginald Aaron Ryle was indeed a fully certifiable crackpot.

His cell phone buzzed.

A woman's voice, vaguely familiar. 'Agent Madsen? It's Shari.'

'Who?'

'Shari Sanayei. From Central Station surveillance.'

Ah. The sergeant who'd come direct from the blast scene to supervise the video searches. The one who had cried, then worked like the devil. Hadn't he given her some fatuous advice about dealing with stress? She probably thought he was an asshole.

'Is this a bad time?' she asked.

He shook his head. 'Sorry. You caught me by surprise. What have you got?'

'Not much. We're still drawing blanks but . . . I want to run something by you.'

'Go ahead.'

'It's personal. Can we meet?'

Before Madsen could reply, a shadow moved into his field of vision. He looked up from the floor, his gaze travelling over combat boots, black fatigue pants, nylon belt, navy T-shirt stretched over improbably large biceps and a thickly muscled neck, finally stopping at a large, grinning face. Zetter's.

The SWAT commander tapped his watch.

Madsen held up a hand to indicate he wouldn't be long. 'Shari, I'm tied up right now. Can it wait until tomorrow?'

'Sure,' she said, but the way she said it told him she wasn't happy about it.

'I'll call you tomorrow on this number.' He hung up.

'Coming?' Zetter asked.

'You bet.' Madsen jumped to his feet and reached out to retrieve his jacket.

The jacket slipped through his fingers, sliding down the side of his desk and onto the floor. The desk tilted oddly. Zetter tilted. The cubicle partitions tilted. Madsen placed his palm against the desk and pushed. The tilt stopped, reversed, then smoothly swung back into line.

'What the hell was that?' Zetter said.

Madsen blinked. The dizziness was already passing. 'I must have got up too fast.'

'You're tired. How much sleep have you had?'

'I got a few hours in. I'm fine. Just give me a minute.'

'Dan, we're boarding a moving boat. If you're not on your toes you risk breaking arms or legs – or worse.'

Madsen waved his arms and hopped on one leg. 'Look, no issues.'

'For now. You need sack time. Go home.'

'I don't think so. This is my operation.'

'And I don't need to be worrying about someone falling overboard. When we get them we'll call you, and you can meet us at the waterfront. Simple.'

Madsen opened his mouth to remonstrate but saw it wasn't

going to get him anywhere. Besides which, Zetter was right. Interviews could easily wait until the pastors were back onshore. And he didn't need any more dizzy spells. Jesus, if he wasn't careful he might eat oncoming traffic on the drive home. 'Maybe you're right,' he said.

'I know I'm right. Get outta here. I'll see you in a couple of hours.'

Zetter left. Madsen retrieved his jacket from the floor and switched off his computer. He walked around the office until he found someone else unlucky enough to be working late on a Saturday evening and arranged for them to release Sorrell the moment the raid was underway. Halfway to the elevator he called Shari back. 'Change of plan. I'm getting out of here. I can run by Central Station if you still want to talk.'

'Not here. Have you eaten?'

'No, but I plan to.'

'Name somewhere near your home and I'll meet you there.'

Odd, Madsen thought. Not over the phone. Not near the station. What the hell did she want to talk about? Or was she trying to make some kind of non-professional connection? She'd said earlier it was personal. Maybe he had missed something. For all his supposed psychological expertise he still got his wires crossed with pretty women. It didn't matter. Either way it would be a pleasant diversion. And he was hungry. 'Yeah, sure,' he said. 'If you don't mind going that way, I'm over in—'

'I know where you live.'

Right. Of course she did.

After a moment, Madsen named a cafe two blocks from his apartment.

Chapter 25

The Persian was thick with coffee fumes and conversation. Madsen liked the place because the food was tasty and inexpensive, it stayed open late – which was a prerequisite for a good many of his evening meals – and it was quirky. The owner had filled it with woven carpets, lithographs of ancient minarets and miniature camels carved from wood. At one time he had even dallied briefly with soft lounges and floor cushions before reluctantly returning to the commercial pragmatism of wooden chairs and tables.

Shari was already there, waiting at a corner table. She had ditched the black uniform for jeans, T-shirt and rubber-soled dockers, the kind with the high lace-up sides. A heavy-metal logo blazed across the T-shirt. He would have called it a tomboy's outfit, except there was nothing tomboy about the way the jeans hugged her curves, nor how her dark hair caught the light.

She brightened when he sat down, but the smile looked forced. 'Thanks for coming,' she said awkwardly.

'No problem. Good to have company.'

'You look tired.'

'It's been a long day. For both of us, I'm guessing.'

She sipped her water, holding the glass tightly enough to turn the tips of her fingers white.

The waitress came. Shari didn't seem interested in ordering. He selected for both of them. A diced lamb tagine, chicken kebabs, vegetables stuffed with nuts and spices. To put her at ease, he tried giving his little speech about plotters, liar-men and wand wavers, how all good cops made mistakes, and that whatever kind of animal he might be, at least he was not OPI. He told his guilt radar joke. It elicited a laugh. A small one, but it seemed to help.

When the food arrived, Madsen spooned a generous quantity of diced lamb onto his plate and began eating. A little too hastily for polite company, but the spicy aromas sharpened his senses and gave urgency to the hollow in his belly. He was pretty sure she would understand.

Shari picked up a single kebab and placed it on her plate. She left it there. Out of nowhere she asked, 'Why did you become a plotter?'

He cocked a wary eyebrow. 'Same reason as everybody. To catch bad guys.'

Shari frowned. 'No, really. I want to know.'

He was about to brush it off with something glib, but the direct question and her utter seriousness made him change his mind. 'My father, probably. He started out a farmer, then made a career in construction. Used to point to houses and bridges and say, "I built that," and that was exactly how he felt, even if he was only the site supervisor. His thing was that whatever you did it had to be practical, had to be *real*, otherwise it didn't count. Catching bad guys is real.'

'So you did it to please him?'

He laughed. 'The funny thing was I went the other way first. Dabbled in history and psychology, bummed around universities. I was going to be a career academic. It used to drive him nuts.'

'What changed?'

'I realized he was right. I was teaching bored kids who couldn't care less about learning, they just wanted a diploma. I started asking myself what I was contributing and wasn't coming up with any answers. Then by accident I got introduced to an FBI profiler. I was good at the practical side of psychology, we hit it off, he introduced me to some other people. And the rest, as they say . . .' He let the words trail off and shovelled in another mouthful of lamb.

'Go on,' she said.

There was no need to go on, really. He had already given a complete answer. As much of an answer as the question warranted, anyway. But something in the way she leaned forward, elbows propped on the table, chin in hands, bright green eyes staring with unsettling intensity, made him decide to say what he normally left unsaid. 'And he died.'

'The profiler?'

'No, my father. Work accident. A truck backed over him.'

'Oh, I'm so sorry.' She leaned back in her chair, concentration broken.

He shrugged. 'That's okay. Anyway—' He tapped the table for emphasis. 'Apart from having no one to rebel against any more, that *really* got me thinking about my life. I joined the Bureau not long after.' He shot her a quizzical look. 'So what about you? What made you want to be a camera jockey?'

She didn't hesitate. 'I'm good at it. No, don't make a face. It's hard to explain. I have a kind of affinity with all that stuff. The sensors, camera nets, algorithms . . . what they can do and what they can't. I always knew that's what I wanted. It took a while to get here, though. I was in Arizona. Flagstaff. They weren't looking for surveillance people, so I joined as a regular cop. Did two years on the streets before they accepted my transfer. Don't get me wrong, I loved the guys and how they looked after one another. It mattered, but it wasn't for me. I learned the basics, and when I heard they needed good operators here, I moved to California.'

'Where they have bigger networks, bigger toys.'

She smiled. 'Something like that.'

'So you want to tell me why we're here?'

The smile disappeared. She picked up her glass and peered into it, absently swirling the water. Outside the shadowy, backlit world of the viddy room her skin was brown and smooth, almost flawless.

'Because I want to keep doing it,' she said.

'Doing what?'

'My job.'

There was a long pause. Shari took a deep breath and began, 'I had a relationship with Adam Carmichael . . .'

Madsen listened without interrupting. He heard about the kind of guy Adam was and why she fell for him, and the affair, and how the time had come to get it into the open. He heard about Wednesday and how they had argued, her rush to the scene and utter helplessness once she got there. And he heard about how she decided everything would stay secret, for Adam, for his wife, for herself. As he listened, Madsen made the connections with her mud-streaked appearance and the vulnerability he had seen that day, and the manic intensity she'd channelled into her work afterwards.

She finished. The hiss of the coffee maker and the murmurs from nearby tables seemed to get louder.

Madsen said, 'So this . . . Yolanda. She's the only one who knows?'

'Yes.'

'And you haven't told Captain McAlister or Holbrook?'

'No. I just wanted to keep working. I need to get the bastards who killed him. That's all I care about.'

'You don't think they'd let you do that?'

'They'd have me out of there in a second.'

'So why me?'

'I needed to tell someone. Someone should know. I need to know I'm not being negligent.'

'And I'm not SFPD. Is that it?'

She nodded. 'I thought I could talk to you. At least then some-one on the team would know and . . . maybe that would be enough.'

Madsen sat back and scratched his head as he tried to think it through. The affair itself wasn't an issue. She'd fallen in love with a cop. A good one, by all accounts. Not nice for the wife, but maybe she was a dragon anyway. Who knew? Certainly he didn't. Technically Holbrook, as head of the investigation, should be told, but Madsen didn't want Shari sent home. Not only was she the best camera jockey he'd seen, she was also the most motivated. And the only person familiar with every viddy frame, TrackBack search and ID trace. A replacement would take days to get up to speed. They didn't have days.

On the other hand, there was his own skin to think about. If he said nothing, then he was breaching multiple regulations, and if it was raised in an integrity test he would have to argue that he'd exercised personal discretion for a greater good – in this instance achieving a faster outcome in the case. That wouldn't impress the OPI boys.

And if she hadn't told him everything and the relationship *was* somehow material to the case, they would lynch him.

But that was unlikely. And for the OPIs to ask a question they first had to know it needed asking, and only he, Shari and this dispatcher friend of hers had any idea . . .

He watched her take a sip of water as she awaited his response. Her hands no longer held her glass so tightly and she sat straighter, as if a weight had gone. *That's because part of it just got dumped on my shoulders*, he thought, *and I'm so goddamn tired I really don't need it. Thank you, Shari, for making me complicit in your little non-truth.*

His face must have betrayed his thoughts, for suddenly she was apologizing. 'God, I'm sorry. It's so unfair of me. I'll go back. I'll tell the captain.'

'No,' he said, raising his hand. 'No. Don't worry. It's fine.'

It was dark outside, and it felt cooler than it had in days. He felt the first raindrops strike his shoulders as he walked the two blocks to his apartment. He thought about backpack man, the weirdness of the dollhouses, all the SACs and division chiefs and assistant directors with their never-ending demands for up-dates, and he wondered if the night would yield any answers at all. He trudged wearily up two flights of stairs and unlocked his front door. Not bothering to turn on the lights, he kicked off his shoes and dropped his jacket on the floor before collapsing, fully clothed, into a bed he hadn't lain in for three days.

Chapter 26 _____

Several miles to the north-west, Curt Zetter watched seven shapes through his night-vision goggles, each one ghoulish green against black ink. They huddled in the grass like a brooding, silent band of gorillas, pulling harnesses, checking buckles and pouches. Busy and businesslike, as befitted the best operators in his squad. A pungent mixture of salt water and mangrove mud assailed his nostrils. To his left, a ghostly dirt track snaked back to the dim outline of a van nestled in the trees. In the other direction, a wooden pier arrowed into blackness, peeling timbers betraying its age and lack of use. He scanned beyond it, his goggles picking up waves as spots of static, but saw no sign of the transport. He listened, but heard only a soft gurgle from under the pier and a flurry of rain arriving on the breeze.

A figure detached itself from the others and loomed in his goggles. Big Jose Rodriguez. A consummate professional, veteran of a hundred jobs and a wingman Zetter could rely on under any kind of pressure. Rodriguez had been wisecracking earlier, as they loaded gear into the van. Tonight was the night, he said, that five NeChristo pastors would be attending confession, and SWAT would be handing out penance. Rodriguez began pulling and prodding at Zetter's harness, making sure it was secure.

Zetter reached down to his sidearm, a SIG Sauer P226 strapped against his right thigh. The grip slotted comfortably into his palm and his thumb fell naturally against the pop-button of the retaining strap. The SIG was his secondary weapon. The primary was the Heckler & Koch MP5 submachine gun slung across his chest. The MP5 had laser sights and a thirty-round magazine, with three additional magazines stowed in button-down pouches on his vest. Each of the other men was similarly equipped, with sidearms chosen according to personal preference. It was probably overkill for the job, but Zetter's philosophy was that if you didn't know exactly what you were getting into then there was no such thing as overkill. Besides, tonight's excursion was a great exercise for the boys. He planned to do it properly.

Rodriguez reached up and checked Zetter's chinstrap. Then he leaned in close and made a thumbs up sign. Beneath the bug-like goggles he was grinning.

At the same moment, distant but unmistakable, the throb of powerful engines drifted in over the breeze.

Zetter reached up to press the rubberized button on the side of his helmet. A tiny red dot blinked three times in his goggles before being replaced with a tiny green 'M' at the edge of his peripheral vision. Mission camera activated.

Minutes later, spray spattered Zetter's face and the roar of triple Yamaha 250s blasted his ears. The rigid-hulled inflatable boat, RHIB to the initiated, was essentially a stripped-down hull with engines, and the men sat on plastic benches, hunched against the elements and gripping handrails to hold themselves in as it thudded across the wave crests. The coxswain stood with his knees bent in a boxer's stance, deftly working wheel and throttle behind a wedge-shaped binnacle.

Without warning the roar dropped to a howl, gradually sub-siding to an angry growl as the hull came down off the plane. Boiling foam caught up and surged past. Then she wallowed, black and sleek and low in the water, slopping uncomfortably with the outboards backed off to a deep burble. She ran no lights.

The small ship a mile ahead and moving north to south across the RHIB's track was lit up like a Christmas tree. Spotlights showcased twin funnels, rakishly angled. Every porthole blazed yellow across the waves. Her name was *Genevieve II* and Zetter already knew that she contained within her generous beam three lounges, a dining room and five staterooms. These in turn were packed with every conceivable luxury, including teak floors, granite countertops, twenty-four-carat gold fixtures and bulkheads specially engineered to reduce the noise and vibration from twin twelve-hundred horsepower diesels. The rear entertainment deck appealed to him the most. It featured a full-sized movie screen and a thousand-gallon hot tub.

The coxswain lined them up on a diagonal track and nudged the throttle forward. On the *Genevieve II*'s radar they would appear no bigger than a small, slow-moving fishing vessel. Slowly, the gap narrowed. The coxswain backed off the throttle slightly, allowing the cruiser to draw a few hundred yards ahead. He adjusted the wheel. Still on reduced speed, the RHIB slipped into the wake of the larger vessel.

Zetter reached over towards Rodriguez and gave his helmet a slap. Rodriguez returned a thumbs up and repeated the ritual with the next man. Each lowered his head and braced himself. Zetter placed his right hand on the coxswain's shoulder. More seconds ticked past. He slid his hand forward where the coxswain could see it and then held it there, two fingers pointed at the stern of the *Genevieve II* and thumb at right angles, in the universal imitation of a cocked pistol.

He dropped his thumb. Seven hundred and fifty horses surged into life. The bow shot skywards. The hull bucked and kicked itself forward in a frenzy of noise and spray, pulling its passengers with it. A surge of electricity fired through Zetter's senses and his heart rate doubled. In an instant the RHIB was back on the plane, slapping the waves and homing in like a missile.

In a few seconds they were hard alongside the gleaming hull, pulling themselves up and over the railing, one following the other.

A crewman, dressed in an all-white uniform and carrying a case of champagne, stood paralysed with terror as masked creatures dropped to the deck around him. Moments later he was face down, wrists and ankles zip-tied.

Two men disappeared towards the bridge. Another two headed aft. Zetter and the remaining four dashed up a set of stairs to the main deck, where they positioned themselves, weapons ready, on either side of a pair of large double doors.

Zetter held up three fingers. Two. One. There was a crash of splintering wood.

'Freeze, FBI!' reverberated through the lounge. The men fanned out, laser dots switching from target to target. Boots thudded on carpet. Screams and expletives came back at them. A dozen bodies were sprawled on lounges and cushions. Males, females, at least half of them naked. A large man wearing a toga and intoxicated to the point of blindness staggered to his feet. Zetter placed a black-gloved hand against his chest and pushed him backwards onto a couch.

The men moved methodically from person to person, binding wrists with zip ties, patting down clothing and shouting 'clear' every few seconds. The shouts gradually abated. An African beat thumped from hidden speakers.

Zetter flipped up his goggles.

Bottles rolled on the floor. Here and there the carpet was stained with spilled food. Half the occupants were staring wide-eyed at the invaders, the other half were too stoned to care. Four males, middle-aged and flabby. Nine females, young and skinny. No sudden movements. No body language to signal danger. Satisfied, he carefully picked his way through the clutter of bodies and cushions. Amid the debris he saw silver trays crisscrossed with generous trails of white powder. He smiled and thumbed his throat mike.

'Alpha leader. Main cabin clear. Report.'

Rodriguez's voice. 'Team one. Bridge is clear. We have three males secured.' Calm. Reassuring.

'Team two. Outside decks are clear. Two males secured.'

Five out of the ship's six crew were accounted for.

'Alpha leader,' Zetter said. 'Let's clear the rest.' He stepped through a door in the forward bulkhead and stood in the stairwell connecting all decks. A few moments later he was joined by the two men coming in off the outer deck. He pointed them towards the dining room and forward lounge and they moved off. Rodriguez descended from the bridge, goggles up, and tipped him a wink. Zetter padded quickly down the stairs with Rodriguez following close on his heels.

The staircase terminated in a corridor that travelled the length of the boat. There were closed doors down both sides and at each end. They started at the stern. Rodriguez crouched and shouldered his Heckler & Koch while Zetter grabbed the latch, turned and shoved. A throaty clatter greeted him. He peered briefly into the forest of pipes and gauges of the engine compartment then shut the door, killing the noise. The next door led to a galley, and they burst in on a white-hatted chef. He threw up his hands in astonishment. Rodriguez zip-tied him. Zetter thumbed his mike. 'Alpha leader. Bottom deck. One male secured.' Six out of six crew. He relaxed a little and moved on. A storeroom. Empty. A stateroom, lavishly decorated in blue and gold with the covers of the king-sized bed thrown back. A trail of white powder spilled across the dresser. Unoccupied. Another stateroom, all clear.

Zetter's headset crackled. 'Main deck secured. Upper deck secured.' The hum of motors dropped a semitone and the deck shifted under his feet. The guys on the bridge were turning towards harbour.

No accidents or mishaps, a mountain of cocaine, and heading for dry land. A job well done.

The thought must have temporarily pushed aside Zetter's in-grained caution, because without thinking and without waiting for Rodriguez, he reached out, grasped the latch on the forward door, and shoved.

A chill ran through him. Disappointment. That was the over-whelming emotion. Disappointment at his complacency, and at setting such a poor example. His SIG was holstered. His MP5 slung uselessly by his side.

He stared down the barrel of a pistol.

The pistol was held by a balding man in his fifties. The man clutched a red satin sheet to his bare chest. His hand shook violently. Zetter felt detached and hyper-aware. His eyes picked up the play of light on the fine silver swirls engraved down the slide of the gun. His brain registered the diameter of the jitterbugging muzzle and noted that it was a .32. He felt the slight lateral tug as the *Genevieve II* stabilized on its new course. His nose detected the combined odour of sex and sweat. He saw how the bed was heart-shaped, and the point of the heart slotted neatly into the vee of the boat's bow. And he registered the two small figures huddled in the sheets at the back of the vee. A boy and a girl. Naked. Neither could have been more than ten years old.

'Put it down, mister, or I *will* take your head off.' Rodriguez's voice, soft and menacing. Zetter could sense rather than see the MP5 barrel hovering over his right shoulder. The bald man's eyes twitched, and his pistol hand trembled like he had a bad case of Parkinson's.

Slowly, still shaking, the silver muzzle began to drop.

Chapter 27

A loud buzz broke into Madsen's thoughts. It took him a moment to realize he was in his own apartment and his own bed. He glanced at his watch. Not quite midnight. He found his jacket on the floor and retrieved his cell phone.

It was Zetter, and he sounded elated. 'Five senior pastors and enough coke to take a whole congregation to heaven and back. And we got one for threatening an agent with a firearm. Your guy wasn't kidding. If I were you I'd give him a nice—'

'Whoa,' Madsen interrupted. 'Did you say firearm?' It was a stretch to imagine anyone stupid enough to pull a gun on one of Zetter's operators, let alone a pastor.

'You got it. And they were knee-deep in hookers. You should've seen it. God only knows what goes on with these guys. But get this. They also had a couple of skinjobs. Kiddie jobs.'

'Kiddie jobs? You mean like . . .'

'Like prepubescent. Like the paedophile priest lives on. Nomura specials.'

Nomura. Madsen was waking up fast now.

Zetter continued, 'That's got to be good news, right? Maybe there's a connection. Nomura and NeChristo? We'll be docking shortly. You'd better get down here . . .'

*

Minutes later the Dodge's tyres hissed along rain-slick streets as Madsen drove to the marina with the windows down, yawning and rubbing his eyes and trying to balance haste with caution. By the time he got there, the *Genevieve II* was already tied up, its yellow portholes mirrored in the rain puddles along the quay. Zetter's boys were leading their prizes down the gangway.

Madsen commandeered a small shed for his interviews. It was spartan inside and smelled heavily of diesel and paint, but it had two chairs and a grimy table, which was all he needed.

He had the pastors brought in one at a time. As expected, the narcotics charges hung heavy. There was fear. They wanted lawyers. And, as expected, the fear turned to confusion, then blossoming relief, as he informed them he was only interested in, and only going to ask questions about, the dollhouse bombing. Anxious to secure favour, each one responded with a rapid stream of answers. Madsen learned that the kiddie jobs were the property of one pastor. They were neither lent nor leased to anyone else. He learned that the supplier was a man with private connections to one of Nomura's Japanese wholesalers, that every other month he smuggled in a container load via the Los Angeles shipping terminal, and that he wasn't fussy about who he sold to, as long as they had cash.

And Madsen established, completely and beyond doubt, that none of the pastors aboard the *Genevieve II* knew anything whatsoever about Grant Avenue.

Sunday

Chapter 28

The young summer intern working the graveyard shift in News-Globe's New York office had volunteered to scan the public submissions inbox. It sounded easy, and she could finish off her media studies assignment at the same time. No one told her it would turn her brain to mush.

The task entailed eyeballing a mind-numbing four hundred emails every hour, each promising a sensational, hard-hitting revelation that would change the world, or at least galvanize a worldwide audience, and none of them delivering anything of the kind. It took a tenth of her brain power to do the scanning and two-tenths to work on her assignment. The rest was dedicated to staying awake. She understood now why this particular inbox was christened 'the shit-box', and why it was always cleared by interns.

As she had yet to see anything that might merit the appellation 'news', she had made a few refinements to her technique. Instead of reading the emails, she skimmed twenty headers at a time. If one caught her eye, she clicked on it and gave it two seconds. If not, she hit the delete button and pulled up another screenful.

A corruption allegation against a mayor in Missouri. Allegation only, nothing to substantiate it.

A tap on the keyboard. *Next twenty.*

An essay on how a Jewish cartel secretly manipulated energy markets. Five thousand breathless words, complete with misspellings.

Next. Another tap.

Thirteen identical emails from one guy on his revolutionary new exercise machine and how it burns fat twice as fast with half the effort.

Jeez, if only! Next.

Alaskans are FLUSHING carcinogenic CHEMICALS down their toilets and KILLING the wildlife.

Next.

The real NeChristo.

Next. But her finger hovered. It might have been the password pasted in the subject line, or perhaps it was because the sender had used an anonymity broker to hide their identity. Either way, something made her decide to give it a few more seconds.

She examined it again.

The real NeChristo. Password = gdn85h6

She opened it and found a link.

http://www.fbi_internal.gov/ops/case3X7495/evid/vidfile2245

On impulse she clicked.

A login screen popped up.

She copied the password from the subject line and pressed enter.

The screen went black. A moment later it turned into a wriggling confusion of phosphorescent green blobs on a black background. A luminous gloved hand appeared and disappeared. A shape swung into view. The shape was also a dozen shades of green and black. A boat? Green worms again.

The seesawing was enough to make her giddy, but eventually she worked out that the wriggly worms were reflected lights on water and she was looking through a night-vision camera mounted on someone's head. Strange symbols and a tiny clock counter in the corner suggested it was military.

Weird shit.

And by far the most interesting thing she had seen in the past two hours.

It *was* a boat. A big one. She watched it loom. Heavily armed figures clambered over a railing. A minute later, whoever was wearing the camera busted through a door and the night vision flared, then switched to brightly lit technicolor. Black-clad figures, 'FBI' spelled out in big yellow capitals on their flak jackets, momentarily blocked the view. The camera panned over naked limbs, upturned furniture, champagne bottles, faces . . .

The intern sat up with a jolt. She had seen one of those faces before, on the news.

'Holy fuck, holy fuck, holy *FUCK!*'

Her hands shook so much that she misdialled twice before getting through to the duty editor.

Twenty minutes later, the chief editor of NewsGlobe marched in, senior counsel following on his heels like a lapdog, and yelled at everyone on the night shift to report to his office.

The meeting was brief. The news value of the piece was not canvassed; the discussion dealt solely with risk. Federal prosecution was raised, then dismissed. They moved on to lawsuits. A figure was mentioned. Another, much higher figure was advanced against it. Upside beat downside. They discussed the other media organizations the video might have been sent to and quickly reached a consensus: their biggest risk, by far, was delay.

The chief editor ordered his team to cut the footage to the essentials, telling them to be sure to 'keep the drugs, gun and kids, and linger on the kids'. It needn't be pretty, he said – they could tidy it up and re-release it later – but it had to be fast. He quickly dictated the words and phrases he wanted wrapped around it. Then he kicked everyone out of his office so he could call the affiliates and prepare them for what was coming.

Chapter 29

Daniel Madsen reached out from under the covers and killed the persistent *eek eek* stabbing at his eardrums. His skull felt like it had been beaten with a rubber mallet. His eyes were sore. And something was wrapped around his neck. He reached up and pulled it away. It was the shirt he had only half-removed before falling asleep. He caught the pungent smell of body odour and winced.

First priority was a shower.

He turned the taps up to full. A steaming torrent pummelled into his neck and shoulders. He stood there, relishing the feeling. After a minute the muscles in his back loosened and his headache eased from terminal to tolerable. He stayed until the hot water ran out.

Extensive digging through the sheets and clothes scattered across his floor turned up a single, barely presentable pair of trousers. A further expedition into the dirty laundry piled up beside the front door secured a shirt that had been worn only once. He dressed, then went to the kitchen where a careful search yielded a dozen slices of stale bread and a banana in an advanced state of mush. He returned to the front door and surveyed the discarded clothes. There was a laundromat at the corner of his block, and next to that a small coffee shop. He stuffed the laundry into a bag and lugged it downstairs and out into the street.

A thin San Francisco fog hung in the air. It filled his lungs and felt fresh and cool against his skin. Parked cars glistened under a film of cold, early-morning condensation.

At the laundromat, he loaded up two machines and filled the slots with coins. Then he went next door and devoured fried eggs with bacon, sausage links and hash browns, and orange juice to wash it all down. The chilled juice was like a tonic, and the headache faded to nothing.

Back in the laundromat he dragged up a plastic chair and zoned out in front of a screen.

The washing machines hummed and clunked.

His thoughts turned to the day ahead. That it was Sunday made no difference. It was important to maintain momentum, keep things moving. He would head down to Central Station first. Check in with Holbrook, then go over names and places and all the case data. If there was a NeChristo reference anywhere, he'd find it.

On the laundromat screen, a trio of sultry sirens appeared – an advertisement triggered by his presence. The volume was turned down and they winked and blew kisses and moved their hips to the thrum and racket of a spin cycle. The Dreamcom logo appeared along with the address of a nearby dollhouse. A bikini-clad nymph stretched out a languid forefinger and beckoned. Madsen wondered if his headache was going to make an early return.

A second advertisement kicked in. No nubile young women this time, just a single, earnest, middle-aged man. He mouthed his sales pitch to camera while holding up a bottle of pills. Over-the-counter antidepressants. Madsen shook his head sadly. The pills were the exact same shade of blue as those he had picked up off the men's room floor in Berkeley. Different chemical, same purpose. The man's 'before' shot – all sallow cheeks and suicide eyes – briefly haunted the screen before swapping to the newer and happier version, holding hands with his imaginary family and dancing, ring-a-rosie style, in front of a mansion with a red BMW parked in the driveway.

Mercifully, the advertisement ended and a news bulletin started. The familiar face of Latitha Williams filled the screen. Big-haired and brassy, Latitha was living proof that women with character and determination could still prevail over bimbettes, at least in the world of newsreaders. She was speaking animatedly about something, but Madsen's eyes were drawn to the background. The giant lattice of the NeChristo dome glittered under the caption 'CHRISTIANS OR KILLERS?' spelled out in big block letters.

Madsen leapt to his feet and bounded to the screen, kicking over a stack of plastic baskets on the way. He fumbled for the volume control and pressed it until Latitha's voice thundered over the sounds of the laundromat.

'Rumours that the New Christian Organization of America is connected to the tragedy have been circulating for days. In the early hours of this morning a series of videos and images were leaked that confirm, in the most sensational way, that the church is indeed the focus of an extensive police and federal investigation . . .'

Madsen's head began to pound. Long seconds passed. Dazed, he backed out of the laundromat. He had to get the Dodge, get to the office. *Forget Central Station*, he thought. *DiMatteo and the director and half the Bureau will be waking up to this . . .*

He broke into a run.

In his Washington home, Senator Erol Arbett scowled at his hallway mirror. He had tied the knot too big, and the gap it left between where his tie ended and where the top of his belt buckle started only served to accentuate his belly. From behind came giggles and half-hearted reprimands from the nanny as she tried to keep the children still long enough to brush their hair. He pulled the knot free and started again. Despite the scowl, he was in a jocular mood. Not counting funerals, memorials and official services, it had been years since he had voluntarily attended any kind of religious gathering, and today would be his very first visit to a NeChristo church. He was looking forward to seeing what the fuss was about.

His wife, on the other hand, was so appalled by the idea she wasn't speaking. Her particular gripe was that Martha Hollingsworth, socialite, fashion plate and her long-time best friend, was in town and they had plans to spend the morning doing some serious shopping. Being asked to forgo this excursion to listen to some hack preacher, as she put it, screwed her day before it started. Arbett had tried telling her that NeChristo services were popular because they were thoroughly modern, relevant and centred on human values. In response she said she didn't appreciate being fed such baloney by a man who couldn't give a fig for values, human or otherwise. Eventually Arbett had put his foot down and told his wife point-blank that it was simply one of those occasions when she was expected to be seen by his side, period. She had been sulking ever since.

Which was why, as he stood in the hall retying his tie for the third time, he was immediately suspicious when Rebecca Arbett came to him and asked, in her sweetest baby-doll voice, if he had just a teeny-weeny moment to come see something on the news?

Reluctantly, and with an eye on the time, Arbett followed her into the lounge room.

Latitha Williams's voice boomed from the screen. 'On Friday an FBI special agent was seen leaving the church's Salt Lake City headquarters. It's believed he polygraphed senior leaders, possibly even Pastor Luke himself. Yesterday further interviews were conducted with church officials in at least seven states, culminating in the detention of Joe Sorrell, a pastor in San Francisco . . .'

The screen showed a short clip of an untidy-looking man in a parking lot, walking towards the viewer with the NeChristo dome soaring into the sky behind. A second clip showed a man in handcuffs looking sorry for himself as he was bundled into the back seat of a car, a hand pressing down on the top of his head. The large owner of the hand had his back to the camera, but the guy holding the door open had the same unruly hair and rumpled jacket as the FBI agent in the first clip. Both shots looked like they might have been taken from behind glass, perhaps in a vehicle.

'Most shocking of all is this video, allegedly taken during an

FBI raid last night somewhere off the California coast. It shows senior pastors being arrested for drug and firearms offences, as well as possession of child dolls, illegal in the United States.'

Arbett's hands dropped slack to his sides and he leaned against the wall. A wave of nausea spread upwards from his stomach.

'Finally there is this sequence of images.'

Three stills of the same man, side by side: a sinister face, all hoodie and sunglasses; a close-up from behind and at an angle, with the hoodie partly dislodged; and an enhanced close-up of an object on his ear. A G-ring.

'A source from inside the San Francisco Police Department tells us this man is the principal suspect in the bombing of the Grant Avenue dollhouse. His identity is still unknown and he is thought to have died in the blast. This has yet to be verified – the San Francisco Police Department and the FBI have both refused to comment – but it is believed the suspect may have been a suicide bomber.'

Arbett made a distant gurgling sound.

Somewhere behind him, a telephone began to ring. Then another. Then a third. Rummaging in her purse, Rebecca Arbett retrieved her own phone and began smugly scrolling through the contacts for her best friend's number. She didn't look up as her husband, shirt tails flapping, ran heavily down the hall to his study.

Twenty-three hundred miles to the west, Gerard Stimson, fifty-seven, fit, and with the hawk nose and patrician manner of a Roman dictator, had risen early and breakfasted in the rose garden of his Beverly Hills mansion, taking his time to enjoy the sounds of summer songbirds. The news was not part of the senior pastor's Sunday morning routine.

He finished his coffee, placed the cup and saucer on the silver tray for collection by his butler, and made his way to the garage where, after a moment's consideration, he selected the '69 Mercedes 280 SL. The raspberry red leather gave a satisfying creak as he slid behind the wheel. The freshly restored six-cylinder engine kicked into life and settled to a purr. Stimson dropped the transmission into drive and glided down the drive and out through the automatic security gates to begin his rounds.

He drove to the North LA church first. The external structure was a one-third replica of the Utah dome and glittered above the trees as he coasted the perimeter. Bypassing the enormous parking lot, he nosed the Mercedes into a private lane that took him through the trees to his reserved space at the back. He stepped from the Mercedes, buttoned his jacket and carefully straightened his creases. As he swiped his security pass at the plain white door his staff jokingly called the 'tradesman's entrance', a distant observer might have marked him as a senior partner in a law firm or the chairman of a bank.

The sounds of electric guitars and synchronized clapping bounced down the corridors. Stimson walked purposefully, patent leather heels clipping polished floors and making echoes of their own. He passed down several corridors and stopped in front of a wall panel, scarcely distinguishable from those on either side. He inserted a small key on a chain around his neck and the panel became a door, swinging open to reveal a narrow circular stairwell. After relocking the door, he climbed the stairs at a brisk pace. Even so, it took a full minute to reach the top. A second door took him out onto a steel mesh platform. Clapping and singing reverberated off the dome's ceiling only a few feet above. To the left and right was a forest of cables and scaffolding for stage lights. In front, a narrow suspended gangway followed the spine of the ceiling to its highest and most central point. Hanging from the far end, at the very centre of the dome, was something resembling an oversized, dark-tinted light bulb.

Stimson made his way along the gangway. Far below, through the mesh, tiny figures with guitars moved about on a stage. Heads bobbed and weaved like wheat in the wind. At the end of the gangway Stimson descended a short ladder into the bulb and made himself comfortable. The seat, joystick and panoramic, slightly dizzying view reminded him of a crane operator's cab, not that he had ever been in one of those.

He began with the preacher's stagecraft. The young buck was in fine form. Bold words alternated with soft. Laughter. A burst of song. *Connecting.* The magic in this one, Stimson mused, was in his wit. Being genuinely funny allowed him to connect to his congregation – much more than passion alone would have done. Stimson's other preachers could learn from that. He made a note to put highlights of today's performance in the weekly training clip.

The band, on the other hand . . . Loud, energetic, sunny smiles, but in his parish that wasn't enough. He expected *sizzle.* The kids had talent, though, and it was only their second week – another forty or fifty hours' practice should do it. He would give them a pep talk. If they couldn't get there in a fortnight, he'd swap them out.

The preacher took the energy up a notch. On cue, helpers began moving down aisles and passing out collection baskets.

Stimson turned his attention downwards. His eyes travelled over the semicircular rows, counting heads, weighing up the attendance. He saw gaps, a lot of them, and for the first time that morning his face was creased by a frown.

Next to Stimson's right knee was a panel of switches. He reached over and flicked the largest one. A monitor in the floor of the pod flashed on, revealing an extreme close-up of a lady's lap. He jiggled the joystick until he picked up one of the collection baskets. With practised movements he tracked it and began a silent, running tally of the notes. There were no coins to complicate his calculations. The baskets had holes, like sieves, ensuring they fell to the floor to shame the ungenerous.

In the dim light of the cubicle, Stimson's grip on the joystick began to tighten. By the time the baskets had traversed the third row, his knuckles shone bone-white, like a row of golf balls.

Chapter 30

'So what the fuck happened?' Mary DiMatteo's angry voice bounced off the walls of her office. Madsen sat in silence. He had already tried to answer several times and each time she had cut him off.

'Yesterday this was sensible,' she continued. 'It was under control. *You* were under control. Now instead of an investigation we are scaring the shit out of the public and doing trial by media, and sticking the knife into America's favourite church, or religious organization or whatever it is they call themselves. *Are you out of your fucking mind?*'

The words flew like bullets. The office walls were cheap and flimsy; everyone else would be hearing them as well. Madsen ached to be out of there.

'As I said. We were low-profile.'

'You were on CNN, NBC and ABC, for Chrissakes!'

'It's a set-up. Dreamcom must have engineered it. We've investigated Nomura, the feminist coalition and a whole bunch of individuals, and there was no coverage of any of them. Just NeChristo.'

DiMatteo slumped in her chair. All at once the tiredness showed on her face. *That*, Madsen thought, *is what teetering between honourable retirement and a pension cancellation does to a person.*

'Who leaked?' she asked.

'Sorry?'

'Who leaked?'

'It didn't come from me.'

'Then who the hell did it come from?'

'I don't know. About all I do know, or think I know, is that they also knew my movements. They must have followed me for days to get that footage.'

DiMatteo's face tightened like she had taken a mouthful of milk and discovered it was curdled. 'The person that knew most about your movements was you.'

'So did a lot of others.'

'Bureau or police?'

'Both.'

She looked him up and down. 'I know you, Madsen, and you know how to play the system. When you have an agenda you know how to get others helping so you don't get your hands dirty. Was there a nod and a wink? Were you involved in any way?'

'Of course not.'

'No more NeChristo interviews.'

Madsen rolled his eyes. 'Our guy is still a member. That hasn't changed. At the very least I need to—'

'No. Lay off them. Get more evidence, granite hard, before you even think about going near anybody. Then check with me. Then, if I am so stupid as to say yes, ask me again, just to be sure. Clear?'

'No, it's not clear,' he said. 'You're cutting off my main line of investigation.'

Her face reddened. 'You must have other leads to work, so work 'em. And before you leave this office, the director wants a list, which means the division chief wants a list, which means I want a list.'

'Mary, I don't—'

She held up her hand. 'OPI are coming to test everyone involved in the case. SFPD has already given clearance for their people to be included. I want the names of everyone who had access to the files. Agents, cops – the lot.' She slid a pad across the desk. 'In order of priority.'

Madsen shook his head in disbelief.

'And be sure,' DiMatteo rasped, an index finger levelled like a gun barrel at Madsen's chest, 'to put your own name at the top.'

Six hundred miles to the east, Pastor Luke's office had been transformed into a crisis centre. Updates cascaded down the electronic screens like waterfalls. Paper was taped to the walls and strewn across the floor. A whiteboard with IMMEDIATE ACTION written across the top in bold red letters had been wheeled in, and a jockey-sized assistant in jeans and T-shirt scribbled tasks and names on it while simultaneously engaged in a heated telephone discussion.

Luke, his collar askew and shirtsleeves rolled up, took up one end of the conference table. Five middle-aged men manned the sides. Behind them, the holographic ball glowed blue and green through the angled glass. It was visibly smaller than it had been when the meeting started.

The jockey at the whiteboard wrapped up his telephone conversation. All eyes shifted to him. 'LA North and Central. Attendance down fifteen per cent. Average yield down twenty-two.'

'Which comes to?' Luke addressed his question to Pastor Richard Hodge, his CFO, who was sitting to his immediate right. Hodge punched the numbers rapidly into a laptop. He had silver-flecked hair and wore suspenders over a pinstripe shirt and a paunch, giving him the look of a grizzled Wall Street trader.

'I make that a thirty per cent revenue hit, all up,' Hodge said.

There was a collective exhalation.

'It'll be a lot worse tomorrow, once everyone has seen it,' he added.

'LA were – ah – keen to emphasize that point,' said the assistant.

'Did they say how Stimson was?' Luke asked.

'Pissed.'

'I'll call him later.' Luke glowered to his left, where his member services chief stared unhappily through the glass at the Ball of Connectedness. Judging from his outfit he had been on the way to the golf course when he received the call. 'Frank. What's the impact on memberships?'

Frank blinked. 'Oh. Sorry. Call centres are swamped on the east and west coasts. We're getting a lot of cancellations, mostly new members. That's all I know. It's still too early for a projection. We should have one in another twenty minutes or so.'

Luke frowned. He switched his attention to the red-headed dandy to Frank's left. His head of communications. 'Bobby?'

'Press statement is being pushed to everyone we can think of. They want you fronting interviews, the sooner the better. Message and Q & A guides have been sent to all pastors and flock leaders. Pretty basic, but better than nothing. We should have an updated version within the hour . . . I need to know what to tell pastors about earnings projections, too. They'll be asking.'

Luke turned to Hodge, who was still tapping at his laptop. 'Richard?'

'Based on this, cash flow to tank for two weeks. Maybe a forty per cent hit for the month.'

'Jesus, I'm not telling anybody *that*. We'll have a fucking riot.' Addressing Bobby again Luke said, 'Let's hold off until this afternoon. We'll have more data. It might look better then.'

Bobby nodded and returned to his notes. 'We're preparing a letter to the San Francisco Police Department and the FBI offering to assist—'

'Fuck 'em.'

Bobby waited for an elaboration. When none was forthcoming, he drew a line through something on his notepad and continued: 'Last thing is today's G-ring broadcast. In light of events, our message is too assertive.'

'I know. It's already gone out.'

'If we record a new one, we can de-queue everyone who hasn't listened or watched yet, and we can pull the multi-language and overseas broadcasts. That's more than half our audience. I've got the studio standing by.' He looked up hopefully.

'Do it.'

Luke turned to the only other person in the room, his head of security. 'Paulie?'

The tall man in the charcoal suit sat at the far end of the table, apart from the others. He had dark sideburns and might have been good-looking except for his nose, which at some stage had been flattened against the side of his face. His reply came in a soft monotone. 'We're crawling the databases now. The police images are shit, but we have the best face-matching software money can buy. If he's a member, we'll find him.'

'And our latter-day sodomites?'

'Terminations served ten minutes ago.'

'Sorrill or Sorrell or whatever the fuck his name is?'

'Gone.'

Bobby said, 'I'll add that to the next press statement.'

Luke glared around the table. 'Have we missed anything?'

Frank sounded utterly miserable as he dragged his eyes away from the windows. 'The dollhouse protests.'

'What about them?'

'My analysts are saying member turnout for today's protests will be way down. We've had flock leaders calling to say they won't lead them. The venues will be packed with counter-protesters. It'll look awful.'

Luke screwed his eyes shut. 'Recommendations?'

'Cancel,' Bobby said. 'We call it a temporary measure while we ask our community to focus on internal healing.'

'Cancel,' Richard said.

'Cancel,' Frank said, his voice barely above a whisper.

Paulie said nothing.

Luke shook his head in disgust. 'A few bad apples and we hide under a rock. We're going to look like idiots. Okay, cancel, but I want to be ready to restart as soon as the air clears.' Turning to his CFO he said, 'Richard, I need you to fly to San Francisco. Take

Paulie with you. I want you to whip the pastors there into line. For the next forty-eight hours I need them to be the most pious, God-loving, baby-blessing holy men on the planet, and when they talk, they need to stay *exactly* on message. At all other times, they keep their fucking mouths shut. Got it?'

Richard nodded.

Luke's chair creaked as he raised one of his meaty hands high over his head then brought it swiftly down, connecting with the table with a loud *smack*. A glass of water jumped and tipped over. 'Last item. What are we doing about this FBI guy?'

Bobby began, 'We can lodge a complaint—'

'Complaint? I want the low-life fuck *crucified*. I want people digging up all the dirt there is on him. Everything he has ever said, done or screwed. And I want it in a fucking memo shoved down the throat of his boss, his friends, his family and every journalist and talk show host in the country. Paulie, you hearing me?'

Paulie nodded.

'ARE YOU HEARING ME?'

Paulie stood. 'I'll get it started.'

Chapter 31

Madsen left the thirteenth floor and took the elevator down to the SWAT operations centre. He felt angry and frustrated. His stomach churned. A couple of days ago he'd been rolling up dealers. Now he was making lists for OPI. That kind of activity isolated you real fast; he had already noted the averted eyes and silent cubicles as he made his way out of DiMatteo's office. He wondered about the leaker. Dreamcom's motive was understandable. He didn't like it, but he could understand it. But the cop or agent, what was their agenda? Did they think it would force Luke into helping? Did they have some score to settle with the church? Money? Whatever the reason, the Bureau was embarrassed, and embarrassing the Bureau was a mistake. OPI would polygraph everyone who had access to the evidence files, everyone who knew Madsen's movements, and they would find answers. They would talk to as many people as they thought necessary. By the end, most of them would think Madsen was poison.

There was no one in Zetter's office, but the sound of clanking weights floated from further down the corridor. Madsen followed the sound until he found Zetter's second-in-command, Rodriguez, working out on a bench press, his pecs swelling like inflating balloons with each lift.

Rodriguez finished his set and sat forward on the bench. 'Zetter's out,' he said, wiping the sweat from his face.

'Have you seen it?'

'I've seen it.'

'Somebody leaked.'

Rodriguez was unimpressed. 'Yeah, well, it is what it is. We followed procedure. I uploaded the mission files myself.'

'Whoever it is isn't helping.'

No answer.

'Did anyone have an opportunity—'

'Hey. I'm sorry last night didn't work out, but don't be coming in here asking those kinds of questions. Leave that to the OPI faggots. Okay?'

Madsen left Rodriguez to his work-out and meandered back towards the elevator. He didn't relish the prospect of returning to his desk, but he didn't have a definite plan either. The morning had thrown everything into disarray.

A message buzzed on his cell phone and made the decision for him. It was from Carl Steinmann in evidence recovery, asking him to come down to the medical examiner's office.

Madsen rode the elevator down to the garage and a few moments later threaded the Dodge up the ramp and under the boom gate. He felt a surge of relief to see the Phillip Burton building in his mirrors. He turned south. The office of the chief medical examiner was located with the city morgue, courts, SFPD headquarters, highway patrol and half a dozen other police divisions in the Hall of Justice, a long grey battleship of a building south of Market Street and only a few minutes' drive from the federal building. The lingering fog deadened the light and deposited trails of moisture along the windscreen as Madsen drove. Cool tendrils of dampness washed in through the air vents. By the time he arrived he felt a little calmer.

Madsen signed in at the front desk and asked for directions. He navigated his way down a series of corridors, all tiled with the same worn-out linoleum and lined with endless rows of battered filing cabinets. Halfway down one corridor, nestled in a small alcove between two cabinets, he spied the familiar lab coat hunched over an instrument that looked like a pair of binoculars mated to a microscope.

'Carl?'

Steinmann raised a finger for Madsen to wait. After a few moments he rolled back his chair and regarded his visitor sternly. The instrument's eyepiece had left two semicircular impressions at the top of his cheeks. His nose seemed larger and ruddier than ever. 'Mr Madsen,' he said. 'I hear you've had a busy night. I always thought the mass media was too blunt an instrument for a top agent. Weapon of last resort, that sort of thing.'

Madsen forced a smile. 'Thanks for the advice, Carl. And since you ask, no, I didn't do it.'

'I should hope not. Beneath you really.'

'I appreciate the vote of confidence.'

'And I hope I don't find my name on that list of yours.'

Bad news travels fast, thought Madsen. 'You left a message?'

'So I did. Follow me.'

They walked down another corridor, took a sharp right and arrived at a set of heavy doors with a thick glass porthole set into each one. Steinmann leaned on a door and gestured Madsen through. The filing cabinets gave way to white tiles. The temperature dropped twenty degrees. The air stank of formalin. Lurking underneath was another smell. Madsen had once forgotten to pay his electricity bill before going on a two-week training course, returning to find the contents of his freezer dissolved into a pool of warm, fetid slush. It was the same smell. A row of steel autopsy tables dominated the room. Each was heavily stained down the sides and polished to a high shine on top. What you could see of the top. Clear plastic bags of all shapes and sizes were crammed onto every flat surface and overflowed from the basins. The bags had white stick-on labels, each neatly annotated in black felt-tip marker. A lab worker wearing white cotton gloves sorted through the bags, making notes on a clipboard. She nodded as they came in, then returned to her work.

Steinmann said, 'We've recovered most of the remains. Not all, but my team has been thorough.'

Madsen bent to look. The nearest bags contained marble-sized lumps of ash. They looked like they might have been scraped out of a campfire.

'This table is just fragments,' Steinmann said, picking up a bag. 'Whole bodies and, ah, larger chunks, are over there. You see the way these are grouped together? The numbers on each bag correspond to the grid references for where we found it. Latitude, longitude, elevation.' Steinmann pointed to a computer screen. 'We've put everything we've found on a 3-D plot. It's quite interesting. You can see from the patterns how the blast follows the line of least resistance. It also allows us to run a kind of reverse simulation to see where fragments originated. Would you like to see it?'

'No, thank you.'

'Perhaps later.' Steinmann dragged two stools away from an autopsy table and arranged them in front of a narrow work-bench that lined one of the walls. The bench was littered with instruments, containers, keyboards, papers and pens. He withdrew a black plastic folder from the clutter and handed it to Madsen. 'The DNA results. We got priority turnaround. Fastest yet. Came in this morning.'

The hairs rose on the back of Madsen's neck. The team had been so focused on getting a speedy result from the video, he had almost forgotten that there was another way of identifying his killer. He thumbed through the folder eagerly, but his excitement soon gave way to impatience. The pages were filled with nothing but endless sequences of letters and numbers, unintelligible to the layperson.

'What does it say?'

'I'm coming to that. First, what *I'm* telling you is that we can be confident my guys got most of the pieces. We extracted DNA in a good enough state, and we mapped the location and orientation of each piece, both against the site and relative to other human remains, to build a comprehensive picture. Agreed?' He raised an eyebrow as if waiting to be challenged.

Madsen nodded. 'Yeah, I get it.'

'And we received clear DNA results back from the lab.'

'Okay.'

'So, based on this, I am in a position to give you some results. According to the handbook we have to call them preliminary, because the evidence recovery process isn't complete. That's the official position. Unofficially, nothing is going to change no matter how many more rocks we pick over. If I use the terminology that seems to be in vogue nowadays, what I'm about to tell you is not just high probability, but as near as dammit to certainty.' He gave Madsen a look that said this was not a phrase to be used lightly.

'Carl, you got my attention. Let's hear it.'

'We've found all the human beings in that building, and we have firm IDs on all eleven.'

'Jesus, you know who he is! You ID'd our man!'

'No.'

'What?'

'No. I do not have his ID.'

'But you just said—'

A pained expression crossed Steinmann's face. He took a pen out of a drawer and searched for something to write on. Finding nothing on the bench, he reached over to a printer, opened it, and extracted a clean sheet of paper from the refill tray. He cleared a space on the bench, put the paper down and uncapped the pen. At the top of the paper he printed an eleven. Then he printed another, underneath. Under that he wrote out an equation.

$$11$$
$$11$$
$$A - D = 12$$

'Now,' Steinmann said, regarding his colleague seriously. 'As I told you, my team found the remains of eleven people, and we've ID'd eleven. We know who they are.' He placed large ticks against each of the first two numbers. 'Our good friends in SFPD surveillance made their own calculation of how many people were inside.

They did so via their usual method, by taking all the *departures* they caught on camera and subtracting them from all the *arrivals* caught on camera.' He underlined the 'D' and 'A' for emphasis.

'That's right,' said Madsen. 'They counted twelve victims.'

'So the SFPD surveillance people,' Steinmann said, his tone making it abundantly clear where he positioned them in his hierarchy of professional investigators, 'were *wrong*.'

He drew a large 'X' through the twelve for emphasis.

'Shit.'

'And given that the IDs on all eleven of our John Does have been cross-checked with photographs in driver's licence, passport and employment databases, I can tell you, categorically and definitively, that a certain Mr Backpack Man was not among them.'

'He got out.'

'Yes. He got out.'

Chapter 32

The Sunday morning traffic was light, and the sun had burned away the last vestiges of fog, freeing Madsen to hammer the Dodge along the city streets as he raced towards Central Station. Urgent thoughts spun through his mind. The killer escaped. He was still out there. The notion of unseen people on the loose, ready, willing and able to bomb dollhouses, was no longer a theoretical possibility, it was real. If this guy thought it was worthwhile bombing one then he wasn't going to have reservations about two. Or three. Or ten. And they still had nothing. The investigation team needed to fire up and go back to the beginning. Find what they'd missed.

He half-parked, half-abandoned the Dodge in Vallejo Street, checked in past the desk officer and jogged down the corridor. He took the stairs two at a time up to the task force operations room and burst through the door.

To be greeted by death stares and stony silence.

Holbrook was there. As were two other inspectors. Madsen could imagine their thoughts. They hadn't wanted him in the first place. He'd been forced on them by headquarters. Not only had he failed to deliver a fast collar, now they faced the singularly noxious prospect of *more* plotters arriving any day for the express purpose of performing cop-on-cop polygraphs. They probably thought Madsen had leaked the raid himself, to save his reputation or stoke his own publicity. Even if they allowed for the slim possibility that it hadn't been him, they were damned-for-sure certain it was someone in the FBI, and in time-honoured fashion the Bureau would be doing its level best to shift the blame.

He made his way cautiously over to Holbrook and dragged a battered school chair up to the steel-topped desk. Brown rings from a dozen coffee cups stained the surface. The inspector leaned back with his feet up and hands behind his head. The two of them sat, eyeing each other.

'I've just come from the medical examiner's office,' Madsen said. 'Carl Steinmann says our man got out.'

Holbrook's expression morphed from sullenness to confusion and then, finally, utter incredulity.

'What?'

'There were eleven bodies in there, not twelve. His wasn't one of them.' Madsen related the rest of his conversation with Steinmann. When he was finished, Holbrook said, 'He must have been Harry fucking Houdini.'

'I'm thinking sewers,' Madsen said.

'No way.'

'Why not?'

'Why not? Well, for one thing I don't know any buildings that have manhole-sized entrances to sewers on the *inside*. And it's kinda hard to flush yourself down a toilet.'

'Suppose he made a hole? A utilities map would tell us if any tunnels ran under the building.'

'Okay, Sherlock, then why didn't he go in that way instead of using the front door? Better yet, why bother going in at all if you can leave the bomb there and blow the guts out of your target from underneath?'

'Good point.'

One of the inspectors dropped a pile of manila folders on Holbrook's desk. He grabbed another pile and took it away, but not before giving Madsen a look that said he should wear running shoes next time they met. Holbrook called him back. 'Bob, you want to run down drawings of the sewers, electricity, any other underground cavities for me?'

'Cavities?'

'Our federal friend here says backpack man got out.'

'No shit.'

'Express post from the lab.'

'Maybe he teleported.'

'Maybe. Run 'em down anyway.'

The inspector rolled his eyes and left.

'Thanks,' Madsen said, watching him go.

'I don't want your thanks. He never got out. But that's what we do here. Follow up stuff, no matter how shitty, until we find something. Then we build a case.' Holbrook swung his feet off the desk. 'Now if you'll excuse me, I've got a bunch more work to do before your OPI buddies arrive and start punching big fucking holes in my schedule.' Madsen stood. 'Wait,' Holbrook said, eyeing the pile of folders on his desk. He extracted one from the middle and tossed it at Madsen's chest. 'Just in case you feel like doing some real detective work.'

Red-faced, Madsen opened the file. It contained a printout of every name connected to the case so far. Bystanders, victims, families, friends, witnesses, vehicle owners, drivers, employees, activists, protest leaders, and every 'near' and 'possible' match returned by TrackBack in the various queries that had been tried. Each name was annotated with times, locations, connections and relationships. The names on the first few pages had been ruled out in red ink. The printout was an inch thick.

Disgusted, Madsen went downstairs to give Shari the news.

He found her in the corridor outside the surveillance operations room, but instead of returning his smile she averted her eyes and sidestepped, trying to pass.

She suspects it was me, he thought. *Just like the others.*

He stepped back, blocking her path. 'Hey, are you okay? I need to talk to you for a second.'

Shari's stare was icy. Accusing. She opened her mouth to say something but shut it again when boots echoed down the corridor. She bit her lower lip hard enough to turn it white.

A pair of officers approached, nodded politely and shuffled past.

Two rosy points appeared over Shari's cheekbones. She raised her hand, and for a moment Madsen thought she was going to hit him. Instead, she grabbed his elbow. With surprising strength, she pulled him down the corridor, through the entrance lobby, and out into Vallejo Street. Before Madsen could ask what the hell was going on, she nudged her eyes upwards, at the camera suspended over their heads, and to the left, at the side lane where cops were busy picking up and dropping off vehicles. Without a word she turned and strode off in the opposite direction, up the hill.

Madsen followed.

When they were thirty yards from the station she turned and faced him. They stood there, blinking in the sunshine.

'What do I say?' she asked.

'About what?'

'Your OPI people are coming here. They'll polygraph me. What am I supposed to say about Adam?'

Jesus, he thought, *is that what this is about?* Was she really so terrified of being taken off the case? There was no way she was going to be caught, and even if she was, what was the big deal? She did the wrong thing because she thought it was the right thing, because she wanted a result. Because she was committed, zealous even. So what?

'Listen,' he said. 'You're getting worked up over nothing. The integrity test will be an inconvenience, that's all. Don't worry about it. OPI stick to their scripts and they're coming to find out who leaked. That's it. Before you know it, you'll be finished and wondering what the hell the fuss was about.'

She said nothing. Just locked eyes with him. She was still scared.

'Listen,' he said. 'You and I have more important things to worry about.'

'Like what?'

'Like backpack man. He got out.'

Shari stiffened. 'Bullshit.'

'Lab says they have a firm body count and IDs. He wasn't among them.'

'Maybe he was vaporized.'

Madsen shook his head. 'I asked Carl Steinmann about that. He said that even if the guy was hugging the bomb there would still be . . .' He wrinkled up his nose as he searched for the right word. 'Material. Steinmann's team would've found it. He knows his job.'

'Well, I know mine.'

Madsen raised both hands in surrender. 'Okay, sorry. I'm not questioning your abilities. But we have a contradiction and we need to resolve it. Is it possible there was a gap in the coverage? After all, the guy knew how to avoid getting his picture taken close up, and he managed to break the trail by exploiting the cameras that were out of action in Pacific Garage.'

'I can assure you all the units along Grant Avenue, and the alleyway behind, were functioning perfectly. We had full coverage.'

'Didn't the explosion break some cameras?'

'Yes. We lost two units on Grant and I had to turn unit 643 around. We had one hell of a black spot. But that was after the blast. I hope you're not suggesting he took advantage of *that*, because if you are then he had to wait inside, survive a hundred tons of concrete coming down on his head, dig his way out, dust himself off, pick out which units were broken—'

'Okay, okay, I get it. I've already had that conversation with Holbrook. He must have escaped before the explosion and after the last time we saw him on CCTV.'

'That's only two minutes.'

'I know. And the camera coverage was seamless. I'm not arguing, but that's all we have left.' Madsen squeezed his eyes shut, trying to think. 'Look, this might sound ridiculous, but is there any way he could have manipulated a camera? Like to make it transmit different footage while he walked past?'

'Like taping a photo across the lens?' Shari smirked.

'Very funny. I was thinking more along the lines of making a camera stream a recording instead of live vision.'

'No. All city cameras time-stamp and encrypt their footage before transmitting. Even if he did manage it you would see anomalies where cameras overlap. Pedestrians and cars would disappear, light levels and shadows wouldn't synch. You don't need computers to pick that stuff up, it stands out a mile to human eyes. We would have spotted it.'

'Would you check again?'

She shook her head. 'That's a lot of work and it's a dead end. He died in there, Dan.'

'Not according to Steinmann.'

'And I'm telling you, Steinmann got it wrong.'

Exasperated, Madsen turned and made for his car.

'Where are you going?'

'Grant Avenue. Maybe I'll find some inspiration down there.'

Chapter 33

Pastor Luke felt like he had survived a near miss from an artillery shell – winded and bleeding, and somewhat amazed to discover all his limbs were still attached. He slouched in his chair, staring down the well of the building. The floating blue and green ball pulsed. It was half the size it should have been, but it was holding. For the first time since the calamity had unfolded, he was alone.

The replacement G-ring broadcast had been well crafted, a fine balance of anger at the men who had brought shame upon his church, and contrition for having allowed them into it in the first place. The speechwriters had earned their money. He would make sure they got a bonus. The interviews after, however, had been relentless. Excruciating. Delivering his head on a platter again and again. How he'd managed to maintain his composure he would never know. He'd desperately wanted to reach out and slap that smug bitch from NBC right across the mouth.

And every moment in between he had soothed angry members, placated friends and donors of the church, and alternately calmed and cajoled edgy pastors. That son of a bitch Stimson had even gone so far as to question his leadership. The guy ran a tight ship in LA – got the best yields in the country – but that didn't buy permission to run his mouth, and now he knew it.

Very slowly, Luke struggled to his feet and trudged over to a small cupboard in the corner of his office. He withdrew an unopened bottle of Johnnie Walker Blue Label and a crystal glass. He retraced his steps, plonked them down on the conference table and fell back into his oversized chair with a loud *whump*. After a moment he leaned forward, grasped the bottle with one hand and twisted with the other. The seal gave a satisfying crack as it broke. He poured a generous shot and raised the glass to his nose, savouring the aroma. Shutting his eyes, he drained it. Liquid fire descended, bloomed, and radiated outwards.

It was the combination that was so diabolical. The boat mess . . . well, they had dealt with such things before. Pastors were always being tempted by loose women, drug merchants, nasty blackmailing little boys. Their money made them targets. He was painfully aware that the one area where he had not done as good a job as Engels was hiring. A few of his decisions had been too hasty, and he had resigned himself to the occasional clean-up. But five at once! And with *kiddie dolls*, for God's sake! Plus the suicidal maniac wearing a G-ring. Plus that out-of-control agent cuffing pastors in broad daylight. The timing was hideous. An orchestration. Yes, that's what it was, an orchestration. And what an impact! Richard's first estimates had been optimistic: the latest projection was one hundred and seven million in lost earnings and four or five months to get back to pre-crisis revenues. If they had left their filthy images in the bottom of all the collection baskets it couldn't be worse.

Luke poured himself another shot and downed it.

Recovery.

Then payback.

The recalcitrant pastors were history, cut out like a cancer. As for the FBI, Luke allowed himself a grim smile. He would start at the bottom. Buried skeletons, addictions, sexual deviations, rumours. He would hire the best. And they would tap the swollen ranks of embittered ex-cops and asked-to-accept-early-retirement agents. The pleasure would come in revealing the details. Slowly, giving hints about what was about to be exposed. Letting Madsen and the others agonize over when their poison pill would hit the news and bring their careers to an inglorious end. After that, Fillinger . . .

Luke's arms felt heavy. His mind drifted. There was more to do, more broadcasts, more interviews, more everything. But it could wait. For the next hour he would let others do the worrying. It was under control. He let his chin fall forward. It could all wait. Right now he just needed a little . . .

Distant sounds registered. Echoes. *Unimportant. Someone else's problem.*

The sounds became clearer. Closer. A slam. Shouts? Yes, and running.

The door burst open.

Luke blinked. A young staffer from the communications team, cheeks bright red, hands on knees, stood in the doorway gasping. Luke stared in astonishment.

'Excuse me, pastor. I'm so . . . sorry.' The boy fought to get his words out between breaths. 'But there's been . . . another one. Another video.'

'What video?'

'It's worse. Much worse.' The staffer reached over to switch on one of the screens.

Five minutes later a trembling, white-faced Pastor Luke locked his door and placed three calls.

The first was to the church's legal counsel.

The second was to a secretary, instructing him to chase down a quorum of senior pastors for an emergency decision.

The third was to a Learjet halfway between Salt Lake City and San Francisco.

'Richard?' Luke said. 'It's me. Forget everything. This just got a hell of a lot bigger . . . yes, really. When I'm finished you can switch on a screen and see for yourself. Listen to me. It's about survival now. We're going to have to escalate our response *radically.* You're not going to like what I'm going to ask you to do, but I need you to do it anyway. Everything you need will be waiting at the airport . . .'

In Washington, Senator Erol Arbett bunkered in his office. Outside, his secretary could be heard frantically cancelling appointments and fielding incoming calls. Inside, Jet Barnes, Otto Finkeld and Kenny Bosco sat with the senator, watching the screen, transfixed.

Jet Barnes was giving a running commentary punctuated by shrill, uninhibited laughs. 'This is out-bloody-*rageous*! So far we've had a pastor paying not one but two high-class hookers in a hotel, one drunk as a skunk and disgracing himself in a strip joint, and one snorting enough coke to fry his eyeballs. Fuck me, this is the biggest stitch-up I've ever seen!'

Arbett had his head in his hands. He couldn't bear to look.

Otto Finkeld cleared his throat as if trying to remove a particularly unpleasant taste. 'I have to say, these clips were recorded over a long period. Someone has been saving them up. They've chosen to release them exactly when they can do the most damage.'

'Fillinger,' said Kenny Bosco acidly.

'It's a thermonuclear weapon if you ask me,' Jet said. His voice brimmed with admiration.

Kenny glared. Otto snorted. Arbett shook his head in exasperation.

'What I like best are the helpful labels,' Jet continued, oblivious to their hostility. 'None of that "let's mail my secret footage to *60 Minutes* and see what they do with it". Oh, no, this is a master class. Everybody named. Every deviant behaviour dated and placed. It's a bloody *master class!* Uh oh, who's this one?'

Otto sighed. 'Pat Simonsen. Senior pastor for Louisiana. He is – was – well respected.'

'Yeah, like the others. Let's see . . . a motel. Who's that with him? My, my, a very clean-cut young man. In they go. And now that's an inside camera . . . They *are* in a hurry!'

Arbett felt ill. He waved a hand in defeat. 'Enough!'

Otto picked up the remote and killed the screen.

'What's important here,' Arbett said, his voice barely above a whisper, 'is what we are going to do. What's the strategy?' He looked at each of them in turn.

Bosco, red-faced, said nothing. Friday's enthusiastic endorsement of NeChristo neutered anything he had to offer anyway.

Otto took off his glasses and rubbed his eyes. 'Okay, distance and damage control. First we make nice noises to Luke, but privately. We cannot have him saying he was abandoned in his time of need. We need to be positioned far enough from this that it doesn't tarnish you, but not so far that we can't move when NeChristo bounces back—'

Jet cut him off with another high-pitched laugh. 'Jesus, Otto. I really don't think we need bother with all that, do you? It's simple. They're toxic. Radioactive. Get as far away as possible.'

Chapter 34 _____

Still fuming from his reception at Central Station, Madsen stood waiting at the police tape at Grant and Pacific. His cell phone vibrated with incoming messages. Doubtless another fusillade of urgent requests, pointed comments, unsolicited advice. *Give me some peace*, he thought. Angrily, he reached into his pocket and pressed the off switch.

He had already taken a look around the darkened bays in Pacific Garage and, finding nothing, examined the stretch of Grant Avenue leading north, away from the crime scene. Life there was already returning to normal. The debris had been cleared. Store owners were sweeping and cleaning. Workmen crowded the sidewalks, fussing around pallets of replacement windows.

On the other side of the police tape, looking south towards Jackson Street, Grant Avenue was a moonscape punctuated by rubble piles and car wrecks. A crime-lab tent, pristine and white, stood in the centre. Next to it squatted a giant yellow excavator, its belly rumbling. A thin blue haze floated from the dirty exhaust stack.

A bored-looking SFPD officer approached. 'Help you?' he asked. He had to raise his voice a little to be heard over the excavator.

Madsen flashed his badge and asked him to fetch the site supervisor. The cop headed for the white tent.

There was a loud crunch followed by an extended roar. The excavator lifted a bucket of rubble. A few broken bits of plaster fell, making white puffs where they hit the ground. Diesel fumes mingled with the smell of charcoal and grit. The machine swivelled and the bucket descended, depositing its load on a clear patch of ground with an unceremonious rattle. A cluster of crime scene technicians, looking like aliens in dust masks, white coveralls and purple gloves, stepped forward and began sifting.

The officer returned. Accompanying him was the supervisor, a pear-shaped man in a lab coat. The supervisor frowned unhappily behind his safety glasses. His frown deepened when Madsen asked about tunnels. No, they had not seen any. Yes, they would be sure to keep a look out. Yes, he could come onsite, but if he strayed inside any of the zones marked by red tape the supervisor would personally see to it that a load of bricks fell on his head. He muttered something that sounded suspiciously like 'fucking idiot' and stalked back in the direction of the tent.

Madsen ducked under the tape and threaded his way towards the middle of the block. He passed a pile of folded steel – the crushed remains of three, possibly four vehicles that had been parked in the wrong place at the wrong time, now rudely stacked one upon another to make more room. There was a roar, followed by the clank and squeal of heavy metal. Madsen noted the working radius of the excavator and skirted it carefully.

A yawning gap and a Lego-pile of broken slabs were all that was left of the dollhouse. An iron forest of reinforcing rods poked and twisted from the concrete pieces. Long lengths of broken electrical cable looped out and around and in between. Here and there, cleared paths and mounds of neatly sorted debris marked where the rescue units and evidence recovery teams had been. On a whim, Madsen pulled out his HAMDA and switched the sensor array from polygraph to narcotics to explosives. The light glowed bright red. Embedded in the HAMDA's cigar-shaped body was a small rollout screen, three inches square, flexible and transparent, like a sheet of toughened cellophane. He pulled it out. Thin coloured lines crossed horizontally, left to right – except the line labelled D-5, which spiked almost to the top of the scale.

He grunted and put the HAMDA back in his pocket.

Both buildings adjacent to the dollhouse had received heavy damage. The one on the left had its side peeled away from the fourth storey down to the first. Chairs and tables hung precariously. Torn carpet flapped in the breeze. The building to the right had a triangular wedge taken out of the bottom. As the dollhouse collapsed the compression must have built to a point where it exploded sideways as well as forwards, punching a good chunk into the first floor of its neighbour. Across the face of the building a set of rickety iron fire stairs dangled where they had been torn from their mounts. As Madsen traced the metal zigzag upwards, an idea came to him. Every building in the street had an identical arrangement. Suppose backpack man had used the dollhouse fire stairs to get to the roof? He could have crossed to the next building and hunkered down to wait out the blast. In all the confusion he could have picked his moment, descended . . . No. It didn't work. The dollhouse stairs were out front, in plain view. He would have been seen.

Madsen turned to examine the opposite side of the street. The buildings directly across from the dollhouse were a mess of broken windows, chipped and scarred walls, dented signs and dust, but they were structurally intact. His eyes drifted upwards, scanning the sills and ironwork of the upper levels for the two broken city cameras. He found the first. It had a conical dent in the pressed metal casing, smack in the middle of the '4' in '645'. The dent was deep. Whatever made it had likely smashed the insides into spare parts.

There was no sign of camera 644. He knew roughly where to look, but there was nothing but dirty, pockmarked brick. He puzzled over it until he spied a thin metal rod jutting from the wall. The rod was bent forty-five degrees, like a broken arrow. The camera must have been knocked clean off its mount. He strolled along the sidewalk beneath, head down, searching for the casing in the dust.

He was still there ten minutes later, sifting through a mound of gravel with his toe, when someone yelled from behind, 'Agent Madsen, right?'

It was the pear-shaped man in the lab coat. He was sweating, like he had been running.

'That's me,' Madsen said, but the words were lost as the excavator revved its engine. The supervisor cupped a hand behind his ear to indicate he hadn't heard. Madsen leaned in closer. '*Yes, that's me. I'm Madsen.*'

'*Your office has been trying to call you. You need to—*' The rest was drowned in a long, sustained roar as the excavator bucket ascended high in the air.

'*What?*' This time it was Madsen's turn to offer an ear.

'*I said you've got to get down to the airport!*'

Madsen switched on his cell phone and desperately tried to get more information as he drove towards San Francisco International. The request had come direct from DiMatteo. He called her number. No answer. He called her assistant. She confirmed the location was one of the airport hotels – the Chesterton – and reiterated that his ass was needed down there yesterday, but that was it. On impulse he checked his voicemail. Multiple messages, all saying there had been another video. He switched on the car radio . . . and hit information overload.

The new video had hit the media in the last hour. It was long and it was graphic. It contained a bunch of NeChristo pastors in compromising situations. It was dynamite. Fumbling comments offered by NeChristo spokespeople gave the impression of a church in meltdown.

But still nothing on whatever was going down at the airport.

A dozen uniformed officers were standing at the Chesterton's front entrance as Madsen drew up. One stepped forward, examined his badge and pointed. 'Second floor, turn left, all the way to the end.'

Madsen took the stairs to save time. He found another cop at the top, two in the corridor and two more posted outside the door at the end. *Jesus*, he thought, *they got half the department down here.*

His badge was scrutinized again. The cop nodded and opened the door, gesturing for Madsen to enter.

Madsen stepped inside and stopped dead.

It was a conference room, typical for this kind of hotel. A sideboard stacked with glasses at one end, projection facilities at the other, sun-worn drapes across the windows, a long veneer-topped table dividing the room down the middle, chairs along both sides. Standard. Except for the people occupying the chairs.

Facing the door on the left flank was Mary DiMatteo. On the right flank was the potato-faced SFPD chief of police, Bryan O'Halloran. Between them was a shaved head belonging to a man Madsen had only ever seen on the news. Gavin Chang, the mayor's spokesman and right-hand man.

All three stared at Madsen with undisguised hostility.

On the near side of the table sat two men in suits, one wider with silver-flecked hair, the other taller and darker, a tough-looking guy with a flattened nose and a deportment that was all chest and jaw. The man with the silver-flecked hair had removed his suit jacket to reveal a pair of old-fashioned suspenders holding up his trousers. The jacket had been draped over the back of his chair. Neatly centred over the breast pocket was a red and gold pin. A NeChristo pin.

DiMatteo scowled and jerked a thumb over her shoulder to an empty chair.

Madsen made his way over, taking in the other people in the room. Seven or eight assistants. A couple of cops in SFPD uniform. A few others who looked like accountants or lawyers.

DiMatteo turned and whispered, 'If someone asks you a direct question, answer. Otherwise stay out of it.'

'Fine by me. But what the hell is—'

The man with silver-flecked hair cleared his throat. 'For the benefit of the latecomers, my name is Richard Hodge and I am the chief financial officer for the New Christian Organization of

America. I have a few things to say, if you will allow me, on be-half of the church, and with the full authorization of the executive committee.'

Heads nodded solemnly along Madsen's side of the table.

'We believe that our organization has been, and will continue to be, a great force for good. NeChristo has reintroduced Christian values into the lives of millions, offering them comfort, support and a sense of community. We have put faith and stability back into our suburbs. This has been good for the nation and good for the city of San Francisco. Unfortunately . . .' Hodge pursed his lips and tapped the table lightly with his index finger. 'Some very determined people have been trying to destroy us.' The finger extended itself horizontally, first at DiMatteo, then at Chief O'Halloran. 'And some of those people work for you.'

No one moved. DiMatteo was rigid. The back of the chief's neck went bright pink. Madsen could hear his own heartbeat.

Hodge spread his hands wide and looked around. 'This shouldn't *be*. We stand for the same outcomes. We – all of us in this room – are on the same *side*.' Hodge placed both hands on the table in front of him, slowly scanning the assembly from right to left. His tongue flicked out, wetting his lips. 'We specifically re-quested the attendance of Agent Daniel Madsen – is he present?'

A dozen heads turned.

Madsen felt his face burning even as a cold stone grew in the pit of his stomach. He was attending the opening proceedings of his own termination. Like a show trial from the old Soviet Union, everyone was here to vent their spleen over the leaks before send-ing him to Siberia.

'Agent Madsen,' Hodge said. His tone was polite, neutral. 'It will interest you to know that we've searched our member data-bases thoroughly. The man you are after is not and was not, ever, a member of our church. Should you wish to perform your own verification we will of course arrange access to our member rela-tions system for that purpose.'

Madsen blinked, confused.

Hodge snapped his fingers. An assistant with rimless glasses popped the catches on his briefcase and withdrew a bundle of documents, handing them to Hodge. Hodge slid one across to the mayor's man, Chang, another to DiMatteo and another to the chief of police. He kept the fourth for himself. All the documents appeared to be identical.

Madsen's brain flipped like a fish. He had braced for an outburst, accusations, castigations, threats, profanity. Now he was utterly at a loss. Was this the opening salvo of a lawsuit? A claim of damages?

Hodge opened his document at a red tab and addressed Chang. 'You will find here verification of the transfers to a dedicated account.' He flipped to a second tab. 'And here, a legal affirmation that these have been paid out of the holdings of Pastor Luke, myself and the eight other senior partners on the executive committee. Here is the contract ceding control to the city, and here are the conditions under which it can be claimed. They are fairly straightforward. Whoever finds him gets all of it, as long as he is successfully prosecuted. If there are multiple claims, any apportionment will be decided by a panel consisting of one representative each from the mayor's office, the San Francisco Police Department and the US Attorney's office. We don't want any part in the apportionment process.'

Chang picked up his copy and held it over his shoulder. An assistant – Madsen guessed a lawyer – leapt to his feet and took the document to the far end of the room, where he began poring over it, page by page.

There was a long and uncomfortable silence.

Someone passed a folded sheet of notepaper to Chief O'Halloran. He read it and scrunched it up.

The assistant came back and whispered in Chang's ear. Chang grunted. He turned to Hodge and nodded.

DiMatteo looked up from her copy and nodded too.

Hodge raised a questioning eyebrow at Chief O'Halloran.

The chief, still holding the note in his fist, shifted uncomfortably. The folds of his mouth drooped. 'Can I ask when you are planning to announce this?'

Hodge checked his watch. 'The press conference is in five minutes.'

Madsen heard several sharp inhalations. The chief's neck darkened from pink to a rich cherry red. 'This is going to generate an unprecedented amount of interest,' he said evenly. 'I'm not sure if my people are ready. Is there any way we could get you to delay an hour?'

Hodge's nostrils flared and his chin tilted upwards. 'As you will appreciate, due to the actions taken by the authorities represented in this room our church no longer has the luxury of time.' He stood, signalling the meeting was at an end, turned, and made for the door. His assistants fell in behind.

There was a brief chaos as everyone else either rushed to follow or pulled out cell phones and began talking over one another as they tried to relay instructions.

Madsen got to his feet, scratching his head, and found himself breathing expensive aftershave and staring into the flattened nose and squared-off jaw of Hodge's tough-guy colleague, who curled a lip and hissed, 'Just find him. And when you're done we'll have a different kind of meeting.'

Madsen flashed his best I-don't-give-a-shit grin, but it was wasted. The guy had spun on his heel and was already gone.

DiMatteo's rasp came from near his elbow. 'Well, cowboy, you won't have to worry about a shortage of leads now.' She held out her copy of the document. Madsen took it. He glanced down at the cover.

TERMS for transfer of REWARD MONIES
From
THE NEW CHRISTIAN ORGANIZATION OF AMERICA
Into the TRUST of
THE CITY OF SAN FRANCISCO

He inserted his thumb at the first red tab. He read down the page, blinked, then read it again. It had to be a mistake. Perhaps the scandals had affected their sanity.

Shock gave way to a feeling of dread. Up until last night, he had been setting his own agenda. It wasn't getting him anywhere, but at least it was his. From the moment he woke up this morning he had been pushed from one event to another, like he was riding somebody else's train. All day he had been trying to apply the brakes, trying to make sense of where it was going. Now the brakes had been disconnected. He was freewheeling down a hill, a long one, with an enormous hand shoving from behind. What were the words Chief O'Halloran had used a moment ago? *An unprecedented amount of interest*?

Wrong. Dead wrong.

Two hundred million dollars was going to stir up a tsunami.

Chapter 35

As Pastor Richard Hodge spoke into the collected microphones of the press on the first floor of the Chesterton hotel, another broadcast rippled out to G-rings across the United States and beyond. Millions of NeChristo members heard an emotional plea from Pastor Luke. Find this man. Find him and stop a murderer. Find him and restore the reputation of your church. Tell your friends to help. Tell friends of friends.

And when you do find him, call this number.

Recipients who happened to be near a screen tuned it to the NeChristo channel and stared at sinister close-ups of a hooded man in sunglasses as they listened to Luke's words. Others rushed to find a screen as soon as they heard the part about the reward.

By the time the press conference was finished it had achieved saturation coverage on all major news channels and Pastor Luke's plea had been heard in thirty-seven million earpieces, producing the biggest and fastest mobilization of eyes and ears in recorded history.

The tip-offs started coming in.

One hundred every second.

Within minutes all call centres operated by the San Francisco

Police Department and the FBI were swamped. Additional facilities with automated recording banks were hastily requisitioned through the Bureau's criminal justice information services division.

The volume doubled. Then doubled again.

I saw him walking across the parking lot, he's in my hotel, he took my coffee order, he pretends to be a fireman, he's hiding in my basement, he passed me riding across the Brooklyn Bridge on a Harley Davidson and I have the registration number. He is my father, husband, boss, doorman, brother, cousin, friend, teacher, lover . . . The calls came from crackpots, attention seekers, opportunists, jilted wives, ex-girlfriends, disgruntled employees, creditors, revenge seekers, fraudsters and pranksters.

By the end of the first hour, the National Center for Collaborative Crime Detection had redirected ninety trillion bits to thirty-three facilities temporarily requisitioned from police departments, government agencies, universities and telecommunications companies.

Powerful algorithms went to work. They analysed recorded voice patterns for stress, honesty, instability and intoxication. They winnowed, filtered and funnelled while listening at speeds incomprehensible to human ears. And they took what was left and applied a different set of algorithms that parsed sentences and plucked out names, places, nouns and verbs until every building, person, vehicle and thing mentioned in every call was tagged, categorized and indexed.

Thirty-three requisitioned facilities took a data deluge and tamed it into a series of torrents. The torrents were forwarded to the National Crime Information Center in Clarksburg, West Virginia. The NCIC machines cross-matched, compared, correlated, weighed and scored each tag against a thousand state and federal databases.

They began to return a steady trickle of names, each assigned a number between zero and one – a *p-score* – where a higher score meant a higher probability that this was the bad guy.

The names and scores pulsed over the networks, down optical pipes, and back to Central Station.

Shari Sanayei spent the afternoon shuttling between supervising her people downstairs and watching the show in the operations room. Madsen, Holbrook and a half-dozen inspectors greeted the names rolling in with much head-shaking and little action. P-scores over 0.3 were worth investigating. All the names coming in, notwithstanding the NCIC filters, were scoring between 0.1 and 0.2. That was the problem with rewards. They generated so many worthless leads that the real ones got lost. The bigger the reward, the more leads generated.

White noise.

Name number four hundred and seventy-two drew a muted cheer. The p-score was 0.35, the location Atlanta. There was a brief flurry of activity as inspectors pored over case notes, looking for any references or links to that city. Head-shakes all round. Holbrook called Atlanta PD and asked for priority video surveillance of the subject. He said a reference file was on its way so they could match the subject's face with the guy they were looking for. Atlanta PD promised to slot it into their programme.

No one got too excited.

Ten minutes later they got one in Vancouver. A call was placed to the Royal Canadian Mounted Police.

It continued. Endless lists of low-scoring names. A request to investigate was initiated every ten or twenty minutes. Always routine, always half-hearted, dampened by the unspoken knowledge that it was almost not worth doing at all. Occasionally a lead drifted in from somewhere outside North America and Madsen routed a request via the State Department.

There was a surge of energy when someone in Brooklyn, New York, scored a 0.58. More than a dozen people in the immediate neighbourhood had fingered the guy. A conference call was convened with NYPD and the Bureau office at 26 Federal Plaza. They promised to check it out immediately.

They waited.

Terse reports began coming back. Not the guy . . . No match . . . Negative . . .

New York sent a message. 'Close surveillance complete. Subject left building in a vehicle. We conducted a car stop. Interesting character, but not yours.'

Pizzas were ordered. Delivered. Eaten.

Afternoon became evening.

A few minutes before nine, Shari sat against the wall in the operations room. Empty pizza boxes and coffee cups and soda cans littered the desks. Holbrook was slouched in a chair with his feet up, staring at the ceiling. Two of the inspectors played cards. Only one, chin propped on a fist, bothered to watch the names scrolling steadily up a screen. Madsen lay in a corner with his eyes closed and his jacket rolled up under his head. Captain McAlister was no longer stopping by for updates. Perhaps he had gone home. The team had actioned twenty-six names. Twenty-six fingered by multiple callers who believed what they were saying. Twenty-six from thousands, twenty-six where circumstances, locations, descriptions and records fit enough patterns and triggered enough flags to make the radar.

Twenty-six time wasters.

The place was silent. Dead.

Shari rubbed her eyes and headed downstairs. Angie Mertz would soon be taking over the surveillance night shift. She was learning the ropes as duty officer and Shari wanted to make sure she got a decent handover. Not that Angie needed much help. She was sharp, that one, and ambitious. The handover was important to reinforce that she still had more to learn and to remind her not to act above her pay grade: assumptions were dangerous, mistakes easily made.

Shari ducked her head around the door. The main console was unoccupied. Angie hadn't arrived yet. It was another cool night and the street criminals were staying in. The operators were doing routine sweeps, looking bored. She decided to change and wait for Angie in her civvies.

Halfway to the locker room she passed the notice board. Four fresh sheets of paper had been tacked up. Cautiously, she stopped to look. The first sheet was a memo, signed by the captain, announcing that representatives of the FBI's Office of Professional Integrity were arriving in the morning. *Polygraph interviews will begin immediately. To minimize disruption, testing will be spread over three days. Using the shift roster, station personnel have been divided up accordingly. Please check the lists and ensure you make yourself available.*

The second, third and fourth sheets were lists headed Monday, Tuesday and Wednesday. Under Monday, three names from the end, her finger stopped under Sgt S. Sanayei.

She stopped breathing.

Tomorrow.

Nothing would go wrong, Madsen had said. What they don't know they can't ask. Perfectly logical, as if that was all there was to it. But what if, instead of asking about *leaking*, they used words like *inappropriate access*, or *tampering*? Would they pick up her lies then? And Yolanda was on the same list, five names above. How much had she seen? What would she say in her interview? Shari continued on down the corridor. She entered the women's locker room but strode straight through, into the washroom. She barely had time to lock the stall door and face the bowl before a stream of pepperoni-laced vomit forced its way up and out. She doubled over and retched again. She waited for a third convulsion, but it never came. Wiping her mouth, she flushed away the evidence, unlocked the stall, and washed her hands.

A commotion erupted overhead.

Shari dashed back upstairs to find the operations room thrumming with activity. Everyone was talking and jostling to get a look at the screen. Someone yelled for quiet. The inspector at the screen was typing rapidly while Holbrook stood over him.

'Give me that location again,' Holbrook said.

'Place called Little Rapids, Oregon. Just the other side of the state border.'

'Never heard of it.'

'Seems to be a mountain community. Tiny. No cameras, no local police presence.'

'How far?'

'Wait . . . four hundred miles north-east of here.'

Shari pushed closer. She stood on tiptoes but still could not see the details. Madsen was alongside. She stole a glance at him. His eyes were unblinking, unwavering, utterly focused. She whispered, 'Good candidate?'

'Gold.'

'What was his score?'

'Point nine five.'

She closed her eyes. She wondered if she would recognize the guy when she saw him, whether he was among the thousands of faces she had studied on her cameras over the previous four days. *When we have you*, she thought, *then it's finished. I can stop. I can explain everything.*

The original call recordings were forwarded through, and everyone crowded around to listen.

No less than fourteen of the seventeen residents of Little Rapids had fingered the guy. All were credible. All were consistent. They bubbled with excitement. He was a loner. He was volatile. He lived outside the community, ten miles further on, in the wilderness. They said his name was Karl Morris, but the database scans had already flagged that as an alias. They described his recent activities.

The listeners raised eyebrows and nodded to one another. They were in no doubt.

A multi-state, multi-jurisdictional, multi-agency conference call was set up.

Problems were discussed. There were plenty. Remote locale, rugged topography, dangerous target, no law enforcement presence. It had to be a tactical team, it had to be a good one, and it had to fly in. Turf issues were raised, then squashed. A consensus was reached. The FBI would handle the operation. It had a team standing by.

Madsen placed the call to the SWAT team commander. Midway through the conversation Shari heard his voice take on added sharpness.

'Zetter,' he said. 'This time I'm coming along for the ride.'

Monday

Chapter 36

A few minutes after midnight Madsen clambered aboard a Euro-copter AS350 and wedged himself into the crowded compartment. The pilot twisted around briefly to check on his passengers, then gripped the collective in his left hand and eased it upwards, increasing the pitch of the rotor blades. The engine note deepened as the blades clawed at the air. Slowly, the skids wobbled free. The nose dipped and Madsen caught sight of the navigation lights of the sister machine, already airborne and gaining altitude. Then the chopper cleared the Phillip Burton building, gathered speed and clattered northwards through a moonlit sky.

Two and a half hours later the helicopters were across the Oregon border and touching down at a remote crossroads. The spot was one of the few locations in the area flat enough to make a landing.

Two sets of high beams flashed. A pair of SUVs wearing the livery of the county sheriff's department rolled forward. Men and equipment began to transfer across even before the blades had stopped turning.

After a long, winding ascent the convoy drew into Little Rapids. It was dark and still. The tiny cluster of dwellings had once served as a supply post for gold miners but was now just another waypoint to nowhere, eking out an existence from the few adventurous campers and hunters who came through each summer.

The headlights picked up a pale figure coming towards them: Anna-Lee James, the owner of the general store. The sheriff had called ahead and asked if she would act as a guide.

They continued into the pine forest, bumping over bigger potholes and climbing steeper and narrower trails.

Madsen was squashed and uncomfortable. He sat in the back of the lead vehicle with the generously proportioned Anna-Lee on one side and a wide-shouldered Rodriguez on the other. Zetter and the sheriff rode in front. Two more SWAT operators were squeezed behind, in the cargo tray. Equipment was shoved wherever it fit, which meant Madsen had to contend with a stash of body armour under his feet and a gun case across his knees.

Anna-Lee spent five per cent of her time navigating and the rest excitedly retelling the story she had already told in her call to the hotline.

'Karl's a real goddamn – whatcha call it – recluse. Everyone knows everything around here, but you don't ask him no personal questions if you don't want aggravation. Howdy and what'll it be today maybe. Any more and you'll get your head bit off. Know what I'm sayin'? Only two things get him talking, and that's God 'n' Jesus. But he don't talk with you, he talks *at* you, you know? Gets all fired up 'n' quotes from the gospels. Always the same kind of quotin' too, the *angry* kind. An eye for an eye and such. The whole world is sinners as far as he sees it. Especially in big cities. These mountains to him are kinda like a shield, you know. To stop him being infected by city folks. Hell! If he knew half the goings-on behind closed doors in Lil' Rapids he'd be up and moving to Alaska!' She laughed, her eyes bright with excitement.

'Tell us about the threats,' Madsen said. The SUV was negotiating a sharp incline and he had to speak up to make himself heard above the whine of the transmission.

'Karl's been comin' by for supplies going on for two years. One visit a month, give or take. You hear that big old truck before you see it. He stops, gets what he gets, goes across to Ted's for a drink, then back to the hills. Always the same, you know? Two weeks ago he comes by and I got a screen blaring in the store, and it's showing them dollhouses and protests and such, and he goes crazy. Cussin' like it's the end of the world.' She shook her head. 'So this time he goes over and starts drinkin' and drinkin' and before you know it he's preaching to them boys in the bar. Oh boy, the liquor fired him up some. He was shouting. He said people who went into them dollhouses were the worst kind of sinners. When he stomped out of there he was drunker and meaner than I ever saw him. That's how I recognized his picture on the news, didya know that? He was all so twisted-up serious behind them sunglasses. He had the exact same look that day, when he got in his truck.'

Karl's notion of sinning, Madsen mused, apparently didn't extend to driving under the influence.

'And the next time, the *last* time I seen Karl, he was flyin' up the mountain. People drive slowly round here, you know, so you notice. He didn't stop. That truck came in all banging and popping, him all big eyes and hunched over the wheel, and kept right on going, through and out.'

'And that was Thursday,' Madsen said.

'That's right! How did you know? Thursday, round five.'

Five. Which was twenty-five hours and sixteen minutes after the bombing. Which was easily enough time to get out of San Francisco and make his way back to his mountain sanctuary with no police and no cameras and no neighbours prying into his business. Not until two hundred million in cash was waved around. Then his business became everybody's business.

A mile and a half out they slowed to reduce the noise.

At one mile they stopped.

The SUVs were parked side by side, blocking the trail. The SWAT team dismounted. They murmured softly to one another as they organized equipment and unpacked weapons in the darkness. The mountain air was as cold as it was still. Madsen buttoned his jacket. He found a windbreaker and zipped it over the top, then clipped a ballistic vest over the windbreaker. He checked access to his Beretta. It would take effort to dig it out, but with all the artillery the others carried, he was unlikely to need it in a hurry. And it would be no use at all if he froze to death. He helped himself to a pair of night-vision goggles and a radio pack.

Zetter split his men into two groups. He placed Rodriguez in charge of one and took the other himself. Madsen tacked himself onto the end of Zetter's section. Leaving Anna-Lee and the sheriff's men with the vehicles, they plunged into the forest.

Zetter navigated by GPS, taking a wide arc to flank the objective. His section trailed behind in single file, five or six paces between each man. No one spoke. Communication was via hand signals. Madsen brought up the rear. It was slow going. Even with night-vision goggles he found it hard not to trip or lose his footing. He concentrated hard, studying shapes and textures and trying to distinguish between rocks and hollows and shadows and fallen branches in the weird green landscape. Spraining an ankle would be bad, making noise even worse.

The closer they got, the slower they moved.

The last hundred yards were the most difficult. They crept then crawled, a few inches at a time, towards positions pointed out by Zetter. By the time Madsen was in place, the first grey smudges were beginning to appear against the sky.

Then he lay still, waiting for the dawn.

Chapter 37

'Five minutes.'

'Roger that.'

Madsen jumped at the crackle. He had been listening to the heavy stillness of the forest for so long that he'd forgotten all about the radio. He glanced around, alarmed, to see who else had heard. But of course no one had. The offending speaker was an inch across and secured tightly against his right ear by an elastic headband. Even someone lying alongside couldn't have heard. Not unless they were wearing an earpiece of their own. He turned the volume down a notch anyway.

Madsen snuggled down lower, inhaling dampness and the smell of pine needles. A mosquito landed near his right eye. He blinked it away. They had been coming for twenty minutes and he could feel lumps rising on his neck and hands. Worst was the bug that had discovered an opening in his windbreaker and was crawling slowly down his back. He longed to roll over and grind it out of its miserable existence.

Through his binoculars he zeroed in on the cabin, a ghostly apparition emerging in the dawn. A wisp of smoke rose from the chimney and hung there, held close by the heavy air. A woodsman's hideaway, all rough-hewn logs and handmade fittings. On one side was a pick-up, once red, now a battered patchwork of rust and primer. Stacked against the other side was a woodpile almost as tall as the hut itself. And propped against that was an axe. A large one. Madsen's eyes lingered on it. In truth it was the least of their concerns – any man living this deep in the woods had to have guns. But it was still a damn big axe.

'Two minutes everyone. Two minutes.'

Through the canopy above, distant granite slopes turned gold where the first rays skimmed the mountain peaks.

Madsen glanced to his right. Huddled in the foliage, invisible to anyone more than a few yards away, a black helmet pressed against a rubber eyepiece. A tiny butterfly flitted from the undergrowth and oscillated gently upwards, past the helmet. It hovered for a few seconds, as if sniffing the air currents, before meandering away in the direction of the cabin. In seconds it was lost in the shadows.

'Spyfly on the way.'

Propelled by wings only half an inch long, the Spyfly made less noise than a bumble bee. It would cover the distance to the cabin in less than a minute. Its operator would coax it to the top of the wall and land it under the eaves, where it would find a gap before activating its payload: a twenty-milligram high-definition camera. The operator would then be able to call the target's position to the rest of the team.

The seconds seemed to drag, playing on Madsen's nerves. There were a dozen ways for this kind of operation to go wrong. If the guy had installed sensors or tripwires, or was even especially sensitive to the sounds of the forest, he might have clocked them already. The first they would know about it would be the crack of gunfire and bullets snicking through trees. There would be urgent calls as one man fell, then another, bodies convulsing and bouncing as bullets slammed into them, followed by the deafening roar as Zetter's men cut loose, chewing the cabin into a storm of woodchips . . .

'Spyfly twenty seconds.'

Slowly and carefully, Madsen worked his fingers under the

ballistic vest and his jacket and withdrew his Beretta. He placed it on the grass in front of his chin.

'Stand by, stand by.'

'WHO'S THERE!' A voice, deep and angry, boomed across the clearing.

Madsen's eyes snapped to the binoculars, scanning for movement. The window! He could see a tiny black slit. Was he imagining it? No, it hadn't been there a second ago. The dirty yellow curtains were disturbed.

'I know somebody's out there. I got a gun. Come on and show yourself!'

A crackle came through Madsen's earpiece. 'Okay, keep cool, hold position. Everybody take a breath. No firing unless lives are directly threatened.' Zetter sounded calm, his voice soothing, but Madsen knew he would be fuming about being compromised.

Zetter's voice came again, this time through a megaphone. 'Karl, this is the FBI. Your cabin is surrounded by armed agents. We need you to come out. Put your weapon down and come out with your hands where we can see them.'

Silence. Maybe, hopefully, the guy was white with fear, having half-expected his challenge to elicit nothing more than a deer wandering from the forest. Or maybe he was right now propping assault weapons under the window. Or snapping a magazine full of .50-calibre armour-piercing rounds into the receiver of a Barrett sniper rifle.

'Spyfly. We got a negative on the entry. Repeat, spyfly is negative. No eyes on.'

Shit.

The megaphone squawked into life. 'Karl, you need to follow my instructions, and you need to do it now. I repeat, put down your weapon and come out with your hands on your head.'

Madsen watched, his eyes riveted to the curtains. Fuck. The worst scenario was having to go in and get them. Stun grenades were all well and good, but nobody wanted to be first through the door when you didn't know what was on the other side. Odds on this guy was already a multiple murderer. Even if he wasn't, unstable people did irrational things when cornered, and if Anna-Lee James and the good folks of Little Rapids had made one thing clear, it was that Karl was about as stable as a one-bladed helicopter.

Madsen pressed his chest into the pine needles and braced himself for world war three.

The door cracked. An inch, no more.

Madsen didn't dare breathe. He could feel rather than see Karl's right eye squinting out at him from the darkness. In his mind's eye he could see the barrel settle, the crosshairs brushing the top of his skull, the finger caressing the finely cut grooves on the trigger face, taking up the slack, squeezing . . . His scalp tingled. Every follicle seemed to rise until it was standing taut. Sweat stung his eyes. The lenses on his binoculars began to fog.

'West two. I have eyes on. He's at the door.'

'West one. I have eyes on.'

'Alpha leader to West two, keep calling it how you see it. North one and two, stand by to move on my—'

The door swung open. Wide. A shape crouched in the darkness. The dull glint of metal.

Voices exploded over the radio.

'Shit. Gun, gun, gun!'

'West two. I see him, looks like a rifle.'

'Roger that.'

'West two. I have a clear shot, permission to fire?'

'Denied. Hold fire, hold fire!'

'I'M COMING OUT!'

Fuck. Coming out how? Walking, running, screaming, firing from the hip, how? More detail please. Madsen didn't blink. He saw a foot extend slowly out of the darkness, descend, and touch the ground with infinite care, as if it might trigger a mine. He could make out the dim shape of the figure, then the rifle cradled in the arms. Long-barrelled, wooden stock, box mag. An M14. Old, heavy. And lethal. Twenty rounds of .308 Winchester ready to be delivered with twice the punch of an M16.

'West one. I have a clear shot.'

'Roger, West one. Hold fire.'

The megaphone rang out. 'Karl, we need you to put that weapon on the ground. Right. Now!'

The figure took another cautious step. For the first time Madsen had a view of the face through his binoculars. The jawline was smudged by a three-day beard, but it fit. So did everything else: shoulders, height, hair – they all fit. The eyes bulged wide, white showing above the irises. His mouth and nostrils twitched. Stress. Some maxed-out synapses in there.

'Alpha leader to North one and two, stand by to move.'

The figure shuddered, then turned slowly, scanning the forest, looking for signs of his tormentors. He stopped. He was staring directly at Madsen. He uncradled the M14.

Madsen held his breath.

'North one and two. Moving.' On the far side of the cabin Madsen could see black creatures in body armour moving silently out of the woods.

The figure bent, knelt. Very slowly, he extended the rifle in front of his body, then lowered it to the ground.

'West two. Gun is down, gun is down.'

'Go go GO!'

The clearing exploded with running men. The figure, still down on one knee, was hit from behind, slamming the breath from his body and catapulting him face down into the dirt. Bodies piled on top. Two men, MP5s extended at the shoulder, dodged past the melee and took up positions on either side of the doorway.

Madsen got up and ran, Beretta in hand, arms and legs pumping.

By the time he crossed the clearing, operators were already leaving the cabin shouting 'clear' and the man out front had been zip-tied into submission.

Madsen stepped cautiously into the cabin. The interior was gloomy and smelled heavily of wood smoke. As his eyes adjusted he saw it was even more basic than he had anticipated. A hand-made bed frame with a torn mattress and jumble of discarded blankets. A table and chair. A pot-belly stove, cast-iron and black with soot. A few pans. Tins and jars. And books. Lots of books. They lined sagging planks fastened along the walls. Piles were stacked in the corners and under the furniture. They spilled from the table.

Madsen walked along one of the shelves, scanning the titles. *God Forgotten: the Fight to Restore Faith in Our Time*, *The Art of Protest*, *Unleash the People!*, *The New Survivalist's Field Manual*, *Church and State in America*, *Earth Discipline* . . . Religion, politics, activism, philosophy, more religion. And notebooks. Soft exercise books of the kind used by elementary school students. Easily a hundred, all squashed up together. Madsen selected one at random. Like all the others it had been carefully covered in brown paper. There was no title, only two six-digit numbers neatly inked down the spine. Dates. Start date at the top. Finish date at the bottom. He leafed through the pages. Every inch was jammed with dense handwriting. There were no margins. The text ran to the top, bottom and edges. Even the breaks between paragraphs contained tiny sentences in different coloured ink, as if the writer had felt compelled to go back and append thoughts and ideas that came later. Tiny headings, in printed capitals and double underlined, poked through the packed rows of letters. It appeared to be a long, rambling essay on the nature of freedom.

Madsen replaced the notebook and opened another. This one contained detailed descriptions of sins and transgressions committed by the current federal administration. The unbroken sequence of paragraphs continued on for fifty pages.

A hand slapped him on the shoulder. 'Well, Dan, how does it feel?'

It was Zetter, weapon slung, helmet off, grinning from ear to ear. The SWAT leader took Madsen's hand, opened it, and dropped something metallic into his palm. 'It took 'em eighteen years to get the Unabomber,' he said. 'You got your guy in five days.'

Madsen looked down at the object in his hand. It was a G-ring.

Chapter 38

'You're not under arrest,' Madsen said, dragging an old storage chest over to use as a makeshift seat. 'The hand restraints are temporary, for your safety and mine.'

The cabin had been declared safe and the man sat at the small, square table in the centre, avoiding eye contact. He was barefoot and bare-chested, average height, average size. His hands were zip-tied behind his back. There was dirt down the side of his face. More flecks speckled his hair and beard. He appeared to be still in shock.

He said nothing.

'You're an intelligent man,' Madsen said, gesturing towards the bookshelves. 'You must have read and written more than most college professors. I know the last thing on earth a smart guy like you wants is to have a conversation with a guy like me, but I need to point out that it is entirely in your interest.' He pointed to where the HAMDA lay on the table. It had yet to be switched on. 'That thing is your friend. It'll save you a lot of trouble. Answer a few questions and we can clear everything up, right here.'

The only reaction was a hate-filled glare directed at the cigar-shaped cylinder.

'Shall we start with your name? We know it isn't Karl.'

No response.

'The photos and fingerprints will ID you anyway. So why not just tell me?'

More silence.

'Take your time.' Madsen scooped up the HAMDA and slipped it into his pocket. He stepped outside and the SWAT operator pulling security moved into the doorway to keep an eye on things. The SUVs had been brought up and flanked both sides of the clearing. Black-clad men, now free from operational constraints, swapped jokes and laughed loudly as they squared away their gear. Others lounged on the ground with their shirts off, catching the sun. Zetter sat against the woodpile with his MP5 across his knees. His helmet was on the ground next to him, and next to that was a laptop, a tiny model encased in shock-absorbing rubber. It was plugged into a sat-com unit.

'Anything?' Madsen asked.

Zetter shook his head. 'Link must be slow.'

Madsen went over to the sheriff's vehicle. There was a thermos on the front passenger seat. He unscrewed the cap and poured what was left of the contents into a plastic mug. No steam rose from the brown liquid, but the coffee aroma was still strong. He placed the mug in a centre-console cup holder and went around to the back compartment where he rummaged in boxes until he salvaged a chocolate bar. He pocketed the chocolate, retrieved the mug, and headed back towards the cabin.

Zetter had unplugged the laptop and was holding it up. 'We got it.'

Madsen nodded. He took the laptop and went inside.

The man hadn't moved an inch. Madsen placed the laptop and mug on the table and resumed his seat on the storage chest. 'Coffee?'

A glance at the mug.

Madsen took that as a yes. He held the mug up to the guy's lips. 'It's lukewarm, sorry. Better than nothing.'

A tentative sip.

'Chocolate?'

Head-shake.

Madsen retrieved the bar from his pocket, tore the top off the wrapper and held it up. 'Sure?'

No response.

Madsen nodded. He took a bite himself, adjusted the screen on the laptop and began to read. After a moment he turned back and smiled. 'Carroll James Mitnick, huh?'

A flicker. Annoyance.

'I don't blame you for switching. Not that it's a bad name, but Carroll doesn't quite fit the tough mountain man image, does it? Let's see . . .' Madsen switched his attention back to the screen and scrolled down. 'Traffic violations, public nuisance, wilful damage to public property, assault, resisting arrest, multiple counts of everything . . . most of it associated with protests and marches and rallies . . . I'd say you've got a few anger management issues there, wouldn't you? And this is just what we have under your real name. Nothing under Karl Morris. Nothing at all this year. You've been behaving yourself, staying quiet. Storing your anger up, perhaps? Maybe channelling it towards something bigger in, say . . . downtown San Francisco?'

Silence.

'I'm betting when we do a camera search, a really big camera search, we're going to find your face turning up outside a whole bunch of dollhouses. Am I right?'

Tiny eye movements. He was listening. And thinking.

Madsen reached into his pocket and withdrew the HAMDA for a second time. He placed it in the centre of the table. Tapping the steel cylinder he leaned in close, trying to make eye contact. 'This thing will clear you, Mitnick. Clear up everything, right now. You can go back to your breakfast and hunting and whatever else it is you do up here, and we'll saddle up and leave you in peace. Otherwise I have no choice. I have to arrest you and take you back. God knows, cities aren't your favourite places.'

Mitnick switched his gaze upwards, to the kerosene lantern hanging in the centre of the cabin.

Madsen waited, his face a picture of benign patience. A minute ticked past. Then another.

'So. What'll it be?'

Nothing.

Madsen sighed. He hadn't really expected any different. When you cornered real perpetrators they never talked. Why would they when they knew they'd be hanged by their words? When you finally got your man you always had to do it the long way. Arrest, attorneys, a cell to soften them up, then confront them with evidence, convince them there was no hope, no way out, ratchet up the pressure . . .

A shuffle came from the doorway. It was Zetter, waiting with his arms folded, one eyebrow raised in enquiry. Madsen nodded. Might as well get moving.

A mutter. So unexpected and low that for a second Madsen thought he imagined it.

'Did you say something?'

Mitnick looked him dead in the eye. 'I said, "Okay".'

It took a few seconds for Madsen to get over his surprise. Then he offered up a warm smile, reached over to the HAMDA and flicked it on. The green light winked. 'We'll start with where you were last Wednesday, but before that we need to run through a couple of baseline questions . . .'

Chapter 39

Just south of the equator, in the middle of the Pacific Ocean, Nathaniel Addisson, the US chargé d'affaires for Samoa, took a sip of iced tea and frowned. His house was on a hill overlooking the nation's tiny capital, Apia, and he was standing on the verandah, watching the dawn. Below, the Catholic church, the government building and Aggie Grey's hotel resembled white conning towers poking through the sea of nodding palms. In the harbour beyond, a handful of rust-streaked vessels bobbed in the freshening breeze. Out over the Pacific, clouds gathered.

The view, Addisson was fond of saying, was one of the two best perks of the posting. The other was that nothing happened. Not unless you counted dealing with the occasional lost passport or playing mediator when some idiot tourist ran over a pig. And that was just fine. At forty-nine, further efforts to climb the greasy pole amounted to so much wasted energy, and this was as good a place as any to sit out the final years of his career. A small staff handled the day-to-day work, freeing him to pursue his principal hobbies of retirement planning and drinking; when he wasn't receiving trade delegations or attending cocktail parties he racked up gin and tonics with the British consul down the road. His wife socialized with the other expat wives. His children, both attending universities stateside, flew in on their vacations and seemed to enjoy having the Pacific as their playground. The days passed with little asked and little given.

Yesterday's call, however, had broken the routine.

The State Department bureaucrat was insistent. Multiple tip-offs, he explained, all pointing to a mysterious American in a remote spot on Savai'i island. Could Addisson liaise with the authorities to arrange an immediate investigation? *Immediate!* The poor fellow clearly knew nothing about the concept of 'island time', nor the state of your average Pacific police service. Addisson was across the news reports coming out of the States, and highly sceptical. Why Samoa? It was a joke. Or some arrogant tourist had upset the locals and earned a bit of payback. Not worth the fuss. But the bureaucrat wouldn't be swayed, and in the end Addisson had promised to do his best.

When he called the chief of police, with whom he was on friendly terms, peals of laughter rippled back down the line. As promised, Addisson tried to convey the gravity of the matter. After a conversation punctuated by ribald comments and puns he managed to convince the chief that it might even be fun, especially if he came along. They would do it first thing in the morning.

Now, as he waited for the chief's driver, sipping tea and watching the gathering clouds, he wondered if volunteering to go might have been rash. Sloshing about in a tropical downpour wasn't his idea of fun.

He was about to call to postpone when a black-and-white Nissan pulled into his driveway. The driver sounded two taps on the horn.

The chief was waiting at the wharf with a crushing handshake and a twinkle in his eye. Beside him, a police launch bumped and burbled against the tyres lining the edge of the jetty. They boarded, along with half a dozen officers. As they cast off and butted out through the chop, Addisson noticed that two of the men had shotguns. The shotguns looked brand-new, like this was the first excuse they'd had to take them out of the armoury.

The launch made short work of the crossing, but the uneven pitching still made it a relief when the volcanic peaks of Savai'i finally rose above the bow. The instant they nudged the wharf, Addisson grasped the ladder and climbed happily onto dry land, wobbling unsteadily over to a public bench to recover. The chief and his men ambled over and joined him. Plenty of banter and good-natured ribbing followed, and Addisson found himself laughing. The venture was ridiculous. He was ridiculous. It was going to make a terrific after-dinner story at the British consulate.

Fifteen minutes later, a battered Toyota pick-up with a crew cab and an open cargo tray pulled up. The driver exchanged cheerful handshakes with the visitors. They piled in. For the next forty-five minutes they wound their way along the coast road, passing through village after village. White-tipped waves danced on the right. To the left, steep slopes covered in rainforest soared six thousand feet into a woollen blanket of cumulus.

They swung away from the coast. The dark hues of the ocean receded behind them, making way for a dozen additional shades of green. The occasional vegetable plots became less frequent, then disappeared, leaving only the soft shadowy drapery of forest. The dense grey clouds swirled closer.

The first spats of rain hit the windscreen.

In seconds the drops had fattened and were beating a steady tattoo on the Toyota's roof. The wipers thumped and squeaked. Addisson felt relieved to be inside the cab. The three men stuck in the cargo tray were holding a sheet of flapping canvas over their heads.

The drumming escalated to a deafening roar as they turned onto a gravel track, bouncing and splashing through the potholes.

The driver rounded a sharp bend in the track and suddenly braked. They had arrived at a house. Rivers sluiced down the windscreen, but Addison could see enough to make out a simple two-storey residence with whitewashed walls and a pair of columns flanking the entrance. Ghostly pillars of steam hissed off concrete as heat found release in the downpour.

The men piled out. All except Addisson who, with one eye on the torrents of water, was searching the cab for an umbrella.

The chief of police marched up to the door and thumped it, the noise of fist against wood lost in the roar of rain. He waited, then did it again. He called over one of his bigger officers and pointed. The officer gathered himself and threw a shoulder into the door. It must have been solid because he bounced off. He tried the handle. It opened. The chief doubled over with laughter.

They went inside.

Addisson gave up on the umbrella; being left alone was worse than getting wet. He opened the door of the Toyota and scrambled out. Holding his jacket over his head, he splashed the short distance to the house, shook as much water off as he could, and stepped inside.

The interior was dark. Shutters were closed over all the windows. The rain was muted to a muffled thrumming, high overhead. It took a second for Addisson to register that the expensively decorated room he stood in had been trashed. Upturned tables and chairs lay everywhere. Shards of smashed porcelain littered the floor. Splintered frames and torn canvases were all that was left of paintings torn from walls. Someone must have taken their time to go around methodically smashing things. Or maybe there had been a fight. A protracted, desperate fight. An icy feeling crept up Addisson's back. This was no longer a joke.

The chief and his men were no longer laughing.

The men fanned out. Addisson heard the clump of boots as they moved from room to room. The chief bent, grim-faced, to examine what appeared to be a brown stain splashed across the wall. One of the men reported back. More chaos and broken furniture in the other rooms. No sign of anyone, American or otherwise.

A slam. Someone going out the back door.

From behind the house came a shout, followed by a long, high-pitched squeal.

The chief and his men rushed towards the sound. Addison followed, not really wanting to see, but not wanting to be left alone with the brown stain on the wall. He passed through a kitchen, a door, and onto a rear patio. The policemen had gathered in a huddle at the far end of the back garden, where the lawn ended and the rainforest began. They were staring at something on the ground.

The downpour was easing to a steady patter. Soon it would stop, just as suddenly as it had started, and the sun would cut through the clouds and begin turning it to steam again. Tentatively, Addisson stepped from the cover of the patio and moved closer.

He saw the feet first. Ice-white with garish purpling along the toes. Then the shorts. Black. Or navy. It was hard to tell; they were saturated and streaked with mud. The shorts were bunched around the corpse's ankles. *A dead man can't hurt me*, Addisson told himself, and it helped. His fear ebbed. A conflicting mixture of revulsion and morbid curiosity took its place. The rain forgotten, he pushed in closer.

The chief stared at him thoughtfully, then shrugged and stepped aside.

The body lay face down on the waterlogged lawn. Apart from the shorts, it was naked. The head was turned to the side. The torso was bloated, the flesh of the wet, bare buttocks almost translucent. Thin stripes of grass shone vivid green against alabaster skin. The mud streaks and grass seemed to indicate the body had been dragged across the lawn to its present position.

Then he noticed the wounds.

The arms and legs were covered in bites. The flesh was torn roughly, in some places to the bone. Water had pooled in the cavities and dripped steadily from flaccid strips of hanging skin.

Addisson leaned over to see the face.

He reeled back, feeling his knees go to jelly. It was all he could do not to sit down right there in the mud. Half the face was missing. Empty ragged holes stared where there should have been eyes. The lower jaw was a hideous mass of gristle.

Addisson looked around, eyes questioning.

One of the men cocked his head to the side. Addisson looked.

Two pigs, fat and brown and bristling, hovered nearby, resentfully eyeing the intruders who had so rudely interrupted their meal. The nearest one opened its mouth and emitted a long, piercing squeal.

Chapter 40

Wind and turbine noise assaulted Madsen's ears and drowned out all conversation, which was just as well, because he didn't feel like talking. He glanced at the SWAT guys sitting opposite. They were bare-headed and grim-faced, each seemingly lost in his thoughts. They had thrust themselves into a highly charged situation and come out the other end without receiving – or giving – so much as a scratch. In all respects an outstanding job. They should have been like footballers after a hard-fought game – aching muscles, a few bruises, but otherwise all high-fives and basking in the warm glow of victory. Instead, they stared out at the passing landscape and ignored one another.

The rooftops of San Francisco office blocks slid past the plexiglass window, aligning and realigning in a shifting chequerboard of grey squares. The pitch deepened and Madsen's stomach floated up under his ribcage. The chopper settled. There was a lurch and a bump. He popped the door and, two hours after leaving Little Rapids, stepped down onto the roof of the Phillip Burton building. The SWAT team began unloading. He left them to it and headed down to the thirteenth floor, dreading what was coming.

He found DiMatteo on a call, looking agitated. No doubt she had been fielding them all night. First she would have asked for patience. Nothing to report, she would have said. No sense getting excited. Later she would have fed them tidbits to keep them happy. The team is in position. The target is at home and it's looking good. The raid is underway. By now the mother of all shit storms would be bouncing back and forth over the phone lines.

She hung up. 'Where is he?'

'Little Rapids.'

'You didn't bring him in?'

'He didn't do it.'

'He's a *nut*, for Chrissakes!' Spittle flew from her lips, sending an involuntary jerk through Madsen. 'A dozen witnesses saw him threatening to do something about the dollhouses. He came out at you with a gun. You should've had him for resisting arrest—'

'He didn't resist. He did as he was told.'

'You should have brought him in.'

'Mary, he's got a big history, but no outstanding warrants. He was at a dollhouse protest on Wednesday but it was in Portland, not San Francisco. He slept in his truck and the following day, at a diner, he saw the bombing on the news and tore home with his ass on fire because he was terrified – rightly, as it turns out – that people would connect it with his threats. TrackBack corroborated his movements, his face was similar but not an exact match, the sniffers found no D-5 and he pulled clean greens on a polygraph . . . What can I say?'

She glared, but said nothing.

'Jesus, this time yesterday I'm an asshole for going in too hard, now I'm an asshole for being too soft. What do you want, exactly?'

'Good news.'

'What?'

'I need good news.' DiMatteo gestured at her phone. 'That was the director. Not the division chief, the *director*. After this I have to call the mayor.'

Madsen was about to offer some blunt advice on what to tell the mayor when he noticed her hands were shaking. It stopped him cold. Mad, bad, fire-and-brimstone Mary, he could cope with. Scared shitless losing-her-rational-mind Mary was a whole different ball game. In all the time he had known her he had never seen her like that.

He got out of there as soon as he could.

A memo was waiting on his desk. A paper version of one he had already received electronically. Bureau crest in the top left corner. Office of Professional Integrity printed on the right.

Subject: Leaked evidence Grant Avenue investigation.

Interview time: Four o'clock.

Location: Phillip Burton bldg room 13.03.

Interviewee: Special Agent Daniel Madsen.

Then, in a large red typeface and right justified so as not to be missed: *Attendance Mandatory.*

He checked his watch. Just going on twelve. He had four hours. He'd go back to Central Station and keep digging. He couldn't guarantee he'd find good news, but he sure as hell needed to be chasing something new before he came back this way again. Maybe he'd start with that file of Holbrook's. The big one. Christ, when this was over he'd have to sit down and re-evaluate. If this was how it was going to be, then there was only so much he could take. Maybe he'd think about a transfer. Or see a shrink.

The task force operations room was littered with trash and empty coffee cups. A solitary inspector – the same one who had given him the death stares at Holbrook's desk yesterday morning – was monitoring the main console. What was his name? Bob something. Wolleck? Yes, that was it. Whatever, there was no sign of anger or resentment now. The guy's eyelids drooped with fatigue.

'Where is everyone?' Madsen asked.

Wolleck yawned and stretched both arms above his head. 'Out. We got a local. Scored a point three seven. They're over at Alameda checking him out.' His tone said he wasn't putting money on a positive outcome.

'What's the run rate?'

'It's fallen off. We're down to about one reasonable candidate every half-hour. About fifty investigation requests completed, sixty-two on the back list. They're coming from all over now. I got one in from the Ukraine, believe it or not. You want to see?'

'No.' Jesus, a hundred and twelve requests and God knows how many police resources tied up chasing them down. It was out of control. Madsen went over to Holbrook's desk and sat down. The stack of manila folders was still there and the one with the inch-thick printout was on top. Sweeping the clutter aside, he took it down and opened it, casting his eye down the long list of names without enthusiasm.

'Where the fuck is Samoa?' Wolleck asked.

Madsen didn't bother looking up. 'No idea. Why?'

'Some guy just emailed. One of our hand-offs from yesterday. The cops investigated and found a body. Homicide. They've got a passport that says he's a US citizen.'

Madsen sighed. 'Don't tell me. The local hotheads saw a tourist in a hoodie with a red backpack and decided to go vigilante?'

'Not by the sound of it.'

'What's the name on the passport?'

'Ian John Callan.'

Madsen switched on the computer monitor. He dug a keyboard from under a pile of paper and started typing in the details. Callan's driver's licence photograph popped up. He examined it closely. The nose was right. The jawline looked the same. But then again so did mountain man's.

'The guy that emailed. Did he leave a phone number?'

'Yeah, I got it here.'

'Give it to me.'

Addisson answered on the second ring. Excitement bubbled down the line as he recounted the events leading up to the discovery.

'Are you sure it was homicide?' Madsen asked.

'Definitely.'

'Any idea who did it?'

'None. But there was a fight. The house looked like a cyclone hit it.'

'Maybe it was a robbery gone wrong.'

'Not on your life. That kind of thing doesn't happen in Samoa. These people go to church twice on Sundays – literally. And they share everything. No one locks a door, except foreigners. Half the houses don't even have doors.'

'When did it happen?'

'The police think the time of death was inside the last twenty-four hours, but they don't know for sure. It's hard to tell in the tropics. And the body was in a bad way.'

Madsen pondered that a moment. 'Could you do something for me? Would you contact the medical examiner's office there and ask them to send copies of their photographs and fingerprints as soon as they can?'

'Absolutely.'

Madsen thanked him and rang off. He stared at Callan's image. There was something about it that tugged at him, and it was more interesting than anything else at the moment. He hit the print button, waited for the printer to spit out the sheet, then took it downstairs to the surveillance operations room.

The left side of the Wall was a grid of squares. A guy clutching a woman's handbag sprinted from one camera to another while officers on foot moved into position to intercept him. On the right side, a ten-foot-high Inspector Mike Holbrook emerged from a warehouse. He looked pissed. Scratch the Alameda candidate then.

Shari was at the supervisor's console.

'Hey,' Madsen said.

She turned. Her face was pale. 'Hey.'

'You look busy,' he said, gesturing at the Wall.

'It's fine. The operation just finished.'

'Still worried about the integrity test?'

She offered a thin smile.

Madsen handed over the printout. 'Do you want to take a look at this guy for me? See if he's our man? Might take your mind off it.'

Shari examined the face, then placed the printout next to her keyboard. While Madsen watched, she entered the details and brought up the driver's licence record he had just been looking at. This was swiftly followed by Callan's passport photo and images from other government databases. With a few deft keystrokes she set up a query:

FACE COMPARISON
SOURCE: 'IAN JOHN CALLAN' / CA RECORDS
TARGET: 'GRANTAVE_UMV#3' / COMPOSITE MODEL

Seconds later the results flashed up:

ID MATCH: [87 %]

'What does that mean?' asked Madsen.

'It means Callan looks a lot like backpack man.'

'Does it rule him in or out?'

'Ah . . . out.'

'You don't sound convinced.'

'It's a high number. It would be interesting to break it down . . .' Shari tapped her console and a 3-D model of a head appeared. Black patches covered the large areas where backpack man's hoodie and sunglasses had blocked the cameras. The exposed surfaces were covered in densely spaced contour lines and tiny numbers.

'That's strange,' Shari said.

'What is?'

'The consistency. You see the zone numbers?' She pointed as she read them off. '86.9, 87.1, 87.2, 86.9 . . . I've never seen that before. Normally when you compare two faces you find that some features are more alike than others. Their noses are similar but not the ears, the upper lip but not the lower lip . . .'

'Yeah, I get it.'

'All the numbers hover around 87 per cent. Almost exactly the same level of mismatch all over . . .'

'How would that happen?'

'I honestly don't know,' Shari said, shaking her head. 'It's weird.'

'But he's not our guy?'

'No. A near miss, but not a match.'

Weird, Madsen thought. That was a word to get your attention. But sometimes you got weird, and sometimes you got coincidences, and sometimes you got near misses. Didn't he know it.

He bumped into Wolleck in the corridor. The inspector's eyes were lively, with no trace of the earlier tiredness. He wore a conspiratorial smile. 'I did some more digging on Callan. Nothing exceptional. No convictions, arrests. Last registered address in Palo Alto. Nothing interesting at all, until . . .'

'Until what?'

'Until I looked up his tax records.'

'And?'

'He used to work at Dreamcom.'

Madsen's eyebrows shot up. 'Really?'

'He was an employee for six years. But he left. Last year's return has him at some outfit called Datum Tech – down in Santa Clara.' Wolleck held out a fresh printout.

Madsen grabbed it and stuffed it into his jacket. 'Do me a favour, will you?' he said, backing towards the entrance lobby. 'Call Dreamcom's HR department. Ask them to dig out his personnel file and send it over. Call me as soon as you get it.'

'Sure. Hey, where are you going?'

'Datum Tech.'

Chapter 41

The I-101 was bumper to bumper, and it took an hour before Madsen made the exit onto Great America Parkway and drove past the sprawling Santa Clara convention centre. A few blocks later he arrived at the address on the printout and turned into a driveway leading to a modern, sterile business park, exactly the same as those on either side. The buildings were shiny, anonymous boxes panelled in blue-tinted glass and bordered by three-yard strips of close-cropped lawn. Each box was the same. Same two-storey regulation height. Same width. Same sized parking lot. Only a unit number, stark white against the glass, differentiated one from another. Like a giant set of blue dice.

Madsen meandered between the boxes until he spied a white '3'. He parked the Dodge between a gleaming Maserati and a brand-new, heavily customized Porsche, and stepped out. The lot was full of cars, but deserted of people. It was so quiet he could hear the faint roar of the highway and the riffle of a banner in the next business park. The banner said, *CME Storage – proudly awarded 8th Healthiest Employer in the Bay Area!*

There was no one in the Datum Tech foyer either. Just two pot plants, a set of stairs, a desk and a bell.

Madsen gave the bell a slap.

A kid in designer jeans and a black T-shirt jogged down the stairs. The kid didn't look a day over sixteen. When he sighted Madsen's badge a mischievous eyebrow shot up. 'Aha! You must be here about the insider trading then.'

'I'd like to see your boss, please.'

'I'm one of the owners. Will that do?'

Madsen studied him more closely. He'd heard that Silicon Valley entrepreneurs were getting younger, but this was ridiculous. He tried another tack. 'I want to speak to whoever supervised Ian Callan when he was here. Would that be you?'

Another grin. 'That would be Jason, my co-founder. I'll get him.'

Jason turned out to be about the same age, with gangly limbs and a dusting of freckles, but from the outset it was obvious he had a more serious disposition. He greeted Madsen politely and invited him to follow him up the stairs.

The second floor was a zoo, dozens of geeks beavering away in a commingling of green punk hairstyles, pierced lips and noses, long dresses, outlandish shirts, coke-bottle glasses, shorts, trackpants, beanbags, sneakers, bare feet, soft toys and hats. The workstations were luridly coloured and shaped. Customized, perhaps, to suit the personalities of their occupants. One was painted to look like it had been welded together from sheets of scrap metal. Another was shaped and textured like a hollowed-out tree trunk. From the workstations came the clatter of plastic keyboards and the tinny sounds of headphones turned up too high.

There was a single meeting room, a glass-walled box positioned in the centre of the floor and furnished with beanbags and pink designer chairs. As Madsen entered, he noticed someone had handwritten 'The Fish Tank' on a Post-it and stuck it across the door.

The other Datum Tech employees peered in curiously, most probably getting a brief on their visitor's occupation from the first kid. A twenty-something with gold plaits and an MIT T-shirt stared from behind the tree trunk. *Like Alice in Wonderland*, Madsen thought. He was doing his best to get comfortable in one of the chairs, but no matter how he sat, the flowing curves refused to match up with those of his spine.

'Can I ask what kind of trouble Ian is in?' Jason asked.

Madsen ignored the question. 'Let's start with what he did here,' he said, dragging his eyes away from the menagerie outside.

'He specialized in inferring the physical characteristics of objects within images,' Jason said.

'Come again?'

'Sorry. He wrote software to help robots look at an object and guess how large it is, how heavy it might be and so on. Humans do it naturally. Getting machines to do it is hard. You have to combine what they see through their onboard cameras with different types of stored knowledge. It's pretty fundamental to what we do here.'

'Which is what, exactly?'

'Datum Tech makes vision systems.'

'Was he good?'

'At his job? Very. Everybody is good at what they do here. Ian had a quirky way of thinking – always coming up with new ways of doing things . . .'

Madsen swiftly established that yes, Callan got along well with his colleagues, despite being one of the oldest. He worked hard and played hard – especially if there was plenty of alcohol on hand. Outside of work he was into extreme sports like rock-climbing and base-jumping, but he considered these solitary activities, not to be shared. Jason had once hinted he'd like to learn rock-climbing and was swiftly rebuffed. He was not, as far as Jason knew, religious. No, he wasn't married and there was no steady girlfriend, but he did go through a lot of women. One-night stands mostly. Jason knew that because it had caused one or two problems around the office. *A bit of a wild man* was how he summed up his personality.

'Where do you think we can we find him?' Madsen asked, picturing Callan's corpse lying on a slab somewhere, bloated from the tropical heat.

'He finished up last month. I can give you the address we have on file, but it won't be any good.'

'Why not?'

'He had travel plans. Backpacking in India to begin with. To visit gurus and stay in ashrams and get in touch with himself or something. I left a few voicemails asking him to reconsider but received no replies, so I assume he's already gone.'

'Did he leave on good terms?'

'Sure. He was doing great things here. As far as I was concerned it ended a little abruptly, and he missed out on his stock options . . . he had to move on to his next thing, I guess.'

Madsen glanced up. 'Stock options?'

'Oh, like most firms around here we give everyone a slice of the action through an employee stock plan. It's a way to retain good people and keep them motivated. There's a vesting schedule – you have to stay a certain length of time before your allocation can be traded. If Ian had stayed a few weeks longer he would have been here a year and redeemed a third of his options. Instead, he forfeited them.'

'What were they worth?'

Jason shrugged. 'About a hundred and eighty, give or take.'

'Thousand?'

'Thousand.'

Alarm bells rang in Madsen's head. No one, he thought, even if they had plenty of money, walked away from a hundred and eighty grand just before it fell due. Something had happened, something he couldn't ignore. An event, a trigger, an order . . . His thoughts were interrupted by buzzing from his cell phone. The caller ID said Central Station. He excused himself and took the call.

It was Wolleck. 'Dreamcom sent through the personnel records. I also got an update from Samoa. They sent pictures, prints, the lot.'

'Give me a minute. I'll call you back.' Madsen rang off. Turning back to Jason he said, 'Just a few more questions and we can wind this up.'

Jason nodded.

'Did Ian ever talk about his previous employer?'

'Dreamcom? He talked about them every day.'

'Every *day*. Did he have some kind of problem?'

'No, no, I should explain. Dreamcom is our biggest customer. They use our vision systems in their dolls. A year ago they bought a twenty per cent stake in Datum Tech. Win-win. They secured their supply, we got a cash injection plus a locked-in customer. Ian's job there was integrating our systems and they suggested he transfer across as part of the deal. To speed up the exchange of knowledge.'

'You said yes?'

'Of course. Having someone onboard with a deep understanding of your customer's systems is a big help. You can't beat it.'

'Was he unhappy about that?'

'Not at all. Actually, I think it was his idea.'

'So what were his feelings towards Dreamcom?'

'He loved the place. Loved the whole dolly thing and he had a lot of friends there. That's what made him such a great asset. He could call on anybody, at any level, to sort out problems.'

As Madsen drove out of the business park, he tried to reconcile what he had heard with what he already knew. The news that Callan was a trusted insider at Dreamcom meant he would have been privy to many of Dreamcom's business practices. Perhaps he had come across something he didn't like. If so, he'd hidden his feelings well. Then, weeks after suddenly leaving Datum Tech and days after a dollhouse bombing, a bunch of citizens finger him as a suspect and the next thing you know he's dead. Killed. According to Shari, he wasn't the bomber. But he was connected somehow. He had to be. And somebody had killed him, which meant that whatever Ian John Callan was involved in, he wasn't alone.

He called Wolleck back.

'What've you got?'

'Nasty pics. The guy was a mess. Someone beat the living shit out of him. And afterwards, some animals got to the body. I ran the prints. The body matches the passport. It's Callan.'

Madsen grunted. 'What else?'

'Couple of things. He went down to the local village and was acting all furtive, didn't speak much, trying to be quick when he bought his groceries. Trying not to be noticed.' Wolleck laughed. 'Of course that had the exact opposite effect. When the story broke on the news, the locals thought of him immediately. Also, I got the details for the owner of the house and called him. A New Zealander. Wound up his dive-boat charter and returned to Auckland years ago. Rents out the place online, mostly to short-stay vacationers. Our guy books it for six months in advance with the name John Smith and pays up front, via money transfer.'

Madsen whistled. 'That's a big vacation.'

'The Kiwi was pretty pleased with it. Not so happy when he heard about the mess.'

'What about the personnel file?'

'Nothing stands out. Senior systems engineer, project leader, head of integration . . . a whole bunch of technical stuff I don't understand. Seems to have been a model employee. Regular promotions and bonuses. Looking at the number of zeros in his pay cheque I'd say he was doing okay.'

'His last supervisor. Does it mention who he was?'

'Let's see . . . a guy by the name of Mark Pemberton.'

'Is he downtown?'

'It says here he's head of production, at the factory.'

'Where's that?'

'San Jose.'

Shit. San Jose was further south. Going there meant it would take that much longer again to get back to San Francisco. Madsen glanced at his watch. 2:20 p.m. He had to be back for the integrity test at four. Less than two hours. He toyed with the options. Go north and he'd make it easy. South and it was touch and go. He was already back on Great America Parkway. The I-101 North on-ramp loomed ahead. He flicked his indicator and eased into the long queue of vehicles waiting to turn right.

Wolleck said, 'By the way, don't even think of seeing Pemberton without Holbrook.'

Madsen blinked. 'Why not?'

'He's inbound from Alameda and expects you to haul ass back here to brief him on Datum Tech. Said to remind you, and I quote, "It's my fucking case and given all the crap you've brought down there is no way on God's green earth you should be out cruising solo."'

'No trust left there then.'

'Just passing on the message.' Wolleck rang off.

Fifty yards before the on-ramp, an electronic billboard displayed the bright yellow logo of a restaurant chain. As the Dodge drew near, the logo faded and was replaced by a dozen beautiful women cavorting along a beach. The water sparkled, silver on blue. Palm trees lined the sand. The caption said:

Come to Ten Worlds!
Opening tomorrow
Which world will you choose?

Madsen pushed it from his mind and stared ahead, tightening his grip on the wheel. He felt a predatory stirring. He was finding threads. Real ones. They didn't make sense, but each time he pulled one it revealed another. Callan's conspirators were out there somewhere, ready to strike again. *Do you worry about what other people think, or seize opportunities?* he asked himself. *Dance to someone else's tune or make a difference? Your choice.*

The car ahead peeled to the right.

Fuck it.

Madsen swerved, setting off a chorus of furious honks. He passed under the highway, elbowing the Dodge across to the leftmost lane. Then he pitched the car hard left, onto the ramp marked I-101 South.

In the surveillance operations room at Central Station, Shari Sanayei finished marking up footage of a brawl on Green Street. Two males, one female, still onsite, injuries sustained, no weapons sighted. She checked the badge numbers for the patrol officers arriving at the scene and queued the footage for download to their handsets. As soon as it had transferred, she pulled her microphone to her lips. 'Okay, guys, you're on your own for a few minutes.'

Both operators gave her a thumbs up.

She cleared her head and selected the Grant Avenue evidence directory on her console.

After Madsen had left she'd puzzled over the weird match-up results for Callan and concocted several theories, each a little crazier than the last. Unfortunately, no one told all the bag snatchers, drunk drivers and hotheads that she was preoccupied with something else today, and nonstop surveillance requests had left little time for hypothesis testing. Still, by snatching a minute here and there she had already managed to rule a few things out. She was onto something now. She just needed to run some comparisons to make sure.

A long list of camera numbers, dates and times filled the screen. She began scrolling down, scanning. There was one particular file . . .

From the corridor came the sound of footsteps and the rap of knuckles on steel. Shari's stomach nosedived. She listened intently. A door squeaked open. It was the door to the interview room across the corridor.

The captain's voice: 'Yolanda Payne, this is Special Agent Ryan Samuels, with the Bureau's Office of Professional Integrity.'

Another voice. Male, deep, smooth. 'Please relax, Officer Payne, this won't take long . . .'

The click of the door closing.

Five to go. Then me.

Shari took a deep breath and returned to her scrolling with renewed urgency.

Chapter 42

The Dreamcom factory was a slab-sided building with none of the outward flourishes of its other facilities. And it was big. Madsen had time to appreciate just how big as he drove the perimeter looking for a way in. The entrance, by comparison, was modest. A break in the double security fence, a white guardhouse, and a solid-looking boom gate with a round disc tacked to the middle declaring STRICTLY NO TAILGATING.

A large man wearing wraparound reflective sunglasses plodded over. He wore a starched white shirt with red and black security patches sewn to both shoulders. A heavy revolver dangled from his hip.

Madsen flashed his badge. 'I'm here to see Mr Mark Pemberton.'

'Do you have an appointment?'

'No.'

The guard bent to the window and scrutinized the badge, then Madsen's face, then the badge again. He ambled back to the guardhouse and picked up a phone. There was a second man sitting in the shade, an assault rifle cradled across his knees. Madsen drummed his fingers on the wheel. A loud buzz sounded, followed by a clack. The boom gate slid upwards.

A few minutes later Madsen stood in a reception room receiving a crushing handshake from a friendly giant with flaming red hair and a matching beard. Madsen began explaining why he was there, but Pemberton cut him off.

'I know. You're working on the bombing. Anything we can do to help, just name it.'

'You were expecting me?' Madsen asked cautiously.

'You're famous! I must have watched you arrest that pastor outside the baseball stadium a thousand times. And taking down those guys on the cruiser. *That* was outstanding. Which one were you? We couldn't tell with all the goggles and helmets.'

Madsen didn't feel like explaining that he hadn't been on the boat, and that the footage he was referring to had brought nothing but problems. *Better to let it ride*, he thought, *and enjoy the novelty of having someone genuinely happy to see me.* 'I'm here about a guy named Ian Callan. I understand you might be the right person to talk to?'

'Ian used to work for me. Good guy, really smart. What do you want to know?'

'Everything. What he did, his behaviour, who he hung out with . . . I'm not really certain what I'm looking for, so anything could be important.'

Pemberton stroked his beard. 'No problem, but I've got an urgent batch of dollies due out.' He looked apologetic. 'Do you mind if we walk while we talk?'

Madsen shook his head. Pemberton handed him a hairnet and an orange vest marked 'visitor' and led him down a short corridor to a door marked: STOP! BEYOND THIS POINT ALL VISITORS <u>MUST</u> BE ACCOMPANIED BY DREAMCOM PERSONNEL. Pemberton opened the door and ushered Madsen through.

They emerged into a gigantic enclosed space that reminded Madsen of a very long, very large aircraft hangar. The air was heavy with the smell of plastics and glue. Power tools whined. The sharp blast of air compressors echoed off the walls. Industrial-sized exhaust fans roared high overhead. Next to the door, a steel staircase had been bolted to the wall. Pemberton was climbing the stairs and gesturing for Madsen to follow.

At the top of the stairs was a gangway, also of steel mesh, and recessed into the wall was a coffee machine. Pemberton pushed two styrofoam cups under the taps and punched a button. Jets of steaming brown liquid shot into the cups, filling them to the brim. He handed one to Madsen and they leaned over the railing, taking in the view.

The gangway stretched away in both directions until it circumnavigated the entire rectangular space. They stood roughly a quarter of the way along one side and high above the production line. Below and to the left was a cluster of prefabricated offices and a collection of large vats connected by pipes. Stretching away to the right was a vast network of assembly bays filled with tables, equipment stands, storage bins, electric cables, hoses, tools and utility carts. Movable partitions enclosed a few bays, but most were open, delineated only by bright red squares painted on the floor. Tall storage racks punctuated the production line like exclamation marks and driverless forklifts whined softly along the corridors, making stops. Technicians in white overalls and hairnets bobbed and bustled inside the squares. From where Madsen stood they looked like mice in a maze.

'Callan came here from the online entertainment division,' Pemberton was saying. 'Main claim to fame was improving what we call our lust prediction engine.' He chuckled. 'That won't mean much to you, but it's a big deal. Tastes in pornography change, sometimes rapidly. If you do a good job analysing viewing patterns and historical data you can predict the rate and direction of change for each individual customer, which means you can serve up just the right avatar at the right time to get their rocks off!'

He laughed, and Madsen remembered Eva Hartley's forceful description of how everything Dreamcom did was designed to 'escalate' customers to desire greater levels of intensity and more outrageous experiences.

A forklift passed underneath and stopped at a storage rack.

There was a whirring sound and the forks rocketed upwards cradling a green plastic bin. A second whirr and the bin shot into an empty slot. The forks retracted and descended. The lift whined away to another task.

Pemberton started down the stairs. 'When a vacancy opened in my vision systems team,' he said, 'I advertised internally. It was a new field for Ian but he's a smart guy. Learns fast. He did a great job.'

If Callan was such a computing prodigy, Madsen reflected as he followed Pemberton down the stairs, then six months of low-tech isolation on a Pacific island was probably his idea of a nightmare. It supported the notion that he was hiding out rather than taking a vacation.

They stopped at the first assembly bay. White-coated technicians removed long pieces of alloy from plastic bins and connected them together with power tools. Each piece featured unusual grooves and holes, but was otherwise vaguely familiar. At the end of the bay was a wheeled frame resembling an oversized hotel luggage cart. Three completed assemblies hung from it, each a metallic facsimile of a human skeleton.

'I just came from Datum Tech,' Madsen said. 'They said when Callan was here he integrated their systems. What does that mean?'

Pemberton checked something on his clipboard and began to walk. 'The Datum Tech guys build software that recognizes objects and makes predictions about their characteristics. Their stuff is used in that forklift you saw back there, so it can pick up storage bins. It's also used in homecare bots . . .'

'To assist the elderly?'

'Elderly, disabled . . . or fat lazy people with a ton of cash and no desire to bend over to pick up a dropped spoon.' Pemberton's eyes twinkled. 'Now, forklifts and homecare bots are easy. You can glue twenty-cent cameras all over them. No one cares. But you can't do that with dolls. They're restricted to two cameras packaged in two human-sized eyeballs, and they interact using three simultaneous sensory inputs: sound and touch as well as sight. That was Ian's job. Making all those things work together.'

They bypassed the next assembly bay. Madsen caught a glimpse of more skeletons and white-suited technicians pressing colour-coded bundles of wire into deep grooves along the metal 'bones'. Pemberton stopped at the third bay. The two technicians inside wore face respirators and elbow-length gloves. An unpleasant acetone sharpness stabbed at Madsen's nostrils and his eyes began to sting, as if he'd leaned over freshly chopped onion. He watched the first technician prod a pair of bright blue rubber lungs into position behind a metallic ribcage. The lungs appeared to be bags of liquid. His colleague stepped forward with a spray gun. A thick gel shot into the chest cavity, filling the gaps around and under the lungs.

Pemberton pointed to a plastic tub piled high with blue bags. 'Our sixth-generation battery. The biggest R & D project ever undertaken by Dreamcom.' He winked. 'Dolls aren't popular if they have to stop and recharge in the middle of the act.' He noticed Madsen wiping his eyes and laughed. 'The chemicals are nasty, but don't worry, once we seal them up they're perfectly safe.' He began walking again, setting a brisk pace.

'Is there any reason Callan would be unhappy with Dreamcom?' Madsen asked, hurrying to keep up.

Pemberton shook his head. 'Not as far as I know. He was very happy here. Loved the dolls. Some people here like the technology and couldn't care less about the product, but Ian would take dolls home and road-test them! About the only thing he disliked was being bored. On the weekends, he'd ride his motorbike, go hang-gliding, base-jumping, whitewater rafting, that kind of stuff. A classic adrenalin junkie. Ah, here we are . . .'

They had passed several signposts in quick succession: *Plumbing, Optics, Logic*. Under the last one someone had added: *Brain surgeons at work!* Pemberton stopped to consult his clipboard. The sign beside him said *Muscle*.

Madsen examined the bay. Directly in front of him, a much more complete skeleton hung from a wheeled coat rack. Rubberized tubes ran through the abdominal cavity. A silver box no bigger than a pack of playing cards lay under the sternum, connected to the lungs behind via a pair of thick cables, one red, one black. A bundle of much thinner wires branched away from it in all directions. Madsen guessed the box was a combined computer and power controller. With the exception of the 'lungs', now odourless in their hardened gel case, all the components were surprisingly small. The overwhelming impression was of elegant simplicity.

Pemberton approached a large bucket containing what looked like large green slugs immersed in a jelly. Tucking his clipboard under one arm, he reached down and picked out a slug. It was about six inches long. Wet slime dripped from the ends. He took it over to a stand with a lightning bolt painted on the side, then stretched the slug out and touched two probes to the ends. The slug instantly shrank into a tight, fat ball. He tossed the slug back in the bucket. It landed with a wet plop.

'Electroactive polymer,' said Pemberton. 'Put charge in and it shortens like real muscle fibre. A dozen to a shoulder. Three dozen for a quadriceps. Before we had these it was impossible to get realistic movement, let alone feel.' He pointed to the other end of the bay where a technician knelt in front of a skeleton and was threading the tip of a slug through one of many small holes near the hip. He picked up a power tool and tightened a screw, clamping the slug in position, then stretched the slug down the femur and repeated the procedure at the knee.

'Isn't this secret?' Madsen asked.

'Our competitors use mostly the same internal components nowadays. The real secrets are in the software, and of course the skin. You'll see that next.' Pemberton strode off.

Madsen started to follow when he noticed something out of the corner of his eye. High on the opposite wall of the factory, standing on the gangway, was a man. Unlike everyone else Madsen had seen, his head was uncovered. His hair had been drawn back in a ponytail and the factory lights reflected off a large bald spot on his forehead. But it wasn't the absence of a hairnet that had caught Madsen's attention, nor the way the man's fists were locked tight to the railing. It was the way he stared at Madsen with black intensity.

Madsen stared back.

The man broke eye contact.

Madsen turned away. Why shouldn't the guy stare? According to Pemberton, he was famous around here.

By the time he caught up, Pemberton was waiting in front of a bay surrounded by high partitions.

Madsen asked, 'If Callan was so keen on this place, why did he leave?'

'When we bought into Datum Tech, we needed him to go over and be our inside man, so he went.'

'You asked him to go?'

'God, no. I wanted him to stay. I had to find a replacement.'

'Then who?'

'Senior management. And this . . .' Pemberton said, grinning, 'is why they call 'em skinjobs.' He swept aside a plastic curtain.

Rows of skins hung from wires, like clothes on a line. Technicians hovered over them with airbrushes, checking their work against posters tacked along the walls. The posters were nudes, life-sized and posed to the front, back and side, like full-body mugshots.

'Real skin is translucent,' Pemberton said. 'So ours has to be too. You notice they're only painting the finishing touches on the underside? The base colour is pre-mixed into the polymer which, as well as looking right, has to be odour-free, hard-wearing, and textured to feel *exactly* the same as real skin. This recipe is more secret than Coca-Cola. Cost maybe a hundred million to get right. Recognize that one?' He pointed at one of the posters: a petite curly-haired brunette with a wicked smile.

Madsen shook his head.

'You mustn't see many movies. That's Kathryn Fox. Hottest thing in Hollywood. Every man's fantasy. We signed a licensing deal with her last month. Lots of starlets want to be dolled up. Good publicity, notoriety . . . they love it. She should be popular for a few months . . . That's our biggest challenge, by the way.'

'What is?'

'Variety. The market demands it so we give it. Different face, skin, hair and eye combinations, you name it. The problem is, every variation costs.' Pemberton rubbed his thumb and forefinger together. 'We try to compensate by economizing and standardizing everywhere else. We bring dolls back for refits, laser-cutting new curves in the jelly that's layered over the muscles. We build them for seduction and fucking and that's it. They don't do massages, they don't vacuum, they don't talk and they walk at two speeds. But it's a constant battle. They wanted this last batch, for example, to be capable of taking drink orders, as a gimmick for Ten Worlds. I lost that one. So far, thank God, we've managed to stick to only two chassis sizes – standard and petite. That's why we liked Kathryn: she's petite down to the quarter inch. Tastes are changing, though . . .' Pemberton rolled his eyes. 'We're under a lot of pressure to introduce a super petite.'

Madsen thought of the pale, juvenile faces in the forward cabin of the *Genevieve II* and shuddered.

They crossed to the far side of the factory. There was a loading dock there, with a rectangular opening in the wall and a Dreamcom semitrailer backed up with its container doors open. A long row of aluminium coffins lay nearby, side by side along the concrete apron. Pemberton walked slowly down the line, checking off serial numbers on his clipboard. When he reached the last coffin he knelt, popped the catches and pushed back the lid.

Everything Madsen had seen to this point would have looked more at home on a dissection table in Roswell, New Mexico than in a bordello. Now he saw a woman. Platinum blonde, long-legged, statuesque – every bit as perfect as the doll he had encountered in Fillinger's office.

'Eight more and she's on her way,' Pemberton said. 'By this time tomorrow she'll be working alongside her friends in Vegas.'

'Did Callan have friends here at the factory?' Madsen asked. 'People he was close to?'

'Yes, of course.'

'I'd like to talk to them. All of them. One at a time. Can I borrow an office? I have a handheld polygraph with me.'

Pemberton looked up, his eyes wide with alarm. 'Are you serious?'

'Very. It could make all the difference in this case.'

'But production . . . our deadline . . .' Pemberton rose to his feet, his face pale. 'I need approval. Wait here.' He strode back the way they had come, towards the offices.

Madsen was alone.

It was pleasantly quiet. Storage racks bordered the concrete apron on three sides, muting the blast of power tools from the assembly line. A light breeze drifted in through the loading bay, diluting the smell of chemicals and plastic. He stared down at the coffin-shaped container. It struck him as creepy, but it was essentially just a box with reinforced corners and foam padding, similar to those used by roadies to transport sound equipment between concerts. Certainly the doll didn't resemble a corpse, not with that glowing pink skin. He wondered if her chest was warm, and if he would feel a heartbeat.

A high-pitched whine approached. Another coffin floated into view, lying across the arms of a forklift. With a series of whirrs the lift pivoted, deposited the coffin at the end of the line, and accelerated away. Seven more to go.

Madsen wandered over to the storage racks, looking for somewhere to sit. He didn't feel like sitting on a coffin. He glanced at his watch. Shit. It was already after three. He was out of time. If he was going to make the integrity test he had ten minutes maximum before he had to leave. What was he thinking? How many people could he get through in ten minutes? To distract himself he took out his HAMDA, switched the detection array to narcotics and waved it around. The light glowed green.

The whine returned. That was quick. Six more to go.

He switched the array to explosives.

Green. Wait. Was that a flicker?

He frowned. Yes, there it was again. Very faint.

The whine stopped.

Madsen pulled the rollout screen and watched the coloured lines. He began to turn in a circle . . .

The breeze dropped.

Madsen looked up.

A gigantic rack, packed with storage bins, teetered overhead.

For a millisecond he stood. The plastic bins rasped as they slid from their shelves. Adrenalin kicked in. He pivoted and ran.

The first bin caught him beneath the shoulder blade, knocking the wind from his lungs and sending him stumbling to his knees. Rolls of cotton gauze flew past his ear.

The second hit the floor near his ankles and exploded in a shower of flying white fragments.

His mind registered a third bin sailing past his head before a thunderous clang deafened him and reverberated through his body.

Silence.

A distant, retreating whine.

Madsen gasped, sucking air back into his lungs.

He lay face down. His back was a bruise.

He reached up and touched his head. Still there. He opened his eyes and saw a sheet of iron in front of his face. A shelf. He must have missed being decapitated by an inch. Something fell from his cheek with click. A fingernail. There were thousands of them, white and bloodless. The fragments from when the second bin burst. He tried to get up. Nothing doing. His leg was jammed. He twisted and saw a steel beam had pinned his leg at the knee. The beam was a few inches off the ground, held up by crushed storage bins.

His nostrils hurt. He lifted his chin and looked to his right. Panic clawed into his throat. A bright blue rubberized bag, one of the lung-sized batteries, had burst on the concrete a few feet away. Long wisps of white smoke curled off iron where toxic liquid had spattered against the shelf. The rest of the liquid was seeping into a puddle that was expanding and creeping in his direction. Madsen's eyes and nose flashed like hot mustard had been sprayed in his face. His breathing became laboured. Tears streamed down his cheeks. He turned away, sucked in as much air as he could and locked it in his lungs. Then he set his mind to holding it there for as long as he possibly could.

An alarm began to sound, like a diving klaxon.

He had no idea how long he managed to hold his breath, nor when he blacked out. He remembered shouts, running steps, another approaching whine. He was on his back. He floated, then drowned. He tasted salt. At some point he opened his eyes and saw the lights on the factory ceiling moving past like a conveyor belt. He remembered a man's face staring down from a railing, far above. Through the film of tears the face was a blur; there was a smudge that might or might not have been a ponytail, and two dark, piercing eyes. Shark eyes.

Chapter 43

He lay on his back. His chest and neck were soaked.

'I'm going to squirt you again,' said a far-off voice.

Madsen nodded.

Warm relief flooded his eyes and poured down his chin. It tasted salty.

He blinked away the solution.

A young, delicately featured man peered at him. He was holding a plastic squeeze bottle and smiling. Pemberton's anxious face loomed behind the young man's shoulder. He was pulling at his beard and saying something about an accident. Behind him was the blurry outline of a nurse in a white uniform. Madsen wondered why she wasn't helping.

Madsen squeezed his fingers into his eyelids, trying to push back the pain. He heard movement, a door opening and closing, rummaging sounds.

He opened his eyes and, after a significant effort, managed to sit up. A hot starburst radiated out from behind his left knee and his back felt like a football team had used it for kicking practice. He was sitting on a couch with cushions propped all around. Pemberton had gone. The young man was kneeling with his back to him, looking for something in a cabinet. The cabinet had a big red cross on the side. Magazines and video games were scattered on the floor.

Some kind of combined recreation room and first-aid station.

Madsen glanced over at the nurse again and saw that the outfit he had assumed was a uniform was in fact two pieces: tight white shorts and a matching halter top, the latter tied with a bow behind the neck to support a generously proportioned chest. His eyes drifted upwards, taking in the bright red lipstick, beauty spot high on the cheek, impossibly long and impossibly thick eyelashes, golden hair, solitary blonde curl dangling . . .

One of the bedroom eyes tipped him a languid wink.

The same slow, sultry wink from the movies and newsreels. The same one that seduced Mickey Mantle and JFK.

Enough! Madsen shuffled forward to the edge of the couch. Gingerly, he placed his feet on the floor and tried putting some weight on his left leg. Pain lanced upwards, but he didn't think it was broken. He gently pushed himself into a standing position. It hurt like a son of a bitch. No matter. Driverless forklifts did not 'accidentally' push over storage racks, and they most definitely did not suffer a one in a billion malfunction when a federal agent happened to be standing on the other side. Somebody had caused it. Someone in the factory who wanted Madsen out of the way but needed it to look like an accident and didn't want to be near, didn't want to fall under suspicion. Someone prepared to kill to avoid being polygraphed. The guy with shark eyes. Or Pemberton. Or the guy at the medicine cabinet.

Time to get out. Now.

The young man turned and hurried over, his face creased with concern. He held a bottle of pills in his hand. 'No, no, you need to rest—' He stopped. His eyes crept downwards to the muzzle of the Beretta levelled at his belly. His jaw fell open in astonishment.

Madsen hobbled to the door, twisted the handle and backed out, uttering a single word: 'Stay.' The last thing he saw as he closed the door was Marilyn Monroe blowing him a kiss.

He holstered the Beretta and took his bearings. He was in the cluster of offices. There was a door marked EXIT fifty yards away. The shortest path to it was across the production line. The environment suddenly felt alien and hostile and full of possibilities for another 'accident'.

He began to move towards the door, hobbling around pieces of unidentifiable equipment, passing hoses and whirring tools. Shower-capped workers looked up in surprise. He dodged a tool stand and a rack of steel skeletons.

Forty yards.

Over the din of machinery he heard a familiar high-pitched whine over to the left. He moved faster, half walking, half running. He skipped around a plastic bin piled high with steel bones.

Twenty yards. One more assembly bay.

His toe hooked a cable and a loud slap rang in his ears as he landed face first on grey-painted concrete. A woman in a white jumpsuit and hairnet goggled down at him. He picked himself up, his knee screaming in protest, and passed the last row of tables. He thought he heard a shout. The door banged, and he stood in blazing sunshine.

He limped to the Dodge and got in, being careful not to bump the door against his leg. He started the engine and idled towards the guardhouse, mindful of the assault rifle he had seen earlier and not wanting to alarm the occupants. He stopped in front of the boom. The disc in the middle said DRIVE CAREFULLY.

A pair of wraparound glasses leaned out of the guardhouse. Madsen forced a smile. Seconds ticked by.

In the rear-view mirror he saw a door open. A white-coated figure began jogging in his direction, waving.

The boom began to rise.

Madsen shoved his foot to the floor. The Dodge leapt forwards. There was a loud bang as the tin sign on the boom tumbled off the hood. He slewed the Dodge onto the perimeter road and gunned the motor, leaving two looping snakes of rubber in his wake.

*

Madsen's breathing returned to normal. He eased his right foot off the pedal and took stock. First thing he needed was reinforcements. He'd get a posse of agents, turn around and lock the place down. Then line up everyone in the factory – manager, workers, cleaners – the lot. Only way out is past the HAMDA, refusals duly noted. The factory would have a duty roster. He'd work his way through it, smoke them out. A concentration of resources would pay fast dividends.

He switched on his handset and it immediately began buzzing. The caller ID said DiMatteo. He glanced at the dashboard clock. 4:03 p.m. Ouch.

'Where the fuck *are* you?' she hissed.

'San Jose.'

'For God's sake, why?'

'I've just been to the Dreamcom factory. I need—'

'You missed the test.' Her tone was equal parts venom and disappointment.

'Mary, there was a good reason—'

'Shut up. There can only be one reason. You leaked.'

Jesus.

'How did you think you could get away with it?' Mary continued. 'You, of all people. You embarrassed the Bureau. Did you think OPI wouldn't get involved? Wouldn't jump on something that big? Were you hoping they'd *forget* the test? Aw shucks, sorry we missed you, Dan, you were so busy, we'll just have to skip it and catch you next time. Is that seriously how you thought it would go down?'

'That's not what's going on. I'll do the test. You need to listen—'

'Damn right you'll do it. In my office. Eight o'clock tomorrow morning. And you'll be doing it as a suspended agent – effective now. Washington is having fantasies about tearing you to pieces. You're an idiot. Actually, you're a complete fucking lunatic. Certifiable.'

Madsen felt a cold, heavy stone in his gut. He took a breath. 'Mary,' he said evenly, 'whatever happens I'll deal with it, but someone at the factory is connected and he tried to kill me.

Someone is on the inside there. I picked up traces of D-5. For all we know he's preparing to blow up the factory as we speak. I need reinforcements. I'm going to go back and polygraph the entire shift. As soon as I identify—'

'Dan, stop!'

'Just listen . . .'

'Didn't you get my messages? SFPD declared it. Case closed. We're out. Done. Finished. It's *over.*'

'What? No. This guy Callan led me to—'

'Dan. It *was* Callan.'

Chapter 44 _____

Madsen boiled with frustration as he drove north. He had fully expected to muster the cavalry and come charging back into the factory. Instead he'd run headlong into a brick wall.

We're out. Done. Finished. It must have been a godsend for Mary, a gift-wrapped parachute to jump clear of the burning plane. Now she could wash the Bureau's hands of the whole mess and concentrate on repairing the damage and shifting the blame. He could picture the communiqué already: *The FBI congratulates the San Francisco Police Department on bringing its Grant Avenue investigation to a successful conclusion . . .* She was about to get her pension back, so why would she sanction anything on the say-so of a lunatic who had skipped his integrity test? Through her eyes it must have seemed like he had busted way beyond his brief, gotten into trouble, and was turning stones over in a blind panic, desperately trying to find something, anything, to vindicate himself. Not accurate, but not an entirely unreasonable conclusion to draw either. He had pushed on and taken risks. He should have taken more time, covered his ass.

Somewhere on the drive back he made another depressing discovery: his HAMDA was missing. It had been in his hand when the storage rack fell. It had to have been smashed to pieces against the concrete apron. Not as terminal as losing his gun, but not far off. The Bureau didn't like losing expensive assets.

Go home, eat, get some sleep, that was what he had to do. Discounting the fitful naps taken in the deafening cabin of the helicopter, it had been thirty-five hours since his head last touched a pillow. Then wake up and be there at eight in the morning to take his OPI medicine. He'd face sanctions for missing today's test, losing the HAMDA, and anything else they could come up with. The suspension would be followed by a period of restricted duties. Maybe he'd be fired. But at least the truth – his motives, reasoning, conviction, all of it – would come out. And after getting clean greens he would have their attention. He could get his message across. That was the path of least resistance, the rational path. And the only chance of breathing any life back into his career.

The problem with that was someone had tried to kill him. Someone who was inside the factory planning to blow it to smithereens. And whoever it was knew Madsen was onto him, which meant he would be looking for ways to bring his plans forward.

He might not have until eight tomorrow morning.

He might not even have twenty minutes.

He needed to make sure someone was onto it *now*.

The thought consumed him as he turned into Vallejo Street and searched for a place to park among the police cars and vans.

A few moments later he stood in the doorway of the task force operations room, Central Station. The place was transformed. The files were neatly stacked. The discarded paper had been swept up. The computer monitors were off. Several inspectors had drawn up a circle of chairs and were happily shooting the shit. Holbrook had his feet propped on a desk and was doing something that, in Madsen's limited experience of the man, was wholly out of character. He was laughing. He stopped when he saw Madsen.

'Uh oh, it's supercop.'

'Celebrating?' Madsen asked.

'As a matter of fact, we are,' Holbrook said. 'We're adjourning to Rosie's in a minute. You want to join us? Just promise to leave that damn wand behind.' The others chuckled.

'Can I talk to you?'

'Floor's yours.'

'Outside.'

Holbrook looked at Madsen warily. 'Sure,' he said, swinging his feet from the desk.

They stood toe to toe in the corridor, like prize-fighters squaring off before the bell. Holbrook held a distinct advantage in height and width. Other than a loosened tie he also looked relatively fresh. Madsen, on the other hand, knew he looked like hell. He held his hands out, palms open. 'What's going on? They're saying it's Callan.'

'And? Oh, of course, how stupid of me, you were hoping to make that announcement yourself.'

'Not at all. It's just that when I last looked he was a near miss.'

'Surveillance got a one hundred per cent, bona fide match.'

'It was only eighty-seven per cent a couple of hours ago.'

Holbrook shrugged. 'Maybe they didn't get it right first time.'

Madsen paused to digest this. Shari struck him as the type that didn't make many mistakes, but she would be tired too, and something *had* been bothering her when she called a no-match. 'Okay, but even if he's our guy you can't step off the gas. He wasn't on his own.'

Holbrook said nothing.

'Mike,' Madsen said, 'someone tried to kill me down at the factory just now. I'm pretty sure *that* wasn't Callan. You need to organize some men and get down th—'

'Whoa! Hold on there.' Holbrook's eyebrow arched ever so slightly. 'We got a call from the manager and he described it a little differently. Sounded like you went nuts . . .'

'Christ, it was made to look like an accident, but it was meant for me . . . Listen, Callan can't be a lone wolf. It doesn't work and you know it. Let's see . . . he plots against his former employer, blows up a dollhouse and skips the country . . . all fine up to the part where, just when the world's biggest reward is announced and we get a sniff of his location, someone smashes his head in. He didn't do it to himself, did he? And what about our other little mysteries? Like how he managed to teleport out of the blast zone?'

Holbrook wrinkled his nose like there was something offensive in the air. 'There's a thing you learn after twenty years of detective work. Sometimes, no matter how hard you try in a case, no matter how many ways you look at it, you still have some unexplained bits left over at the end. It's inconvenient, but there it is. By the way, I hear you're suspended. Why are you here at all? And when did you say you were taking that integrity test?'

Madsen's shoulders fell. Holbrook thought he was several steps ahead. He couldn't see anything but what he wanted to see. Everyone wanted to close it out. Get it out of their lives. 'Tomorrow,' he said.

'Good. Give me a call after that.'

'This can't wait.'

'Yes it can.'

'I may have fucked up a few things, but I don't run from my responsibilities. Two cops killed and some of the people who did it are still out there. Don't you care?'

With unexpected swiftness Holbrook grabbed two fistfuls of Madsen's jacket and yanked him to his toes. He shook him once, hard. 'Don't talk to me about responsibilities,' he snarled. 'If you're clean, prove it. Do the test. Until then you can shut the fuck up.' Abruptly he dropped Madsen back to his heels.

White shards of pain shot up from Madsen's knee. He refused to show it. Instead, he pulled his jacket down where it had bunched around his neck, nodded, and headed for the stairs. Without turning he said, 'You're making a big mistake, Mike.'

There was no reply.

At the foot of the stairs, Madsen turned to make sure Holbrook had gone, then made for the door marked 'Surveillance Operations'.

Shari was speaking softly into her headset. The operators worked busily at their cameras. Half the Wall was a kaleidoscope of twisted metal – a jackknifed semi and the crushed remains of a hatchback. On the other half a pair of feet, one with a shoe and one without, stuck out from under a white sheet. A spreading circle of crimson was turning the sheet into a Japanese flag. A camera panned over the gathered bystanders, zooming in so close to the cop taking witness statements that Madsen could see the chew marks on his pen.

'What happened with Callan?' he said.

Shari spun. Even against the fluorescent backdrop of the Wall, Madsen could see the alarm on her face. She glanced at the operators and put a hand over her microphone. 'I can't talk to you,' she whispered.

'You got him to match. How? What changed?'

She bit her lower lip. 'I filtered out some bad data.'

'What data?'

Shari darted another look over her shoulder.

Madsen caught the look and frowned. *What the hell are you hiding?* he wondered. Aloud he said, 'Shari, listen. Our lords and masters have taken to this like a lifeboat in a storm. They've got their bomber and all they care about right now is putting out a press release. But Callan wasn't on his own and I seem to be the only one that cares. I need to know what you know.'

'You need to go.'

'What's going on?'

'You need to go.'

Madsen took a step closer. They were inches apart, almost touching. 'What data?'

She pressed her lips together.

'Did you give this to them?' he asked. 'The mayor, the Bureau, the chief, they've been desperate for a way out. Now they've got it – from you. Holbrook just fed me some bullshit about the loose ends being something you live with, but all the loose ends, everything weird about this case, the TrackBack failures, the

Harry Houdini escape, the leaks, the contradictions . . . they *all* came through this room.'

As he spoke Shari's eyes widened. 'No,' she said.

'Why are you doing this? Is it because of Adam?'

Tears spilled down her cheeks. 'You can go to hell.'

The two operators had turned to watch the unfolding drama. Madsen just had time to register that they were looking past him, rather than at him, when his arms were yanked back and pinned beneath his shoulder blades. Powerful hands lifted and propelled him from behind, out of the room, down the corridor and through the entrance lobby. A shove sent him sprawling into Vallejo Street.

'If you want to self-destruct, do it on your own!' Holbrook yelled.

Several uniformed officers stopped to watch. Madsen picked himself up, his back on fire and his knee throbbing, and limped to his car. He fell into the driver's seat, exhausted, and thoroughly defeated. As he fumbled in a pocket for his keys, his fingers brushed something unfamiliar. He took it out and examined it. It was a scrap of paper, torn from a notebook. Pencilled across it in tiny, hurried letters was one word: *Persian*.

Madsen didn't know how long she would be, so he parked with a view of the Persian's front entrance, reclined his seat and waited.

A bus clattered by and squealed to a stop thirty yards further on. There was a hiss and a crash as the door cranked open. Tired commuters intent on losing their suit ties and high heels clunked down the steps. They cast long shadows as they passed. None bent to look inside the Dodge. If they had, the red-rimmed eyes staring back might have sent them hurrying on their way.

The bus roared and clattered on in a haze of carbon monoxide. No Shari.

An hour and three more buses passed before she came. The last yellowing rays of sun lit the sky and the street had dimmed. A cab pulled up. She stepped out dressed in her civvies – jeans, T-shirt and high-top dockers and disappeared inside the cafe without so much as a glance over her shoulder.

He followed and joined her at a corner table, the same one they'd had the last time.

They regarded each other cautiously.

Shari was first to speak. 'They came at me today, your OPI people. It was just after I confirmed it was Callan. People were happy. I was starting to hope the interview would be a formality. But they grilled me on the leaks, the images, the viddy evidence. Everything that went wrong in this shitty case. I thought it would never end.'

'I'm sorry, Shari.'

'They really thought I was part of it.'

Madsen said nothing.

'They got nothing because there was nothing, okay?'

'Okay.'

'I was surviving. I was fine, just like you said. Until they asked about Adam.' Shari's green eyes flashed. Her hands, resting on the table in front of her, balled into fists. 'They *knew*.'

Christ, when she had sought his advice he had told her the test was an inconvenience, nothing to get worked up over. *OPI stick to their scripts*. 'Are you going to be okay?'

She shrugged.

'How did they know? For what it's worth, I didn't say anything.'

She nodded. 'It was Yolanda. I don't blame her. She must have been torn up inside, and I put her in a dreadful position. Let's face it, if I'd come clean at the beginning I wouldn't be in this mess. As it is, they took me by surprise. I lied. I deleted evidence. Game over.'

'Deleted evidence? What evidence?'

'There was recorded audio of me and Adam arguing. It was captured and stored in the Grant Avenue files. A candid discussion about us, nothing to do with the case, but it was only a matter of time before somebody else came across it. I deleted it.'

'Jesus. You didn't tell me *that*.'

There was a long, uncomfortable silence. The waitress stopped by to take their order. Shari shook her head. Madsen ordered coffee. When the waitress had gone he asked, 'Are you suspended?'

'Effectively. The captain was furious. He had no choice but to let me finish my shift because there was a big accident at the Broadway Tunnel plus two homicides. It was chaos. That was when you saw me. As soon as Angie arrived to take over, I was told to take a hike. Go home. Stay there. Don't talk to anyone. Don't come back until called. It's hanging over me. I guess he's trying to work out what else I might have done. For now, I have no credibility. When I tried to show him what I found he wouldn't listen. None of them would . . .'

Madsen frowned. 'Show him what? What did you find?'

'I'll get to that. First you have to know that the OPI guy in charge, the one that did the interview, is gunning for you. He's nasty.'

'What's his name?'

'Samuels.'

'Ryan Samuels?'

'Yes.'

'Dresses like one of those feds from the nineteen fifties – crew cut, sharp suit, spit-polished shoes, the whole deal?'

'That's him.'

Madsen sighed. 'This day just keeps getting better. And I applaud your character insight: he's a nasty son of a bitch.'

'Well, once he knew I wasn't the leaker, he started asking about you, preparing for your interview . . . the one you didn't show for. No one is supposed to talk to you. If they knew I was here . . . God knows what would happen.'

'And what about you? Do you think I'm the leaker?'

'No – yes. Honestly, I don't know. All I know is you care. You want to get the people who killed Adam as much as I do and you won't let anything stand in the way. You proved that again this afternoon, when you came and accused me . . .'

Madsen shifted uncomfortably. 'I'm sorry. I was out of line.'

'But you were right. I wasn't telling you the truth. At least not all of it.'

Madsen fell silent. So she *had* been hiding something. He could tell from her expression that she expected an angry reaction, but he wasn't upset. Whatever had held her back before, she was here now to make amends and tell him what she knew. He allowed a smile, and the tension between them eased a little, displaced by something a fraction warmer. 'So what did you find?'

She took a deep breath. 'Okay, let me back up a little. You remember the uniform differences I got between the two faces? Callan's and backpack man's?'

'Sure. You said it was weird.'

'Yes. It bothered me, and after you left I tried to come up with an explanation. First I wondered if the licence and passport photographs we had were old, because ageing might explain it. I checked. They were taken this year. Then I ruled out plastic surgery because you'd get bigger differences where the work is concentrated – on the chin and nose, for example – and no differences in other areas. I decided a mask *could* work . . . if backpack man was just Callan with a thin layer of, say, liquid latex, that could definitely achieve a slight difference all over, but it didn't make sense: if you go to the trouble of using Hollywood-grade make-up for a disguise . . .'

'Then why go halfway? Why not make your face look *really* different?'

'Exactly. Finally I started thinking about—' Shari lapsed into silence. The waitress had arrived with Madsen's coffee. She placed it on the table and asked if there was anything else. Madsen shook his head and she moved away to serve another table.

Shari sat forward. 'Finally, I started thinking about pollution. We used footage from a lot of cameras to build our composite of backpack man. In effect, our model is an average of all those inputs. If there was a big distortion in one camera, like from a faulty lens, maybe that could have thrown the average off a little. So I tested for that. I began making composite models of backpack man using just one camera at a time, beginning with the best footage we had, which was from the camera in the dollhouse bedroom.'

'And?'

'And straight away I got a hundred per cent match-up. First

time. Eureka. I told the team and . . . like they say, good news travels fast.'

Yeah, Madsen thought. *Except down to dumb fucks doing factory tours in San Jose.* He leaned back in his chair, nodding slowly. 'So it was Callan.'

'Callan was the bomber. No question.'

'But you said you tried to show the captain something and he wouldn't listen . . .'

'I'm coming to that. I still didn't know which camera was distorted, so I decided to keep looking.'

'And?'

'The very next camera produced a model of backpack man that was an eighty-three per cent match-up with Callan. Wow! I picked the bad one straight away! What were the chances? I tried another, just to be sure. Whoops, eighty-three per cent again. Uh, oh, now I was confused. Two cameras bad? Distorted by exactly the same amount? I don't think so. I tried more city cameras, the CCTV cameras in stores across the street, the bank cameras . . . eighty-three per cent. They were *all* the same!'

'Jesus.'

'Then I tried the second interior camera. The one in the doll-house stairwell . . .' Her voice dropped to a whisper: 'A hundred per cent.' An anxious frown creased her brow. 'I tried to tell them, but it's like you said, no one wants to hear. They cut me off . . .'

Madsen screwed his eyes shut and shook his head. He had lost track somewhere. 'I don't get it. What's the significance—'

'Don't you see? The bedroom and stairwell cameras each produced a model that matched one hundred per cent with Callan. All the outside cameras lined up on only eighty-three per cent. They modelled a different face.'

'Not Callan's?'

'No. Someone else.'

'Are you saying he had an accomplice?'

'Yes. That's exactly what I'm saying.'

Madsen exhaled slowly. He was stunned. It made sense. Two similar people dressed in identical clothes. The surveillance team had assumed, perfectly naturally, that all the footage was of the same guy. Then they did the sensible thing and utilized all the data available to construct the best possible model. Except it wasn't. The model was a blend. A fusion of two people. It would never completely match either one individually. It certainly explained the weirdly uniform differences when they had tried to match it with Callan's photographs.

And this afternoon Shari had separated the footage correctly, into two categories. On her system somewhere there were now two models. One of Callan and one of an accomplice. An accomplice who was still alive. An accomplice who, only a few hours ago, had tried to decapitate Madsen with a storage rack.

Proof.

He pushed back his chair and got to his feet.

Shari looked up. 'Where are you going?'

'Back to Central Station.'

Chapter 45

Shari Sanayei never imagined she would steal from a police station.

She spent the drive back to Vallejo Street trying to talk Madsen out of it. At first she said he shouldn't do it at all. He could wait for his integrity test, then make people listen. Not an option, he said. The threat was immediate. Then she said it wouldn't work. There would be uproar if anyone saw him, and even if he managed to talk his way into the surveillance room he didn't know how to get the files off the computer. He didn't care, he said, he'd work it out.

Then she said she'd do it. He'd argued about that too, but she pointed out that she could walk through the front door and go directly to the surveillance room. If anyone asked, she would say she'd left her wallet behind. Angie was supervising night shift. She was a subordinate. Shari could send her somewhere, get her out of the room for a few moments. She knew exactly where the files were and where to jack in a memory cube. The download would be done in ten seconds. No one would see: surveillance rooms were one of the few places in the city that didn't have any security cameras. If no opportunity presented itself she would simply walk out empty-handed. Easy. She would be in and out in three minutes.

Now, as they watched from the darkness of Madsen's Dodge,

she was having serious doubts. The spotlights that threw 'Central Police Station' into dramatic relief over the entrance suddenly looked terrifying. She could conjure up any number of ways for it to go wrong.

A yellow shaft stabbed the laneway alongside the station. It grew and lengthened into a rectangle. The shutter door on the garage. A police cruiser pulled out. It turned onto Vallejo and rolled, unhurried, to its nightly rounds.

The yellow rectangle shrank, then disappeared.

Shari cracked the door. In the darkness she could feel Madsen's eyes on her, sense his concern. Without a word, she got out and crossed the road.

The entrance lobby was empty except for the desk officer behind the perspex. One of the older guys. Cuesta. He glanced up from his magazine, bored. Shari nodded. Cuesta nodded back. She crossed to the security door. The sign above it warned: BEYOND THIS POINT PERSONS WILL BE SUBJECT TO SEARCH. She waited for the buzzer.

Nothing happened.

A voice from behind called, 'Shari?'

Fear rippled beneath her ribs. She forced herself to turn.

Cuesta leaned forward, his face grim. He cleared his throat. 'I just wanted to say . . . I heard about you and Adam. I'm sorry.'

She nodded and gave a wry smile. 'Oh.' *That didn't take long to get around.*

'Yeah, he was a great guy. I'm gonna miss him.'

'Me too.'

She turned back to the door, hoping Cuesta would get the message. There was a long silence, then a loud buzz and the clack of bolts.

She took a deep breath and pushed.

Shari passed the patrol room. Inside, a group of uniforms loitered around a screen, sipping instant coffee and watching a sitcom before heading out on patrol. The dispatch centre was next. Radio calls and the clatter of keyboards floated into the corridor. She had almost made it to the surveillance room when she heard someone on the stairs, coming down. Her heart skipped a beat. All the administration people had gone home; the only people working nights on the upper floor were inspectors and commanders.

The wallet excuse suddenly seemed completely inadequate.

The interview room. The door was just to her right, and the glass porthole was dark. Empty.

Without thinking she pushed the door open. It squeaked. She stepped inside and eased the door closed. The latch clicked home and she flinched. Big mistake. If she were found hiding there, in the dark, no excuse on earth was going to sound rational. The person on the stairs reached the bottom. Shoes clapped linoleum, coming closer. The steps slowed. Shari shut her eyes.

A burst of laughter echoed from the other end of the corridor. A shoe scraped. She heard the tap of receding footsteps. From the direction of the patrol room came Captain McAlister's voice: 'Hey, you boys are supposed to be out already.' A chorus of groans. More laughter.

Shari cracked the door. No one in sight. The captain must have gone inside the patrol room. She crossed briskly to the surveillance room, turned the handle and entered.

Angie wasn't there. Her jacket was draped over the master console chair. A lone operator idly cycled cameras. Romero, one of the rookies. After a manic day, the surveillance team was enjoying a quiet night.

Ten seconds. That's all it will take.

Shari slipped silently behind the master console, then inched open a drawer, retrieved a memory cube and slotted it in. She slid the keyboard towards her and paused. Romero would hear the typing. She stared at the back of his head, trying to think of a way to handle it. She smiled. Romero's head was tilted, propped on an elbow. His right hand rested lazily on the console. Centre screen on the Wall, an ample-chested woman in a tiny skirt and heels tottered down Columbus Avenue. As she passed from view, Romero lifted his index finger and nudged the joystick, cycling to the next camera.

Shari picked up a headset and slipped it on. She tapped the mike. 'Glad to see you looking after that lady's welfare, Officer Romero.'

Romero jumped. His ears and neck turned a deep shade of red.

'I'm not going to make a fuss,' Shari said. 'But all the same . . . you won't forget to, ah, protect and serve the less *attractive* citizens of this fine city, will you? How about a by-the-book sweep, west to east?'

Romero sat bolt upright. The woman disappeared as he got busy.

Shari whipped off her headset and got busy herself. Her fingers flew over the keyboard. She opened up the Grant Avenue evidence directory and sorted the files by type, looking for the models she had created earlier. She held down the control key and began clicking, selecting files. Her hands shook. Partway through she slipped, deselecting everything. She started again, from the beginning. *Too long!* On impulse, she selected the entire directory and dragged it to the memory cube. A blue bar appeared with a time estimate.

Her heart sank.

One minute fifty-five seconds.

She glued her eyes to the timer, willing it to go faster. She watched with such intensity that the first she knew someone was behind her was when Angie's irritated voice asked, 'What's going on?'

Shari froze. Then, putting on her best smile, she slowly turned. Angie stood there, one hand holding a coffee mug, the other on her hip. She was peering over Shari's shoulder at the screen.

The wallet excuse wasn't fooling anyone now. 'Angie,' she began shakily, 'I need you to check something. Can you—'

'You're not supposed to be here.'

'Angie, listen. A second person was involved in Grant Avenue. Everyone insists there was only one, but there was someone else. Agent Madsen needs to get people to listen.'

'The plotter?' Angie was aghast. 'You can't talk to him. Don't you know there's a warrant for his *arrest*?'

'What?' Out of the corner of her eye, Shari saw Romero turn and stare, wide-eyed.

'He turned up at the Dreamcom factory, demanded to poly-graph half the shift, then caused some kind of industrial accident. He pulled his gun and threatened people. He was going to *kill* someone. Then he tore out of there. Dreamcom are screaming about damages, terrified employees, disruption to their busi-ness . . .' Angie frowned. 'And you've seen him . . .'

He's sitting fifty yards away, Shari thought. *If anyone checks the GPS on his Dodge they could go out the front door and slap cuffs on him.*

Angie's eyes narrowed. She stepped forward to get a better look at the screen. 'What the hell are you doing?'

'If you'll calm down a second, that's what I'm trying to explain.'

'Oh my God . . .' Angie backed into the corridor. 'The captain needs to know about this . . . right now!' Her coffee mug dropped, made a *thunk*, and sprayed a fan of brown liquid across the linoleum. Shari heard Angie taking the stairs three at a time.

Shari turned back to the console. The pale blue bar crawled across the screen in tiny, excruciating increments. Romero was on his feet, uncertain what to do.

Angie yelled to someone from the top of the stairs.

The bar stuttered to a halt. Disappeared.

With a hand shaking so violently she had to steady it against the side of the console, Shari reached out and unplugged the memory cube.

Muffled thuds came from overhead. A door slammed.

Shari fled.

She took two steps towards the exit then realized she would never make it past the patrol room and out through the entrance lobby. Fighting panic, she reversed course and ran further into the building. The corridor branched left and right to the deten-tion cells. Dead ends. She kept going, towards the T-junction at the end. Left to the locker rooms and rest rooms. Nowhere. She turned right.

The garage.

Behind her, at least two pairs of shoes thundered down the stairs. A shout echoed in the corridor. The surveillance room door banged open.

She reached a steel door, opened it, stepped through.

The garage was a brightly lit cavern full of gleaming squad cars. The big shutter door was at the far end. Shari hurried between the cars, trying to look casual while moving as rapidly as possible. She passed a mechanic in blue overalls tinkering beneath a raised hood. He took no notice. She arrived at the shutter. Next to it was a grey control box with two palm-sized plastic buttons – one green, one red.

She slapped the green one.

An almighty screeching of dry metal echoed through the cavernous space. She didn't look back. As the shutter passed her knees she dropped to the ground and rolled underneath.

Chapter 46

Daniel Madsen knew something had gone wrong the instant he spotted Shari coming from the laneway instead of the main entrance. He started the engine as she sprinted across Vallejo Street. The passenger door slammed and he accelerated smoothly from the kerb. 'What happened?'

'Take the next right.'

'Why? Where do you—'

'*Just do it!*' she shouted. He did.

'And again,' she said. 'Now left.'

He followed her directions.

'Pull over.'

'Here?'

'Yes. Here.'

They were only two blocks south of where they'd started, but her tone brooked no argument. He brought the car to a halt. To his astonishment she leaned over and began fumbling inside the pockets of his jacket. She withdrew his handset and shoved it in the glove compartment. She turned back and searched the other pocket. 'Where's your polygraph?'

'I don't have it. It was smashed.'

'Give me your gun.'

'Why?'

'Just give it to me.'

Reluctantly, Madsen drew the Beretta and handed it over. He watched in astonishment as Shari checked the chamber was empty, reversed the pistol so she held it by the barrel, then smashed the butt against the dashboard. She did it a second time, harder. Tiny pieces of broken plastic fell away. As she gave it back, understanding dawned on him: the tag. Every Bureau asset carried a GPS tag as a precaution against loss and theft . . . and it doubled as a backup for tracking an agent's location. Nothing could be done about the GPS embedded in his phone, but the gun's tag was glued to the base of the grip. She had busted it off.

Shari climbed out, came around to the driver's side door and pulled it open. 'Leave the keys.'

He holstered the Beretta, threw the keys under the seat and followed. 'Where are we going?'

'Just come with me.'

There was an alleyway across the street, narrow and unlit. Shari made a beeline for it. They plunged into darkness. The air stank of damp rotting trash. Madsen found himself slipping on patches of something unidentifiable and slimy. Where the hell was she going? She was acting like she'd lost her marbles. On the other hand, going blindly down here after her didn't score highly for rationality either.

They arrived at a chain link fence. Shari stopped and held a finger to her lips, then pulled Madsen close and cupped her mouth to his ear. 'Don't talk,' she whispered. 'The camera here is covered in grime but the microphone works.' She grasped the fence and began to climb.

Madsen watched incredulously. He examined the fence more closely and found a gate, but it wouldn't budge. A rusty padlock secured the bolt. Reluctantly, and favouring his sore knee, he hauled himself up. He swung a leg over the top and lowered himself down the other side. He felt Shari's hand grab his sleeve and tug him towards a tiny passage running off the side, between two buildings. They moved off along it. Each time she neared a window she bent to clear it. Madsen followed suit, his leg throbbing in protest. They crept across a yard stacked with pallets and stinking of rotten fruit, cabbage and wet cardboard. They crossed another fence into another alleyway. It was the same size as the first one, but the atmosphere was different. It smelled earthy. It gritted underneath Madsen's shoes. The windows yawned black and empty. At the far end, several strips of tape were stretched across their path. They ducked beneath, and stopped.

Not a single light shone. Large dinosaur shapes loomed in the darkness.

'Know where you are?' Shari asked.

'Grant Avenue.'

'Let's sit. Over there, in the doorway. You've got some explaining to do.'

'*I've* got some explaining to do? How about you start with what happened in there and why we're in the middle of a bombsite?'

'Angie saw me. God knows how it looked. She sounded the alarm and I ran. We're here because it's close and the cameras are down. Now I need you to tell me what happened in San Jose. Why is there a warrant for your arrest?'

Arrest! Madsen listened in horror as she repeated Angie's words. He guessed Pemberton had made the calls. When DiMatteo heard Dreamcom's version of events she must have believed it. Must have snapped. Whatever trouble he was in before, it was now a hundred times worse.

Madsen took a deep breath and began recounting what had happened at the factory. He took his time and told it as fully as he could. He detailed his conversations with Pemberton, what he'd learned about Callan, the sequence of events before the rack toppled and his final moments there. When he told her about pulling his gun and his desperate scramble to get out, he became embarrassed as he recognized how easily his actions could be misinterpreted and manipulated to look like something else.

She listened without interrupting and when he finished she didn't speak for a long time. As he stared at her in the darkness he felt a profound sense of gratitude. A couple of hours ago he had clumsily, shamefully accused her of manipulating evidence. Now, with a much more serious accusation levelled in his direction, she could have – should have – turned him in. Instead her first impulse was to take him someplace where she could hear his version.

A siren squall rose and fell in the distance.

After a moment she asked, 'Why are they blowing up the factory now?'

'What do you mean?'

'Well, you said that's what they're planning, so why did they do *this*?' she said, gesturing at the devastation around them. 'We all assumed it was part of a campaign to generate fear, to scare customers away. The entire task force has been freaking out over another dollhouse being hit. So why the factory? Did they change tactics?'

Madsen tried to think of a sensible answer. Dollhouses were soft targets and by far the most effective way to hurt Dreamcom. Bombing the factory would kill employees, disrupt production, but in the long run it would be much less effective. Dreamcom would eventually get things going in another location and beef up security. The story would fade away. The public wouldn't care. She was right. It didn't make sense.

But the HAMDA had picked up traces of explosive. He couldn't ignore that.

Shari was apparently thinking the same thing. 'How sure are you about those traces?' she asked.

'Very.' He remembered it clearly. He had been standing near the loading dock. Pemberton had gone. He'd switched the HAMDA's detection array from narcotics to explosives. There was an initial, clean scan. Then just the faintest flicker. Very small. Then another. He had pulled out the rollout screen and begun turning slowly in a circle. Tiny traces had registered on the screen. D-5. Fluctuating. But why? Air movements, that was it. He had felt cool air flowing past his skin. Then, just before he'd looked up to see the rack towering over him, the feeling stopped.

'The breeze.'

'What?'

'There was a breeze blowing where I picked up the trace. Coming in through the loading dock . . .' He trailed off. It would be so easy. In the trailer, packed in the coffins . . . Madsen's eyes widened in horror. He started scrambling to his feet. Shari grabbed his arm, pulling him back. 'Where do you think you're going?'

'I got it wrong. It wasn't the factory. They were loading dolls on an eighteen-wheeler. That truck will be rolling down the I-5 right now, heading for Nevada. It'll be there by morning. The Ten Worlds opening. They've been advertising it everywhere. It will be filled with people, celebrities, media . . . there'll be *thousands!*'

Chapter 47 _____

'*I have to get someone to stop that truck!*' Madsen tried to pull away but Shari gripped his arms tightly, refusing to let go.

'Think!' she hissed. 'They think you're crazy, remember? You've been leaking, lying, threatening, trying to kill people. You skipped your integrity test. The moment you call or show your face you'll be arrested and locked in a cell.'

'I'll insist on a polygraph.'

'And you'll get one. Tomorrow.'

Madsen sagged. She was right. He was never going to get a hearing before morning.

'What about this,' she said, fumbling in the pocket of her jeans. She held up something small, close to his nose so he could see. A memory cube. 'I copied all the models. Can't we give them to a journalist? Get them broadcast?'

He thought for a moment and shook his head. 'Same problem. The models aren't pre-packaged and self-explanatory, with all the dots joined up for viewers. We'd have to find a journalist prepared to listen while we went through and explained everything. We'd have to convince them we're telling the truth. That's not going to happen tonight either.'

He sat, put his palms to his temples, and squeezed. If he was going to think, this was the place to do it – dark, silent and dead. For two days he had been propelled by events beyond his control, trapped in a flat spin. He had to take charge, get back in the driver's seat. He had to *get it done*. His mind whirred. *No support, no place to turn, every road leads to arrest, delay. Just one constant: time is ticking. Tick, tick, tick.* He sat and thought for a full two minutes. Slowly, then more emphatically, he began to nod. There was only one thing he *could* do. It would mean kissing goodbye to whatever was left of his career, but what was a career if he couldn't live with himself? He got to his feet. This time Shari did not try to pull him back.

'What's the plan?' she asked.

'Vegas.'

'And then?'

'Warn them. Intercept the truck. I'll work it out when I get there.'

'If you go near an airport you'll be stopped.'

'I'll drive.'

'In your Bureau car? They'll pick you up in five seconds.' She got to her feet, reached out and took hold of both lapels of his jacket. Leaning in close, she said, 'You haven't got a clue.'

She was right: he didn't. But there were no other options. And somebody had to do it. Suddenly he realized what she was leading to. 'No,' he said firmly. 'I've got you in too much trouble already.'

'True, but you won't get a hundred yards without me. I'm coming.'

Madsen argued, but she won the debate with five words, sharp and emphatic: *For their sake. For Adam's.* He shut up and listened. To get down to Vegas, she explained, they needed to keep buying time. At some point, probably soon, the police or the Bureau would decide they needed to locate Madsen and pick him up, and when surveillance operations were engaged they needed to have a head start. If they didn't panic, kept moving and kept their wits about them, they could stay ahead long enough to do what they had to do. Their biggest priority was a vehicle. A clean one, not directly associated with either of them.

But before that, before they could go anywhere, they needed a change of clothes.

Madsen suggested raiding one of the smashed-up stores but realized even as he said it that the only clothes they'd find on this section of Grant Avenue would be souvenir T-shirts, and the store owners had probably cleared everything out anyway. Shari didn't reply. She was already moving off in the darkness, heading south, towards the Jackson Street intersection. Madsen followed. Ahead, past the cyclone fencing and police tape, the streetlights glowed, bright and intact, and Madsen could see Shari's dark silhouette peering under broken cars and into shops and doorways. It stopped and bent low. As he came closer he saw she was kneeling beside an alcove. He could make out a soft, round shape there next to her, on the ground.

Shari reached in and shook it.

The shape jumped. 'Waddyoowan . . .' High-pitched words, frightened, slurred.

'I'd like to buy your coat,' Shari said.

'Why doan yoo fuckoff.'

Shari pulled out her wallet. 'How much do you want for it?'

'Snof'sale.'

'How about fifty bucks?'

They settled for seventy plus Madsen's jacket as an exchange.

A second bum, just a few yards away, had obviously been listening, because after a short but intense negotiation he relinquished his coat for a hundred and forty – all the cash Madsen and Shari had left between them.

Both coats were large and had hoods. But there was a downside. They were filthy, and when Madsen pulled one on, the stink of stale sweat made him want to gag.

So much for clothes. A vehicle was an altogether different proposition. It was no use trying to retrieve either of their private cars. The tags would be picked up by the first camera they passed. Stealing a car anywhere in the area was likely to invite an instant response from watching eyes. Which left begging or borrowing. It was going be one hell of a challenge. There weren't many friends

Madsen could drop in on at this time of night, let alone ask a favour.

Not many, but maybe one.

It was a long walk. In ordinary circumstances it might have taken Madsen a half-hour, but tonight he would be lucky to do it in three times that. He shuffled slowly, hood up, head down – trying to look like a bum searching for a warm place to sleep. He shuffled along wet sidewalks, hosed clean by store owners before closing time. He passed rows of graffiti-tagged steel shutters and listened to the electric buzz as he passed under streetlights. He threaded between cardboard boxes overflowing with garbage, smelling nothing over the stink of his own coat.

He walked alone.

Two people together, Shari had insisted, was bad. Too obvious. She rattled off the streets and laneways – the ones that were quieter and those that avoided close-up cameras – and made him repeat them back until he got it right. And try not to limp, she said. TrackBack will zero in on that in no time and no matter how often you change clothes, your gait will give you away. Then, with a brief squeeze of the hand, they separated to walk unseen but parallel courses. Guilt ate away at him. She had confided in him about Adam, made herself vulnerable. He'd repaid that trust by accusing her of lying, then letting her get caught stealing evidence and now dragging her deeper into a mess that should have been his alone.

He headed south, then west, then south again, doing his best to keep his sore leg in step with his good one. Chinatown tea importers, tarot card readers, souvenir merchants and jewellery traders gave way to banks and narrow boutique hotels and the bright display windows of home decor and fashion stores. He passed people, some alone, some in company. Couples, late-night tourists, office workers, homeless men. Two men holding hands politely stood aside to let him pass. Most averted eyes or pretended he didn't exist.

A searing beam blinded him and flicked away and his heart

raced as he registered a police cruiser nosing past, probing the shadows with its spotlight. The cruiser growled off, leaving him hyper-alert for the sound of the next vehicle that passed. A cab.

The streets became dark again, punctuated by occasional splashes of neon. Heavy bass music thumped from hidden clubs. Doorways offering nothing but a stairway and a promise spilled white light across the sidewalk. Madsen rounded a corner and spotted the bright red and yellow sign advertising his destination. Resisting the temptation to speed up, he continued his steady shuffle all the way into the parking lot. As soon as he was behind the privacy wall, he pulled off his coat, grateful for the chance to breathe the fresh night air.

Shari stepped from the shadows into the bright store lights, her coat already rolled up under her arm. 'What took you so long?'

Eddie's Adult Emporium had three attributes that Madsen considered priceless in the present circumstances. The first was being within walking distance. The second was that it was surveillance-free. Not only did it have a high perimeter wall to shield customers from city cameras, but it was exempt from the Stream Share Act, courtesy of its status as a registered adult entertainment establishment, so no police access to CCTV either. The third attribute was Eddie himself. He was friendly. He was pragmatic. And he owned a car.

They pushed the plastic curtain aside and went in. Eddie was seated at a stool, watching something on a portable screen propped on the counter. He was wearing a canary yellow jumpsuit. A straw boater was perched on his head. Two customers, both middle-aged men, browsed the displays. No sign of Scotty.

Madsen made for the counter.

'Eddie,' he said. 'I need a favour. Can we talk?'

Eddie turned, his expression was serious and cold. He regarded Madsen for a brief moment, then turned back to the screen.

'Eddie, what's up?'

No response.

'Eddie?'

328

'Please go away.'

Madsen glanced around. The other customers weren't paying attention. Shari was standing at one of the clothes racks, pretending to check out the costumes. She raised a quizzical eyebrow and tapped her watch. Turning back, he tried again. 'Eddie, talk to me.'

'Why?' Eddie asked sadly. 'You had principles once. Behind the badge and white charger and self-righteousness, you had principles.'

'I still do.'

'So when did you start persecuting people for their sexuality?'

'I've never done that. Where did you get that idea from?'

Eddie turned. His eyes glistened. 'What do you call it when you plaster a man's face all over the news, just because he fucks little plastic dollies? He wasn't hurting anyone. He just didn't live up to your standards.'

'Hang on a second. The guy you're talking about threatened a cop.'

'And if your face and your bedroom secrets were about to be dragged across every screen in America, wouldn't you reach for a gun?'

'Eddie, someone else leaked the boat video. I didn't expose him.'

Eddie levelled a finger at Madsen's chest. 'Yes, you did. You went after that man and you exposed him just as surely as if you had dragged him naked through the city streets. You haven't learned yet, have you? Everyone has a little darkness inside. It's not a choice, it's just there. You wave that wand of yours and you dig it out, but as long as it stays inside it doesn't hurt anyone. Don't you see? Who's next? Trannies? Gays?'

'You know me better than that. I've never let you down. I've kept every confidence, respected everything you've told me. There isn't time to explain but you need to trust me. It's an emergency. I need your help.'

Eddie held up his hand. 'I don't want you near me. Sooner or later you'll hurt me too. I can't help. Find someone else.'

Chapter 48 _____

Agent Ryan Samuels of the FBI Office of Professional Integrity was in his pyjamas and about to slip into a neatly turned down hotel bed when he got the call. He registered no surprise as he listened. He had exposed the sergeant's lies, and it had been a shock to her. In his experience people often did stupid, impulsive things afterwards. Doubtless her actions this evening would get her in more hot water. That was the SFPD's problem. But when the caller got to the part about Madsen, his eyebrows shot up.

He retrieved a freshly ironed shirt from the wardrobe and dressed quickly, pausing to make the knot in his tie just so. Grabbing his room key from the slot, he stepped over the room service tray in the corridor and strode briskly to the elevator.

A few minutes later he joined Holbrook, McAlister, Mertz and Romero in the surveillance operations room at Central Station. Holbrook was grumpy and bleary-eyed, evidently none too happy about being extracted prematurely from his celebrations. His breath smelled of beer. Captain McAlister looked like he was attending a funeral. Romero looked like he was in shock. Angie Mertz waited expectantly, her eyes bright.

Samuels nodded.

Angie punched something on her console. A section of Vallejo Street with Central Station in the background appeared on the Wall. Shari sprinted across the road towards a battered blue Dodge. Madsen's. An instant later Samuels was watching the same vehicle from a different angle and parked in a different place. The caption above said Stockton Street. Shari looped around the car, yanked the driver's door open and led Madsen across the road and down an alleyway. The view changed again. Blurry figures running in darkness. The clock counter stopped.

'Where'd they go?' Samuels asked.

'TrackBack lost them in there,' Angie said. 'They can't have moved or it would have picked them up again. I've set it up so the instant they pass a camera we get an alert. Romero is manually scanning the surrounding streets as a backup, and I've called in officers to set up a perimeter.'

'Exactly what did she take?'

McAlister answered. 'The Grant Avenue evidence directory. She copied the entire thing.'

Samuels stared at the image of the two shadowy figures, frozen, hand in hand. One with an arrest warrant out on him for his bizarre actions at the Dreamcom factory. The other now apparently in the business of stealing evidence. *What the devil are you two up to?* he thought.

Samuels rode with Holbrook over to Stockton Street. A squad car and a pair of uniforms were already waiting. A brief examination of the Dodge turned up Madsen's handset and the broken pieces of plastic on the dash. Using flashlights they probed the dumpsters and filthy, windowless walls of the alleyway. When they arrived at the chain link fence, one of the officers retrieved a pair of bolt cutters from the squad car and made short work of the padlock. Moments later Samuels found himself investigating a narrow passageway and the yard behind a fruit and vegetable market. He found several locked doors, any one of which their quarry might theoretically have entered and bolted behind them, but he dismissed them as soon as he shone his flashlight through a second chain link fence. The alley beyond was full of dust and mud and glittering fragments of broken glass.

Twenty minutes later he was peering into an alcove flooded with the light from four converged flashlights. One of the sorry-looking men inside was curled up in a foetal position, arms tightly folded, knees drawn up to his chest. A piece of blanket, ragged and torn, was wrapped tightly around the top half of his body. The other had a patchy beard and was sitting with his back to the wall, one arm raised in an attempt to shield his eyes. He looked in worse shape than his friend. Except for his jacket. That was new.

Samuels leaned in close, trying to ignore the smell.

'Where did you get that jacket?' he asked.

'Fuck you, 'smine.'

'I don't think so.'

'Doan take it. Alf! Tell 'em I swapped fairnsquare.'

The man with the blanket said wearily, 'It's his. Fair and square. Now how about you guys leave him alone?'

Standing, Samuels borrowed a radio from one of the officers. He thumbed the mike and asked for Central Station surveillance.

Angie's voice came back. 'Viddy ops. Go ahead.'

'Look for two homeless people exiting Grant at either Jackson or Pacific, before we got the perimeter up.'

'Roger. Wait one.' A long pause. 'I've got one on his own. Crossed Jackson heading south at . . . twenty-one fifty.'

Samuels checked his watch. It was already past eleven. 'Keep looking.'

Another pause. 'Okay, make that two. I'm tracking . . . Stand by, I'll patch the loops to Inspector Holbrook's cell phone.'

Holbrook pulled out his handset. Samuels moved over beside him to look. Two videos, two figures. In many respects they were clones: one clad in khaki, the other in tattered blue, both trudging along, hoods up and tight, heads down, careful not to allow any part of their faces to be caught by a street camera. They moved steadily and without pausing, never looking in shop windows or otherwise acknowledging anything or anyone.

Holbrook muttered something.

'What did you say?' Samuels asked.

'I said it's spooky. Almost exactly like watching backpack man all over again.'

The radio crackled. Angie's voice. 'They arrived at an adult retail store at twenty-three hundred. We've got good visuals on the entrance and surrounding streets and I've recalibrated TrackBack to recognize our two wanderers. They haven't come out. Stand by for an address.'

Holbrook's Chrysler and a black-and-white squad car swept into the parking lot of Eddie's Adult Emporium nose to tail, peeled left and right and slammed to a stop. The officers pulled out flashlights and began to search the lot. Samuels strode directly up to the entrance with Holbrook in tow. Inside, several customers gawked at him. A middle-aged man in a jumpsuit and a straw hat sat at a stool behind the counter. Samuels ignored the customers and made for the counter.

The man in the jumpsuit was bent forward, repairing something with a soldering iron. It was some kind of electronic device bristling with rubberized appendages, the largest of which was shaped like a fist. An access panel lay open and a bundle of wires and circuit boards dangled from its innards.

Samuels held out his badge and said, 'Special Agent Ryan Samuels. I assume you're Eddie?'

A barely perceptible nod of the hat. After an interval, Eddie unhurriedly placed his soldering iron in a holder and looked up. A jeweller's magnifying glass covered one eye. The uncovered eye regarded his visitor without a trace of surprise. He reached up and removed the magnifying glass, leaned forward and appraised first the badge, then the owner, the way someone might appraise a particularly large and malodorous dog turd.

'This won't take long,' Samuels said. 'You have a couple of visitors. They arrived here twenty minutes ago. I'd like to talk to them.'

'Can't help you,' Eddie said quietly

'I think you can.'

'Guess we think differently then.'

'We've got them on camera.'

'Not in here you don't.'

'We know they came in.'

'If you know so much, why are you talking to me?'

Eddie replaced the eyeglass and bent to examine a circuit board, leaving Samuels staring at the top of his straw hat. Samuels looked around in exasperation. The customers had fled. Holbrook was slouched in the doorway, watching proceedings with an amused expression on his face. Turning back, Samuels said, 'If they're not here, then you won't mind us taking a look around.'

Eddie held the circuit board up to the light. 'Be my guest. The immersion booths are in the far corner, if you get the urge. The one on the end has Kathryn Fox downloaded. Remember your manners and use the proper receptacle. And don't steal anything.'

The cops began searching the displays and booths while Samuels made for the door marked PRIVATE. Much to his annoyance, Holbrook made no effort to move from the doorway. A few minutes later Samuels was back, red-faced and empty-handed. 'All right, Eddie, no more fucking around. Where are they?'

Without looking up, Eddie said, 'I really don't think you're getting the picture.'

'No, I don't think you are.' Very slowly, Samuels reached over with his thumb and forefinger and plucked off the hat. He dropped it to the counter. Then he withdrew his HAMDA from his jacket pocket and thrust it under Eddie's nose. Eddie leaned back and pressed his lips together. His uncovered eye shot Samuels a withering, hate-filled stare.

Holbrook said, 'That won't be necessary.'

Samuels spun around, astonished.

Holbrook grinned. 'Eddie, what if I said I've just had someone run checks on all the vehicles leaving these premises over the past half-hour.' He tipped Samuels a wink. 'Nothing fancy. Just regular, boring police work, tag numbers, owners, that sort of thing.'

Eddie said nothing.

'And what if I told you,' continued Holbrook, 'that one of those vehicles was a white Toyota hybrid?'

Eddie's cheeks flushed bright red. After a moment he removed his jeweller's glass, raised his chin and looked Holbrook square in the eye. 'I'd say I don't know what you are talking about.'

Holbrook made a show of withdrawing his notebook and flipping it to a blank page. He raised a questioning eyebrow. 'Would you like to report it as stolen?'

'No, thank you.'

Holbrook shrugged. 'Tell you what, when they dump it I'll give you a call so you know where to pick it up, just as a courtesy. Don't ever let it be said that the San Francisco Police Department doesn't care.'

They were outside in the Chrysler when Samuels saw Eddie step through the plastic curtain and walk down the side of the lot. He stopped and stared at an empty parking space. His hands crept to the top of his head and gripped two fistfuls of hair. A moment later, the night was split by a long, enraged shriek.

Tuesday

Chapter 49

Shari Sanayei drove carefully, staying a few miles an hour under the posted speed limit. She was wearing a pink plastic jacket with the collar up. A Marlon Brando-style crushed motorcycle cap was pulled low over her eyes. The late-night traffic was light and she was making good time. Unfortunately they were travelling north-east, not south, but all going to plan that would change in a few minutes. She peered ahead, looking for the turn-off.

When she had dragged Madsen out into the parking lot to reveal the purloined clothes and the car keys she had grabbed from a hook in the back room, he had shaken his head in admiration. 'You pick up some interesting skills in viddy ops,' he'd said. More wisecracks, mostly directed at her driving, followed as they crossed the Bay Bridge. There were fewer between the MacArthur Freeway and Highway 24. By the time they had exited the Caldecott Tunnel his sense of humour had dried up altogether.

Understandable, given his accommodation.

She looked down at the two wretched coats lying across the passenger footwell and addressed the lump in the middle.

'How are you doing?'

'Terrible.'

'Not long now.'

The headlights lit up a turn-off sign. Lafayette. She flicked on her indicator.

A few moments later the Toyota nosed along dark, leafy streets. When she found the one she was looking for, she turned into it and cruised several hundred yards until she reached an unbroken stretch of trees. She pulled over and switched off. On the opposite side of the road were a couple of driveways and some widely spaced utility poles. The houses were invisible, set well back from the road.

'We're here. Remember, I'll be moving slowly but I don't want to come to a complete stop. Five minutes.'

'See you in five.' His voice sounded cheerful again.

Leaving the key in the ignition, Shari switched the dome light from 'door' to 'off', scooted over to the passenger side, opened the door and slithered to the kerb. She shut the door behind her and crawled into the trees.

The park was as she remembered it. Large, with a duck pond and playing fields in the middle, and a small forest of trees around the edges. This side of the park opened directly onto the road. The other three sides backed onto long rows of residences, with pathways running between some of the houses to connect the park with the surrounding streets. The question was whether she could pick the right path in the dark.

Staying close to the trees, she followed the perimeter. The fifth path she came to looked familiar, with tall, thickly grown hedges lining both sides. She hurried down it, stopping twenty yards short of where it met the street. Turning ninety degrees left, she pulled the hedge apart with her hands and pushed her way through, stepping into a front yard. The house was handsome. Two storeys, with gabled windows and a neatly tended lawn. The lights were off. In the drive, moonlight reflecting off the polished black paint, was a brand-new Ford Bronco.

She crossed the lawn to the front door and searched silently among the flower pots. Finding the key in its usual place, she brushed the soil away, slipped it into the lock and held her breath, praying that no alarms or dogs had been installed since her last visit.

The key turned. The door swung silently inwards.

The living room was in total darkness.

No sirens. No barks.

She felt her way, moving a few inches at a time lest she kick something. After an eternity she navigated through the living room and into the kitchen. The clock on the microwave emitted a pale blue light. The benchtops were clear and the cupboard doors closed. Pots and pans hung from hooks in order of size. The aroma of the evening meal lingered. Vegetarian, with plenty of spices. She went to the drawers.

The Ford key was where she expected it to be, in the third drawer from the top. There was also a small flashlight. Holding it between her teeth, she carefully opened each of the other drawers and examined their contents. She found a roll of electrical tape in one and slipped it in her pocket. From another she retrieved a notepad and pen and wrote, *Sorry Mahdi, I had to borrow your car. Love, Shari.* Leaving the note on the bench, she pocketed the key and retraced her steps, stopping briefly to exchange her pink jacket and Marlon Brando cap for the considerably more fashionable items hanging next to the front door.

A few moments later she stared apprehensively up at the bedroom window as she released the handbrake on the Bronco and let it roll backwards down the driveway. It made a small bounce and coasted into the street. She turned the ignition. The big engine sounded insanely loud as it caught and fired, then fell to a low grumble as she knocked the shift into drive. She let the car idle away from the house.

No lights came on in her mirrors.

At the corner, she turned right and aimed for a dark patch between two houses, the gap where another path connected the park to the street. Keeping her foot away from the throttle, she eased the wheel over to the right, letting the Bronco crawl the kerb at walking pace.

A hooded figure detached itself from the shadows, pulled open the passenger-side door and climbed aboard.

'Going my way?' Madsen said.

They drove for several blocks then pulled over. While Madsen checked for cell phones in the glove compartment and door pockets, Shari reached under the dash and yanked the power cable to the sat nav. Then they made a U-turn.

When they were safely on the I-680, heading south, Madsen said, 'What will he do?'

She pictured her cousin coming downstairs in his dressing-gown and seeing the note as he retrieved a box of cornflakes from the cupboard. 'He'll explode,' she said. 'This is his pride and joy.'

'And then?'

'Start calling me. And when he gets no answer, he'll call the rest of the family. Then he'll curse and shout and plot revenge. But he won't report it stolen.'

'He's a good man.'

'Like a brother to me.' And she hated doing it to him. But if she had asked permission, he would have wanted to know why, he would have asked questions, and he would have said no.

After a brief pause, Madsen said, 'My brother's a marine, over in Virginia. If this truck was his, he'd hunt me down and shoot me.'

Samuels spent the whole journey to Lafayette clenching and unclenching his jaw while watching surveillance loops on the centre console. The traffic cameras had picked up good front-on shots of the Toyota leaving. He was certain Sanayei was driving. No sign of Madsen. It got worse on the last loop. The Toyota parked in a leafy area with poor lighting and poor coverage. The nearest camera was more than sixty yards away on the wrong side of the street. All he could make out was a single shadow moving around in the vehicle and the top of the kerbside door opening and closing.

They found the Toyota unlocked, keys still in the ignition, and empty, save for a noxious-smelling coat draped over the driver's seat. Nothing in the back. A spare tyre and two large cartons of adult toys, unopened, in the trunk. They probed at the shadows and trees with their flashlights, but the space was immense. Dozens of exits. All kinds of hiding places.

They called in a local K-9 unit.

The Alsatian leapt into the vehicle and snuffled enthusiastically at the coat before dragging its handler off into the woods. Samuels jogged after them with Holbrook huffing and puffing behind, struggling to keep up.

A few minutes later, Samuels stood at the end of a narrow pathway watching as the dog turned wide circles, alternately rustling through the bushes on the left, sniffing along the schoolyard fence on the right, and visiting an empty spot where the path intersected the street.

Holbrook stood near, hands on knees, labouring to catch his breath. His brow glistened in the moonlight.

'I don't get it,' he said.

'Get what?'

'This. Everything.'

Samuels regarded the inspector with ill-disguised contempt. 'What's not to get? Madsen is unstable and delusional. He leaked video evidence to the press, almost derailed your entire case. And it's getting worse. After his brain snap at the factory he needs to be locked up before he kills someone. Isn't that enough?'

'He's out of control, no argument. I had to physically throw him out in the street. But Shari? She's a good cop.'

'Not that good. She's helping him. Stealing evidence for him.'

'Why?'

'I don't know why.'

Neither spoke. The dog whined and panted and padded in circles in the darkness.

Samuels said, 'What I do know is this: they're running rings around us while we're crawling around with flashlights. Now might be a good time to stop with the half-baked chicken shit. Otherwise they're going to pop up for another circus act, and when they do you and I are going to come out looking like a pair of clowns. Here's the plan. You raise hell with your chain of command, I'll raise it with mine. Let's get drones, helicopters, TrackBack and enough dedicated computer time to crunch everything coming out of every fucking camera in a hundred miles, and let's close this thing out.'

Chapter 50

They were more than halfway to Los Angeles and thirty miles short of the Bakersfield turn-off when the fuel light came on. Madsen had been expecting it. It was his second stint behind the wheel and he had been monitoring the gauge. He tapped the down arrow on the cruise control, shedding five miles an hour to buy a little more economy. Shari slept, curled up in the passenger seat with her cousin's jacket as a makeshift pillow. Her long black hair had flopped forward over her face. She looked pale in the dim light of the instruments.

Tyres thrummed on asphalt. Giant steel power pylons marched across an endless stretch of California flatness.

Madsen shifted in his seat, trying to ease the ache down the left side of his back, and pondered the bigger of two questions on his mind. Could they catch the truck before it reached Ten Worlds? They had the advantage of two drivers. They could keep going nonstop, one at the wheel and one sleeping. Assuming the truck driver was solo, he'd probably stop and rest every three or four hours. They would gain on him each time. Against that was the head start which was . . . what? At the factory Pemberton had been waiting on eight more dolls to roll off the production line before the truck could leave. That became seven when the forklift delivered another. The next forklift had tried to kill him, so he had no way of estimating the rate of production. It could be one doll per minute or one per hour . . . And what if the truck had left with two drivers anyway?

He shook his head. The truth was, he just didn't know.

A distant glow crested the horizon.

The glow sharpened to a puddle of light.

The puddle became a service area, an all-night diner, and a long row of dormant eighteen-wheelers.

As good a place as any.

Madsen flicked on the indicator and eased onto the exit ramp, wrestling with the second question that had been kicking around in his head for the past hour: how to get gas with no cash and without resorting to credit cards.

He let the Bronco coast down the long line of trucks and scanned for red and black livery among the bright colours, giant logos, painted advertisements and polished chrome. The trucks were silent and still, with curtains drawn over the sleeper cab windows. He was envious. The long-haul drivers inside would be stretched out on flat bunks, snoring into real pillows before waking fresh to continue down to San Diego and the Mexican border, or making the turn for Nevada, Vegas and points east.

A movement caught his eye. A pair of skinny legs in high heels disappearing behind a sleeper cab door. The door shut.

More trucks. More colours. No red and black. No Dreamcom logos. But maybe a solution to his problem.

He let the Bronco roll to the far end of the lot, away from the lights, and killed the engine. More than anything he wanted to crank back his seat and close his eyes. Instead, he reached over and lightly shook Shari's shoulder.

She lifted her head sleepily. 'Where are we?'

'I'm stepping out for a bit. Stay here, okay?'

'Where are you going?'

'Cash. See you in ten.'

He clambered from the Bronco like an old man, stretching and limping and feeling needles radiate from his knee as the circulation returned. He skirted down the line of trucks. Kenworth . . . Mack . . . silver Texaco trailer . . . blue Freightliner . . . Peterbilt. That was the one. Curtains drawn, light leaking around the edges. Plus additional confirmation in the form of a tiny Mazda sedan, very old and very second-hand, parked behind the trailer.

Madsen waited in the shadows, watching the door. The smell of air brakes and motor oil hung in the air.

Five minutes passed.

A clunk. A splash of light.

A pair of bare feet stepped onto a short chrome ladder below the door. Skinny legs emerged, followed by a miniskirt, a hand dangling a pair of high heels, a slung handbag. The woman stepped onto the gravel and bent to clip on her heels, one at a time. The door slammed. She retrieved a brush and lipstick from her bag and tottered to a chrome panel on the side of the cab, her heels making hard work of the gravel.

'You busy?' Madsen asked.

The woman turned, surprised. Her face looked well travelled – she'd lost a tooth somewhere along the way. She said, 'Take a number, baby,' then dissolved into a fit of hacking laughter. When she recovered she said, 'Where's your truck?'

Madsen flashed his badge.

The smile gave way to world-weary resignation. He gestured for her bag. She relinquished it and watched sullenly as he carefully sifted through the tissues, lipsticks and assorted debris. He held up a syringe, then a twist of plastic cling wrap no bigger than the tip of his pinkie. Inside the plastic was a white, soapy substance.

'Soliciting and possession,' he said.

'They got feds doing this now?'

'They do tonight.'

'Don't take me to jail.'

'When was the last time?'

'Friday. How about a little sugar instead? On the house.'

'No thanks.' The syringe and cling wrap disappeared into the bag. A second later, like a conjuring trick, his hand reappeared holding a wad of twenty-dollar bills. Hiding the twinge of guilt he felt inside, he said, 'But I'll still cut you a deal.'

Gas wasn't the only thing they needed. Madsen hadn't had lunch or dinner and in a few hours he'd be missing breakfast as well. Shari wasn't complaining, but she had to be starving too. It would only take a minute. Leaving her at the pumps with the Bronco, he ambled over to the diner, taking the precaution of crossing the brightly lit forecourt with his hood up and wearing a pair of sunglasses he'd found in the glove compartment. A little odd in the middle of the night, but what the hell – the place bristled with bubble-domed security cameras and raising a few eyebrows was a whole lot better than leaving his face exposed. He pushed his way inside.

The smell of coffee and fried bacon and the hiss-scrape of the griddle gripped Madsen's stomach and started it rumbling. The prospect of going without food instantly took on life and death dimensions.

He glanced around. A dozen or so truckers were scattered around the cheap plastic tables, gazing, semi-comatose, at a wall-mounted screen. They were watching NASCAR. On-screen, smoke streamed off tyres and cars cannonballed into one another. To Madsen's right was the food counter, a wide one made out of scuffed sheet metal, and above that a generously illustrated menu. Madsen ran his eye down the list. Burgers, steaks, fries, shakes, twenty-four-hour breakfasts . . .

His belly growled.

There was one customer waiting at the counter. An old guy. Short, bald and wearing a uniform shirt from one of the big produce companies. When Madsen stepped up behind him to make it a queue of two, the old guy turned and wrinkled his nose in disgust. The coat. Madsen smiled apologetically and took a step back. He watched the NASCAR, trying to take his mind off the wait. A long snake of race cars circled. A green flag waved. The snake broke up as cars pulled out to overtake. The action faded to a black background and an invitation:

Heading to Las Vegas? Call into Ten Worlds . . .

Madsen shook his head in disbelief. No getting away from the things. Shifting his attention away from the screen, his eyes were drawn to a guy sitting against the back wall, a dough-faced giant with tattooed arms and a roll of fat where his neck should have been. He wore a yellow Pennzoil cap and denim overalls with the sleeves torn out. Black finger-streaks of grease decorated his chest. The cap was too small and perched high on his head. Combined with the greasy overalls it made him look more like a locomotive engineer than a trucker. In between forkfuls of food, he was staring directly at Madsen.

The old man pushed past carrying a plate loaded with pork chops and fries and smothered in onions and mushrooms and gravy. From behind, a voice drugged with boredom asked, 'What'll it be?'

Madsen moved to the counter. The server barely blinked. Evidently she had smelled worse things than his coat. He gazed longingly up at the menu and decided, reluctantly, that hot food wasn't the smart option. It would take precious minutes. He was being scrutinized. He stank. He chanced another glance over his shoulder. The giant under the Pennzoil cap had stopped chewing and was eyeballing him with lively interest.

'What'll it be?'

Moments later, Madsen hurried back across the forecourt with two bottles of water and an armful of pre-packaged sandwiches.

It took an hour and a dozen phone calls for Samuels and Holbrook to wake metropolitan police commanders, chiefs, agents in charge and division heads, and to finish explaining and re-explaining what was going on and what they wanted to do. It took a second hour to get necessary authorizations and resource allocations drawn up, signed and countersigned.

Credit cards for Daniel Madsen and Shahida Sanayei were flagged with the banks for an instant alert on transactions.

Voiceprints were registered with the telecommunications carriers for an instant alert on calls.

Composite models of their faces were generated and synched across municipal, traffic and police camera networks for an instant alert on sightings.

A search was set up. The composite models were fed into TrackBack. Two starting points were selected: Eddie's Adult Emporium and a park in Lafayette, twenty-two miles to the northeast. Computer facilities were reserved at a dozen universities. A hundred municipal cameras surrounding each location were directed to begin feeding the facilities.

On the Wall at Central Station, the search zones were represented by two circles on a map. Samuels watched the circles expanding slowly outwards, like ripples on a pond. The process was steady, continuous. Eventually the circles touched, then overlapped, then merged into a single, peanut-shaped blob.

After a time, amoeba-like tentacles began creeping outwards along roads and highways as billions of stored bits were sucked from cameras north, east and south of the city.

Chapter 51

A *brump, brump* vibrated through the steering wheel, cutting into Shari's consciousness. Her eyes snapped open and she jerked the Bronco away from the verge.

Beside her, Madsen rubbed his eyes and cranked his seat into the upright position. 'My turn already?'

'Soon.'

'What time is it?'

'Not quite six.'

Madsen grunted. After a moment he said, 'You really gave me a headache.'

'How's that?'

'Ever since Carl Steinmann told me backpack man got out of that building I've been trying to work out how he did it. Holbrook called him Harry fucking Houdini, which summed it up pretty nicely. I just about gave myself a brain embolism conjuring up possible escape routes. Now, because of you, I have to come up with a way *two* people could have done it.'

She didn't reply. She had mentally walked through the video analysis a hundred times herself, looking for something she'd missed. And she had made Madsen recount every detail of what he had seen and learned at Datum Tech and the factory and about

Callan, hoping there might be a clue, some logical connection she wasn't seeing. She was good at her job, obsessive about the details. If she couldn't work it out, someone like Madsen, who relied so heavily on speed and intuition, hadn't a chance.

She shook her head. They needed more information, a fresh perspective. 'Do you still think it's NeChristo?' she asked.

'Well, a two hundred million dollar reward makes a pretty convincing statement that Luke didn't sanction it. But I still think it was one of the other pastors, or some splinter group of radicals who decided to take NeChristo's anti-dollhouse crusade a little too literally. You can't ignore the G-ring. There's a connection somewhere.'

In her rear-view mirror, Shari watched a pinprick of light split and resolve itself into a pair of headlights in unsettlingly quick time. A sedan. She thought she saw a glint. Something mounted on the roof. 'Uh-oh,' she said.

'It's just common sense—'

'No. Behind. I think it's Highway Patrol.'

She checked her speed. A whisker under sixty-five, but earlier she had switched off the cruise control when the drowsiness started to bite. It gave her something to concentrate on. Creeping over the limit for a couple of seconds seemed a small risk to take compared to waking up as the Bronco speared off the road and into a ditch. Well, her strategy had worked. She wasn't remotely drowsy now. She cursed herself for being so stupid.

The vehicle sailed closer, slowing to match their speed. She could make out antennas and roof bars. The gap closed to a hundred yards. It stabilized. The driver was apparently content to sit there.

Madsen leaned forward to look in the side mirror. 'What's he waiting for?'

'I don't know. But he has our number.' She had seen it a thousand times. When a cop made up his mind he was going to pull someone over there was a *tightening* in the driving, like a big cat tensing before the pounce. The gap told its own story. In the city, a hundred yards between you and a police car was benign.

When it was between the only two vehicles on a straight stretch of highway bisecting empty desert, it was tailgating.

The instant the patrolman ran Madsen's name his warrant would pop up. It would be over. They would never catch that truck.

A second pair of headlights appeared, a mile behind the first and closing. Fast. 'He must have been waiting for backup,' she said. 'Which means they already know it's us. Maybe the hooker called you in.'

Madsen shook his head. 'She never saw the vehicle.'

The new set of headlights came on rapidly. Faster. Closer. Flicking across to the outside lane.

Madsen said, 'He's coming in real hot.'

'Maybe they're planning to box us in. I'm pulling over.'

'No, wait . . .'

The headlights barrelled on. Shari heard the rising howl of a performance engine. *Jesus*, she thought, *this guy means business*. Her heart hammered.

A missile blasted past.

Long and low, with a two-tone silver paint job.

A Corvette.

Its brake lights flashed twin red circles. The nose dipped. Its quad exhaust pipes popped and spat as it decelerated.

Too late.

Strobes and flashers lit up Shari's mirrors. The Highway Patrol cruiser moved leisurely into the outside lane, then pulled alongside. Shari kept her eyes straight ahead, feeling the patrolman's silent stare as he motored past, releasing her in exchange for a juicier victim. Blue and red shadows crisscrossed the landscape. The Corvette flicked on its indicator in defeat. Hunter and captive paired, slowed, and slid in tandem towards the verge.

Shari allowed herself to exhale.

She watched until they disappeared in her mirrors, then set the cruise control and returned her attention to the highway. Far ahead, at the junction of sky and desert, the velvet blackness had softened to a deep purple and was beginning to bleed into the first glow of crimson.

'We got a hit.'

Samuels leapt from the chair where he had been dozing. 'Where?' The search had been underway for hours and so far they had picked up absolutely nothing.

'Citizen Eyes. Can you believe it?' The excitement was evident in Angie's voice as she worked the console. Romero was the only other person in the room. Holbrook had gone to Eddie's for another look and hadn't returned.

It was surprising. Citizen Eyes was an old programme that encouraged citizens to send images from their cell phones if they saw anything resembling terrorist activity. The volume of nuisance submissions got so high that the task of evaluating threats had to be turned over to computers, which didn't improve matters much, because they couldn't tell the difference between what was real and what was a joke. It should have been retired years ago.

Angie tapped her keyboard and an image appeared on the Wall. A hooded figure carrying two bottles of water and what looked like a bunch of sandwiches. It was not a great image. The figure was partly blurred, as if he had been moving quickly. But the head was facing the camera and positioned directly underneath a harsh fluorescent light. Even behind the sunglasses the face was clear.

Madsen.

'It was taken at a truck stop on the I-5,' said Angie. 'Submitter said he was acting weird. That's all he put in his description, "acting weird".'

Samuels shook his head. He was running an enormous co-ordinated search, certainly the biggest currently underway in California, possibly the biggest in the United States. He was exploiting every city, state and federal surveillance asset he could get hold of. And his first hit had come from a random snap from a trucker's phone.

'Give me a location,' he demanded.

'Going up now.'

On the Wall, the image of Madsen shifted to the left. A map of San Francisco appeared on the right. The map zoomed out until most of the state was visible. A marker glowed on the I-5, just north of Los Angeles.

Jesus, he thought. They've been travelling.

Aloud he said, 'Is this truck stop on Stream Share?'

'It's a chain,' said Angie. 'Those guys share everything. We'll have full access inside and out, plus the last forty-eight hours' archive on tap. Give me a sec to log in.'

A few moments later the still image was gone, replaced by a grid of squares, each one a CCTV camera monitoring Madsen's progress as he exited the diner and strode, head down, across the forecourt. He approached the passenger side of a black Ford Bronco.

Samuels leaned forward. 'Give me the driver.'

Angie slowed the loop to a stop. She cycled the cameras until she found one with a view of the driver's side.

The figure behind the wheel was female, with long dark hair.

'Bingo,' said Samuels. 'That's both of them.'

'Processing the tags now . . . It's registered to a Mr Mahdi Sanayei. Address in Lafayette.'

Samuels shook his head. 'A fucking relative.'

'Right.'

'Okay, upload it. If they haven't changed vehicles in the last two hours we've got them.'

Samuels sat back to watch. After a few moments, a green dot appeared on the map, just south of the original sighting. A label identified it as the traffic camera at Exit 257 on the I-5. More dots appeared to the north and south. Samuels ignored those stretching back to Lafayette. Ancient history. The southern trail formed a long looping curve to the east, like a J written backwards. Traffic cameras in Bakersfield, Tehachapi, Boron, Barstow came thick and fast.

They stopped.

The last dot was a Highway Patrol vehicle. The forward-facing camera had registered a sighting twenty minutes ago. Just to the right of the dot was another, different kind of line, orange and arrow-straight, much straighter than the others, and cutting a long diagonal from north-west to south-east.

'Shit,' Samuels said. 'They crossed the state line. Can you tap Nevada cameras?'

'Yes, but we need to make a formal request and it has to come from higher than the captain. It'll take maybe a half-hour to organize.'

'Don't bother. I know a faster way.' Samuels pulled out his cell phone. He looked up the Las Vegas field office and searched down the personnel list for the special agent in charge. He found him eight names from the top: *Collins, Graham. SAC.* He hit the call button.

After a delay he heard ringing. The ringing continued. He let it go on. Five seconds . . . ten . . . twenty.

A tired voice answered. 'Collins.'

Samuels identified himself in a few terse sentences, then got straight down to business. 'I've got two fugitives headed your way, one of them a suspended agent, the other a police officer. The agent is armed and should be considered dangerous. I've got vehicle details. I need you to get Nevada Highway Patrol and Vegas PD online to pin it down immediately. Can you take some of your boys and—'

'Samuels, did you say?' The voice was weary, unimpressed.

'That's right.'

'From OPI?'

'Yes.'

'Uh huh. Well, everyone here is flat tick today, Agent Samuels. We'll do our best, but if they're headed here we aren't going to get much in the way of immediate help from the Vegas surveillance teams. They're busier than hell.'

'If this is because I'm OPI, then just let me know and—'

'Whoa, there. Keep your hair on. It's just a bad day. They've got a new casino opening up. The biggest yet. Mega crowds, mega cars, road closures, the whole circus. The police department has half the force out there just doing traffic control.'

Casino. The word stirred something in the back of Samuels's mind. A vague recollection. Something he had seen advertised . . .

He asked, 'Does that casino have a dollhouse in it?'

'From what I hear they've got so many skinjobs they'll have trouble squeezing in people. Why?'

Samuels didn't answer. He was moving the pieces around, fitting them together. The picture emerging was so terrible he could hardly believe it. It would mean the two of them had derailed the Grant Avenue case from the beginning. The leaks, the chaos at the factory . . . it was all to slow the investigation, to delay their discovery. He was crazy and she had a motive: her lover . . . the dolls that had corrupted him . . . their maker . . .

Collins said, 'Look, everything is a little wacky and out of control. Send over the brief, by all means, and I'll get it on the list somewhere. It might just take—'

Samuels gripped his phone. 'Collins, listen up. That casino is where they're headed, and they aren't going there to play slot machines . . .'

Chapter 52 _____

Tom Fillinger felt his seat press gently into his back as the Gulfstream banked for final approach into McCarran International. He looked out through the window and surveyed the Las Vegas sprawl until he found the blaze of colour that marked out the strip. Halfway along, three glass fingers jutted from a flattened cylinder, like candles on a birthday cake. The upper floors of the Ten Worlds accommodation towers were aglow, gleaming and flashing in the first horizontal beams of sunlight.

The vast entertainment complex beneath shone even brighter.

The cylinder was six hundred yards across, and a skin of light-emitting polymer covered every square inch of exterior surface. According to the engineers, the skin was equivalent to installing ten trillion LEDs. One giant electronic billboard. Even from this height Fillinger could discern the scene playing across the surface. Shapely hips in grass skirts shimmied in front of the lost, jungle-choked temple. A little closer and he would see the ancient stones glistening with moisture and butterflies dancing among the vines.

The Gulfstream levelled out. The co-pilot switched on the intercom and announced they would be landing in a few moments.

Fillinger glanced across the aisle to where his lieutenant was sitting. Radim Ivanovic was reclined, eyes shut, apparently asleep. The ugly little prick had been quiet ever since take-off. The incident at the factory must still be on his mind. Time he lightened up. The war was fought and won, the police had the bomber, the advertising blitz was a success and the marketing boys were reporting that Vegas was packed with visitors. Best of all, there wouldn't be a single NeChristo protester to spoil the opening.

It was going to be a great day.

Pastor Luke pressed the buzzer for his security gate and padded back to his living room, where he fell into his armchair. He felt the stubble on his chin and pinched the sagging skin under his eyes. Today the make-up artists would earn their keep transforming him into the joyous leader his public expected. To his left was a scaled-down holographic replica of the Ball of Connectedness, and next to that was a panel blinking a steady stream of financial updates. He refused to look at either. Instead he gazed outside.

Like all the other residences in the reclaimed parklands, his home was embedded in the side of a small artificial hill. It was energy-efficient, unobtrusive and at one with the environment. Outwardly it was much the same as all the others, which conveyed a certain humbleness and egalitarianism. Of course his excavations ran six times deeper, which nobody could see, and his hill was taller, which was only appropriate. French doors separated his lounge from his patio. They slid into recesses to provide an unobstructed view of the NeChristo dome half a mile away.

He contemplated the dome now, from his armchair, watching it glitter in the morning sun.

His visitors entered. Unlike Luke, they were both dressed formally, in business suits. They had arrived unannounced. Pastor Richard Hodge was first. He had rung the bell. Urgent business, he had said. Well, there was plenty of that going around. Beside him was Gerard Stimson. That was a surprise. The old iron ass ran his parish like a zealot. He never left LA if there was even the smallest problem to attend to, let alone in the middle of a full-blown crisis.

He looked the same as always: like he was sucking on a large, very sour slice of lemon.

Luke waved them to the lounge. They sat. Hodge fidgeted and twitched like he had ants in his underwear.

'So, gentlemen,' Luke said wearily. 'What news is so awful you couldn't wait for me to get to the office?'

Hodge opened his mouth and closed it again, as if he didn't know where to begin. He cleared his throat. 'Drew Zomaya and Bill Beale resigned last night.'

Luke nodded. That was good news, not bad. He'd asked for their resignations personally. The only wonder was that it took them so long. 'A disgrace to their parishes,' he said. 'The good people of Louisiana and Massachusetts deserved better. But surely you didn't come here at this time of day to tell me that? Tell me something I don't know.'

Hodge tugged at his suspenders. 'Last night there was an incident at one of the New York services. People in the congregation forced their way on stage and seized the microphones. For a whole hour they took turns hurling insults at the leadership. Our members feel betrayed.'

'They have been betrayed,' Luke said.

'It's not enough,' Stimson said softly.

'What isn't?'

'Zomaya, Beale . . .'

'Those two are the last of the tainted bastards. They're all gone. Out. Who else do you want to fire?'

Neither man answered.

Hodge fidgeted and looked down at his feet.

Stimson stared Luke straight in the eye, like he was sighting him down a hunting rifle.

Ah, thought Luke, *I get it. You've come to question my actions. My authority. My leadership.* No wonder Richard was so damn nervous.

He smiled. 'I think you mean me.'

They said nothing.

'Well, before you say any more, remember this: I fought for this church. I grew the organization and the membership. I made it what it is. I've been here from the beginning. Let me remind you—'

'The question,' interrupted Stimson, holding up his hand. 'The question is not what you've accomplished, but what the rest of us can salvage. The NeChristo brand will be worthless before long. Our members won't value being part of the community. They won't wear their G-rings in public. They will not, no matter what we do or what we say, be inspired to give.'

'The best pastors,' said Hodge, 'will go independent, and their flocks will go with them.'

'So let them!' shouted Luke. 'They'll soon learn it's the partnership, the networks, the coast-to-coast coverage that gives them scale. Without it they're nobodies. They're nothing!'

'Without them *we* are nothing,' Stimson said. 'By acting decisively now we can salvage something. A core. Enough to claw our way back.'

'And only my head will do. Is that it?'

'They expect it. We have to give it to them.'

'And who's going to lead it if I go? You?'

Stimson said nothing.

Luke nodded. 'You always coveted it, didn't you? From the beginning. LA was never big enough. But Gerard, my dear naive Gerard, you can't take my job by dawn assassination. It's much harder than that. You're going to have to work! First you have to go around to all the others. Convince them. You have to win their support. Get the numbers.'

'We already did,' Stimson said. 'Last night.'

Luke stared, trying to discern whether he was bluffing. He would have had to connect with each of the committee members, work them over, convince and cajole, make promises, secure pledges. All in one night. He would have needed help . . . but of course he had it. Hodge must have done the legwork. Used his connections and position, set the direction, agitated for change, advertised where his own allegiance lay. And that meant they must have secured the numbers, because if Hodge was even slightly uncertain of the outcome he wouldn't have dared show his face here.

Fuck.

He should have known, should have sniffed it out. If he had not been so preoccupied fighting fires . . . But there would be waverers. Pastors who would be tense, worried about whether they had chosen the winning side. He knew which ones to go after. Their midnight courage would dissolve when they heard his voice. And a few would have stayed loyal . . .

As if reading his thoughts, Stimson said, 'The committee is unanimous. Feel free to make as many calls as you like. You can request a vote or we can bring them together, I don't mind which, but you'll only delay the inevitable. And of course, more delay means more damage. Or we can have the press release out in an hour.' He nodded to Hodge, who withdrew two documents and a pen from his folio and slid them across the coffee table.

'This is the best way,' continued Stimson. 'It's the *right* way. It's good for you and good for the church. The separation fee is more than generous.'

The arrogant son of a bitch, Luke thought, *thinks he can engineer a mutiny and sweep my legacy away, but he has no idea who he's taking on. This will be the biggest fight he's ever seen. Damn the church. He has no right.*

Briefly, Luke contemplated leaning over and punching Stimson in the face.

But he didn't.

Instead, he picked up the documents. Two copies of the same contract. One for him, one for them. He leafed through the top one. The terms were as you'd expect. Confidentiality clauses, non-compete clauses, immediate effect. Administration services plus two secretaries and a jet at his disposal to arrange his relocation. He got to the figures. The amount was . . . appropriate. More than expected, actually. Indeed the church could hardly afford it in present circumstances. Stimson must have wanted to eliminate any chance of haggling.

Luke made some rapid mental calculations, beginning with the cash flow and equity position he would hold if a protracted leadership struggle left him at the helm of a much diminished church. He balanced these against the number in front of him.

The comparison prompted new thoughts. Was a fight really such a good idea? The organization was a mess. There was already a ton of repair work to be done without adding to the damage. Maybe it was always going to be Stimson. Stimson the iron ass. Stimson the puritan. He would be a linchpin, a known quantity the others would stand behind. At least it wasn't Richard. That cowardly fucking Judas couldn't even look him in the eye. And where was the fun in rebuilding NeChristo anyway? He had done that once already. He could recharge. He could take this money and use it to start something else, something new.

Fuck them.

Let them clean up the mess.

He reached for the pen and began to sign.

When he was done, he tossed the contracts on the table.

Stimson picked up a copy, checked it, then folded it and placed it in the inside pocket of his jacket. He got to his feet. Hodge hesitated. He looked torn, like he was feeling emotional, like he wanted to say something, maybe make a little speech about how sorry he was that it had come to this . . .

Luke said, 'You know where the door is.'

When they had gone, he stared out at the dome he would never return to and searched his feelings for any sense of nostalgia or loss. He found none. It was already in the past.

Chapter 53 _____

Madsen stared out at flat Nevada landscape as he drove. The sky had paled to a mild eggshell blue. The sand stretched out on all sides to distant, dun-coloured hills. They were travelling at just under sixty-five. All the windows were down. Cool, dry air whipped through the cabin. He wore the sunglasses and had his hood up. Next to him, Shari had her cousin's cap pulled low. A hundred yards ahead the box-shaped rear of a Winnebago swayed gently as it rode the undulations.

Still no truck.

When they found it, the plan was simple. Stop it. Detain the driver. Find the explosive. Coffins first, then trailer, then cab. Inside and out. Not much of a plan, but he had a badge and a gun. He could make it work.

If they found it. They were running out of time.

He nursed a bottle of water between his knees, taking frequent sips to ease the pounding behind his temples. His left knee throbbed and he desperately wanted to get out and stretch. But that would waste precious minutes. At least he was no longer worrying so much about pursuers. They hadn't celebrated when they passed the brown and white *Welcome to Nevada* sign because the close encounter with the California Highway Patrol had still been too fresh. Nevertheless, it was an important milestone. According to Shari, it meant additional delays transmitting information across jurisdictions. And now, as they approached the outskirts of Las Vegas, they had daylight and dozens of vehicles for company.

Shari stiffened. 'Incoming.'

'What?'

'Dead ahead. See it?'

Madsen squinted. Floating directly ahead, just above the Winnebago, barely visible against the sky, was a speck. He moved his head to be sure it wasn't dirt or an insect stuck on the windshield.

The speck darkened.

Instinctively Madsen reached up and drew his hood tighter.

As it closed the distance, the speck gained shape and detail. Two tiny silver spikes seemed to grow from the sides. They were long and thin and lined up with the horizon. Wings. The centre mass fattened and the lateral spikes were complemented by two smaller ones, projecting downwards to form the upside down 'V' of a tail. The drone shot down the highway towards them holding altitude at a hundred feet, then flashed overhead. Madsen heard the chatter of a high-speed propeller and just had time to register *NHP* stencilled underneath the gunmetal grey fuselage. Nevada Highway Patrol.

The propeller noise died away. The drone shrank in the mirrors.

Shari had twisted to watch through the rear window. 'It's turning,' she said. 'It spotted us. Pull over.'

'Are you sure?'

'We've got maybe thirty seconds.' She was grabbing something out of the glove compartment.

Madsen simultaneously flicked his indicator, jinked the Bronco to the shoulder and hit the brakes.

Shari was out before they had stopped. She ran around to the back and disappeared. Madsen had no idea what she was doing. He pulled the handbrake, climbed out and followed. He found her kneeling in the dust next to the rear bumper, using her teeth to tear strips off a roll of electrical tape. He watched, aghast, as she applied the strips to the licence plate and refashioned a three into an eight. Smoothing the tape with her thumb, she stood, then pushed past, heading for the front bumper. 'Get ready to go,' she yelled, pointing.

He looked and saw the drone banking far out over the desert, skimming the hills, cutting a graceful arc through the sky. It had completed one half of a giant circle. Soon it would be coming around for a second head-on run. He clambered back into the driver's seat and waited with the car in gear. Seconds later she bobbed up in front of the hood, sprinted around and leapt aboard. He disengaged the brake and slammed his right foot down. The Bronco fishtailed onto the highway. Ahead, the drone was completing the circle, levelling out. The wings aligned with the horizon and became spikes again. The front profile of the fuselage became a tiny flattened football. It seemed to be flying lower and slower this time, like it was making a bombing run and didn't want to miss.

It arrowed in for the second pass.

The rude chattering blasted through the open windows before fading rapidly. Shari twisted and tracked it through the rear window. Madsen watched in the mirrors. This time the drone kept on going until it disappeared.

He asked, 'What the hell just happened?'

'It picked us up, and it wasn't random. It was looking for us.'

'How do you know?'

'Normal pattern for a traffic drone is high and to the right of the road. That way they get better hang time approaching vehicles from behind, plus it's less distracting to drivers. That one was half-height, head-on and fast. It's been re-tasked to scan every tag of every vehicle inbound to Vegas as quickly as possible.'

'If someone asked it to do that, then they already know where we're headed and what vehicle to look for.'

Shari nodded. 'And we've moved up someone's priority list.'

She was still holding the roll of electrical tape in her hand.

Madsen glanced at it, then her, his eyebrows raised. He said, 'Why did you bother? It got the tags on the first pass.'

'The slow pass was to confirm. That was the one that counted.'

'You only changed one number.'

'As far as the drone is concerned we were a completely different vehicle.'

'It can't be that easy.'

'It is – sort of. There's a catch.'

He glanced across. 'What catch?'

'Unless the altered number miraculously corresponds to another Ford Bronco, colour black, home state California, we will generate a mismatch in some motor vehicles database. An anomaly flag will be assigned to us.'

'Which means?'

'Which means at some point we'll get checked. We'll be pulled over.'

'That's a fucking big catch.'

'If we stayed with the old tags we'd have been picked up in two minutes.'

'And now?'

She shrugged. 'No way of knowing. Anomalies can be generated by data entry errors, vehicle accessories, modifications, mud spatter on the plates . . . all kinds of things. They're common. Low priority. How long we've got depends on how busy the local police are. And luck.'

They motored on in silence, passing the first rows of houses. Suburban boxes, brown tile on brown brick. In the centre distance, rising proud of the urban sprawl, reflections sparkled off a small cluster of improbable shapes and spires.

Madsen said, 'I've still got some cash. How about we ditch this and hail a cab?'

Shari shook her head. 'Cab companies have an open pipe policy to law enforcement. And you can forget the sunglasses. With a hi-def security camera twelve inches from your face you'll be matched and splashed on a police viddy Wall before your ass touches the seat. We're stuck . . . unless we can borrow another car.' She shot him a wry smile. 'Know any friendly people in Vegas?'

Madsen screwed up his face. 'I know people, but they're not friendly.'

Chapter 54

The short helicopter ride from McCarran to Ten Worlds gave Fillinger a bird's-eye view of the gathering crowds. They lined the overpasses and stood in groups and clusters along the sidewalks, in open spaces and at intersections. Along the length of the strip, bisected by a thin line of palm trees, the traffic was already down to a crawl, the yellow cabs standing out among the muted blues, greys and maroons. Cars and crowds all seemed to be heading in the same direction, towards the sound and colour blazing from the walls of the entertainment complex. Fillinger grunted with satisfaction. Like moths to a flame. Magnificent. The whole thing was magnificent.

In the seat beside him Ivanovic wasn't seeing it. He still looked like someone had shot his grandmother.

The glittering pillars of the accommodation towers loomed ahead. The pilot adjusted the controls and gently coaxed his machine towards the giant black 'H' on Tower One. Next to the landing pad was a strip of red carpet flanked by a greeting party of several dozen staff standing at attention. Their red and black uniforms flapped in the downdraught as the chopper descended the last fifty feet. The skids settled smoothly onto the pad.

A man in jeans jammed a white cowboy hat on his head with

one hand and twisted the door latch with the other. Wind and turbine noise flooded the cabin.

'Howdy, pardner!' Jim Bonitas yelled.

Fillinger grinned. 'Great day for making money!'

'You betcha. And we got plenty down there waiting to part with it.'

'Any news on our friend?' Fillinger asked, stepping down from the machine.

'Flew in last night.'

Fillinger clapped his hands in delight. Seventy-two hours ago Senator Arbett had refused to return his calls. Now he had flown in for the grand opening. It didn't get any better.

The red carpet led towards the elevator. They walked side by side, nodding and smiling at the staff.

'The presidential suite is yours if you want to rest up before proceedings,' offered the Texan.

'I'm not waiting another second. Let's go and meet our VIPs.'

'Fine by me. Just one thing,' Bonitas said, a concerned frown crossing his face. 'I hate to bring this up, but the last forty dolly birds? They ain't here. They need charge-up time and we want 'em humping and pumping by noon.'

'Stop worrying. The power cells are pre-charged at the factory. They'll be ready and working in no time. The truck will be here soon.' He glanced over his shoulder. 'Right, Radim?'

Ivanovic nodded. 'Any minute.'

Chapter 55

Madsen flicked his indicator and eased into a gap, exchanging one slowing queue of vehicles for another. The tall buildings marking the beginning of the Las Vegas strip were less than two miles away. He peered ahead, searching for the angular outline of a semitrailer. Nothing.

Dammit!

The traffic was robbing them of time. It had to be connected to the Ten Worlds opening. The truck was still ahead. Maybe it had already reached its destination. Part of him had begun to watch for a black smoke cloud boiling above the skyline.

The congestion had one upside. The cops would be busy, which reduced their chances of being picked up for the altered licence plates. The guy he knew with wheels was a few streets east, not that far, but like he'd told Shari, he wasn't friendly. With only a couple more miles to go, he would take his chances.

He tapped the brakes. The lanes ahead were merging down to one. Lines of people-movers, taxis, limousines and convertibles bumped forward, a few feet at a time. A giant orange arrow rippled from left to right.

'This isn't good,' Shari said.

'Just a traffic diversion.'

'It's manned.'

Madsen looked. Past the arrow, alongside the turn-off, was a black-and-white patrol car. It was parked on the verge under a sick-looking palm tree, with an officer reclining against the driver's door. The officer's arms were folded and his blue reflective sunglasses were trained in their direction.

Shari said, 'Either he'll pick up the tags or his car camera will. Can you turn?'

Madsen checked to his sides. The close-packed traffic left no room for manoeuvre. The only turn-off was the one ahead. 'No.'

'Use the sidewalk?'

'Bad idea. Guaranteed to grab his attention. Let's hang tight.'

The Pontiac in front rolled forward. Madsen stayed close, using it to shield the front licence plate. He kept his eyes on the blue shades. They didn't move. Madsen imagined a pair of steely eyes glaring back.

As they crawled towards the turn-off, Madsen casually reached down and flicked on his indicator. The cop was a statue. Maybe he was asleep.

The Pontiac turned right and Madsen followed, placing the Bronco a foot from its bumper. Halfway through the corner he switched his attention to the yellow cab in his mirrors, braking gently and trying to coax it closer so he could shield the rear plate.

It didn't work.

The corner opened up to two lanes and the cab driver pulled sharp left and accelerated past, taking the trouble to say what he thought of Madsen's stop-start driving with a long blast of horn. The blue shades snapped around. The cop bent to the patrol car window and peered in at something. Then he straightened, un-clipped his mike, and brought it to his mouth.

Shari was watching in the side mirror. 'He's calling it in. We'll be up on a viddy ops Wall soon, with units being directed to inter-cept. We've got five minutes max.'

Madsen's mind raced, rethinking his options. He watched the gap widen between themselves and the patrol car. One hundred yards. Two hundred. The road curved. The moment he broke line of sight with the cop, he spun the wheel right and jammed his foot to the floor.

The Bronco hesitated for the microsecond it took for the transmission to kick down, then it lurched, surged and bounced up over the sidewalk. The V8 roared. They carved a diagonal path across a parking lot and shot past a sign welcoming them to *Magicca! – Witches and Wizards Superstore*. People dodged out of the way, then blurred as they sped between two buildings towards the street behind. Madsen rotated the wheel left and the Bronco dropped from the kerb. It slewed viciously as it scrabbled for traction.

They hurtled onwards. A traffic light turned red. Madsen slowed, judging the speed of the cross traffic. Choosing a gap, he punched his foot down and the Bronco shot through. A chrome grille dipped outside the driver's-side window as he narrowly missed the nose of a pick-up.

Two blocks down he prepared to make a left. As they flew towards the intersection, the lights switched from red to green. Madsen aimed for the left-turn bay, trying to beat the oncoming traffic. Too late. He slammed the brake pedal. The Bronco juddered to a stop.

A long tanker truck rumbled across their path. Twin stacks belched thick clouds of diesel. The driver glared. Precious seconds ticked by until the last pair of giant wheels rolled past.

Madsen hit the gas and the tyres squalled as the Bronco surged forward. Out of the corner of his eye he saw Shari grip the safety handle with both hands. A few moments later he found what he was looking for. A shabby single-storey building with a faded sign that said simply: *Gold bought here*. He swept into a parking lot swirling with dust and litter. The Bronco slid to a stop between a beaten-up Volkswagen and an ancient Mercedes.

'Three minutes,' Shari shouted as they clambered out and ran to the entrance.

The interior managed to be simultaneously bright and bleak. Display cabinets crammed with shiny watches, bracelets, rings, pens and knives lined the sides. Guitars of all shapes and sizes hung along the walls. Dejected people queued at a service counter under a poster comparing the relative merits of pawning and selling.

Madsen made for the back. There was a crude partition there, with a panel of one-way glass, a door and a fat security guard. As the guard stepped forward, Madsen shoved his badge in his face and told him to take a hike. He pushed the door open.

The office was much as he remembered it. Dingy and cluttered with filing cabinets, electronic goods and dust. The only natural light came through the one-way glass. There were two desks. One was buried under junk. Unlike the last time he visited, it was un-occupied. The other desk held an in-tray and a small mountain of cash.

Behind that desk sat a dwarf.

His face was concave and heavily scarred, like he had gone the full twelve rounds with Mike Tyson and Tyson had been allowed to wear knuckledusters. He goggled at Madsen.

'You!'

'In person,' Madsen said.

The dwarf drew his lips back in a grimace, baring identical gold incisors. 'Seven years was too long, you son of a bitch.'

'It seemed fair to me. He shifted a lot of contraband.'

'He's a total motherfucker for settling accounts. When he gets out . . . Last time I saw him he mentioned something about using your entrails as a hood ornament.'

Madsen shot him a wide smile. 'Do you still have motorbikes?'

A long silence. 'You took my daddy away and you want to do *business*?'

'Yes.'

An expression of wonder crossed the dwarf's face. His eyes flicked over Madsen's filthy coat, then to Shari, lingering on her chest, then back to Madsen. He put his pen down and scrutinized Madsen warily, then scratched his head. After a further period of silence, he slid from his chair. 'Follow me.'

Dozens of motorbikes were crammed into the workshop behind

the store – customized Harleys, stylish Ducatis and a variety of powerful Japanese machines. Steel pipes had been fashioned into clothes racks and bolted along the walls. An assortment of helmets and leathers hung from the racks.

Madsen walked along the bikes, examining them.

Shari made for the racks. She stripped off her jacket and grabbed another.

The dwarf watched, amused.

Madsen spied a Suzuki trail bike at the far end of the workshop. The fuel tank was dented and the front mudguard broken. Judging from the layers of dirt encrusted on it, the previous owner enjoyed motor cross and didn't own a hose, but it had one feature that made it considerably more desirable than the others: a key in the ignition. He threw a leg over the seat and kicked the stand. Shari tossed him a helmet.

The dwarf wrung his hands. 'Buying or trading?'

Madsen pulled on the helmet, leaving the chinstrap unbuckled. He kicked the start lever downwards and the Suzuki crackled into life. The suspension dipped as Shari jumped on the back and wrapped her arms around his waist. Madsen revved the bike. He leaned over and yelled, 'It's a loaner, okay? There's a black Ford Bronco in your lot for security.' He aimed the bike at a side door and popped the clutch.

As they shot into the sunlight he heard the dwarf scream, 'You can't afford my terms, plotter man. You hear me? You can't fucking afford them!'

Madsen turned north, towards the strip, and opened the throttle wide. The Suzuki wound up like a buzz saw, firing vibrations up his spine. Shari's grip tightened as he ratcheted up through the gears. He felt strangely exhilarated. They were totally committed now, with no alternatives or complexities left to worry about, fused together and bent on a single aim: to get that truck.

He turned and shouted over his shoulder, 'How much time left?'

'None.'

On cue, a cavalcade of red and blue lights materialized dead ahead, accompanied by a chorus of wails and the urgent hammer of engines. Madsen steadied the throttle. The gap shrank rapidly. A thump of air hit his chest as the first vehicle shot past. He counted two, four, six patrol cars. And two vans. The vans had SWAT markings down the sides.

'They're still going for the Bronco!' Shari shouted.

Madsen was too stunned to reply. Christ, he thought. *All that for us.*

The traffic thickened. He aimed the Suzuki at the gaps and twisted his wrist, darting between vehicles.

Two blocks further on, he slowed.

They found gridlock, the crowds and the target, all at the same time.

Chapter 56

As Madsen threaded the bike between the lines of vehicles, he found himself staring up at a gigantic iridescent cylinder. *Ten Worlds* was blazed across it in giant red letters. The letters disappeared and the entire structure shimmered with ancient cities, steamy jungles and thundering waterfalls. Shari tapped his helmet and pointed. The sidewalks were packed with pedestrians and camera-toting tourists. A nearby overpass groaned with rubber-neckers. Above, three glass and steel towers soared skywards, each connected to the others via a web of delicate, transparent walkways. The truck had beaten them. Steinmann said there was enough D-5 left for eight or nine more Grant Avenues. What kind of Armageddon would he see if it all went up at once? Could it bring down one of those towers? Would the walkways twist and flex and snap, or would they shatter like glass?

No time to think. *Go.*

He walked and elbowed the bike forward, using the sidewalks, looking for gaps, looking for a way in. He crawled past the main public entrance, a monorail station, the entrance to a multistorey car park . . . There. A boom gate marked SERVICES. On the other side a wide ramp leading downwards, into a tunnel.

He jockeyed the bike around the end of the boom and gunned it down the ramp.

The tunnel was wide and tall and the Suzuki's flatulent echo was deafening. Orange overhead lights cast weird interlocking shadows as they raced along. When the end was fifty yards away, Madsen put the bike in neutral and let it coast the rest of the way.

They stopped at the entrance to an enormous, circular cavern. The centre was an open expanse of concrete. Running all the way around the outer perimeter was a raised runway, a flat ring of concrete perhaps four feet high and twenty yards wide. At various points around the ring, trucks had been backed up for unloading, cabs pointed inwards, like the markings on a clock face. Behind the trucks, driverless forklifts with yellow strobe lights bustled back and forth around the runway, shuttling heavy crates and pallets of boxes to oversized freight elevators which yawned in the cavern walls. Thumps, bangs and the whine of hydraulic lifters echoed across the space.

Madsen scanned the trucks. They bore the markings of transport, catering and supply companies. All but one. The truck at nine o'clock on their left was red and black with a Dreamcom logo emblazoned down the side. As he watched, a forklift backed out of the container with a coffin across the prongs. His heart sank.

We're too late.

The D-5 could be in any of those coffins, and once they disappeared into the elevators it would be impossible to keep tabs on where they went. He tracked the forklift's journey. It moved towards a freight elevator and stopped, gently depositing the coffin. Not in the elevator, in front of it. And not on the ground, on another coffin. They were stacked there, five wide, three layers high.

Not too late.

Madsen kicked the bike into gear, yelled at Shari to hold tight and gunned the throttle. The Suzuki accelerated across the open space. As he neared the truck he aimed for a set of stairs leading up to the runway. He felt Shari's fingers dig in. The front wheel hit the bottom step, followed an instant later by the back wheel.

The suspension scissored. The revs shot up as they rocketed over the lip. He leaned the bike over. The tyres stuttered, scrubbing off speed, then bit. He accelerated along the runway, towards the truck.

Two men in orange safety vests and helmets stood near the container doors, staring open-mouthed at the bike hurtling towards them. The Suzuki skidded to a halt. Madsen killed the motor, kicked down the stand and dismounted. Fumbling for his badge, he shouted, 'Stop unloading, now!'

Neither man made a move.

'Now!'

One of the men carried a clipboard and looked like he might be a supervisor. 'I'm not authorized,' he said.

The other man began backing away.

'Stay where you are!' Madsen yelled, drawing his Beretta. 'Get on the ground!'

The man did as he was told. Shari moved over to keep an eye on him.

The supervisor was white with fright. He put up his hands.

Madsen pulled off his helmet and leaned in close until their faces were inches apart. 'This truck is carrying explosives. I need you to secure the load – all of it.' As he spoke he heard a whine and a forklift zipped past. It disappeared into the truck container and a moment later reversed out with a coffin across the forks. Madsen pointed to it. 'Stop that thing.'

The supervisor's eyes twitched between the gun and Madsen's filthy coat. 'You're crazy . . .'

Madsen shoved him down beside his colleague, pressed the Beretta into Shari's hands, and ran after the forklift.

His damaged knee was no match for the machine. It pulled away rapidly, but he kept going, half-jogging, half-limping, knowing that the lift would slow when it neared the elevator. He began to catch up. Reflections played across polished alloy as the coffin was manoeuvred into position. The coffin descended the last few inches. The moment the aluminium cases kissed, the lift began beeping. The forks retracted . . .

Suddenly it reversed, directly at Madsen. He dived out of the way. The lift stopped and turned in a tight circle, squaring up for its return run to the truck. There were handles on the side. Madsen grabbed at one. Ignoring the pain firing down his left side, he bent at the knees and jumped. He sprawled across the engine casing, his nose stopping an inch away from a red plunger switch marked *EMERGENCY STOP*. In one swift motion he looped his hand up towards it, but the lift accelerated with frightening force towards the truck, sending his body sliding backwards. His palm slapped steel casing. He groped forward and slapped again.

The effect was instantaneous. The yellow strobe died and the whine stopped and the machine jolted to a halt. Madsen somer-saulted through the forks, hitting the concrete with a thud.

He got painfully to his feet and regarded the now-silent machine with wonder. *One problem solved.* Shari was calling out, asking if he was okay. He waved her off, limping back towards the stack of coffins.

There was no time for niceties. He reached up, grabbed a coffin with both hands, and pulled as hard as he could. It slid, slowly at first, until he had it teetering over the edge of the stack. He yanked again and it crashed down to the concrete. He popped the latches and threw back the lid. A doll. He felt the padding. Nothing. He reached up and hauled down a second coffin. As he pulled frantically at the latches, he heard the clunk of elevator doors behind him, then a whine. *Another goddamn forklift!* He threw back the lid.

A searing flash obliterated his senses.

Chapter 57

Madsen felt like a blunt axe had been embedded in the back of his skull. Splinters stabbed at his brain. He couldn't see but he could hear, which meant he hadn't been blown to smithereens. From far away he heard urgent shouting and something that sounded like . . . applause. Out of the darkness came images. Coffins stacked one on top of another. His own hands reaching, pulling, flicking latches. Then from the side a shadow, an ugly twisted mask radiating hate. Dark eyes. Shark eyes.

The shouting resumed, closer this time. He concentrated, trying to understand. It was a woman's voice. Hoarse and fearful, calling his name. Shari's voice.

He opened his eyes.

He was lying on the floor, on his side. Shari was a few feet away, facing him. Her jeans and T-shirt were torn. Silver duct tape bound her ankles and her arms were behind her back. Relief flooded into her face as she saw he was conscious. Then her eyes hardened and flicked upwards, past his shoulder. She pressed her lips together and raised her chin in silent warning.

He tried to sit up but found he couldn't. His ankles and wrists were clamped and he had lost most of the feeling in his left arm.

But he could lift his head. And twist.

He looked around.

They were lying at one end of a room perhaps thirty feet long and fifteen feet wide. The room had been divided lengthways. One half appeared to be a high-tech workshop. A steel bench extended along its length and hundreds of tools, shiny and arranged neatly according to size, packed the wall. Above the tools, up near the ceiling, a dozen computer screens hung at forty-five degrees.

The opposite side of the room looked like a row of shower stalls in a locker room, except the curtains were black and rubberized, and hoses and cables snaked from the ceiling in lieu of showerheads. From where he lay, Madsen could see a dozen pairs of feet under the curtains. They wore delicate gold-ribboned sandals. They stood still, toes neatly aligned and pointing away from the wall.

At the far end of the room was a door, which was closed. In front of the door lay an aluminium coffin, which was open.

Kneeling in front of the coffin was a man.

He had his back to them but Madsen recognized him anyway. His hair was tied back in a greasy grey ponytail.

The man bent over the coffin and grunted. Slowly and with considerable effort, he dragged a metal drum up and over the lip of the casing, then eased it to the floor beside two other drums.

Madsen's senses sharpened. He noticed the butt of a handgun protruding over the far edge of the workbench, within easy reach of the man. The grip was unmistakable. His Beretta.

The distant applause came again. Madsen looked up and saw the computer screens were actually CCTV displays monitoring exotic settings: an empty medieval throne room on the left, the deep greens of a jungle paradise on the right, and multiple views of deserted Roman streets in between. All except one. The centre display, where the sound was coming from, showed a huge auditorium packed with people. Two figures were approaching a stage. One of the figures wore a white cowboy hat. The other was tall and silver-haired. People stood and cheered as they passed.

With all the strength he could muster Madsen bent forward and hauled at his wrists, trying to stretch and break the duct tape. He shut his eyes and clenched his jaw and forced the pain from his mind until he felt his shoulders tearing from their sockets.

Nothing. The tape didn't give. He sagged, involuntarily letting out a low groan.

'Woke up, huh?'

Madsen looked up. The man had turned around. The black eyes fixed on him were neither hate-filled nor angry. The only emotion to be found was dispassionate curiosity, which somehow seemed much, much worse. He was not tall, but he looked like he might be strong. Perspiration dripped from his chin. His sleeves were rolled up, revealing sweat-matted hair on his arms.

'Who the fuck are you?' Madsen rasped.

No answer.

Instead, the man reached over to the workbench. For a moment Madsen thought he was going to pick up the gun but instead he retrieved what appeared to be a small blue fire extinguisher with a long coppery nozzle and an oversized trigger. He walked over to Madsen, working the trigger with a series of clicks and snaps until a flame erupted from the nozzle with a *whoomp*. He made an adjustment and the flame narrowed into a conical blue jet. Madsen caught the heavy whiff of propane and felt superheated air rippling over his skin. Squatting, the man grabbed a handful of Madsen's hair and twisted. 'Radim Ivanovic at your service,' he said. 'Feel free to scream as much as you like. The room is soundproof.'

Madsen was still processing the words when he heard a low roar and a sizzle. A blinding pain detonated behind his ear. His eyes bulged. A violent spasm racked his body, expelling air and spittle through his lips. The sizzle stopped. Madsen's head dropped to the floor with a *thunk*. He sucked oxygen into his lungs in long ragged gasps. The sickly smell of burnt flesh and hair stabbed at his nostrils.

'That's a taste, so you know I'm serious,' Ivanovic said. 'Now I'm going to ask some questions. The important thing to keep in mind is that if you hesitate it isn't you I'll be working on, it's your

383

girlfriend. I thought I might barbecue her nipples first. So tell the truth, and quick answers, please. Okay?'

Through a blur of tears Madsen saw Shari writhing, pushing herself further into the corner. He nodded.

'I can't hear you.'

'Okay.'

'Good. Why did you come here?'

'You know why.'

'Tell me anyway.'

'To try to stop you.'

'From doing what?'

'Blowing up this place.'

Ivanovic blinked, as if that information was a big surprise. After a long pause he said, 'Why didn't you stop when you got Ian Callan?'

'Because I knew there was more than one person responsible.'

'More detail, please.'

Madsen said nothing.

Ivanovic waved the propane torch in Shari's direction and raised his eyebrows.

Madsen said, 'He must have had help getting away after he set the bomb. The way he left his job. Someone killed him before we could interrogate him. I knew there was somebody else. And I knew they were inside Dreamcom.'

The shark eyes tilted and leaned in close. 'Ideas, hunches, suggestions. These are not good reasons, plotter man.'

'When I was at the factory, I detected explosives in the truck. I knew.'

There was another wait. A long one. Ivanovic seemed to be deep in thought. He began to nod, slowly at first, then with more conviction, as if coming to some sort of conclusion. He stood and turned off the propane torch. 'Thank you,' he said. 'I'm a very organized person. I don't like . . . gaps.'

Madsen said nothing.

Ivanovic put on a sad expression. 'A shame you couldn't convince anyone else of your crazy theories, except your dumb bitch here. You two had to come alone . . .'

'No. The police know we're h—'

Crack. A boot stomped on Madsen's knee. The bad one. White noise shot into his brain.

'Don't bother. I know all the answers from here. Over the past hour we've been getting calls from the FBI, the cops, everyone, warning us you are coming, to watch out for you. You are dangerous. You have explosives. Big panic. Then you actually did arrive. And they followed. They're searching the complex now, all jumped up and armed to the teeth and ready to shoot you on sight. They think you're crazy. They think it's you attacking Ten Worlds.'

Madsen said nothing. It felt like ground glass grating behind his kneecap. But even through the blur of pain he could see how chasing the truck to Vegas could have been misinterpreted as the precursor to an attack. It explained all the cops and SWAT vans.

Without another word Ivanovic tossed the propane torch on the workbench, strode back to the other end of the room and bent over the coffin. He began hauling out another metal drum.

Madsen's mind raced. He couldn't break the tape, couldn't do anything to stop the guy directly. If the SWAT teams were searching the building he needed to delay, give them a chance to find this freak before he set his bomb. He had to keep him talking. 'Look at those people,' he called out. 'In the auditorium. They've got families, children. They didn't make the dolls. They aren't evil. They aren't sinners, no more than anyone else, anyway. They're here for a party.'

Ivanovic said nothing. A fourth drum thumped to the floor. He pushed it with his foot until it fell on its side, then gave it a shove. It made a sloshing sound as it rolled towards the centre of the room. He selected another drum and repeated the procedure. Madsen ploughed on. 'Didn't Pastor Luke teach you forgiveness? His message was non-violent protest. NeChristo does good in the world. It stands for—'

'NeChristo,' Ivanovic said mildly, 'is dead. They started this war by putting a gun to our head and we finished it. We killed their credibility and we killed their protests. In just four days we annihilated them.'

Four statements, none of which made sense. But at least the lunatic had temporarily stopped what he was doing. Madsen said, 'I thought you were with the church.'

'That's because you're a complete fucking moron. You did everything we wanted you to do. You picked up on the G-ring, you brought them into the open, found the pastor with the kiddie dolls . . . *You* put the heat on. All we had to do was feed the media and let public revulsion do the rest.'

'Who sent you?'

Ivanovic watched Madsen's confusion with growing amusement. 'No one.'

'Then why are you attacking Dreamcom?'

'I'm not. You are.'

'But the D-5 . . .'

'There isn't any. We used that truck to dump what was left after Grant Avenue. You probably picked up the leftover residue. I'll be sure to have it cleaned.'

Madsen stared at the metal drums.

Ivanovic chuckled. 'Acetone. Best I could come up with at short notice. Or rather, the best *you* could come up with at short notice. You see how nicely it fits? We have CCTV of you attacking the loading bay, ripping open doll cases. After that you came up in the elevator, found the drums here in the dolly workshop. In your frenzy you didn't care. You just wanted to burn the place down. But when you set it alight, oh dear, the fumes overwhelmed you . . . By the time we put the fire out there was nothing left to find but two lumps of ash. You get to die for your crusade, the cops get closure, we get closure. Everyone's a winner.'

Ivanovic went back and selected another drum. Instead of tipping it on its side he unscrewed the cap, pulled a rag from his pocket, and held it to the opening. Using his knee, he tilted the drum slightly and slopped clear liquid over the rag. 'This didn't have to happen,' he said, looking over in mock sympathy. 'You could still be in San Francisco. Safe. Happy. Your problem was you didn't know how to stop. Even when we gave you Callan you didn't know how to fucking stop.'

Madsen was frantically trying to understand . . . the church was destroyed . . . he was saying Madsen had been manipulated to play a part in its downfall, but at some point had deviated from the script . . . there was no explosive in the truck . . .

Suddenly it came together.

All of it.

The reason he had been looking for Callan's co-conspirators within Dreamcom was because they *were* Dreamcom. Fillinger – it could only have come from him – had taken a monstrous, hideous, calculated gamble, then coolly and calmly played the police, the Bureau, the media . . . everyone . . . to destroy his enemy and win back support. He was a psychopath. He had ordered the Grant Avenue bombing himself. His audacity was breathtaking.

And it had paid off.

Ivanovic advanced with the fuel-soaked rag in hand. He was smiling.

'They'll polygraph you,' Madsen said.

'They don't know I exist.'

'Fillinger then.'

'No one suspects him of anything.'

Ivanovic pushed the rag over Madsen's mouth and nose. Madsen jerked his head back but the rag followed. He refused to breathe. The rag stayed. The acetone felt cool against his skin. Vapour stung at his eyes. His head began to swim.

Shari said, 'We analysed the Grant Avenue video. They'll get you.'

The rag lifted. Genuine surprise registered on Ivanovic's face. Madsen stared in astonishment. They were the first words Shari had spoken since he regained consciousness.

'How?' demanded Ivanovic.

Shari said nothing.

'I said, *how?* What did you find in the video?'

Shari pushed against the wall and levered herself into a sitting position. Thrusting her chin forward defiantly she said, 'You'll find out when they hunt you down.'

Ivanovic stood and wiped his hands and retrieved the propane torch from the workbench. There was a *snick snick* and a low roar as he lit the flame. He moved towards Shari.

'Do what you like, you sick fuck. I won't tell you.'

'You don't have to. When I fry your nose like an egg, your boyfriend will tell me everything . . .'

Chapter 58

Just a few steps more. Shari Sanayei willed her assailant closer. For ten minutes she had been working her wrists frantically along a rough edge of skirting board behind her back, sawing through layer after layer of duct tape. She levered her arms apart and felt the threads of the last strip tear free. Whether her hands would be any use was an open question: the tape had been so tight she had no feeling left in her fingers.

She sat with her back to the wall. Ivanovic advanced, leering, waving the flame back and forth. By folding her legs and jamming her heels under her buttocks she managed to wriggle up to her knees. She spat. Saliva struck Ivanovic's cheek. 'You haven't got any balls,' she yelled. 'You play with skinjobs, don't you? No idea what to do with a real woman. Do you slap them? I bet you do, you coward, because plastic can't slap back . . .'

Ivanovic's nostrils flared and his black eyes shone. 'You won't be so chatty when your lips are gone and your tongue is a fucking candle,' he said. His voice was low, menacing.

The flame tip lifted and brushed the wall near her head, causing the paint to bubble and peel. She could hear the roar, feel the blast of heat across her scalp. She heard the crackle of shrivelling hair. An acrid smell bit the air.

'*Stop!*' Madsen shouted.

The heat and the roar diminished slightly.

Madsen said, 'We found a second person in the video. There were two at Grant Avenue. Callan and another. There are computer models. Sooner or later the police will find the models and work it out. They'll come looking.'

'Really?' Ivanovic said.

'Yes.'

'Anything else?'

'That's it, I swear. Leave her alone.'

A relieved grin spread across Ivanovic's face. He began to laugh. 'You never worked out a damn thing. There was *no one* there, you stupid fuck! No first person, no second person, no one!'

With no conscious thought, no plan, just adrenalin and terror and firing synapses, Shari thrust with both legs and launched herself forwards and upwards. The top of her skull crunched into Ivanovic's nose. His head ricocheted. Her swollen hands clubbed at the torch, connected, sent it tumbling from his grip. He stumbled and fell backwards to the ground. With her ankles still taped together, she fell too, landing on his legs, her face to his groin. Instinctively she opened her mouth, thrust forward and clamped down hard with her teeth. She pulled and thrashed with her body. There was a dull pop, like a rubber band snapping, followed by a hideous mewling scream. Blows rained down on her back. She pulled her knees up, curling into a protective ball, and thrashed again. The scream became a wail. The blows fell faster. One smashed into her temple.

She saw static. Her jaw slackened. She rolled away. Through vision starred with fireflies she spied the torch on its side, a few feet away, the flame hissing and rippling at the air. She humped, seal-like, towards it, reaching forward with numb, rubbery hands. Her cheek hit the floor. There was a hand around her ankle, pulling her back. *Fuck you, fuck you, fuck you.* She kicked out as hard as she could. Once. Twice. The hand didn't let go.

But she gained an inch.

Her outstretched fingers touched cold metal, clawed at it,

grabbed hold. She twisted her body and thrust the flame to-wards her tormentor. Ivanovic tried to scrabble away, but the blue tongue followed, searing a thin trail of angry red as it swept across his cheek. The flame hovered and the red darkened to the colour of spilt wine.

Ivanovic roared and jerked. His hands flailed.

Shari ducked, steadied, thrust again. '*Fuck you!*'

Flesh puffed up over his eye. Skin blackened, crackled and peeled. The exposed fat sputtered, giving off a putrid stink. Ivanovic's feet found purchase. With an almighty kick he flew backwards, cannoning his head into the wall. He lay there writh-ing and moaning, his hands over his face.

'*Shari, the gun!*' Madsen's throat felt like sandpaper. He could see the figure in the corner was still conscious, but Shari wasn't listening. She turned the gas valve on the torch until the flame sputtered out, then humped over to the workbench. There were tool drawers underneath. She dragged herself up to her knees and started opening them. After rummaging for a few moments she withdrew a box cutter and swiftly sliced through the duct tape around her ankles. She did the same for Madsen's hands and feet. Then she sat on the floor, head down. Spent.

Madsen worked frantically to rub blood back into his limbs. He found he could stand. He limped towards the far end of the work-bench, willing his left knee not to buckle, reaching for the familiar shape of his Beretta.

Shari yelled.

Madsen spun.

Ivanovic was on his feet at the other end of the bench, one hand clutching the side of his face, the other grabbing at the tools. His fist came away with a heavy, long-handled torque wrench. He lurched towards Shari, holding the wrench like a hammer.

In a single smooth movement, Madsen's arm swung around and up, the Beretta already in his hand, his trigger finger taking up the slack even as the sights glided into alignment.

A thunderclap.

A familiar thud through the wrist.

Ivanovic staggered. There was a hole an inch forward of his ear, a quarter inch above. A spray of crimson speckled the wall behind. The wrench clattered. His body thumped to the ground.

A cold emptiness descended on Madsen. He had purchased the Beretta himself, put a thousand rounds through it knocking down silhouettes at Quantico and punching holes in paper targets at ranges across the country, practised with it two-handed, one-handed and left-handed, drawn it to threaten, dissuade, secure and protect, but this was the first time, ever, that he had fired it at flesh and blood.

Just one shot, not even a double tap, and a man lay stone dead.

Shari rushed towards him. Her arms slid under his, pulling him close. Her face burrowed into his neck. Wet tears and heat radiated from her cheeks. He shut his eyes and embraced her, allowing his lips to brush her head where the hair had been scorched.

Shari released her grip. 'We're not finished,' she said, wiping her face with her T-shirt. 'When they find us, they're not going to listen to fairytales about Dreamcom bombing its own dollhouse and manipulating and framing us. No one is.'

Madsen stared at the fuel drums, Ivanovic's blackened, ruined face and his own warm Beretta and saw she was right. They looked like fanatics. Killers. If their own people found them now they were finished. If they weren't shot on sight they would spend weeks futilely pleading their case. Weeks during which Fillinger would pull strings, exert influence . . .

Applause rang from the speakers.

He stared up at the CCTV screens. The man in the cowboy hat was thanking his guests and exhorting them to enjoy the show. He stood back from the lectern. A beaming, silver-haired Tom Fillinger stepped forward in his place.

On the right-hand screen, a swarm of men – a mix of Dreamcom security personnel and heavily armed, black-suited SWAT officers – moved cautiously through a jungle, checking huts.

'I'm not letting him win,' Shari snarled, moving to the door. 'Coming?'

'Where?'

'To that auditorium.'

Chapter 59

Madsen leaned on Shari's shoulder for support as he stepped from the workshop into a narrow, cobblestoned street. The dark hues of late afternoon, exquisitely painted on a huge domed ceiling, soared over stucco walls, porticos, wooden eaves and terracotta rooftops. Hidden spotlights splashed delicate pinks and reds over the western horizon. The place was silent.

Behind them, the door clicked shut. Madsen turned and saw that this side had an iron loop for a handle and was panelled in rough-hewn oak. It was recessed into a graffiti-covered stone wall. The graffiti were in Latin.

'Pompeii,' he said.

'Creepsville.'

'It's deserted. No customers yet.'

They moved cautiously along the street, peering down alleyways and into houses, unable to shake the ghostly eeriness of the place. They passed an alcove and found themselves face to face with an enormous marble phallus. It jutted from a tiny statue of Priapus, god of fertility and procreation, his bearded face split by a lecherous grin. They kept moving. Madsen hobbled as best he could.

Shari glanced back at him. 'I need you to play back everything you heard yesterday, at the factory.'

'Why?'

'Just play it back. Something that bastard said just now. I need to be sure . . .'

Madsen recounted the highlights of his conversation with Pemberton as best he could while she fired questions back at him. The questions appeared to have no logical order, making it impossible to fathom her reasoning.

Movement. From the corner of his eye, above and behind.

He spun and drew a bead with his Beretta. His knee gave. He tottered and sprawled backwards, still staring down his sights. A dark-haired beauty in a short white tunic smiled and leaned further over the balcony above, making a show of her ample cleavage.

A doll.

'Jesus Christ,' he muttered.

Shari hauled him up. 'Come *on*.'

'Knee's no damn good.'

'Do your best. Judging from the arrangement of those CCTV displays, that SWAT team is in the world next to this one. When they finish with the huts they'll be coming here.'

They passed the entrance to a domed building echoing to the sound of running water. Madsen caught a glimpse of a swimming-pool-sized bath and hot water vomiting from the mouths of stone beasts. Ghostly nudes paraded in the steam. He began noticing more movement in windows and doorways. A maiden beckoned from behind a temple colonnade.

They stopped at a square that looked like a town centre. Streets branched off in six different directions. To their right, fixed high on a wall at the mouth of the widest street, was an arrow and a small sign. It was green, modern and electric and said EXIT.

He pointed at it.

Shari hesitated. 'The streets widen that way, and the room bows outwards along the horizon.'

The effect was subtle, but after staring for a few moments he could see what she was talking about. 'So?'

'So the complex is circular, and the worlds must be arranged around the sides, like wedges in a pie. The exit sign points outwards, which is where the public thoroughfares and fire escapes must be. That auditorium, on the other hand, was round, which means it can only be in the centre.' She jerked her thumb towards the smaller streets to the left. 'That way.'

As if to underline her words, distant sounds came from somewhere over to the right. Multiple voices. Male.

Shari turned and dragged Madsen in the opposite direction, towards a narrow alleyway. Madsen's knee screamed in protest as he staggered and stumbled over the cobblestones. In the dark interiors on either side he saw glimpses of wall paintings: bordello scenes, ritual flagellations and red-skinned satyrs ravaging curvaceous water nymphs. Flickering oil lamps threw garish shadows. Lustful temptresses stared from the recesses. A young woman, reclining on the floor with her bare feet folded to the side, followed Madsen with mournful, pleading eyes. Her tunic was torn. A heavy chain stretched from the wall to an iron collar around her neck. She blew a kiss.

The passage tapered until it became possible to reach out and touch both sides, then terminated at a stone wall with a wooden door. It was identical to the one at the workshop. Madsen tried the handle. It was locked.

'Use your gun,' Shari said.

'I'm not sure—'

'We haven't time to be sure!'

Madsen placed the Beretta's muzzle in the space between the doorhandle and the frame, then snapped off three shots, shattering the silence. Clouds of splinters tore from the timber.

The door wouldn't budge.

He moved the muzzle an inch to the right.

Three more reports echoed off the ceiling.

Seven gone, five to go, he thought, mentally calculating the rounds in his magazine. Not much for a gunfight.

A square of pulverized wood ripped away like cardboard. The door swung free.

Urgent shouts floated across the town.

Chapter 60

The door led into the side of what appeared to be a service corridor. Concrete walls curved away to the left and right. Modern strip lights hung from the ceiling. They tumbled inside and Madsen pulled the door to as best he could. There was no way to latch or lock it. He leaned back against the wall, sweat running off his face. The rush down the alley had taken most of his remaining energy. His knee was useless. He needed rest.

Shari said, 'Wait here,' and ran to the right. In seconds she was around the curve and out of sight. He marvelled at her resurgence. She had come up with some kind of idea and it was driving her, redoubling her motivation. He had no idea what it was, nor could he see any way out. He could hardly move. In seconds men would come pouring through the door. If Fillinger's goons were first he was a dead man. If it was a cop, it was fifty-fifty.

Running steps echoed down the corridor. Shari. 'Come on,' she said, hooking his arm over her shoulders. 'It's not far.'

He lowered himself to his foot and began hopping along beside her. The corridor seemed to be one long curve. Ahead, on the inside of the curve, an archway appeared. A sign hanging from the corridor ceiling said *A/V Room*. They reached the archway and Madsen found himself looking at the base of a steel staircase. The stairs arrowed steeply upwards.

He took a deep breath and began the ascent, yanking on the railing with his left hand and hopping on his right foot, one agonizing step at a time. Shari alternately pushed and pulled.

Halfway up, his good leg gave way. He sank down, lungs heaving, neck and chest soaked with sweat.

'Almost there,' Shari said. 'Keep going.'

'Jesus, I'm trying. I just need a sec.'

From below came the distant echo of a door slam, followed by multiple running footsteps.

'*Let's go!*' Shari whispered.

He hauled himself to his feet and continued the excruciating climb using both hands on the railing and hopping sideways, crab-like. Stars swam in front of his face.

Four stairs to go.

Three.

Two.

She hooked her hand under his belt and lifted him up the last step.

A plain grey door greeted them. Gasping for breath, he tested the handle. This one turned. He nodded at Shari and shouldered the door inwards.

There were three people inside, two men and a woman. They wore headsets and sat on swivel chairs with their backs to the door, working a console studded with knobs and sliders. In front of the console was a large window. The room reminded Madsen of a recording studio.

Propping himself against the doorframe, he rasped, 'On the floor!'

All three turned as one, locked eyes on the levelled Beretta, and froze.

Shari stepped forward, grabbed one of the men by the collar and yanked him from his chair, sending his headset flying. She pushed him to the ground. His two colleagues needed no further encouragement and quickly slid down to join him.

Shari took the middle swivel seat and studied the controls.

Madsen closed the door. There was a lock below the handle. Small. Next to useless. He turned it anyway. Gesturing at the three prone figures with the Beretta he said, 'Faces to the wall, please. Hands behind your head. Interlace your fingers. Cross your ankles.' He waited until all three had complied, then hopped over to the console and collapsed into a swivel chair beside Shari.

They were at the back of the auditorium, perched high above a sea of heads. Below, platinum-haired dolls paraded down the aisles serving refreshments. Long lenses, each sporting the logo of a media network, bristled like bazookas from platforms and vantage points. Miniature airships glided through the air dispensing puffs of confetti. On the stage opposite, the distant silver-haired figure of Fillinger stood at the lectern. Behind him was a giant-sized screen – it had to be sixty feet tall – upon which an attractive couple in royal robes quaffed wine from gem-studded goblets while gazing into one another's eyes. As Madsen watched, the shot pulled back from the royal couple to reveal an ornate fourteenth-century bed, velvet drapery and a mirror-lined hallway straight out of Versailles.

Shari pulled the memory cube from her pocket and plugged it in. A directory opened on the console monitor. She began scrolling through the files.

Madsen spotted a cluster of burly men at the side of the auditorium. Some wore suits. Bureau. Most wore the tan uniforms of the Las Vegas police. They were craning their necks, scanning the crowd.

He said, 'They don't know we came up here yet.'

'They will soon.' Shari double-clicked on a file. Then she reached over to a rocker switch on the console, took a deep breath, and pressed.

*

On the big screen behind Tom Fillinger, the Versailles scene went black, replaced an instant later with a drab building in an ordinary modern city street. A sign on the side of the building said *Public Parking 24 Hours – Early Bird Specials!* A door opened. A man stepped out. His face was hidden behind sunglasses and a grey hoodie. He carried a red backpack. He pivoted on his heel and began walking down Pacific Avenue. He walked steadily, ignoring everything and everyone, face to the front, never varying his pace. A metronome. A man on a mission.

Shari pulled out a keyboard and began to type.

Madsen shivered. His nerves were taut. She was driving and he was just a passenger. Whatever she was doing it was going to play out in the most public way imaginable. In front of the world's media. Live. Down below, Fillinger beamed at the crowd. All Madsen could see of the vast audience were the backs of heads. No way of telling who or how many had noticed the new video. There was a toggle switch near the headphone jacks labelled SPKR ON/OFF. He reached down and flicked it to the ON position and the speaker in the A/V room came alive. Madsen could hear the excitement in Fillinger's words as they filled the room: *'Any patron who enjoys the charms of three or more worlds goes into a daily lottery draw for a luxury suite with two dedicated attendants to pamper him, or her, in any way they please . . .'*

Behind Fillinger, backpack man had passed the bank. He had turned away from the first camera. He had turned away from the second one. He had passed a young woman pushing a stroller in the opposite direction.

Shari stopped typing and glanced up. Madsen saw a line of four-foot-high capitals appear across the top of the big screen: THIS MAN IS WALKING THROUGH CHINATOWN, SAN FRANCISCO. HIS DESTINATION IS THE DOLLHOUSE IN GRANT AVENUE.

The typing resumed.

'Members of our Platinum Club,' Fillinger said, waving an arm expansively across the guests in the front rows. 'You get the privilege of total immersion! Once a year, for a week, all the facilities at Ten Worlds will be turned over to you. A complete escape from the stress and worry of reality. You'll forget there is a reality! You will live like royalty as a resident in the world of your choice, fully staffed, every whim catered for, everyone at your beck and call. Your dreams and fantasies come true. Seven days of heaven!'

On the big screen, backpack man had arrived at the intersection of Pacific Avenue and Grant Avenue. He had pivoted and stopped at the kerb. The lights changed and the traffic going up the hill slowed and stopped. He began to cross.

In the audience, heads were turning left and right. Madsen imagined the puzzled glances and whispered exchanges.

The men at the side of the auditorium were staring and pointing up to the A/V room. One of the uniformed officers was speaking into a mike.

Another line of text appeared: HE WILL GO INSIDE TO THE SECOND FLOOR AND DETONATE THE BOMB IN HIS PACK.

Down below, movement rippled through the audience like a breeze across a poppy field. Heads bobbed and twisted and turned. A new sound came through the speaker. Deep, low, in the background, barely audible, almost a vibration. Distant but not so distant. Getting closer and louder with each passing second. Rumbling and malevolent and gathering momentum. It sounded like an avalanche. Or an approaching train.

Fillinger paused. He looked confused. He raised his voice, trying to assert himself over the noise. 'We wanted to offer two weeks, but the doctors and the insurance people said that could be too much fun for our older guests . . .' He grinned uncertainly. The grin fell and he shook his head and frowned.

Behind him the hooded man had crossed Pacific Avenue and passed the souvenir T-shirts and cheap umbrellas and Chinese fans. He was in front of the jewellery store marching onwards, face to the front, never slowing.

Shari's fingers danced. The keyboard clattered. More text

appeared. HIS HEELS STRIKE THE SIDEWALK AT PRECISE INTERVALS MEASURABLE TO A FRACTION OF A SECOND.

At the side of the auditorium, the uniforms had disappeared. They were on their way.

Backpack man strode past a middle-aged couple, one holding a camera, then past a boarded-up entrance, a grimy sign that said *Fung Long Import Export Co.*

Fillinger looked frustrated, angry.

A man wearing a headset ran down the aisle towards the stage. He waved both arms in big wide arcs over his head.

Very slowly, Fillinger turned a hundred and eighty degrees. His silver head tilted back at an angle.

The guy with the headset leapt to the stage.

On the screen, backpack man arrived at the Grant Avenue doll-house, pivoted on his heel and stepped inside. A fourth line of text appeared. HE IS A SKINJOB. A DREAMCOM PRODUCT, SENT BY DREAMCOM.

Fillinger's knees buckled. The guy with the headset reached out and caught him under the armpits.

In the space of a few seconds the rumble became a roar. A roar punctuated by distinct boos and whistles and angry shouts.

'This came from my conversation with Pemberton?' Madsen asked.

Still typing furiously, Shari said, 'They build them to walk at two speeds.'

'And backpack man does that?'

'Slow near the intersection, fast everywhere else, nothing in between.'

Madsen nodded thoughtfully. 'So they sent a wind-up toy.'

'That's right.'

'And it never did come out.'

'Probably still wearing the bomb when it went off.'

'Which left no body, no DNA. Just another pile of parts in the wreckage . . .'

She said nothing.

'What about Callan?'

'Never there. Fillinger probably had him go and film the interior shots a few weeks before.'

Madsen nodded. Callan was an insider, a man trusted to look after Dreamcom's interests. And a risk taker. Fillinger probably asked him in person: do a video, take a vacation, collect a payment. Not that it won any favours. As soon as he looked like being discovered, they killed him.

Shari punched the ENTER key hard enough to make the keyboard bounce.

The screen in the auditorium said: TWELVE DIED TO WIN PUBLIC SYMPATHY, TO NEUTRALIZE THE NECHRISTO PROTESTS.

Fillinger had disappeared. Below, people were gesticulating, shouting, standing in the aisles. A large man was being propelled towards an exit by two minders, with another two in front clearing the way. A dozen telephoto lenses swivelled, tracking his progress. The guy reminded Madsen of someone he had seen on the news, a politician maybe. He heard Ivanovic's words in his ears . . . *no first person, no second person, no one.* Straightforward and uncomplicated. No bomber, no escape, nothing to trace, no one to find. Shari said city cameras couldn't be manipulated to transmit substitute footage and they hadn't needed to. Fillinger handed his CCTV vision over on a memory cube, pre-packaged with a glimpse of G-ring. Not too obvious, just enough to set things moving in the right direction. Then it was business as usual. Dirt files on the church, a bent cop willing to leak salacious evidence for cash . . . all of it feeding a ravenous pack of media sharks.

Shouts and the thunder of boots on metal. It sounded like a battalion coming up the stairwell.

Shari pushed the keyboard away and slumped in her chair.

On the big screen, the second floor of the dollhouse exploded. A boiling cauldron of dust and smoke shot towards the camera.

The last line of text read: FILLINGER MURDERED HIS OWN PEOPLE. HIS CUSTOMERS. ALL OF THEM.

Fists thudded into the door. The room reverberated to yells of *'Police! Open up!'*

Madsen stared out at the words. It seemed a suitable ending. He pressed the release catch on his Beretta. The magazine fell free and clattered to the console. He racked the slide and the remaining cartridge tumbled to the carpet. Leaving the slide locked open to show the empty chamber, he swivelled his chair to face the door and calmly placed the pistol at his feet.

He said, 'They never figured on the reward flushing out Callan.'

'They never figured on an agent dogmatic to the point of stupidity.'

'I could say the same about you.'

The door smashed from its hinges.

Bodies flooded in, tripping, snarling, reaching, grabbing. Madsen hit the floor hard, face first. A knee slammed into his back and crushed the air from his lungs. A palm mashed down on the back of his head. He tasted carpet. There was a thud from behind as Shari received the same treatment. Lightning shot through his shoulders as his arms were hauled back. A handcuff zipped shut, then another, grinding and biting into flesh. A boot hit him hard beneath the ribs. Someone grabbed a fistful of hair and yanked his head back as far as it would go.

A flint-hard voice spat, 'Do you know what this is?'

Madsen forced his eyes to focus. A fist swam into view and he flinched, expecting it to catapult into his face. It stopped, hovering an inch from his nose. Projecting from the fist was a cylinder. It was stainless steel and cigar-shaped. A familiar light winked from the tip.

He tried to nod but found his head locked in place.

The owner of the voice leaned in close, hissed into Madsen's ear. 'You need to say it.'

Madsen felt a shiver deep within his belly. It worked its way upwards and radiated out. There was no way to control it. It gripped and shook his chest and convulsed his shoulders in short, rapid spasms.

The grip on his hair tightened, twisting him sideways so his assailant could see. But Madsen was neither choking nor crying nor shaking with fear.

He was laughing.

Epilogue

Hideki Yoshida waited with his yellow spiked head bowed slightly.

At the other end of the conference table Noriyuki Nomura, president and chairman of the board of Nomura Entertainment Enterprises, sat very still. His hands were placed symmetrically to the left and right of his leather folio. Nomura's skin had drawn tighter with each of his eighty-nine years and his cheeks were now very hollow, accentuating the lines of his skull. His eyes were closed, giving the impression he might be sleeping. Behind him, rain spattered soundlessly against the windows and the Ginza nightlights ebbed and flowed in a rippling montage of pinks and greens.

The old man worked his jaw back and forth, as if lubricating it.

He began to speak. The words came slowly, but with the strength and timbre of a man one-third his age. 'Tell me again, Yoshida-san, do we get everything we need?'

Yoshida swallowed nervously. Over the past week that question had been asked many times. His superiors had asked it. He, in turn, had interrogated the lawyers and accountants, and they had asked it of their staff. He had even gone so far as to examine all the relevant documents himself. On each occasion the answer had been affirmative. The deal was watertight. But it didn't stop his anxiety levels rising every time he was asked the question again. This was his last chance to say no. In a few minutes, the documents in the folio across the conference table would bear the final signatures. The deal would be done. The time for excuses and recanting would have passed.

He said, 'Yes, Nomura-san. I am sure.'

'He is the sole owner?'

'Yes, Nomura-san.'

'He secured all patents, stock, machines, production facilities?'

'Yes, Nomura-san.'

'I would have preferred to buy direct.'

That too, had been said many times. Yoshida bowed lower. 'I take full responsibility, Nomura-san. He submitted his bid immediately, much more quickly than I anticipated, and the Texan accepted. My offer was already too late.' Yoshida was ashamed. Because of his delay, the company now had to pay almost double to acquire Dreamcom's technology assets.

'I know what you are thinking,' the old man said, 'but his price does not concern me greatly. He makes a profit for being bold and for being first, that is to be expected, and in truth it is still a bargain. No, what worries me is his insistence on having sole distribution rights for the United States.'

Yoshida said nothing.

'This man is an unknown quantity, but when our embargo lifts, this condition means we will have no choice but to do business through him. Our success will depend on his success. Do you take responsibility for *that*?'

This time Yoshida did not hesitate. 'He is shrewd and tenacious. Highly motivated to make money. He will generate big profits for us. Of that, I am certain. He will be here soon. You will see for yourself.'

The old man grunted. Outside, water swept and rippled down the glass.

'Tell me,' he said. 'What happened to this . . . Madsen?'

Yoshida's head bobbed up, relieved at the change of subject. 'There is a great embarrassment over his case. The Bureau is conducting an internal review of its . . . Professional Integrity Office. There is to be reorganization, disciplinary actions, many changes. He is on leave until this is completed, but in my opinion he is disillusioned. He will not go back.'

'Could he be useful?'

Hideki Yoshida cast his mind back to their encounter in Los Angeles and the seamless way Madsen had switched gears, pushing the legal boundaries of interrogation and cleverly baiting himself and Traviano for a reaction. He paused to find the right words to sum the man up. Finally he said, 'He has a sharp mind, Nomura-san, and many interesting qualities, but he is headstrong, driven by passion. I do not recommend approaching him for his services.'

The old man seemed to consider this for a moment. 'And his companion?'

'The sergeant has already returned to her duties, but in my humble opinion what happened to her lover has made her an enemy to anyone in our line of business.'

'Keep an eye on her. One day she will again be asked to make choices, tell half-truths to protect someone. Then she may be vulnerable.'

No, thought Yoshida, *I do not think so. Not that one.* Aloud he said, 'As you say.'

The minutes passed. The wind shifted, sending the rain in from a different angle. The watery sheets made new patterns as they fanned across the glass.

Yoshida's cell phone vibrated. The message read simply, *He has arrived.* Turning to Nomura he said, 'He is downstairs now.'

The old man nodded.

A few moments later there was a knock. The two men stood.

The door opened and a secretary ushered in their guest.

The creases in the generously tailored double-breasted suit were sharp and aligned. A dusting of silk cherry blossoms cascaded tastefully down the weave of the tie. The guest stepped forward, made a long, low bow, and greeted Mr Nomura in formal, deferential Japanese.

Chairman Noriyuki Nomura returned the courtesy, replying in carefully articulated English, 'Welcome to Nomura Entertainment Enterprises. I have heard many great things about you and I am certain today is the beginning of a long and prosperous partnership. It is a pleasure to finally meet you and shake your hand, Luke-san.'

Acknowledgements

A great many people helped get this novel over the line.

First and foremost to my family, who gave their patience, love and support throughout: thank you.

I owe a special debt of gratitude to: Christopher Little, my literary agent, and Bill Scott-Kerr and the stellar team at Transworld, for taking this to the world. To Elizabeth Cowell, my editor, for all her wise and wonderful work. To Kathryn Fox, crime novelist extraordinaire, for her generous and indispensable advice and for her introduction to Jason Sitzes, who gave early, pure-gold feedback. To Lee Findlay and Gus Panucci, writers and fellow travellers, for precious gifts of energy and encouragement and suffering early drafts along with Danny Crawford, Brian and Donna Anderson, Arnold Mitt and Graham Rawlinson. And to the special agent in Arizona who gave hours of her time enlightening me on inter-agency politics, on condition of anonymity.

A long list of people never saw the manuscript but made vital contributions along the way. My sincere thanks especially to: Ken, Theresa and Ceridwen Dovey for offering guiding lights they thought of as small, but which burned very bright in the darkness. To Rachel Thomas at Berkelouw Books, and Parham Salimnejad and all the crew at Persia Belle, truly generous people who kept me going with their great company, friendly words and endless cups of piping hot coffee. And to my father Bill McCabe, Paul and Jo Shaw, Stephanie and Romain Saulnier, Deb Jeffreys, David Matthews, Stuart and Dorothy Kennedy and everyone else who gave thoughtful advice and encouragement when it counted.

I also want to acknowledge a lifelong debt to the late Helen Dancer, a journalist who cared, and who told me many years ago I *had* to write, refusing to take no for an answer.

Everything good in this book is due to the kindness and generosity of these people. All the mistakes are mine.

Bruce McCabe was born in 1969 and lived in Kenya, Fiji and Japan before returning to Australia, where he graduated in science from the University of Sydney. He worked for a variety of tech firms before making his name as an international expert on human factors in technology adoption and innovation. Along the way he published several hundred magazine, journal and newspaper articles, became a provocative weekly columnist in *The Australian* and earned a PhD in computer science. He travels widely as a public speaker and advisor to businesses, governments and science labs, writes constantly, and lives in Sydney with his wife, two children and a Staffordshire bull terrier named Suzi. *Skinjob* is his first novel.

Bruce can be found online at: www.brucemccabe.com